# Jeeni Criscenzo

Copyright © Jeeni Criscenzo, 1996

Publisher's Cataloging in Publication
*(Prepared by Quality Books, Inc.)*

Criscenzo, Jeeni
   Place of mirrors : lessons of the ancient Maya / by Jeeni Criscenzo. --
1st ed.
      p. cm.
      LCCN: 96-76576.
      ISBN 0-9652318-1-X


   1. Mayas--Fiction.  2. Reincarnation--Fiction.   I.Title
   PS3553.R51P53 1996              813'.54
                                   QBI96-30064



Jaguar Books
30043 US Hwy. 19 N., Ste 136, Clearwater, FL 34621-1032
10 9 8 7 6 5 4 3 2 1

♻ This book is printed on acid-free, recycled 60# Envirotext
Printed in the United States of America
Set in ITC Century by The Production Dept., Clearwater, FL
Jacket & Book Design by Jeeni Criscenzo

*To Joey,*
*my consort, friend and love*
*throughout time*

# Preface

*What I have been*
*I am not yet,*
*From proud peacock*
*To free egret.*
*Transcending this moment of being*
*I become more than a moment in time.*
*Tomorrow is yesterday's memory*
*And eternity is mine.*

This story transcends time—from the present-day life of a character some will think is an awful lot like the author, to almost 1400 years ago, when a man named Hanab Pacal ruled a Maya territory known today as Palenque, Mexico. Thanks to recent breakthroughs in the decipherment of the inscriptions of the Ancient Maya at Palenque and other sites throughout Mexico, Guatemala, Honduras and Belize, we now know about Hanab Pacal, his ancestors, his descendants and many of the important events of their lives. The present day people and events in this story are loosely based upon my own experiences and research, with creative liberties taken to enhance my reader's enjoyment as well as for the preservation of the privacy of the individuals involved.

~

A common mistake is to refer to the Maya as a "lost civilization." The Maya people are still very much alive and living near many of the sites of their ancestors. Their lives are still guided by highly spiritual beliefs that predate Christianity. A complex and precise calendar system is dynamically woven into their spiritual life, marking more than just the passage of time. In the Maya Ritual Calendar, each of the twenty days represents an abstract thought that is modified by its use and position—much the way astrologers determine a horoscope by the relative position of the stars and planets in the zodiac. These ritual days are sequentially paired with thirteen numbers in a continuous rotation that repeats itself every 260 days. When a Maya child is born, the combination of the ritual day and number of their birthday becomes the child's name. Because both the day and the number are rich in spiritual and astrological meanings, Maya children grow up with a blueprint of their destiny clearly defined by their name.

One of the twenty ritual days, *Etznab*, is written with a glyph that looks like crisscrossing stair steps. It graphically represents the Maya's fascination with mirrored reflections and their esoteric wisdom that time and place are only illusions. As recorded on his sarcophagus, Hanab Pacal, who ruled Palenque from 615 to 683 AD, died on an Etznab day—thus entering into that magical realm of mirrors...

# BOOK ONE
# The Awakening

# Christina

From the small window of the 747 I could see the bright light of the planet Venus just at the tip of the crescent moon. That beautiful occultation would not occur again for seventy-five years — a lifetime. Perhaps I'd watched Venus and the moon make love once every lifetime.

There was nothing unusual in the way it began – my first glimpse into this strange, eerie state of timelessness in which I now drifted. In fact, it was really quite a mundane beginning, that sticky, August afternoon when I stood surveying the rows of haphazardly labeled door buzzers in that ever-so-slightly-neglected lobby of an old apartment building on East Fourteenth Street.

On that particular day I was so preoccupied with things that seemed to matter at the time, that it took me several moments to realize that my summons on the buzzer marked 7B had produced no reaction: no fuzzy voice demanding my identification; no buzzing sound of admittance at the door; nothing! Thinking that perhaps I'd gotten my appointment mixed-up, I reached into my briefcase and pulled out my leather-bound organizer and flipped it open to August 17, 1987. You see, at that point I still had this sense of my existence as being positioned within these measured increments of hours, and minutes, and days. In fact, it wouldn't be an exaggeration to say that I was overly obsessed with time.

My appointment book concurred that my meeting had indeed been scheduled for 4:00 and a quick glance at my watch reassured me that I was exactly on time. My innocence verified, I hit the buzzer again with the self-righteousness of a Fundamentalist preacher.

But neither buzzers nor curses produced any response from the doorbell marked "7B". As usual, I was in the right place, at the right time, but I'd already decided that Reverend Blaze, with whom I'd scheduled this appointment, was completely irresponsible — and probably even worse. Muttering something to that effect, I impatiently tried the buzzer again. Although there was no sound at the door to indicate that I'd been heard, I tried rattling the door anyway, but to no avail.

What I remember most clearly about that day, and I do remember everything, from that day on, with astonishing clarity, was the way I was startled and appalled by my image reflected in the glass entry door. It wasn't such a terrible image, mind you, but the glass distorted my figure in a way that was extremely unflattering. I stared at the reflection of a thirty-five year old woman in a navy blue, linen, business suit and felt nothing even remotely akin to satisfaction. "If I could just get ahead a few bucks," I thought half aloud, "I'd join a health club and get back into shape." But it wasn't the few extra pounds, exaggerated by the glass, that should have disturbed me. What I didn't see then, but memory serves me well enough to see now, was a profound weariness about my eyes. The shapely legs, emphasized with four-inch high heels; the smart, close cropped haircut; the perfectly matched accessories; were all useless in camouflaging the despair that had begun to clutch at my soul. But, while even a stranger had only to look at my eyes to know that I was struggling with an overwhelming sense of failure, I was oblivious to it. All that I was thinking about was the possibility that I was wasting my time — and as I explained, time had begun to take on an excessive significance in my life.

Time had become my enemy and my master. Late charges, interest penalties, eviction notices and threats of doom from the IRS — these are the weapons time wields as days tick by when your luck has run out. It was astonishing how quickly these vultures of time had gathered over my ailing business. Only two months earlier I'd walked into my ad agency thinking that all was well with the world, believing the sage adage of Capitalism that "if one works hard, one will be successful." That's all it had been — two months since my biggest client informed me that they were dropping my agency. I'd been reduced to the image reflected in that door, waiting to see an old lady about a silly, little brochure. Alenka had assured me that this was a live one and a silly little brochure might pay the rent, not for my office (that was history), but for my apartment uptown.

These were my thoughts as I stood in that stuffy lobby contemplating the worried reflection in the glass. Alenka had warned me that Reverend Blaze was a little on the flaky side, a has-been telepathic, but I was in no position to be choosy where my next meal was coming from. I paced the hot and somber lobby waiting for this irresponsibly late and slightly flaky woman, who would help finance my desperate attempt to survive. Suddenly a tiny, flustered woman, carrying a grocery bag in each arm, pushed open the front door. Although we'd never met before, she seem to recognize me immediately.

"You must be Miss Rossi! You're early. I wasn't expecting you until 4:30," she whispered to me in a cadence that seemed to me like poetry.

I thought to myself, "Some psychic, she can't even get her appointments straight." For a moment I was concerned that she could read my cynical thoughts, but she gave no indication of it as she fumbled with her packages to unlock the entry door.

"Here, let me help you with those bags," I offered as I stooped to relieve the petite woman of her bundles.

"For the celebration tonight!" she explained, referring to the bags as she handed them over to me and turned her key in the lock.

"Celebration?" I inquired. She seemed so certain that I should know what she was talking about that I thought I'd forgotten something important. I tried to remember if there was anything else scheduled for the day in my appointment book. Fortunately, she did seem to read my mind at this point and hurried to squelch my panic by explaining that this was the day of the Harmonic Convergence.

"Why don't you join us?" she offered as the elevator doors opened before either of us had pressed a button. She seemed to smile slyly as I took note of this, but I refused to acknowledge it's unusualness – I'd seen elevator doors open just as you needed them. I was sure it was just coincidence. Trying to recall what the Harmonic Convergence was, I remembered seeing a short piece about it on the prior night's late news. It had something to do with some "Hari Krishna" types chanting about the end of the world in Central Park. I declined her invitation and waited nervously for the elevator to reach the seventh floor.

"So what exactly do you need this brochure for?" I asked, trying to bring the conversation quickly to the business at hand. Something about the woman made me certain that this was not going to be a big budget project. But just then the elevator doors opened and I watched my potential client bustle past me and down the hall without answering.

I followed her to a door with a picture of a colorful wheel-shaped design taped to it, and the words "Harmony and Peace to All Who Enter" written in green marker just below the wheel. Just above the mandala, a decal proclaimed that this was the home of a distributor of Sunrider Health Products. I was beginning to imagine the thrill of strangling my friend Alenka and her useless leads.

Just inside the door was a hallway lined on both sides with shelves of health foods, vitamin supplements and natural beauty products. Assuming that this must be why Reverend Blaze required the brochure, I asked her why the manufacturer didn't supply her with product literature.

"Oh they do," she whispered, dragging out the "oooo". "You can put those bags in the kitchen," she added, nodding to the tiny kitchenette on her left. I put the bags down on the single square foot of counter space that wasn't covered with health food boxes and canisters.

"Would you like some iced tea?" she asked, pouring two tall glasses full without waiting for an answer and bringing them into the living room.

An unusual scent lingered in the room, not altogether unpleasant but quite unfamiliar. In a blue and white, oriental, ceramic bowl on the coffee table was a handful of tiny, velvety, grayish-green leaves that appeared to be partially burned. Reverend Blaze must have noticed my puzzled expression and she explained that the bowl contained sage, which she burned to cleanse her apartment of any evil spirits that her clients might bring in with them. As if to imply that I could be guilty of carrying such ominous contaminants, she flicked a cigarette lighter and lit several leaves in the bowl. A thin wisp of smoke rose up and snaked around the room in a slow, sensuous dance.

The room was decorated in "early attic" with nothing matching and everything seeming to be sentimentally valuable but realistically worthless. The sofa was covered with a hand sewn quilt that must have been prized before it was worn to its present threadbare condition. On an old wooden table in front of the curtainless windows, clusters of colored stones and crystals caught my attention. "I love crystals!" I exclaimed, thinking of the prisms I had hanging in my kitchen window and oblivious to the difference between a "natural" crystal and a cut prism.

Reverend Blaze walked over to the window and studied the stones as if she'd never noticed them there before. Then she turned to me and studied me as well. Turning back to the stones, she chose a chunk of a marbleized, greenish rock which she handed to me.

"Hold this and tell me what you feel," she gently instructed in a voice that again reminded me of poetry.

I put my hands around the smooth, cold rock. It was the fifth straight day of a heat wave and the air conditioner in the apartment was failing miserably, so I welcomed the coolness in my hands. But suddenly a strange sensation seemed to come over me; a sense of incredible relaxation that ran through my fingers, up my arms, into my neck, and down my spine. I felt as if the pressure of gravity had increased and I'd been helplessly impelled onto the sofa. Frightened by the sensation, I gingerly put the rock down on the coffee table and took a sip of the iced tea. It had a bittersweet taste unlike anything I'd ever tasted; biting at my tongue so that it tingled while simultaneously soothing it with sweetness.

"What exactly is it that you need a brochure for?" I murmured, afraid to disturb the peacefulness of the room while trying to focus on the purpose of our meeting.

"I need to tell people what it is that I do," Reverend Blaze said slowly and deliberately as she settled into an old, ladder-back chair alongside the sofa. "I take people on a journey — sort of like a guide, into their past." She paused and examined my face for a reaction. "I can see that you're skeptical and maybe you wouldn't be the best person to write about this, but Alenka insisted that you have an open mind. Would you be willing to let me guide you through a past life regression so that you can have a better understanding of what this is all about?"

I was amazed at how comfortable I felt with this woman. Her voice seemed to soothe me, floating around the room like the wisps of burning sage. Alenka was right, I was open minded and I'd even begun to explore some metaphysical concepts before I'd started having all of my business problems. In fact, the idea of reincarnation seemed quite plausible to me. Suddenly it didn't seem to matter that this was not a client that would fill my coffers. "I guess that would be all right," I answered almost as softly as my enchantress.

Reverend Blaze smiled reassuringly. "Fine," she sighed and picked up a large cut crystal bowl from the table beside her, and rested it on her lap. She picked through the various colors of candles in the bowl, each burnt down to a different length, and finally decided upon two tall, slender, green candles — one lime green and the other a dark forest color. Then, almost on second thought, she selected a short, white, votive-type candle. These she melted slightly on the bottoms with a cigarette lighter and affixed them onto a plate on the coffee table and lit them.

"Green — you seem to need the nurturing power of green. Yes, much green should be around you," she murmured as she handed me the malachite stone again. "Here, lay back on the sofa and hold this on your chest," she directed me. I obeyed and once again felt a wave of relaxation move through my body.

Reverend Blaze continued, "I want you to close your eyes and imagine yourself as having no body. Just let your physical self melt away; first your feet slowly dissolving; and then your legs, so slowly disappearing until there's nothing there." She went on describing the various parts of my body melting away into nothingness while I allowed the suggestions to enter my mind. When it seemed that there was nothing physical left to me, Reverend Blaze directed me to move through the vastness of time and space to a time when I was choosing a physical life in which to incarnate. While one part of me never lost sight of the reality that I was lying on a sofa in an apartment on 14th Street in New York City in 1987, I could hear myself responding to the hypnotist with words that seemed outlandish to the person I still knew was Christina Rossi. But the words I spoke came easily, without any thought on my part, as though my mouth had become an instrument that was being played by a stranger.

"Can you feel yourself in the womb?" asked Reverend Blaze? I could feel my face contorting as I strained to see beyond the warm blackness that encircled me. But suddenly I was overcome with anxiety.

"What's wrong?" I heard Reverend Blaze ask from a far away place.

"It's all wrong. It won't work this way," I moaned.

"What won't work? Don't you want to be born?"

"Oh yes, yes, but I can't do what must be done with this body."

"What's wrong with the body? Is it deformed?"

"Yes, the foot is bent out of shape! It'll be useless."

"It's necessary — don't worry — it's of your own choosing. Let yourself be born."

Once again I could feel my face contorting as I struggled to emerge from the womb. Then I relaxed again and quietly announced, "It is done, I am born a male on the same day as the mother of the gods. And I am the child of the mother, and she is the resplendent one!"

"Where are you? Can you see your mother? Can you describe where you are?" I heard the psychic ask.

"As with the other teachers, so it is with me — to elevate humanity to be fitting company for the gods."

Reverend Blaze paused a few moments as she tried to absorb the magnitude of that reply and I must admit feeling a bit proud of my ability to astound her. "When do you begin this monumental task?" she finally asked.

I remember thinking at the time that her choice of adjectives was astonishingly appropriate, because my task would indeed involve the creation of monuments. But I simply replied, "When I am twelve in your years, I will begin. It will be at the number of days from the beginning that is the perfect number; the day when all cycles are in alignment; in that moment I assume what is mine by divine appointment."

"Could you take yourself forward twelve years to that time?" asked Reverend Blaze in a soft, motherly voice. "Do you think you could do that for me?"

Involuntarily I clenched my fists and curled my toes tightly and then slowly stretched out my fingers and toes as if I was being remotely controlled. In a few moments the spirit that was me, but that I didn't feel connected to, spoke out in the voice of a proud, determined youth. "It is done and I am here!" the voice declared.

"To whom am I speaking and where are you?" Reverend Blaze inquired quickly, excited by my spirited response.

"Woman, you speak to the Ahow of Ahowob" announced the voice coming from my reposing body. "I am Mah Kina Hanab Pacal; He of the Jaguar Sun; He of the World Tree; He of the Place of the Water Lily; Child of the Mother of the Gods; Holy Bacab of the Maya."

"What is your role, Ahow?" queried Reverend Blaze.

"My role is that of Holy Bacab, to appease the gods, keep the days and honor our ancestors. I will lead and strengthen my people so that they will never again be suppressed by gods nor men. I will inspire them to build magnificent temples of such splendor that the gods will bless and protect us. And I will leave the legacy of my greatness in the spirits of many descendants and recorded in stone to last until this cycle of humanity is complete."

I could hear myself speaking and while my words seemed fanciful and incredible, I was powerless to control what was being said.

Reverend Blaze must have noticed that my conscious mind was beginning to force its way to the surface, because she interrupted my speech. "Ahow can you take us to the time of the ending of your life?"

"I will take you to the end of my time in your world!" declared the voice of the boy and then almost instantly came another voice - an anguished whisper. " I have failed. Ahhh, I have failed most miserably," my lips cried.

"In what way have you failed?" Blaze questioned gently.

"My weakness has tried the patience of even the most forgiving gods. I am shamed to see the faces of my ancestors. They will condemn the anger and pride that have blinded me. They will shun me for my transgressions. Oh, I am so very weary with myself. I'm so unprepared for the tests that await me in Xibalba."

My hands crossed on my chest as the despaired voice of Ahow murmured, "I await my last breath in this womb. I am adorned with the sacred green stone and the shimmering green feathers of the flying serpent. Now they annoint me with the red powder that will send me to Xibalba. I hear so much wailing around me. They do not cry for the loss of their Holy Bacab, they cry for mercy. Ah, Kawil, I pray that the blood of the children of Ik will appease you. He beckons me in the distant light. Now I too will plead for mercy!

"I have failed!" I cried out with pathetic anguish. I began sobbing convulsively and my crying shook me to consciousness. The memory of what had just transpired remained quite vivid as I sat up and tried to hide my teary face in my hands. My recall of the experience seemed too clear to have been the result of hypnotism. I felt like I had just made a complete fool of myself by making up this ridiculous fantasy for a stranger who just sat staring at me now. "I have to go," I suddenly blurted. "How long was I out," I asked, pretending that, despite of my feelings of never losing consciousness, I really had been hypnotized.

"Out?" questioned Reverend Blaze. "I never put my clients out. I just help them to remember. You know Christina," she paused while trying to carefully phrase her next words, "You're carrying that sense of failure around with you like a ball and chain. How many lifetimes are you going to suffer through, before you forgive yourself?"

"What did Alenka tell you?" I snapped, thinking about my failed business, the threat of financial doom lurking over my head, and my second marriage that was on the rocks.

"Are you trying to tell me that everything that's going wrong in my life is because of my failure in another life, hundreds of years ago?" I didn't wait for an answer. Seething with embarrassment and frustration I continued, "I'll tell you what I think. I'm experiencing some tough times right now, so naturally I'm going to make up a story about being unhappy with myself. But tell me, how is this fantasy supposed to help me with reality? I'm sorry, Reverend Blaze, you'd better find someone else to write your brochure for you. I'm really not as open-minded as I thought." I quickly slipped my feet back into my high-heels, picked up my briefcase and marched out the door.

# Kit

Kit's lithe twelve-year old body was sprawled across the living room sofa, the phone receiver propped between her right ear and one of the dusty-rose velvet pillows that ran across the back and arms of the L-shaped sectional. A can of diet Coke, dripping droplets of condensation, and a straw basket of tortilla chips were perched at the edge of an end table that had been strategically positioned so that she could avail herself of these essential nutrients without loosing ear contact with the phone. The hand that wasn't delivering sustenance to her mouth was perched, at the ready, on the TV remote control that was set to switch at the flick of a button between two different music video stations, so that hardly a moment would elapse between the last note of a song and the mid-song interruption of another on the alternate station.

Considering that Kit's right ear was occupied with the conversation of whomever was on the other end of the receiver, and the capacity of her left ear was completely saturated with the incessant musical pulsations blasting from the television, it wasn't surprising that I'd been able to unlock the door, enter the apartment and approach my daughter completely unnoticed. When Kit suddenly became aware that someone was standing at her feet she almost jumped out of her skin in terror before she realized it was me.

"Mommy! Why don't you just scare me to death!" she shrieked.

"Sorry" I mumbled as I slipped off my heels and picked up my daughter's feet and placed them on my lap as I settled onto the sofa. Kit was immediately aware that something was wrong and simultaneously flicked off the television while she informed the person on the phone that she would call them back. She was keenly sensitive to my moods and often felt frightened by the anxiety that she detected in me during the past months. It seemed that all of my attempts to protect my daughter from the desperate situation that was unfolding around us, were futile with such a perceptively intuitive child.

"Did you loose another account today?" Kit asked as she sat up and moved closer towards me, almost in tears from the insecure way it made her feel to see the devastated expression on my face.

I put my arm around her without turning towards her and struggled to speak without breaking down into tears. "I've lost everything, Kitten," I stammered. "The whole business is down the tubes and Paul and I are splitting up. I just don't know what to do anymore." Although my protective, motherly instincts realized that Kit was too young and insecure to burden with the frightening consequences of my failures, a deeper, more primitive need compelled me to pour out my heart to the one person I knew would love me unconditionally, no matter how poor my judgment; how unwise my decisions; or how foolish my actions. This evening the mother would become the child, as I tried to fathom our imminent future.

Kit had been aware that my second marriage wasn't going along smoothly. While Paul and I never fought or said anything mean to, or about each other, as she'd witnessed with her father, there was a strained tension when Paul was around, which lately, wasn't very often. I didn't explain to the teenager that I suspected that my husband was a homosexual, but I had to let her know what the consequences would be in the dissolution of another marriage.

"We can't afford to live in the city," I explained, "So we might as well let Paul keep the apartment." Paul's financial situation wasn't too much better than my own and I knew it would be unreasonable to expect any support from him. While my bankruptcy would eliminate all of our debts, I had to admit that financing my business had already depleted both of our assets. If Paul had been a terrible disappointment to me sexually, it was I who had managed, in the three short years of our marriage, to bring economic ruin to both of us. He'd paid a steep price for his desperate attempt to prove his virility.

I suggested that we spend the weekend apartment hunting on Long Island. Not only was the rent less than in the city, but I'd been led to believe that it would also be cheaper to live in the suburbs. We wouldn't have to pay for parking and food would be cheaper outside the city. I assumed that I'd be able to find a job near wherever we lived and therefore didn't consider the cost or time of commuting into New York.

Although I didn't fully explain the reasoning behind each of the things we discussed that night, I felt that Kit had a right to participate in those decisions that would affect her. For almost three years, my daughter had suffered the loss of my attentions while I had been distracted by a new marriage and preoccupied with a new business. The bond between us had been pulled taunt and as we sat talking late into the night, I began to realize how close I'd come to destroying our relationship through sheer neglect.

Before Paul and the business, survival had been a team effort for Kit and me; our pasta and peanut-butter and jelly diet didn't seem to matter as long as we had each other to lean on. Except for one, brief attempt to fit into the corporate structure, I had always worked as a freelance designer at home and had always been there for her. Now, even when I finally did get home, there was nothing left of me emotionally to give my daughter. I'd subconsciously put her on hold three years ago, promising myself that as soon as things got back to normal I'd give her more time and attention. But somewhere during those years she'd matured enough to resent the loss of her mother's attention. She filled that void with endless, mindless telephone calls with her friends, accompanied with the perpetual, hypnotic, flickering of video images on the TV screen.

I couldn't help feeling an overwhelming love and admiration as I looked at my daughter that night. She was developing into a real beauty, having somehow sidestepped that awkward, gawky stage that often precedes puberty. "The boys are probably beginning to hover around her like bees around a fragrant new bloom," I thought to myself as I admired her. Kit was exceptionally creative and had shown herself to have quite a talent for drawing. Her teachers always had to qualify their complaints that she talked too much with the admission that her grades were beyond reproach.

As much as I was fighting back despair that night, I also began to sense that, for everything I'd lost, I was also recapturing something valuable that had almost, imperceptibly and perhaps irretrievably slipped away. I hoped that what I could offer of myself now, would somehow compensate for the most difficult decision we had to make that night — the start of school was only two weeks away and I still hadn't been able to come up with the first tuition payment for the private school Kit had attended for the past two years. Part of the reason we would have to move out of the city was so that Kit could go to a decent public school. We would have to find an apartment quickly if I was going to get her enrolled in time for the start of school.

I watched my daughter's face carefully as she absorbed the idea that she wouldn't be returning to school with all of her friends in

September and for the first time I began to experience an over-whelming sense of guilt for my failure. My daughter would have to suffer as a result of my ineptitude as a business woman.

Once I'd opened guilt's ugly door, the self-reproach came pouring through in droves. I began to wonder if it had been my ambition that had turned Paul off to women. Had my futile escapade into the world of business, not only emptied our coffers but also emasculated my husband? Next came thoughts of the women who would follow behind me in the business world. Would the banks that had believed in me enough to loan me money, use me now as statistical proof that women were a bad credit risk? I even agonized about my uncle who had been so proud of his niece, "the business tycoon". He wouldn't be bragging about me now.

After Kit went to bed, I went to the freezer and took out the bottle of vodka I always kept chilled. "God made booze for nights like these," I said half aloud to the picture of my mother on the wall in the hallway. As was my custom of late, I brought the drink to bed with me. But instead of sipping it slowly, I gulped it desperately and then curled myself into a fetal position and cried long, convulsive tears of grief for the death of my dreams.

Several hours later, my tears spent, I was still awake. I watched as the lighted digital clock flicked from 12:17 to 12:18 and marveled at the vast stream of thoughts that could pass through my mind in only that one minute. Crazed with the endless emptiness of the night, I calculated that there would be over 360 more minutes until morning and decided to get another drink in an attempt to finally fall asleep.

But then it was 1:30 and then finally 1:31 and still sleep would not rescue me from my morbid tirade of thoughts — mostly fearful, dreary speculations about the future. I wished there was a way to remove myself from the agony of those thoughts.

"If only I could skip the next few years and just look back on them when I've successfully overcome all of this," I thought.

Then I remembered an experience I'd had at my friend Alenka's apartment several weeks earlier. Alenka espoused many metaphysical teachings and had insisted one day that I learn how to relax through meditation. Together we'd sat cross-legged on the living room floor, humming the mantra "Oooohmmm" and visualizing a circle representing nothing, while listening to a tape of synthesizer music that Alenka had explained was "new age music".

At first I had gone along with the exercise just to appease my friend. Part of Alenka's charm was the way she was always eagerly embracing new ideas. I never wanted to dampen her spirit, even when I thought she was approaching the bizarre. It had been Alenka who'd talked me into participating in a seminar that previous summer that included walking barefoot over a bed of hot coals. Since I'd survived that experience unscathed, I was more open minded to the new experiences she was always suggesting.

That didn't mean that I was willing to readily accept some of the beliefs Alenka embraced. But as it happened, on that afternoon that she was teaching me how to meditate, I'd had the experience of viewing my body from above it. Later, when I'd told Alenka about the sensation, she'd been overjoyed.

"I knew you were gifted! People practice meditation for years and are never able to do that!" she'd exclaimed. "And you just let yourself relax, just once, and you're having out of body experiences. You're wasting yourself in that business."

Naturally, I had been less enthusiastic. If it didn't put money in the bank what good was a "gift"?

But as I turned the clock that now said 1:32 to face away from me, I decided to try the meditation experience again. I had no "new age" tapes to play and I was too tired to go to the stereo anyway, so I decided to try it without music. Sitting, cross-legged in the middle of my bed, I visualized a circle and softly hummed the "Ooohmmm" chant. Within minutes I felt my body relax as the fears I'd been dwelling on moved out of focus. Suddenly a thought came to me so clearly that it seemed that a voice was actually speaking it…

"Nothing is everything."

The concept was far afield of everything I'd been thinking about that night and yet it seem completely right to be thinking it.

"Yes," I thought, "It's so simple a child could understand it. Zero is the potential; the seed from which everything can come." The circle I'd been visualizing began to glow against the dark background that it was floating in, and then, as it moved further away, it grew to fill my entire field of vision. Within it appeared an idyllic landscape. In what seemed to be the faint light of early dawn, I could see lush, misty grasslands stretching out to infinity. The view came so clearly into focus that I felt as if I'd actually stepped into it. The sounds of early morning surrounded me: bird songs of every description, from the soft and melodious to the sharp and demanding; the distant barking of dogs and the howls and roars of animals I couldn't identify; the sound of water flowing over rocks in a stream not too far in front of me; and the almost soundless flutter of an egret landing in the dewy grass beside me. I looked up to see the glowing rim of the sun beginning to show itself over the distant horizon. It seemed to be rising so quickly that I could actually perceive its movement.

Then, shortly after the entire disk of the sun became visible, a dark circular shadow began to intrude into the glowing sphere, as though it were devouring it. Silence gradually replaced the chatter that had just surrounded me as I watched as the sun continued to rise. The dark shadow steadily slid over it, consuming the virgin light of dawn. It was as though the world had changed its mind and decided to go back to sleep. Soon the shadow had positioned itself directly over the sun. Except for an eerie reflection at the edges of the horizon, the glowing circle that remained cast no light on the world below or the sky above. In the reestablished darkness, the sky was alight with stars. I immediately recognized the constellations Pisces and Aries, although they seemed to be positioned differently. A bright, greenish star seemed out of place just above the Pleiades, and it took me a moment to realize that I was seeing Venus as the Morning Star. I reasoned that the bright reddish star just to the southwest of the hidden sun would be Mars. I looked back towards the sun which was struggling to tear itself free of the ominous shadow. The glowing circle was becoming brighter on its right edge when, again I heard the words, "Nothing is everything." This time though, I realized that the words were coming from my own lips. But the voice was not mine!

A strange feathery sensation settled onto my thighs and I looked down to see the egret sitting there on my crossed legs. Suddenly, to my horror, I realized that I was looking down at the copper-colored body of a naked young boy. "This is only a dream!" I shrieked and the sound of my voice shook me back to consciousness.

I was still sitting cross legged in the center of my bed and my cat, Daisy, who had settled into my lap, was looking up at me sleepily, probably wondering why her mistress had disturbed her sleep. I reached over to the clock and turned it back around. It was 6:30. Thinking of Dickens' Christmas Carol, I murmured, "So they did it all in one night," and reluctantly dragged myself into the shower. I was more exhausted than I'd ever felt before in my life.

# Charlie

It's funny how you can know someone for years in a superficial way, never really knowing them, and then, Wham! something happens, the time is right, and suddenly you see this person from an entirely new perspective. That's how I fell in love with Charlie. He swears he loved me from the first moment he met me, and maybe that's true. But I must admit, although I was always comfortable around him, I'd never thought much about him, except that he was the most reliable printer in New York City.

But then my life turned upside down, and I'll never be certain whether Charlie was the reason or the cause, not that it matters…

The day after my strange dream with the eclipse, I noticed a classified ad in the New York Advertising Club newsletter that seemed to be written just for me. It read "2 bdrm. apt. on LI. Reasonable rent for career single." The phone number seemed vaguely familiar as I dialed it and when a voice answered "City Ink!" I realized that it was Charlie DiMartino who had placed the ad.

Several months earlier Charlie's wife had died after a long and debilitating illness. Not that he had made much of it — the only way I knew about it was when Charlie's secretary, Maria, had explained that he was at his wife's funeral one day when I'd called his office for a quote. Actually, I'd been surprised to hear that Charlie was married; he never spoke about his family and he'd always appear at business or social functions unaccompanied. Charlie was always in the spotlight at these events, he had a natural flair for amusing and charming a crowd and he was often asked to MC an awards ceremony or provide entertainment for a party.

In the few moments before Charlie picked up the phone, I thought I'd figured out the whole scenario and presumptuously greeted him with, "So Charlie, you're finally going to move out here to the city."

"Hell no!" Charlie replied, "Where'd you ever get a crazy idea like that?"

"Well I thought this was your apartment you have advertised." I stammered, feeling uncomfortable about making the wrong assumption. "I thought maybe you were subletting it."

"Christine, the whole world doesn't live in apartments," Charlie laughed. "I have a big, old house in Hicksville that's just too big now, so I've decided to make half of it into an apartment. Do you know someone who'd be interested in renting it?"

"Actually, I was calling for myself," I explained quickly, pausing to gauge Charlie's reaction.

"Oh?" he questioned, waiting for me to offer further explanation.

"I'm splitting up with Paul. You know I closed the agency last month and I've pretty much given up on the City. I'm going to look for work out on the Island — maybe a copywriting job with a small agency.

"How much is the rent?" I quickly changed the subject away from my brief encapsulation of my personal life.

"For you, I'd have to think about it," Charlie softly replied. I didn't realize that my interest had caught him completely off guard. As I explained, I was oblivious to his attraction to me and the fact that my call seemed to him like an answer from heaven. But I mistook his hesitation to give me a price as reluctance to rent the apartment to me.

"Why don't you come by, and we'll discuss it?" he offered after a long, uncomfortable silence. His voice had taken on a soft and inviting tone which didn't seem to fit with my perception of being a persona nongrata. But I agreed to a time later that afternoon and bid an uncertain good-bye.

Pulling open the heavy glass door with the "City Ink" logo stenciled boldly in red across the front, I was too preoccupied with my own problems to notice the pungent odor of inks and other chemicals that I usually found so unpleasant. In fact, for a moment I almost forgot why I was there. Maria, Charlie's matronly secretary seemed surprised to see me.

"Christina, we haven't seen you around in a while. How are you managing these days?" she asked in her usual concerned manner.

I replied with a detached "Oh, I'm getting by," as I peered past her into Charlie's office. He was at his desk and motioned to me with a wave of his arm to come in. I nodded an obliging smile to Maria as I walked past her to his office.

Charlie's office was as comfortable and unassuming as he was. The furniture was good, solid, quality oak, but old and worn and scarred with burn marks. Cigarette ashes were on the rug and butts overflowed from his ashtray. I couldn't remember ever seeing Charlie without a cigarette and the stale smell of smoke that penetrated his office actually masked the ink fumes.

"Sit down, sit down," he blurted happily, his pleasant mood in sharp contrast to my own gloomy disposition.

"Good God, Christine, what's happening? First you close shop and now you're leaving your husband? What did the guy do to make you leave him now when you're flat on your ass broke?"

I was sure his question was an assault on my intellect and an outright denial of my ability to pay the rent. I could feel my face flush with embarrassment as tears welled up in my eyes. As I struggled to compose myself enough to reply, Charlie was looking straight at me with a scrutinizing expression. As seemingly endless moments passed with no one saying anything, Charlie's face softened to sympathy for the poor woman standing before him on the verge of tears.

"Let's go get a cup of coffee," he suggested as he put his arm on my shoulder and steered me around and out of his office. "Maria, I'm going for coffee," he called back to his secretary. Glancing at his watch he added, "Hell, it's almost five, I'll see you in the morning." "Looks like you need something stronger than coffee," he said with a wink and led me out to the street.

I liked the feel of his hand on my shoulder although I wasn't sure why. Charlie was at least fifteen years older than me, but his careless appearance made him seem even older. He was barely taller than me in my heels, with a gut he made no effort to contain. Yet, in spite of the initial disheveled impact of his appearance, he exuded a friendliness and charm that most people found irresistible.

"So what is it? Is he mean to you? Is he cheating? Or does he have some strange tropical disease," he asked in a last ditch attempt to find out what was going on in my life.

I managed a nervous laugh, "One from column a and two from b."

Charlie let out a long low whistle and guided me into the pub next door to his shop. "What'll you have?" he asked as he pulled out a chair for me at a table in a quiet, back corner.

"A cool million, on the rocks," I answered dourly and Charlie was halfway to the bar before he realized what I'd said. I watched him as he swung around back towards me with the smooth grace of a dancer and shook his head approvingly as if to say I was OK.

"If they don't know how to make that, neither do I," I offered, "so I'll settle for a Vodka Gimlet." Charlie again pirouetted around towards the bar like Fred Astaire and ordered our drinks.

It wasn't the alcohol that loosened my tongue that evening, so much as the way Charlie had of listening to me as if everything I said was of profound interest to him. I found myself telling him every detail about "Operation Termination" a term I had coined for the painful experience of going out of business, and I bemoaned the personal bankruptcy I'd been forced into as a result. I explained how I had been too naive for business and watched as he apologetically nodded his agreement. As the night wore on, I told him all about the sexual disaster my second marriage had turned out to be and my painful decision to move out of the city. We talked about my relationship with my daughter and how all of this had affected her.

And then, when I felt completely comfortable, I told him about my strange experience with Reverend Blaze and the related dream that I'd had the previous night.

Charlie made a better audience than anyone I'd ever known; asking questions along the way; steering me towards new topics; and somehow encouraging me to reveal my deepest thoughts. He ordered more drinks, and then hamburgers and fries, and then more drinks, all the while seeming to absorb every detail of my outpouring saga. When at last I realized that I'd bared my soul to this virtual stranger, I abruptly stopped talking and stared at him in amazement.

"I don't know why I told you all of this. What is it about you that just made me open up?" I asked. "You should be a shrink."

"Sometimes we just have to talk to somebody," he whispered gently. "You'd be surprised how many people that you'd think never had a care in the world, have been through some pretty bad shit. I've been through enough of it myself to recognize when someone else is suffering. When my wife was sick and dying, the hospital bills wiped me out. I almost lost my house. I'm only now beginning to see the light at the end of the tunnel," he explained, encapsulating his whole life history in just two sentences.

What Charlie didn't tell me that night was how captivated he was with me. My story had kept him genuinely spellbound and he could not help wondering about his good fortune to finally spend time with me. It was some time later that he actually confessed these things to me, but at the time he simply offered his help.

"Why don't you and your daughter come out and take a look at my apartment on Saturday? We'll work out something for the rent, maybe you can do some of the design work for some of my customer's jobs."

For the first time that evening I could feel the weight of despair start to lift. "Every time I'm on the edge of a cliff," I exclaimed, "God sends me a miracle!"

"Hey, I'm no miracle. I just hate to see you so miserable. And that husband of yours has to be nuts, I think you're a very sexy lady," he added.

I couldn't help noticing how my body was responding to Charlie's attention. He wasn't the kind of man you'd swoon over on first sight, but his sensitivity and intelligence were more seductive than any muscle-bound young stud. I imagined his arms around me and it sent a flutter through me. Embarrassed by my thoughts, I looked at my watch and realized it was 11:00. "Oh my God, my daughter's probably organizing a search party by now!" I gasped.

Charlie was equally startled by the time and quickly paid the check. "My car's just around the block. Can I give you a lift home?" he offered. I was always pleased to avoid taking the subway at night and I couldn't afford a cab, so I was delighted to accept his offer. But beyond the logical reasons, there was this strange new illogical one.

As we walked around the block I felt his arm move across my back and his hand rest firmly on my shoulder. "You know, you're a pretty sexy guy, yourself," I whispered. Charlie said nothing, he just looked at me surprised and smiled. We didn't say much as he drove me uptown. I suppose our newly confessed attraction felt uncomfortable. The free and trusting way I had felt while I was pouring out my heart to him that evening seemed to have faded. But as we pulled into the U-shaped drive to my apartment building, Charlie took my hand and gently kissed it.

"I've enjoyed this evening," he whispered more seductively than my husband had ever spoken me, even on our honeymoon.

I tried to respond, but no sound would come from my startled lips, so I silently mouthed, "Me too," and sat there immobilized by the way Charlie was staring at me. For the first time I noticed the unusual coloring of his eyes — each shimmering green center surrounded by a dark gray circle. "You have the most fascinating eyes," I whispered.

"The better to look at you, my dear," he laughed, just as Bobby, the doorman, opened my door. I gave Charlie's hypnotic eyes one last glance that I hoped would clearly communicate the way I felt. But my thoughts were abruptly interrupted by the doorman.

"Will Paul be returning this evening?" the big, burly man mumbled as he held open the car door, eyeing Charlie suspiciously. I knew that Bobby felt a sense of protective responsibility for Paul because they had both been at that building for so many years, but I resented his presumption of "keeping an eye on me".

"Paul will be out of town for another week... at least," I snapped at him, my annoyance clearly evident in my tone as I stepped out of Charlie's car. "I'll talk to you tomorrow," I called to Charlie in a much softer voice than I had just answered the bothersome doorman. Charlie threw me a kiss and drove away.

# Alenka

"Mrs. Rossi, your daughter's been looking for you!" the doorman called to me as I rushed past him to the elevator. I threw my hands up in the air in mock surrender and hurried onto the elevator. The way Kit kept tract of my whereabouts sometimes made me feel like a child still reporting in to my mother. While I tried to understand that my daughter's concern for me was something I was grateful to have, this evening, I resented being admonished by the doorman for coming home at the perfectly civilized hour of 11:30. By the time the elevator had reached the twenty-eighth floor, I had calmed down enough to realize that I could have spared Kit a great deal of anxiety by just calling her to tell her I was OK.

Since I'd already anticipated my daughter's frantic greeting and was prepared to make an honest apology and explanation by the time she opened the door, I was almost disappointed to walk in and find her calmly chatting with Alenka at the dining room table. I began my speech anyway but Alenka just waved her hands in front of her face and said, "Cut the crap! You needed a night out! I came by because I've been thinking about you a lot lately, and found poor Kit here pacing the floors, worrying about you. I told her to remind you of this the next time she gets home late from a date."

"Thanks, you're a real pal!" I said sarcastically.

"Mommy, Alenka says you were having dinner with a wonderful man who's going to change your life. Is that true?" Kit asked as she got up and draped herself affectionately on my shoulders.

I shot my friend a surprised glance. "Will you please try to curtail your fortune-telling around my daughter. She believes all this stuff you tell her.

"Kitten, I wouldn't exactly call the man I just had a few drinks with, the man of my dreams. We just talked.

"Really Alenka," I groaned, "I don't see how an unkempt printer who's old enough to be my father is going to have any impact on my life."

Alenka pretended to look back and forth at the ceiling while humming. "You've been in the cold world of business far too long, my friend. What you demean as fortune telling is plain old women's intuition. It's every woman's birthright. Unfortunately, too many of you are suffocating that natural ability under all of your dress-for-success business suits."

I pretended to look down into my blouse for my suffocating intuition. "And all this time I thought they were boobs!" I exclaimed.

I had to admit that Alenka's uncanny ability to predict events had proven correct too often to be ignored. But, as always, whenever something made me uncomfortable, I made a joke of it. Kit, on the other hand, was completely enchanted with Alenka and willingly accepted anything she said as gospel truth. This tall, flamboyant, Czechoslovakian woman was just eccentric enough to be acceptable to her rebellious, teenage mind. She loved listening in on our conversations about Alenka's diverse and unconventional romantic escapades, and her somewhat bizarre psychic experiences.

Alenka had already helped herself to the opened bottle of wine in the refrigerator, and a box of Oreos. I was glad my kooky friend had not adopted the rigid health food eating regiments of many of her New Age cohorts. She believed in partaking wholeheartedly in all of life's pleasures, and it was that attitude that I found so exhilarating about Alenka. Having been raised with the morbid, Catholic-Italian mentality of self-denial, I saw Alenka as living proof that indulgence of the flesh was not necessarily a precursor for damnation of the spirit. I was sure that this earthy, individualistic woman had the wholehearted approval of the gods. Why else would they have blessed her with such insight into their realm?

"So Mary Blaze tells me you had quite an intriguing experience yesterday." Alenka mumbled with a mouthful of chocolate cookies.

"Sure, I'm flat broke and you set me up with a kook instead of a client." I grumbled.

"Did you a favor, you mean," Alenka retorted in her motherly tone. "There are no accidents in this world. The things that happen to us, the people we bring into our lives, they all have a reason. Trust me, sometimes you have to loose everything before you can begin to realize what you really have."

Alenka's words reminded me of the dream I'd had the night before. I went on to tell her the details of my past life regression and the subsequent experience I had while meditating last night. "I'm not sure whether I actually had that experience as a meditation or if even the meditating was a dream. I just know that I remember it more vividly than any dream I ever had. Do you think the crazy story I told Reverend Blaze inspired the dream?" I asked my dearest friend.

Before she could answer, Kit, who had been captivated with every detail of my story, spoke up. "We studied a little bit about the Mayans in school last year," she offered, ignoring my perplexed question. "Our teacher said that no one knows where they came from or why they seemed to just suddenly disappear. Maybe, if you can remember more, you can solve the mystery."

I laughed uncomfortably. "You don't seriously believe that I was actually remembering a past life. Even if reincarnation is possible, and I'm willing to concede that it could be, why would a great ruler return as someone whose whole life seems to be a total failure!"

As the words escaped my mouth, I suddenly realized that that was exactly how I had described my previous life as Ahow. I glanced towards Alenka as she just nodded glibly with her eyes raised in an "I told you so" expression.

"Do you know the significance of yesterday?" Alenka asked. "It's the beginning of the Harmonic Convergence. According to the predictions of ancient civilizations, this is when the second coming of the Messiah begins. But this time, Christ doesn't come as a solitary messenger. This time our salvation comes as an awakening in the universal human spirit. Don't you think it's significant that your remembrance of a past life should have occurred on this day?"

My curiosity was awakened. "Then you don't think I just made up that whole story because of everything that's going wrong in my life right now?" I asked.

"Just the opposite! I think that the story you told — mind you, I didn't say 'made up' — is directly related to what's happening in your life right now. It's not because of it, more likely it is the cause.

"Remember the first time I did a reading with you? I told you that you were building over existing structures that were too shaky to support you? You were completely out of place in the ad agency business. You're just too sensitive and talented to be prostituting your creativity on Madison Avenue. And as for your marriage, it was a learning experience you chose to have when you chose this incarnation. Look at what you've learned about compassion for other people's human weakness. What I can't understand is, how come you're so tolerant of weakness in others and you can't concede to any in yourself?"

I turned nervously towards Kit. Charlie was the first person with whom I had ever discussed the sexual problems in my marriage. But I knew that Alenka was clairvoyant enough to have figured out the problems I was having with Paul and I wanted to keep the ensuing conversation from my daughter. "Kitten, don't you think you should be getting to bed," I suggested.

"Oh sure, just when the conversation gets hot and juicy!" she cried as she stood up to leave.

"Honey, I really don't think this conversation is appropriate for a twelve-year old, young lady," I explained. Kit looked at Alenka as if to say I was "out of it", but the red-head just made a brushing motion with her hands for her to leave the room. Kit gave me an obliging peck on the cheek then bestowed Alenka with a warm hug and kiss. I understood the message her exaggerated affection toward Alenka was meant to convey, but ignored it, giving her rear end an affectionate light tap as she walked past me to her bedroom.

"When's Paul coming home?" Alenka asked as soon as Kit was gone.

"Good question," I replied. "He's on tour with the band. You know how musicians are, he doesn't want to answer to anybody. He called last Friday from San Francisco..." I offered every bit of information I could except for what was really bothering me.

"You think it's somebody in the band?" Alenka asked, clearly alluding to her understanding that I suspected Paul was involved in a homosexual relationship. I nodded, hardly surprised that my friend seemed to know something I'd taken months to figure out. In a way I was glad I didn't have to explain the situation — saying it out loud would have been much too painful.

Alenka knew enough to change the subject. "So tell me about this guy you had dinner with tonight," she queried brightly.

"What's to tell you, that you don't already know," I answered. Although Alenka insisted that she wasn't actually able to read minds, it often seemed like her ability to know things before you chose to talk about them was an invasion of privacy.

"He was really very nice, and for some strange reason I felt completely at ease with him — sort of like I've known him all my life."

"Or all your other lives?" Alenka offered.

Alenka and I talked late into the night about reincarnation and karma, about how our friendship had carried us through so many changes, or as Alenka insisted, through so many previous lives. One thing that became apparent was that neither one of us knew anything about the Mayans. I wasn't even sure if they were contemporaries of the Aztecs or Incas, or even where they actually lived. I planned to stop by the library the next day to find out more and to call an astronomy friend of mine at the Hayden Planetarium to discuss the eclipse and the constellations I saw in my meditation.

Astronomy had always been of interest to me, although there were few nights clear enough to see much more than the moon through my telescope out on the balcony. But I knew enough about it to know that it might be possible to determine the date of the eclipse in my dream, by calculating the position of the stars and the planet Venus, assuming that I was viewing the event at sunrise.

It was well past midnight before Alenka pulled out the sofa bed in the living room. She worked as a nurse at the Mt. Sinai Medical Center which was further uptown so it made no sense for her to take a cab all the way downtown so late at night. As I helped her tuck the corners of the sheets under the mattress, I realized that this would probably be the last time she would be staying at this apartment. We looked out the south window that filled the entire living room wall, picking out the traditional lighted landmarks: Citibank; The Empire State Building; the Chrysler Building; and further down, the two, glittering, twin rectangles of the World Trade Center. I handed Alenka a couple of pillows and a light blanket. Following my friend's gaze out the window, I sighed, "I'm going to miss this place. There's something about seeing all those buildings that still sends chills up my spine." It was the first time either of us had alluded to my impending move.

"I'm going to miss these all night gossip sessions," Alenka added with a note of melancholy.

~

That night, as I lay in bed, I thought about the way I'd been aroused by the simple touch of Charlie's hand on my shoulder. It seemed like years since I'd had any kind of sexual encounter and I realized that I was aching for, not only the physical gratification, but the safe reassurance of a man holding me close. I wondered if my attraction to this unassuming, gentle man was only due to my starving sexuality, or if, as Alenka had implied, he was part of my destiny. I fell asleep imagining what it would be like to make love with him.

# Maya Mirrors

Early the following morning I took the subway down to 42nd street and quickly walked the two blocks over to the Library. One thing I was certain to miss when I moved out of New York City would be the Public Library. Each time I climbed those imposing front steps that served as seats for the friendless and the homeless and others just passing the time or waiting for someone or something to happen, I always felt as if I was approaching a temple of the most revered of all gods — The Source of Knowledge. But today that sense was particularly intense, in fact I could almost swear I could hear the chanting of crowds of worshipers from the street below me, as the lions, so proudly perched at the precipice, turned their faces towards me and let out a ferocious roar.

Once inside, I quickly assembled a stack of reference books and periodicals about the Maya and became so deeply engrossed in what I was reading that the hours slyly slipped by into late afternoon. I poured over book after book and discovered that there was evidence of Maya society flowering hundreds of years before Christ. Between 600 and 800 AD their civilization flourished throughout an area that includes today's southern Mexico and the Yucatan Peninsula, most of Guatemala, all of Belize, and parts of Honduras and El Salvador. The Maya were preceded by a sophisticated, although mysterious culture referred to as the Olmecs, who seemed to spring from nowhere sometime before 1200 BC on the east coast of Tabasco, Mexico. The Olmecs are believed to have influenced the ancient city of Teotihuacán near modern Mexico City and Monte Albán in Oaxaca as well as many early Maya sites.

Most of the older books about the Maya were based on conjecture since the remains of their hieroglyphic-type of writing was yet to be deciphered. But, in some of the more recent articles I read that great strides were being made in interpreting those glyphs.

It was obvious from what I read that the Maya had accomplished incredible architectural feats, especially considering that they were achieved without the use of the wheel, draft animal, or metal tools. They observed and accurately recorded the movements of the moon, planets and stars. Their calendar was at least as accurate as our own and was used to predict such astronomical phenomena as eclipses, as well as cycles of luck or misfortune. They had a simple mathematical system which used only three symbols: the dot, the bar, and a symbol for zero as a place holder — something Mediterranean cultures of the time didn't have!

Most of the older literature referred to the Maya as a peaceable people who performed colorful rituals. But more recent references told of bloodletting, human sacrifice and warfare. Although each of the Maya centers was independently ruled, apparently there was extensive trade and an exchange of artistic and intellectual ideas, as well as goods, between them. Great roadways connected many of these sites.

A chart in one book showed the symbols for the twenty days of the Maya calendar system that were matched consecutively with a cycle of thirteen numbers. The name of the twentieth day sign, Ahau, caught my attention. Spoken aloud, it was identical to the name I'd given myself while recounting my past life to Reverend Blaze! I was even more astounded to read elsewhere that Ahau was a title given to Maya rulers.

Enthusiastically, I flipped through the colorful pictures of Maya items on display in the Museum of Anthropology, in Mexico City. Like the sorry victims I saw in a photo of a mural on one of their temple walls, the Maya had taken me captive. One photograph showed a life-sized jade mosaic mask from a funerary crypt at a ruin known as Palenque. I recalled being "covered with sacred green stone and the green feathers of the flying serpent" when I recounted my death as Ahow to Rev. Blaze. The mask in the photo had been found with the skeleton of Maya ruler. The text explained that his corpse had been adorned with dark green jadeite jewelry — a necklace and pectoral, delicately carved earplugs, bracelets made of hundreds of beads, rings on every finger, a large bead clasped in each hand and another in his mouth. Other photos of carvings showed Maya dignitaries bedecked in elaborate headdresses of quetzal feathers.

Looking at each new photo in the book was like discovering another piece to a puzzle. I felt my heart racing with excitement as I uncovered the evidence to support the story I'd recounted during my regression. My education had never included anything about the Mesoamerican civilizations, nor could I recall ever hearing anything about the Maya, except perhaps vague references to the Aztecs, Incas and Mayans as people who had lived somewhere in Central or South America. There was no way that I could have so accurately conjured the details I had described to Rev. Blaze. Contrary to my initial reaction, I was now convinced that there had to be some validity to the story. But where did it come from? Was I actually recalling my own past life, or was I somehow channeling the memoirs of a long dead spirit?

If my stomach hadn't suddenly started protesting it's absence of nourishment, I probably would have stayed in the quiet of the library for days, lost in the world of the Maya. Squinting from the harsh sunlight, I stood at the top of the hot library steps and looked up and down Fifth Avenue, trying to reconcile my existence in the twentieth century with the ancient places I'd been reading about all morning. The lion statues poised at the top of the steps reminded me of the stone jaguars that guarded some of the temples I'd just seen in photographs. Was the vague sensation of recognition that haunted me déjà vu, or the product of an overactive imagination? Preoccupied with the question, I lugged my stack of books down to the subway to return home. I'd promised Charlie that we would meet him at his house in Hicksville that evening.

~

Charlie's directions to his house were simple enough and I was only ten minutes late when I turned my old Buick into the driveway of the cedar-shingled duplex. I tried not to let the pile of construction debris I noticed at the front curb prejudice my opinion of the house, but Kit suffered from no such sense of restraint. "This place is a dump, Mom," she whined.

"Shush!" I enjoined her as I put my hand over her mouth in an exaggerated display of embarrassment. "That stuff is probably from the renovation he's been doing to add on the apartment. Why don't you wait to see the inside. And for godsake, keep your criticisms to yourself!" Despite what I said to my daughter, I mouthed a silent prayer as I recalled some of the pigsties I'd looked at the last time I was apartment hunting. A pile of junk at the curb was nothing compared to some of the places I'd seen. I'd be happy if this apartment didn't smell of rotten garbage and nothing went scurrying away when I opened the cabinets.

Charlie welcomed us into his side of the house and, aside from the same lingering residue of cigarette smoke that was so pronounced in his office, Charlie's home was neat and exceptionally well decorated. The aroma of spaghetti sauce simmering in the kitchen made me feel like I was visiting my mother's house. It was a sensation I hadn't experienced since my mother had passed away five years earlier.

When I introduced Kit to Charlie, he complimented her on inheriting her mother's good looks. She responded by scrunching up her face in disgust, and I quickly explained to him that most girls find the thought of looking like their mother quite repulsive. "What do I know about girls?" Charlie grumbled as he lit up a cigarette, "I've raised four sons. Come to think of it, they wouldn't want to look like their mother either!"

Kit's face suddenly lit up with interest. "How old are they?" she asked, eagerly glancing around for some indication of their presence.

Charlie laughed, a loud, uproarious bellow that momentarily changed his whole appearance for the better. "They're too old for you, my dear! And besides, I wouldn't recommend any of them to a nice young lady like you. They're nothing but trouble, the whole bunch of 'em." He took a deep draw on his cigarette and I couldn't help but notice his sad expression when he referred to his sons. I was so proud of my daughter that it seemed remarkable to me that a parent could look so pained by the mere mention of their children.

We followed Charlie back outside and around to the side of the house where the new entrance to the apartment was still unpainted. Kit nudged me as we walked through the door and I turned to see her holding all her fingers crossed behind her back. While I couldn't accredit her superstitious ritual for what we saw, it couldn't have hurt. The living room was big and sunny with freshly painted beige walls and a thick, plush beige carpet. The kitchen was wallpapered in a ribboned Early American pattern and a big, cheery window opened out to the neatly landscaped backyard. I looked out the window and remarked on the pretty flower bed and patio. Charlie drew in my compliment with a puff on his cigarette and then hurriedly exhaled so that he could respond. "You can use the patio and yard anytime, there's a gas grill too if you wanna barbecue."

The rest of the apartment was as close to flawless as anything I could have imagined. I could easily picture my almond lacquer furniture fitting in with the nondescript vanilla of the floors and walls. Some of the windows already had blinds or curtains on them which would really save me a lot of trouble and money. "This place is per-fect, Charlie. You're a gift from heaven!" I exclaimed, using the moment to give him a friendly kiss.

Charlie flickered his cigarette, á la Groucho Marx, and replied, "Keep it up, honey and I'll lower the rent." While we all laughed, I thought about the way that quick kiss made me feel. There was no denying the physical attraction between us. From the way Charlie was looking at me, I knew he was also keenly aware of that attrac-tion. "So, whatdaya think? Do you want the apartment?" he asked.

I looked toward Kit for confirmation, while I assured Charlie that we would definitely take the place. "Can we move in next week?" I asked. "I'd like to get Kit into school at the start of the semester."

"Sure, you can start moving in today if you want," he responded, obviously delighted, and then added, as if the thought had just occurred to him, "I've got some spaghetti sauce brewing. Do you have any plans for dinner tonight?"

The aroma coming from Charlie's kitchen was even more tempt-ing than his company and Kit and I both happily agreed to stay for dinner. Kit hurried off, explaining she was going to "check out the neighborhood," and I followed Charlie through the inside door that connected the two apartments, to his kitchen. He stirred his sauce and started water boiling for the pasta so casually that I guessed that he'd been doing it all his life. I felt perfectly content, sitting at his old oak table, watching him cook as we talked like two old friends.

Our conversation was so effortless that we continued talking non-stop throughout dinner, with Kit edging into the conversation now and then, her tone becoming more and more sarcastic. I didn't notice her growing annoyance as she watched Charlie and me dis-cussing the problems of operating a small business while clearing up the table. I hardly took note when she went off to the living room to sulk in front of the television, while we continued talking over coffee. In fact it was dark out when Kit finally came and plunked herself in our midst and defiantly announced that she thought it was about time we went home.

While Kit traipsed out to the car, grumbling to herself that living in this place was going to be a "total waste," Charlie pulled me close to him and kissed me long and intensely. His mouth felt warm and intoxicating on my lips and the strength of his arms around me, pressing my breasts into his chest, made me want to crumble in his embrace. As he lightened his hold and our lips parted, I stood star-ing speechless into his glistening green eyes. "Do you think I could get you to fall in love with me?" he whispered as he gently put his hands on my cheeks.

"Do you ask all of your new tenants that question?" I resorted to humor to mask my feelings. But the spell of romance was abruptly shattered when we heard the blast of Kit leaning on the car horn, obviously unwilling to share my attentions any further that day. Mildly provoked, we made hurried arrangements to speak on the phone the following day.

In response to my admonishment for her impatience, Kit leaned back in the passenger seat and defiantly propped her feet on the dashboard, scuffing it with her sneakers. "Get your feet off there!" I snapped, having my fill of her impertinent behavior. She dropped her feet to the floor and glared insolently at me.

"I'm not moving there!" she announced. I think Kit knew how much I hated it when she started an argument while I was driving, especially on a road like the Long Island Expressway that required my full concentration.

"We'll discuss this when we get home," I replied as calmly as I could.

Kit brooded silently for several minutes and then spewed out her anger in one blatant condemnation. "You're still married, and you're kissing another man!"

I wasn't expecting such a harsh judgment from my own daughter. Although I'd been too preoccupied with my business to look for romance or even simple physical gratification during the three celibate years of my marriage to Paul, I no longer considered myself married, nor bound to any promises of fidelity. During one of my arguments with my husband, when I'd pleaded with him to do something, anything, to satisfy my needs as a woman, he'd coolly told me to do whatever I had to do, as long as it didn't involve him. That was over a year ago, and yet this was the first time I'd even come close to doing something about my unmet needs. But how could I explain these things to a twelve year old girl who wanted everything in life to be clearly defined as either right or wrong.

I decided to just let the issue rest until we arrived home. But by the time I'd found a parking space on the street, three blocks from our apartment building—I could no longer afford to park in the garage under our building; walked my sleepy daughter to the apartment; waited for the elevator; unlocked the three locks on our door; helped Kit slip off her shoes and covered her up with her clothes still on; there was no opportunity for discussion of my marital status or sexual needs. In fact, as I sat on the edge of my daughter's bed and smoothed her hair, all I could think about was how nice it was going to be to drive home to an apartment where I could park in the driveway and walk right in the front door.

"Poor baby," I whispered to my sleeping daughter, "You try so hard to be brave and grown-up and then the little girl just erupts and demands to be noticed."

The subject of my relationship with Charlie wasn't brought up again in the following days, we were too busy making arrangements to move. While Kit was anxious about going to a public school, she seemed to be excited about the opportunity to meet new friends. During the previous year, as our financial situation had become more and more of a problem, she'd been having trouble keeping up with the social prerequisites of her crowd at the private school she attended. She would find a different kind of problem in Hicksville, where few of the friends she made had her degree of self-sufficiency and street-smarts.

# Reflections

During the four long years of his wife's illness, Charlie DiMartino hadn't paid much attention to his personal appearance. Looking at the widower now, it was hard to imagine that he had been a real "ladies' man" in his youth, capturing the attention of the opposite sex with his charm and spontaneous humor as well as his superior skills on the dance floor. His charisma, then as now, was further enhanced by an exceptional sensitivity towards women. As he had explained to me, that first evening when I poured my heart out to him, he'd always been "simpatico with women." Even after years of marriage to a sickly and demanding woman, he continued to have an unusual empathy for the female's lot in life.

Life had not been kind to this gregarious, yet gentle man. He'd long ago resigned himself to the responsibilities of providing for his growing family; shelving his dreams of being an entertainer, while he earned a living working as a printer. The financial success of his printing business brought him little satisfaction as it further separated him from his dreams.

Charlie's sons hadn't inherited their father's keen wit and intellect, nor had they acquired the savvy that he had used to succeed in business. Instead, Charlie had wasted his talents smoothing the ruffled feathers of teachers and police in the wake of his sons' wild forays. He'd grown weary of engaging the services of attorneys and contending with irate creditors, ex-wives and employers, as his "fearsome foursome" carried their wild, irresponsible escapades into their adult lives. That weariness had etched itself around his eyes and anyone who looked carefully could see that Charlie had resigned himself to living out the rest of his life alone, without purpose or happiness.

If you listen to Charlie, he'll swear that it was "love at first sight" with me — that the first time he saw me he knew that something electric was going to happen between us — that it was just a matter of time. As for myself, I must admit that until that moment when he kissed my hand, I'd only seen the sad, albeit charming, man, never suspecting the prize concealed within. But, according to Charlie, from the first moment he saw me, he knew that making me part of his life was crucial to his happiness.

He didn't have to wait long. Less than a week after I had said I would take the apartment, he came home to find me helping two young men unload my furniture from a rental truck. I had said that I wanted to start moving in right away, but I think Charlie had assumed that meant bringing over some plants or pictures or perhaps measuring windows for curtains. Never for a minute did he imagine that I would show up that week with a truck packed with all of my belongings.

But that was exactly what he saw when he pulled into his driveway that evening. He just sat there watching from his car, as I jumped down from the back of the truck to greet him, oblivious to the fact that my sweaty tee-shirt was clinging to my breasts. With my hair pulled back in a red bandanna, and my face shiny with perspiration, I didn't feel particularly attractive

"I didn't think you'd be moving in today!" he called out from his car. He must have realized by the sudden change in my expression that I'd mistaken his surprise for disapproval. "Oh, I mean, it's OK. But if I'd known, I could've helped you," he was quick to explain.

I was feeling the effect of the combination of physical exertion and the relentless heat of the August day. Resting on the bumper of the van, I groaned, "You can still help if you've got something cold to drink in your refrigerator."

"Sure," he replied, "Do you want me to bring it out to you, or do you wanna come inside?"

I looked up into the nearly empty truck. "We're almost done here. Give me a few minutes to pay these guys and get cleaned up and I'll meet you in your apartment," I called out as I stood up and grabbed the last chair sitting on the tailboard and carried it into the house.

By the time I tapped at the inside door that connected our apartments, Charlie's section of the house had cooled to an exquisitely comfortable temperature. As I walked into the chilled air I applauded the technology that could "make such a beastly, hot day feel soooo delicious." Charlie watched me as I walked around his living room nervously picking up chachkehs; smoothing the fabric on furnishings; or, as I was doing just then, sliding my finger up and down the cool, moist glass of my drink. I sensed a tension between us and thought that maybe Charlie was having second thoughts about renting the apartment to me, or that he found my disheveled appearance unattractive. I wasn't sure what he was thinking, but I was keenly aware of the intensity of his attention.

In an effort to conceal my nervousness, I began to rattle on about my harrowing experience driving the rental van down Lexington Avenue. Pausing only moments to sip my drink, I described the claustrophobic experience of driving a truck through the Midtown Tunnel. Without interrupting, Charlie walked around behind me and began to slowly massage my neck. I didn't resist. Unconsciously, soft moans of relief escaped me as he rubbed just the right muscles in my neck. Gradually he worked his kneading fingers down my spine, all the while keenly attentive to my reactions. I could feel my voice become softer, interrupted by soft sighs. He gently took my drink and placed it on the table and began to kiss the back of my neck. Still I offered no resistance as he slowly continued his delicious seduction.

By the time he'd turned me to face him and passionately kissed me, I was feeling sensations I hadn't known for a long time. I began to return his affections, pulling him closer to me. He led me into his bedroom and sat on the edge of his bed as he pulled me towards him. My eyes closed as I allowed myself to completely experience the pleasurable sensations he aroused in me.

Charlie was so pleased with my reaction that he actually let out a laugh of delight. Over and over, he brought me to one climax after another that evening, apparently astonishing himself by his own ability to continue our lovemaking for so long. Finally, breathless and exhausted, we lay beside each other in wonderment, and a little embarrassed by our gluttonous, sensual feast. It was obvious that we were about to embark on the most extraordinary romance either of us had ever imagined.

~

The following evening Charlie joined me while I was setting up my telescope on the back deck.

"Is it possible to find in one person intellectual and sexual fulfillment?" he crooned seductively.

Never even looking up from the eyepiece I was peering into, I replied, "I think most men are scared off by my eccentric intellect."

"And what about your eccentric lovemaking?" he whispered as he moved closer to me. He'd succeeded in getting my full attention with that question and I stood up facing him and gently touched his cheek.

"What we experienced last night was unusual. I don't know why it was that way, but," I stopped in mid-sentence, groping for the words that would give us an out if we never again achieved the level of exquisite pleasure we'd reached on our first encounter. Instead, I changed the subject. "Isn't it a beautiful, clear night! Even with a full moon, you can see the stars. Do you know the constellations?"

Charlie was embarrassed to admit that he knew absolutely nothing about the sky. "I think that's the Big Dipper," he said pointing to a large square formed by four bright stars.

"That's the Great Square of Pegasus," I gently explained. "The Big Dipper is much more visible in the Spring."

"You mean, the sky changes? You can see different stars at different times?" Charlie asked, genuinely surprised.

"Oh yes!" I cried out, delighted to have an interested audience. "It's so sad that most people have completely lost touch with the sky. Do you realize that even ancient civilizations, that we consider to have been barbaric, knew all about the stars and the planets. Even the youngest child could have told you what direction you were facing and what season it was, by looking at the night sky. Throughout all of history, and even before history, this has been our connection with the divine.

"When I look up into this infinity my problems become insignificant. The universe goes on and on and what I do or think is less critical to the universe than even one cell is to my body. And yet that single cell is, in miniature, a complete universe."

I realized that I was getting too philosophical. "You see how I scare them all away?" I asked.

Charlie was confused by my question. "The stars?" he asked, struggling to figure out what I meant and apparently disappointed that I'd abruptly stopped my explanation of the sky.

"No, men!" I laughed. "I get so engrossed in things that the rest of the human race finds absolutely boring. Sometimes I feel like all that anyone ever wants to talk about is who won last night's game and who's screwing who."

Charlie laughed. "I've spent my whole life feeling that way. Where were you thirty years ago?" He put his arms around me and held me close while looking up at the perfectly round, white moon. "What's that 'W' shape almost directly above us?" he asked softly.

I looked up without removing myself from his embrace. "That's Cassiopeia, the queen mother of Andromeda," I said and turned slightly to point upward. "Look down from there, about midway between the Great Square and the "W". Do you see that faint smudge?"

Charlie squinted at the sky and then suddenly found the soft, starry spot I was referring to. "Yeah," he whispered, "What's that?"

"That's another whole galaxy! Here, take a look at it in the telescope," I said as I looked into the small eyepiece and focused the instrument on the spot in the sky. When I had it just right I motioned for Charlie to look into it. Through the lens the smudge would look larger to him, though not much more defined, although he could probably decipher a more dense concentration of white in the center, and see that the whole cluster had an elliptical shape. I explained that with a much more powerful telescope he would see a distinctive shape of swirls around a brilliant core.

When it seemed Charlie had had quite enough of star gazing, I mentioned in as offhand a fashion as I could, that my daughter was spending the weekend with her father.

"Are you trying to tell me something?" Charlie asked seductively. "By any chance does all this gazing into the night sky also evoke thoughts a little less philosophical?"

I gave him a look that said everything he wanted to hear and he put his hand out towards the sliding door to indicate "After you."

Our lovemaking that night was actually better than the first time. We enjoyed unsurpassed sensual experiences on into the night. Who could have imagined as our love feast continued throughout the weekend that it would continue with the same exquisite perfection for the rest of our days together. To our constant amazement, each successive encounter always seemed to supersede the previous ones. Each time, as we lay, exhausted and completely fulfilled beside each other, we would wonder if it was just that the intensity of such a perfect reality overshadowed any memories of our past experiences. But as days turned into months, we would eventually stop questioning the possibility of such perfect ecstasy constantly improving, although we would never stop marveling that it continued to do so.

As the months passed, something else extraordinary began to happen. My interest in the Maya began to border on being an obsession. I would come home from the library every few days with a new stack of books about the Maya. I memorized the symbols, names and meanings of the glyphs used in their calendar and I learned how their sacred and solar calendars interwove with cycles within cycles. The current Great Cycle began in 3113 BC and is scheduled to end in 2012 AD. I began to play with the mathematical possibilities of this system, and learned how to transfer Maya dates into our contemporary Gregorian dates.

Charlie encouraged my interest. Each evening, while Kit was busy with her homework or talking on the phone, or doing both things simultaneously, we would sit at his kitchen table, sipping coffee and talking. Charlie always seemed to love listening as I would unravel the details of my latest discovery. For instance, one evening I pulled out a legal pad covered with calculations and proudly showed it to him. "I've found the key I've been looking for!" I announced. "You know how I've been going over and over everything I said in that past life regression trance I had last August, looking for a clue to who I was describing? Well, instead I've found a clue in that dream I had about the eclipse.

I went on to explain, "Today, I went to visit my friend, who works at the planetarium. I asked him to use that new computer program he's been bragging about for the past year, to determine if there was a total solar eclipse, visible from Mexico, around the years 600 to 700 AD. What he came back with was this!" I showed Charlie a printout with markings that appeared to indicate constellations. In the top corner was the date, March 30, 610 AD. 9:55 AM, Central Standard Time.

"It was visible shortly after dawn from Mexico," I explained. "And this is what the sky would have looked like on that date at that time when the sun was completely blacked out. It's exactly the sky I saw in my dream that night after the regression. Even Venus is just above the Pleiades the way I saw it." I pointed to a cluster of dots on the paper with a circle marked with a symbol that appeared to be the circle and cross of the sign for female.

"So what does all this mean?" Charlie asked, not trying to conceal how puzzling all of this was to him.

"Well, if I was a young boy of six or seven on this date, that would have made my birth around 603 or 604. That corresponds to the birth date, in some books, of Pacal at Palenque," I responded, suddenly serious.

"And who, pray tell, is Pacal?" Charlie responded, trying to keep the mood from getting as heavy as he suspected it was getting.

I opened a book to a page I'd marked with my now obsolete business card and showed it to him. "This is a coincidence that's too amazing to ignore!" I exclaimed, showing him a photo of a temple at a site called Palenque in Mexico.

"They discovered a tomb beneath a secret passageway found

beneath the floor of this temple. The skeleton they found buried there seems to be of an important person, probably the ruler Pacal. It was covered with jade — a jade mask and necklaces and bracelets — just like the way I'd described being buried to Reverend Blaze."

Charlie looked at the photo and the drawing beneath it that showed how the hidden stairway led to the tomb beneath the pyramid. "Well that could be the way they buried all of their dead kings. Why would this particular tomb be significant?" he asked.

That was exactly the question I expected him to ask and I was ready for the reply. "Look at the date they discovered the tomb!" I exclaimed as I pointed to the place in the text that had shaken me when I first read it. "June 15, 1952! That happens to be my birthday! Doesn't that seem incredible; that the day I was incarnating into this life, someone was discovering the remains of someone I may have been before!"

Charlie took a long drag on his cigarette as he struggled to comprehend all of the papers I'd spread out on the table in front of him. "You're really taking this thing seriously. My God, you've researched this like you were looking for a cure for cancer or something." He paused, nodding to himself as he crushed the last bit of his cigarette into the ashtray. Then looking directly at me he asked, "Where do you go from here? What do you think you're supposed to be doing with this information?"

I had no answer and made no attempt to provide one. But as the days passed, I felt myself becoming more and more preoccupied with "my Maya".

My evenings of conversation with Charlie had become as delightful to me as our lovemaking. I looked forward to that time with him all day long. Charlie had become the best friend I'd ever known and I couldn't imagine how I would have gotten through those months without him.

I'd been struggling to make ends meet with my sporadic freelance design work, although I never would have admitted it. Still, I'd insisted on continuing to pay the rent we'd originally agreed upon, in spite of our relationship. Charlie would help out, without blatantly injuring my pride, by buying groceries or paying for extras.

But he knew, when I spoke wistfully of going to Mexico one day to study the Maya ruins, that I was talking about something way out of my fiscal reality. What I didn't know that evening, while I attempted to unravel the mystery of my past life, was that he had planned a surprise for me, for Christmas, that would change both of our lives in ways we could never have imagined. While tickets for a month-long safari through the Mexican ruins wouldn't look very extraordinary gift-wrapped under the Christmas tree, no gift ever given would ever have such a profound effect on both the giver and the receiver.

As I look back now on all of this, I can see how we are just the servants of destiny. Just before our trip, serious problems came up with Charlie's business that made it impossible for him to leave, and it was Kit who went to Mexico with me. It was as if the gods had stepped in to rearrange their playing pieces to suit their obscure whims.

# BOOK TWO
# The Search

# Mexico City

"Wait! Where are you going?" I cried out to the young Mexican man who was walking away from the mini-bus that Kit and I had just climbed into.

"Two more people coming on de next plane. I be one moment only," he called back in broken English as he continued walking back towards the airport parking lot.

I had been warned about the Mexican "moment" — it could last for hours — and my patience had already been stretched too thin to wait for even another real moment. I raced out of the bus after the boy who had already subjected us to an hour's wait while a representative of the tour agency assembled the hotel and meal transfers for our journey. It was now one thirty in the morning and I and my daughter had been traveling since six o'clock the morning before. We had changed planes in Dallas to a Mexican airline and had endured a long, crowded flight that landed in five other cities before finally arriving in Mexico City at midnight.

As I caught up to our departing driver, I grabbed him by his shoulder and spun him around to face me. "Take me and my daughter to our hotel. Now!" I commanded, surprising myself with my arrogance. Just at that moment I realized that I had left Kit alone in the mini-bus on a dark, seedy street behind the airport. Without waiting for his response I gripped the boy's arm and escorted him back to the tour agency vehicle.

"Señora, I lose my job if I no get other tourists," the young man pleaded as he allowed me to pull him. But I would hear nothing of his problems.

"Forget about your job, if you don't get me and my child quickly and safely to our hotel you are going to lose your life!" I shouted, half-crazed with exhaustion. Then I noticed a group of men standing around a doorway halfway down the block. I literally pushed the young man towards the driver's door, unleashing a tirade of complaints as the day's weariness and frustration gave way to fear for our safety.

"I didn't bring my daughter all the way down here to be assaulted by a bunch of thugs on a dark street. I could have stayed home for that!" I screamed as I climbed into the side door of the mini-bus and slammed the doors shut. Warily, I eyed the group of revelers on the sidewalk, while our driver fumbled with his keys and started the van, murmuring his own litany of complaints in Spanish.

Kit sensed my anxiety and moved closer to me on the bench seat. "I want to go home," she whispered in the tiny voice of a frightened child.

I looked out at the uninviting dark streets as the rattle and rumble of our bus broke the sleepy quiet of the March night. But I was too exhausted to notice much more than the fact that is seemed to take forever to reach our hotel. When the jitney finally came to an abrupt halt in front of the Hotel Reforma, I gently roused my sleeping daughter and fumbled through the papers I'd been given at the airport for the transfer ticket. Kit had explained to me that she'd learned in Spanish class that the best place to exchange our money was at the airport, but everything had been closed when we arrived. Uncertain as to the value of the dollar, I handed the driver a three dollar tip, thinking it was a small amount, but all that he deserved after his shabby treatment. To my surprise the driver's face lit up as he fanned the three single bills in his hand. I would learn later that a tip equivalent to 7,000 pesos was exorbitant and certainly no way to express dissatisfaction!

Neither I nor Kit noticed much about the hotel that night. In fact, we did little more than take off our shoes before collapsing onto the twin beds in our old but tidy room. I attempted to find a comfortable position but the pillow was so hard that I finally tossed it on the floor in disgust and wadded my blanket into a cushion for my head.

Kit had no problem. She was already asleep as soon as her head touched the bed. Watching her small breasts move slowly up and down under the words "Bon Jovi" that were scrawled across the old tee-shirt she'd been wearing all day, I envied the peaceful serenity that her absolute confidence in my protection afforded her. Sometimes the realization that the welfare of this innocent and beautiful young woman was my responsibility, left me feeling overwhelmed. "I'm not even doing such a great job of taking care of myself," I thought. "How do I protect her and yet prepare her for the real world?" I knew, from my own painful experiences, that intelligence and sensitivity were difficult traits to carry through puberty. Charlie had been right; it was indeed important to take this trip now — important for both of us. "If there is only one weapon I can give her to wield against all the enemies of happiness, it will be my example of self-sufficiency," I mused as sleep slowly softened the edges of my consciousness.

"Mommy wake-up, it's morning and we're in Mexico!" cried Kit as she shook my shoulder. I opened my eyes to a strange sunlit room as I felt the last edge of my dream slip away. Although I could remember nothing, I had the distinct feeling that something very important had just happened. But I quickly forgot about it as I realized that today we would begin our long awaited adventure. We would be spending three days in Mexico City on our own before joining the other members of our party that would travel into the interior of Mexico — to the places most tourists never even realize they miss.

Kit sat cross legged next to me on the bed and spread out a map of Mexico City that she'd found on the bureau with some other literature.

"The first thing we have to do is find a Casa de Cambio to exchange our money," she declared. I had appointed Kit official money keeper as a substitution for the month of math classes she would be missing. She was taking the responsibility very seriously and had already found out what a good exchange rate was, and how much money we could spend each day.

"The first thing we have to do is take a shower!" I exclaimed as I raced her to the bathroom. "I can't believe we went to bed smelling like a couple of pigs."

"Remember, use the bottled water to brush your teeth," I called out as I stepped into the shower. I didn't mention it to Kit, but I carefully checked the floor of the old, tiled shower stall for crawling creatures before venturing into it. The water was sufficiently warm, but the pressure was little more than a trickle and I whispered a silent prayer that sometime in the next month, I would be able to experience a decent hot shower.

Kit's reaction was not so restrained. "Mommy, is this what the shower is going to be like for this whole trip?" she whined after less than a minute under the water.

"No," I laughed, "It could get worse. Just be thankful it's warm."

We almost had to pass on brushing our teeth because the two green bottles of "Agua Mineral" conveniently placed on the back of the sink, required a bottle opener to be opened. I had to laugh when I realized that my daughter didn't know what a bottle opener was.

"Is it possible that you've managed to go your whole life with only twist-off caps and pop top cans?" I asked her teasingly as I searched the bathroom and bedroom for a bottle opener. "Voilá!" I exclaimed as I discovered the jagged metal device screwed onto the bathroom door frame and skillfully positioned the bottle in its grip. Kit wasn't impressed by my dramatic antics.

Together, we attempted to explore Mexico City without the aid of a tour guide for the first day, but our command of the language was not what we thought it was, and we spent most of the day lost.

Along the broad Reforma Avenue, street vendors hawked their wares all around us, selling everything from chewing gum to cleverly cut papaya. While waiting for a traffic light to change we watched a young man gulp a swig of kerosene and spit it towards a torch in his outstretched arm, producing a dramatic fiery burst that gave the appearance of "breathing fire". He followed this display by walking among the stopped cars collecting "payment" for his performance. He certainly had anything I ever saw on the streets of New York beat, but I couldn't help wondering what kind of future he faced.

We managed to find our way to the Shrine of Guadeloupe. The modern shrine and the original basilica with its adjoining chapel stand near a hill called Tepeyac where legend has it, the Virgin Mary appeared to a poor Indian in 1531. Her image was miraculously transferred to the Indian's cloak, which now is displayed behind the altar in the modern shrine. The original old cathedral has been closed up because its east towers and the chapel are sinking into the unstable lake-bed that Mexico City is built upon. Sadly the old basilica was far more attractive than the modern new church built to replace it, which lacks the charm and character of its predecessor.

In the courtyard we watched as pilgrims, most of them mothers carrying babies in their arms, struggled on their knees across the stone plaza towards the cathedral. In marked contrast to their intense devotion, tour guides rudely interrupted a celebration of the Mass going on inside the shrine to bring their groups of tourists to see the famous cloak. In voices loud enough to distract even the most devout of the faithful praying in the pews, the guides pointed out the dark color of the Virgin's skin and her eye where what appears to be a reflection of the poor Indian can be seen in an enlargement.

"Whatever the Virgin's intention had been when this miracle took place, it's all been turned into a mockery — a money making tourist trap," I whispered to Kit as we stepped onto a moving walkway that took us past the cloak behind the altar.

Even Kit seemed to grasp the irony of the situation as we walked out of the church and past the kneeling women, their knees bleeding on the scorching concrete. "Do you think God is any better to these people for doing this?" she asked. I just shook my head as I thought of all the suffering the indigenous people of this continent had endured. It seemed that God bestowed more good fortune on the owner of the tourist concession at this shrine than to the poor petitioners working their way painfully across the square. Noting the blood on one woman's knees, I thought of what I had read of the bloodletting rituals of the Maya. "Why did a people capable of such esoteric acts of faith, end up like this?" I asked myself. But I was soon to see people in much worse conditions and it wouldn't be until we were far outside of Mexico City that I would finally see Indian people living in the dignity, if not the grandeur, of their ancestry.

As we made our away around the city we witnessed more poverty and deprivation than either of us had ever seen before, even on the streets of New York City. On our way to a market, Kit watched horrified as a mother sat on the sidewalk selling trinkets (begging is forbidden, so many of the homeless offer worthless trinkets for sale), while her infant daughter, filthy from crawling on the streets all day, picked up a piece of garbage from the sidewalk and put it into her mouth. In a way, I knew it was good for Kit to learn that there are places in the world that make even New York's homeless seem well off, but by the end of the day we'd both experienced more of the horror of poverty than we could stand.

On our way back to the hotel we passed an herb vendor, known as a yerbero. His medicines, which looked to be just dried plants and twigs, were displayed on the sidewalk in an assortment of plastic bags and old glass bottles. Neatly printed cards explained their use in Spanish and we were able to translate some of them: "To Stop a Cough," "For Mouth Pain," "To Improve the Memory." Kit suggested that we purchase the one that said "To Stop Smoking" for Charlie but the ingredients looked far from inviting and I passed on it.

We were feeling the effects of our arduous trip the day before and by late afternoon we called it a day. I was starting to feel a head cold coming on and wondered if it didn't have something to do with the smog.

Back in our hotel room we watched an old black and white American movie with Spanish subtitles and munched on oranges we'd bought in the street market. It was a simple super but we were both asleep before the movie was over.

That night I dreamt of making love with Charlie and woke up missing him terribly. We had agreed that he would try to call us, but since it was so expensive to telephone from Mexico, I wouldn't attempt to call him. We'd only brought five hundred dollars with us to spend over the next four weeks and since our hotels, meals and tour were already paid for, it would be enough — unless I wasted it on one extravagant telephone call, which could easily cost as much as fifty dollars.

Still, as I laid in bed thinking about Charlie, imagining his arms around me and my face pressed snugly against the warmth of his shoulder, I began to wonder how I was ever going to endure four long weeks without him. In fact, I was beginning to wonder why I'd ever been so fired-up to make the trip in the first place. To add to my depressed feelings, my head cold had fully bloomed and certainly did nothing to lift my spirits.

# Teotihuacán

By the time we'd climbed aboard the modern, air conditioned tour bus for Teotihuacán the next morning, my enthusiasm was reviving, in spite of my sniffling and sneezing.

In the course of researching the history of the Maya civilization, I'd run across a lot of information about Teotihuacán. This once great city, located only 28 miles northeast of Mexico City, was built approximately 2,000 years ago by a highly advanced civilization that could rival imperial Rome. Teotihuacán was an urban metropolis, complete with temples, palaces, markets and apartment-type housing for as many as 200,000 inhabitants. Then, about 900 AD, it was mysteriously abandoned.

There is evidence that a great fire may have had something to do with its demise — or perhaps occurred subsequent to it. The Maya Classic Period was also nearing it's end at the same time. Archaeological evidence suggests that the two civilizations exchanged more than goods — including art, ideology and royal marriages.

No one knows for certain what these people called themselves. The city was long abandoned when the Aztecs, who revered it as a sacred place, called it Teotihuacán, or the Place of the Creation of the Gods. In their myths, this is the place where the last creation of humans occurred.

The city is laid out on a grid with the Pyramid of the Moon on the north end. The Avenue of the Dead extends almost south from it for 3 miles. More a series of plazas than a street, the Avenue of the Dead is lined with platforms and buildings. The largest of these, the Pyramid of the Sun, looms over the site. In the geographic center of the city is a large platformed area known today as the Citadel. It was here that our tour bus pulled into a black-topped parking lot.

Kit and I followed the group of tourists off the bus and through a modern souvenir shop. Our guide, Julio, was a tall, flamboyant, mustachioed man with such a heavy Spanish accent that we couldn't understand a word he said. I was glad I was already well read on the site. To gain access to the site it was necessary to walk through a souvenir shop to reach the Avenue of the Dead. After what we had seen in the Cathedral of Guadeloupe, I thought to myself, "Here we go again. Have all the ancient sites in Mexico been converted into tourist traps?" To my dismay, I saw that the asphalt paving continued outside the modern entrance structure, right up to the first section of the Citadel. "My God, they've paved the whole place!" I gasped in disbelief. All the photographs I'd seen in books about the site had shown it as it was prior to such sacrilegious "restoration".

"They've turned the Place of the Creation of the Gods into an amusement park!" I cried out to those around me. But with the exception of one elderly gentleman, the other tourists didn't seem to care and I realized that not everyone appreciated the sacred significance of the site. To most of them, it was just an amusing diversion.

We followed our guide, who was now sporting a straw hat with a band of multicolored ribbons flowing from the back, so that he could be easily spotted. We climbed up the stone steps of a platform that was one of four tiered structures joined by a wall. As we walked across the platform and carefully descended the steps on the opposite side, we were looking out into the sunken interior plaza. The guide explained that it had been misnamed the "Citadel" by the Spaniards because of its high embankments which they had mistaken for the walls of a fortress. Within the plaza, restoration had been carried out in a more sensitive manner and the grounds were not covered with asphalt as I had feared, but were simply well traversed grass.

We followed Julio's colorful hat across the plaza and around a four sided platform in the center to the large structure in the back of the plaza. This was fronted with a four tiered section known as the Adosado with steps in the front going to the top. We didn't climb this, but instead circled around this structure to the partially restored Temple of Quetzalcoatl. Here a wooden walkway took us past the exposed, intricately carved lower section of the temple. Carved serpent heads framed with feathers jutted out from the facade where their bodies, carved in low relief, wiggled over sea shells and the goggle-eyed masks of the rain god. You could still see traces of red and green paint on the stone.

Walking back across the plaza, we were inundated with vendors selling clay whistles shaped like birds and jewelry and trinkets.

Others hawked soft-drinks in glass bottles that looked to be as old as the ruins themselves. I noticed that, unlike the rest of our group, the elderly gentleman who had shared my dismay with the asphalt paving, was actually encouraging the young peddlers by handing out Chicklets. I smiled and commented on the eager following he'd gathered.

"I've been all around the world, and I can vouch that kids everywhere love Chicklets. I always bring them with me," he explained as he continued to hand them out like a doting grandfather. I couldn't help thinking he would make a great commercial although I'd sworn off thinking about advertising for the duration of the trip.

Just then, our guide blew a whistle and motioned with his hands for the group to gather around him. "I feel like a school-girl or something," I groaned as I started to follow the rest of the group over to where the guide was summoning us. But the old man with the Chicklets laughed and explained, "He wants us to get back on the bus to drive around to the Pyramid of the Moon. But we'll miss half the show if we don't walk up the Avenue of the Dead. It doesn't look that far. Care to join me?" he asked as he indicated the broad swath that cut between the ruins ending in the distance with a magnificent stone pyramid.

I eyed the distance skeptically, noting what seemed to be stone dividers that crossed the road intermittently. My cold was progressing to the point where it was making me feel tired and the heat of the day was compounding my sense of fatigue. But the prospect of separating from the almost sacrilegious group of tourists we had arrived with was too tempting to resist. A tall man of about sixty, wearing a bright red baseball cap, strode up to us and addressed the elderly man with a smooth southern drawl.

"You comin' Elmer?" he asked.

The old man, who I now knew was Elmer, adjusted his tan fishing hat and winked at me as he replied, "I just asked these two lovely ladies to join me in a stroll. Care to join us?"

The tall man took a moment to consider Elmer's suggestion, carefully surveying the walk before us. "Looks like a bit of a stroll Elmer," he said slowly, "You sure you're up to it?" He winked mischievously at us as Elmer bristled by the implication he wasn't fit enough.

"You bet I am," he declared and set off in the direction of the distant pyramid. Kit immediately picked up on the spirit of adventure and raced off ahead of us, up the causeway. The three of us exchanged introductions as we followed her in a pace more appropriate for the temperature. Elmer introduced his gangly friend as "Bill" and explained that they were neighbors from South Carolina. I chose to refer to my origin as New York City.

It took us almost fifteen minutes to catch up with Kit at the first "divider". As we got closer to this obstruction, we realized that it was actually a steeply staired wall which took us quite some time and effort to climb. Finally at the top, we paused to consider the precarious climb down the other side. To my dismay I counted off at least four more similar walls crossing our route and began to doubt the wisdom of our "stroll". Then I noticed that some people were walking along a winding path off to our right. It ran alongside the Avenue, at the same height as the wall we were now standing on. I suggested that we walk across the wall to pick up the path. It wasn't long before we realized that this was the preferred route as we were inundated by youngsters pedaling all sorts of souvenirs.

There was a feeling of festivity in the air. All around me the music of the vendor's carved whistles floated like a song from the ancient inhabitants of this place. Kit was ahead of us, happily weaving her way between the tourists and peddlers on the narrow path. But as we walked along, I started to realized that the distance to the Pyramid of the Moon was much farther than any of us had realized. The structure was so much larger than I had imagined that my sense of distance had been completely distorted.

By the time we'd reached the Pyramid of the Sun, which was half way to the Pyramid of the Moon, we could see the colored tassels of our tour guide's hat in the midst of a group of people approaching us from the other direction. "I guess we've missed out on seeing the Pyramid of the Moon," groaned Elmer as he pointed out our group on the Avenue.

"Yes, but those people have no comprehension of the size and grandeur of this place," I exclaimed, justifying our decision. Kit and I started enthusiastically toward the steps at the base of the Pyramid of the Sun, but Elmer and Bill discussed the prospect of the climb and decided to wait for our approaching party where they were sure to join others who would prefer to pass up another climb that day.

This would be the first of many difficult and often dangerous climbs for my daughter and I. The colossal structure rose to the height of a twenty-story skyscraper in five sloped sections, each smaller than the one below, the uppermost section having once been the base for a temple that had long since disappeared. We climbed the lowest section by one of two stairways that flank a small plaza and altar complex. Then we followed the platform to the wide central staircase that scales the second section. By the time we'd reached the platform at the end of that section we were thanking the gods for a flat surface to walk on, even if only briefly. Sporting her youth and agility, Kit taunted me as she gingerly worked her way up one of the two narrower stairways that brought us up the third section. I followed, panting for breath, and finally sat down in agony on the ridge that topped the third section. "Kit, do you see what I see?" I gasped as my daughter sat down beside me. The two of us looked in disbelief at the next flight of stairs. The fourth section of stairs was actually in two parts, the first being almost perpendicular while the second sloped in an angle similar to the sections we'd already climbed. We watched as other visitors struggled to climb and descend that steep lower half.

"It's like climbing a ladder," Kit explained as she started towards the stairs, confident that she had it all figured out. The depth of the horizontal section of each stair was hardly more than the length of one's toes, while the risers were a good foot high. Going up was even more difficult than it looked and I tried not to think about going down as I followed my fearless child up the fourth and fifth sections. When, at last, we reached the summit, the struggle was immediately overshadowed by the sense of exhilaration I felt as I surveyed the ancient city from this perilous view point.

To my left I could see the Pyramid of the Moon fronted by its own magnificent plaza. To the right stretched out a grand aerial view of where we had been, with the Citadel and the Temple of Quetzalcoatl. And looking back in the direction we had just climbed, were the walls and platforms of the Avenue of the Dead and the mounds of yet unrestored buildings beyond.

A fragrance that reminded me of my school days in art class, filled the air and it took me a moment to identify the source of the turpentine-like smell. Exactly in the center of the platform an Indian sat cross legged, meditating. A glass containing a burning candle was positioned in each of four corners around him. I assumed that he was burning copál, an incense made from the resin that is so sacred to the Indians that it has been described as the "scent of the center of heaven". "That is exactly where we are," I thought as I watched the Indian bob and sway as if he were in a trance.

Smoke rose from the bowl in front of him, twisting like a snake into the air above me, its fragrance arousing in me the hypnotic state I'd experienced under Reverend Blaze's spell. For a second I thought that I saw a jaguar in place of the man but the sensation and the vision passed as quickly as it came. I looked around me quickly and realized that no one else had witnessed the strange apparition.

As Kit walked the perimeter of the platform, snapping pictures and pointing out features, I squatted on the ground near the Indian and tried to collect myself. A tattered young girl came alongside me and eagerly spread out her collection of jewelry for what she immediately perceived as a non-moving target. "You buy?" she queried enthusiastically. It's against my nature to hurt the feelings of one so young, so I tried to feign interest. But I was irritated by her interruption and wouldn't buy anything even though the prices for what the girl claimed were silver items were unbelievably low. One can't help but wonder if this child actually climbed this pyramid each day to sell her wares. Had she discovered that people who climb the pyramid to the top were more likely to buy?

Far below us, on the Avenue of the Dead, Julio was blowing his whistle and Kit nervously summoned me to begin our descent. The climb down was not as exhausting as the climb up, but without a doubt it was more frightening and in many places I chose to navigate the steps the way a baby does, on my bottom, facing outward, one careful step at a time. I also tried the zigzag/sideways technique I saw others using. The process of descent took my complete attention, and I quickly forgot about the eerie vision I'd seen at the top.

Kit stepped lightly down the treacherous stairs as if she was dancing. When she reached the last section, impatient with my caution, she decided to explore a narrow ledge that brought her towards the center of the front of the pyramid. Refusing to respond to my calls, she followed this to where she found an opening in the base of the structure that was blocked off with only a piece of wood diagonally propped across it. "Mom, look what I found!" she cried out with gusto. I was left with no choice but to follow my reckless child to the mysterious cave. We peered into the dark abyss but couldn't see further than a few feet. It appeared to be an intentionally dug opening but there was no indication where it led. From behind us we again heard the guide's whistle and hurried off to join our group.

~

By the time we returned to our hotel, my sinuses were throbbing with congestion and my eyes were tearing. "What I need is a nice bowl of hot chicken soup," I groaned and we decided to eat at the hotel restaurant that night. I found exactly what I wanted in the English description of Sopa Azteca on the menu. It was described as a chicken soup with hot peppers, tomatoes and tortillas served with lime and avocados. The first spoonful was deceptively delicious in those few moments before the fiery message of the chilies reached my brain. Then my nose started running, my eyes watered and I began gasping for water. But to my dismay, only the "taboo" glass of ice water was at the table. I swirled around in my chair looking for our waiter but he was no where to be seen. Finally I saw the busboy at the other end of the room and motioned for him to come. "Agua Mineral," I gasped, fanning my tortured mouth with my hand.

"No Señora, No tiene agua mineral. Coca?" he offered apologetically.

"Si, Coca, Rapido!" I cried in agony. But the young man moved slowly towards the bar and explained in what seemed to me to be an extraordinarily lengthy discussion that I needed a Coke. Nonchalantly, the bartender reached into a case and pulled out a battered green Coke bottle and pried open the cap. My watery eyes cried real tears as I watched him pour the contents of the bottle over ice cubes that I had no way of knowing if they'd been made with purified water. As the bus-boy casually brought the glass over to me, I contemplated asking him for another drink without the questionable ice cubes. But by now I was in real, physical agony from the hot chilies. I suspected that I had been "set-up" with the hot soup to start with and was now being further provoked by these two imbeciles.

Kit tried to calm my paranoia as we waited for the man to finally arrive at our table. She shook her head disapprovingly as I grasped the glass from the insolent young man and immediately gulped down its contents. "You're not supposed to use ice cubes," she admonished me. "They could be made with impure water."

"Well hopefully they didn't have a chance to melt." I explained as I handed the emptied glass back to the bemused busboy. "I'll have another. No ice this time." A look of enlightenment crossed his face, as if he'd never heard that tourists aren't supposed to drink the water. I ignored him and watched as Kit ate her mild chicken burritos. "Next time I get adventurous with food, I'll make sure I have the water first," I groaned as Kit laughed.

# José

I awoke to the irritating beep of my travel alarm clock. I'd set it early to give myself and Kit plenty of time to pack and have a quick breakfast before 8:00, when we were scheduled to meet the group we would be traveling with for the remainder of our trip. As we stepped out of the elevator, dragging our luggage out into the hotel lobby, I was surprised to see only a few people standing around. The two gentlemen we'd met at Teotihuacán were talking with a middle-aged couple who were dressed in matching khaki, safari outfits. I joined them and asked if they were part of the group that would be touring the Maya ruins. I was delighted to learn that Elmer and Bill would be part of the group which I had assumed would be as large as the crowd we had traveled with to Teotihuacán. Only one other couple was in the lobby — a tall, garishly dressed gentleman who was loudly arguing with the desk clerk and the woman with him, apparently his wife. She was trying to calm him, but he would hear nothing of it. His loud British accent reverberated through the lobby, to the poor woman's obvious embarrassment.

The people standing with me, stopped their conversation to watch him as the argument increased in volume. "I hope they're not coming with us," Kit whispered to the general agreement of the others.

Just then, two Mexican men came through the hotel doors. One, in his mid-thirties, was round-faced and plump, and looked nervously at the disturbance at the desk. The other was slightly older, but taller, with a strong, square jaw and intense eyes that added drama to his exceptionally handsome appearance. He strode up to the desk clerk, and although he spoke in Spanish, I could tell by his strong, authoritative tone that he would settle the disagreement.

Now the Englishman was clearly at a disadvantage as the desk clerk and the stranger discussed the problem in a language he couldn't understand. Our bemused group watched as the

Englishman, unable to contain himself, demanded that the two men speak in English. At this point the tall Mexican turned to him and putting his hand on the pompous guest's shoulder, steered him away from the desk clerk. In a loud whisper he explained, "Señor Weinstein, according to our records, you requested that you and your wife would select your own dining arrangements. Therefore you are not on the American plan. This has been figured in the lower price you have paid for this tour. Please understand, Señor, we cannot change things at this time. The others in this group have "AP" on their hotel coupons. That means that they have already paid for their meals. But I am sorry, Señor, you and your wife must pay."

He continued to speak to the surly man as though he was speaking to an idiot, but the man didn't seem to notice that he was being insulted. "Now, if you would please take care of your bill we can begin our journey. We have a lot to do today." The Englishman returned to the hotel desk, grumbling to himself, while the two Mexican men walked over to the rest of us.

Again, the tall, handsome man did the talking, this time smiling with such charm that I felt a shudder of excitement inside me. "Buenas Dias, Señora," he crooned in an obviously sensual tone towards me. Then he acknowledged the rest of the group with a smooth, melodious accent. "I am José and this is Vincenté. We will be your guides for this tour and we are going to be together for the next three weeks." Here he paused and raised his eyebrows slightly towards me. He pulled some papers from the pocket of his crisp, white guayabera and read, first to himself, shaking his head in obvious disappointment. "The Fontaines and the Weinsteins will be traveling with me." He paused to grimace. "Señors Beckman and White, Señora Rossi and the Señorita will go with Vincenté. Follow me, please. The bell boy will bring your luggage." He briskly led us out of the hotel and around to the side of the building where an old, tan station wagon and brown Volkswagen minibus were parked.

The short, pleasant man, who had been introduced as Vincenté, finally spoke; directing me, Kit, Elmer and Bill to the minibus. This was hardly what I had envisioned as the vehicle we would travel through the country with, for the next three weeks. I looked at it's worn seats and prayed the engine was in better condition.

Kit was equally dismayed. "Does this have airconditioning?" she asked hopefully.

Vincenté laughed and replied in a thick accent, "Si, you open da windows and you have air conditioning. Don't worry, you will be very comfortable." His manner was reassuring enough to be believable, and Kit climbed into the back seat happy to finally be on our way. I was just grateful that we hadn't been paired-off with the obnoxious Englishman, although the station wagon seemed like it would be a little more comfortable. I slid onto the middle seat and Elmer sat beside me. Bill climbed into the front passenger seat and we started for Cholula, with the station wagon following behind us.

After passing through a dismal area of rickety, makeshift shanty-towns known as ciudades perdidas, (the lost city) that surrounds Mexico City, the scenery along the highway changed to something similar to a New England landscape. The hills were speckled with pines and deciduous trees and quaint little villages which were poor but certainly more picturesque than the slums we'd just passed through. Eventually the landscape flattened out and the road stretched out straight before us like an exercise in perspective in "Art 101".

In the distance loomed twin, ice-covered mountains. Vincenté explained that they were volcanoes. "They are called Popacatepetl and Ixtaccihuatl. See how the second one looks like the silhouette of a sleeping woman? The Indians called it 'Sleeping Beauty' and thought it was a god," he explained. Kit spent the next fifteen minutes trying to pronounce the names that Vincenté had rattled off so easily.

The journey continued with an air of festivity. I noticed that my cold symptoms had disappeared almost as soon as we left Mexico City and Elmer suggested that I was probably particularly sensitive to the pollution in the city.

"It has one of the worst smog problems in the world," he proclaimed, adjusting his glasses to look over them at me.

"He should know!" announced Bill. "I'll bet you can't name a place in the world that Elmer hasn't been."

Kit and I took him up on his bet and listed every out-of-the-way place we could imagine. Each time Elmer would proudly reply, "Yup, been there!" Even Vincenté got into the act, suggesting absurd little countries I had never even heard of before. But still, Elmer proclaimed, "Yup, been there too."

Our arrival in Cholula was unremarkable. The ruins of what is touted as the largest pyramid in the world are surrounded by a small, ordinary Mexican village. Because most of the mound is enshrouded with soil and vegetation, one could easily drive past it without ever knowing you missed it. Perched atop the hill is a church, called the Church of the Remedios. José, who had joined us as we walked around the area of the exposed ruins, explained that the Spaniards built churches over all the Indian temples in their efforts to convert the Indians. Because Cholula had many temples, it is now famous for its abundance of churches.

He pointed out the architectural features of the site and told the group that the Cholula Indians were part of the Post-Classic period and were massacred by Cortes' army. But he hinted that the site may have had origins that preceded the Cholulas by 1500 years. Pointing to a statue of volcanic rock about four feet in diameter, he suggested that it was very similar to the statues of the "fat god" found on the Pacific Highlands and attributed to the Olmecs.

On the way back to our vehicles we stopped in a dreary little shop and bought very ripe bananas and warm Cokes. It was a pathetic snack, but no one was used to the late lunch (usually the main meal) and the even later super that Vincenté and José advised us was the Mexican custom and would now be our schedule.

Sitting on stone benches outside the dingy shop we finally had a chance to meet the two couples that were traveling in the station wagon with José. The middle-aged couple whom we'd seen talking with Elmer and Bill in the lobby that morning introduced themselves as Linda and Dave. They were French Canadians, he an architect, she a sculptress. The loud-mouth, who'd been arguing with the desk clerk earlier, was Andy Weinstein and he informed us that his wife's name was Janet. I felt sorry for her – he didn't even let her get a word in for her own introduction.

Still hungry, we traveled on to the city of Puebla. This is a colonial city with very distinctive architectural features. A beautiful, blue and white ceramic tile is used as an accent on most of the buildings, either covering the entire lower half of the building, or spaced evenly throughout the brick. Bricks were plentiful and we saw many brick kilns along the road to the city. These looked like little, roof-less, brick houses, about ten-feet square. Another feature that I found particularly delightful, was the wrought-iron balconies, made all the more romantic with terra-cotta pots brimming with bright red geraniums.

Many of the buildings seemed to have "icing" on them, a white, ornate trim that gives them the appearance of gingerbread houses. This style is carried to the extreme inside the Cathedral of Santo Domingo in the famous Altar of the Virgin of the Rosary. There, the gilded plaster is so ornate, it boggles the mind. "I can't understand how they can justify such extreme, almost obscene, decoration of a church, when all around there is poverty," I whispered to no one in particular, as we were leaving the church. José heard me and calmly replied that the Cholula Indian are known for their religious fervor. "It was the very same fervor that inspired them to build their pyramids."

We stopped next at the Cathedral of Puebla and José took me aside to point out a glass encased, life-size statue of Christ in the tomb. I watched as an Indian man caressed the glass so reverently that I felt I had invaded an intensely private act. Within the glass enclosure were hundreds of gold charms of arms, legs, hearts and other body parts. When we were outside, José explained that when a prayer to this Christ is answered for health to a certain part of the body, the grateful Indian will give a charm to the statue.

"Judging by the number of charms, there must be some power to their prayers," I commented.

José nodded. "You see now what I was trying to tell you about religious fervor," he softly replied. He led me back inside the cathedral to join the rest of the group and, in a reverent whisper explained the history of the church, pointing out the creme-colored, arched ceilings adorned with just enough restraint on the gold-leaf to make it pleasant and airy. As I listened to his knowledgeable narration, I felt myself drawn to his delightful combination of sensitivity and dynamic magnetism. One moment he was almost offensively machismo, and the next, he was almost gentle. There was something extremely attractive about the combination.

We finally stopped at a little restaurant in Puebla for a lunch of chicken and rice. Then, content and full, we continued on to the small city of Tehuacan. After a brief stop in the town square or zocalo, to do some shopping, we arrived at the Hacienda Spa Peñafiel.

I was pleasantly surprised. People I had spoken to in Mexico City had complained that this hotel was old and unpleasant. But I found it charming and a welcome retreat after our first day of traveling. Built in the thirties for the casino trade, which was subsequently banned in Mexico, its once lavish decor was badly in need of attention. "This place reminds me of an old maid still wearing her tattered wedding gown," I remarked to Kit as I flopped down on the antique twin beds in our room.

There wasn't much time to relax or to freshen up before we were to join our group again for a little introductory party and dinner. Just as we were about to leave the room, the phone rang. I was beside myself with excitement when the operator told me I had a call from New York.

"How ya doin'?" Charlie asked in his characteristic way of starting a phone conversation. His voice sounded remarkably clear, and to me it was the sweetest sound I'd heard in days.

"Charlie! I miss you so much," I cried into the phone. I wanted to see him and touch him and tell him about everything we'd seen and done. "I've got so much to tell you, I don't know where to start." I felt the pressure of the cost of seconds. There was no way I could even begin to tell him all that I wanted to say. "I miss sitting at the kitchen table, drinking coffee, and just talking with you," was all I said instead.

"Yeah, me too," he replied. It was unusual for him to be at a loss for words.

I detected a sadness in his voice. "Are you feeling OK? You're not smoking are you?" I queried, remembering his promise to try to quit while I was away.

"I'm feeling fine!" He tried to brighten up his tone. "I only have one cigarette a day. It's nothin'. Geez, it's hard getting through to you down there."

"You're lucky you caught us, we were just on our way to dinner." I was almost crying. "God, I miss you, Charlie. I love you so much. I just wish you could be here."

Charlie's voice was getting fuzzy. "Love you too, Honey. I cooked you up a whole batch of spaghetti sauce. Don't know what else to do without you…"

We didn't get a chance to say anymore. Our line was disconnected.

I was shaking with emotion. Here I was, in Mexico at last, and I felt like taking the next flight home. Suddenly everything around me felt foreign and lonely.

"Common Mom, we're late," complained Kit. I didn't really feel like socializing. I was suddenly very tired and confused. But there was something else bothering me; something that seemed to be happening in my dreams since the trip began. It seemed like destiny had brought me here. I wondered why destiny had also arranged that Charlie would not accompany me. Distracted with my thoughts, I followed my daughter to the hotel dining room where our group was already seated at two tables that had been pushed together.

"I've saved a seat for you, Señoras," quipped José, pointing to the two chairs beside him. I sat in the chair furthest from him, much to the amusement of the others who already seemed to be privy to his interest in me.

"Forgive me but I am very concerned," he said in his smooth, melodic accent, leaning over Kit as if she wasn't there. "I tried to call your room, but the operator said you had a call from New York. It's not bad news, I pray?"

José's concern seemed to me to be poorly disguised flirtation. I'd heard about the stereotyped, smooth-talking Latin men and brightened up for the game of cat-and-mouse I was being challenged to play. "That was my rich and handsome boyfriend, just calling to tell me how much he misses me," I replied with exaggerated vanity.

"Ah! And why is he not here with you, may I ask? I would not be so foolish as to let such a beautiful woman travel so far without me, if I were this rich and handsome boyfriend," José retorted.

I forgot my feelings of homesickness as I reveled in the moment. Not only was I enjoying the flattery, but our spirited dialog had caught the attention of the rest of the group and I loved being the center of attention. To the amusement of everyone, we continued our teasing and bantering of innuendoes throughout the evening. But by the time Kit and I retired to our room, neither I nor my sparring partner was sure who had won.

The tantalizing combination of fascination and repulsion between us had been ignited. But what the others saw as playful entertainment, hid explosive emotions that I would soon learn had festered in our spirits through centuries. Little did I know, that the dreams I could now only faintly recall, were the memories of unresolved pain and passion I would now have to finally face.

# Oaxaca

The following day we traveled through the Sierra Madre Mountains. The drive was so arduous that it took us five hours to travel only 150 miles. The mini-bus was leaking fumes and this, combined with the curving motions of this difficult mountain road caused everyone in the back of the bus to get car sick. Fortunately for me, I started out sitting in the front passenger seat and Vincenté and I escaped any real discomfort.

Instead I was treated to the breathtaking scenery of the distant mountains which appear to be naked. Brush stroked with the shadows of clouds, the rolling hills are almost sensuous in the way each peak fades to a softer gray. At times it seemed like I was looking at an enlarged view of an extraordinarily embossed surface without vegetation. But once we were in the mountain we could see that it was actually covered with a scrub type of brush and enormous candelabra cacti.

Meanwhile all of our efforts to keep the rear windows of the mini-bus propped open were unsuccessful. When we realized that only those in the back were suffering with nausea we worked out a rotation for the front passenger seat to give everyone a chance to feel decent enough to enjoy the scenery. When it was my turn to be in the back, I tried using meditation to keep from feeling sick and the trick worked well enough that I taught the others how to do it too.

Our journey took us through lush valleys where water was abundant. Here, the Zapotec Indians grew sugar cane, mangoes, papayas, avocados and watermelon. The beautiful Gacaranda tree with it's lavender flowers was everywhere. I noticed a lot of red barked trees that appeared to be dead, but Vincenté explained that during the rainy season the Madronios tree bursts into bloom.

We saw plantations of sugar cane along the road, in various stages of growth and harvesting. Not native to Mexico, (it was brought in from Cuba), sugar cane has become a prized crop of the Zapotec Indian. Harvesting is accomplished by burning the standing crops. What remains is the stalk of the cane which the Indians cut with machetes and pile high in trucks.

Many of the Indians of this region live in round houses made of the sugar cane stalk and covered with palm. As I watched them, it seemed to me that the residents of these simple houses wanted for nothing in the shadow of the magnificent mountains, along the sparkling green waters of the Rio Salida and Rio Grande.

We stopped at a roadside stand and bought mangoes ripened to a juicy yellow. Easily peeled, they were a tangy treat but their smell reminded me of sulfur. While the group stretched their legs and attempted to calm their stomachs, José, with a smirk, pointed out that rest rooms were located in the back of the fruit stand.

Kit and I went around back and peered apprehensively into the dark wooden outhouse. But we were surprised to see a modern porcelain toilet. Unfortunately, the stink that assaulted us made it clear that this was merely a "prop"; the bowl didn't flush, but simply sat, perched atop an open hole in the ground. Kit, whose stomach was already queasy from the drive, rushed away to keep from vomiting. But I urgently required the use of the facility and tried not to breathe as I quickly relieved myself.

To add insult to injury, after realizing that there was neither toilet paper nor a sink, I was greeted outside the outhouse by an old man who demanded fifty pesos for the use of his tocado.

José had come around to the back, apparently anticipating my reaction. He made no effort to hide his amusement as I tried to tell the old man what he could do with his hole in the ground. José tossed the man a coin and steered me by the shoulders towards our vehicles as I angrily protested that in the United States pay-toilets had been outlawed because they discriminate against women. José continued to laugh as he explained to the rest of the members of the group that I was about to make a political case out of fifty pesos. I appealed to the other women to explain my position to our "male chauvinist tour guide", but they were just happy they had passed up the opportunity to relieve themselves in such a disgusting place.

I climbed back into the mini-bus feeling filthy and irritable as I watched José stride back to his car still laughing and shaking his head. I would have liked to have smacked his arrogant face!

As we continued on I forgot the outhouse episode as I allowed the cool green of the mountains to soothe me. The mountains loomed around us in varying shades of gray green. And closer to them, the zigzag cuts of the road in the sides of the mountains revealed layers of gray-green malachite deposits that the Indians used to make stone objects. The river also glimmered green and all around huge mango trees laden with fruit and sugar cane fields waiting for harvest were a deep rich emerald. "This country is most definitely blessed by its beauty," I thought to myself.

After the long winding climb up the mountains came the long treacherous descent down into the city of Oaxaca. Again everyone in the back of the van began to feel nauseous and no amount of meditation seemed to help. Elmer showed us how to use acupressure by pressing on our upper lip to keep from actually vomiting, but by the time we reached Oaxaca everyone had a sore upper lip except Kit. She was lucky to have been in the front seat for this long roller-coaster ride.

Oaxaca is a city of 120,000 people and seemed modern compared to the villages we'd passed through, but nothing like the skyscraper cities of the United States. After briefly stopping at our hotel we set out for the ruins of Monte Alban.

Before going on to the ruins, we stopped at a little restaurant at the mountain-top site and enjoyed warm chicken sandwiches and watermelon nectar. The view from the patio, overlooking the city below, was breathtaking.

Walking up into what appeared to be hills, which José explained were most likely pyramids overgrown with vegetation, we arrived at a tomb. Although we were permitted to climb down into it, it was too dark to see the colored murals which covered every wall. This disappointment hardly prepared us for the breathtaking sight we would encounter over the next "hill" we climbed.

There, stretched out before us, was a giant, sunken, rectangular plaza, surrounded with buildings and platforms, that is, quite literally, on an artificially flattened mountain top. The view defies words! A huge three-part structure was positioned in the center of the plaza along with an arrow-shaped structure that is believed to have functioned as an observatory.

After climbing down to the plaza we walked along the right perimeter to a structure at the far end known as the Danzantes Building because some people have interpreted the humanoid figures depicted there as dancers. These "slates" seem to fall into three categories. Some had Negroid features that are similar to depictions of the Olmecs at other sites. One of these had a long Oriental type of "pig-tail". They were all "dancing" in such a way that they appear to be deformed or some sort of contortionists.

A second group of stones shows people similarly misshapen and with similar features to the first group, but they seem to be swimming, rather than dancing.

The third group depicted men with almost Phoenician appearances — with beards, Semitic noses and Egyptian attire and accessories. Their faces are expressionless, as if they are in a trance. These statues predate most of the other structures and I wondered if perhaps they could be a record of prior attempts in the creation of humanity.

I tried explaining my theory to the other people in my group but they didn't seem to find it too probable. A pipe fence didn't allow us to get close enough to these carved slabs to touch them, but further on I noticed that some of the stones in the walls of the structures were also carved with images. I went up to one that depicted a man with his hand up, palm facing out, and placed my palm directly on his. Immediately I felt a vibrating rush in my hand and instinctively pulled my hand away, then cautiously touched the carved hand again. Once again, I felt a buzzing sensation going into my hand. José noticed me touching the building and came over to see what I was doing.

"Touch this," I exclaimed, "It's alive!"

"You're not supposed to be touching these things," José admonished as he approached me.

I reluctantly pulled my hand away from the stone and without thinking I reached to the back of José's neck and touching him I said, "I forgive you, there's no more need to suffer."

"What are you talking about?" José asked as he reached to the back of his neck where I'd just touched him, looking bewildered and curious.

I was just as puzzled by my own action and words as he was. "I don't know. It just seemed like something I was supposed to say," I replied abruptly and walked away trying to escape the feelings of embarrassment I was experiencing. José just stood there for awhile touching his neck and staring at me as if I'd become one of the strange figures depicted on the stones.

As I continued walking around the perimeter of the site, hoping that José would just forget our strange interaction, I began to sense that I was getting closer to discovering the reason for my obsessive interest in the Maya. Somehow the words I'd just spoken to José had something to do with my dreams, that I still couldn't recall... and the strange story I'd told to Reverend Blaze... and the vision on top of the Pyramid of the Sun... it would all come together soon, I knew it. But how I wished José would stop staring at me!

Back at the Hotel Victoria, Kit and I rushed into our swimsuits for a luscious dip in the pool. I couldn't remember ever enjoying the sensations of the water and the warm breezes as much as I did that day. It was as if the vibrations that had entered my hand, had permeated my entire body and I felt vitalized, exuberant and in love with life!

The hotel restaurant was on a patio facing east so that as Kit and I sat eating chicken molé (chicken in a dark brown sauce of chocolate, spices and peppers) we could watch the almost full moon edge itself up over the mountains. Even with the brightness of the moon we could still see the constellations. As I expounded on how delightful the evening was, and our view of the sky, Kit began to look at me with the same dubious expression as José!

I went to bed that night thinking that if I had to choose the most perfect spot on earth to build a city for the gods, Oaxaca would be the place.

We began the next day with a shopping trek in the zocalo in Oaxaca. Kit bought a beautiful white shawl, woven in a delicate lacy pattern, for only eight thousand pesos - the equivalent of less than four dollars. The 20 de Noviembre market beckoned us with its spicy fragrances of cinnamon, cocoa and coffee. One vendor was offering boiled grasshoppers. Vincenté, noticed us looking at these "delicacies" with revulsion and explained that legend has it that whoever eats the grasshopper will inevitably return to Oaxaca. I assured him that I would make every effort to return to this fascinating city without the help of the grasshopper. Kit shook her head in agreement as she went on to look at the other more tantalizing treats being offered in the market.

Our next stop was the pottery shop of don Valente Nieto. Working on the patio of his home, don Valente continues to create the intense black, polished, clay pieces that his mother, doña Rosa made famous. We watched as he shaped the clay into a beautiful urn without a turntable, using instead two saucers inverted back-to-back and turning the piece with his hands as he formed it.

While Kit and I were looking over the beautiful pottery pieces he offered for sale in his workshop, Kit started to complain that she wasn't feeling too good. Within minutes she was rushing outside looking for a bathroom. She was perspired and her color was awful and I knew that somehow, she'd been stricken with the greatest dread of all Mexican tourists — Montezuma's Revenge!

José drove us back to our hotel without saying much to me. I mistook his silence for concern that Kit would make a mess in his car. But after we arrived and he had assisted Kit into our room, he took me by the arm and led me out into the hallway.

"Did you bring a prescription for this with you?" he asked. I felt very guilty as I apologized for not properly preparing for this problem. José seemed to be struggling with what to say next.

"Are you a healer?" he demanded almost accusingly.

"What do you mean?" I stammered, feeling defensive of his tone, but confused by his question.

"How did you know that I've been suffering with neck pains for as long as I can remember?" he demanded, his tone getting even more threatening.

"I didn't know. I'm sorry. What do you want? Why are you yelling at me?" I cried.

"You don't know!" José yelled, and then suddenly he must have realized that I really didn't know what he was talking about. "My neck, you touched it yesterday and it's cured. I've tried everything - everything! My own father was a shaman and he couldn't do anything for me. He said that an ancestor was angry with me and had put a curse on me. And now it's gone — for the first time in my life the pain is completely gone."

His voice softened as he changed the subject to Kit's illness. "If you can heal, then you'd better try to help your daughter because she will become dehydrated very quickly. I've seen this problem destroy strong healthy men in a matter of hours."

"I don't think that I'm a healer," I explained to him. Maybe your father was right and the pain in your neck had something to do with your past — a past life... We can discuss that later, right now I need to get this prescription you mentioned. Do you know a doctor around here?"

José shook his head, "No, but I know what to give her. Will you trust me to use a herbal cure of my people? I usually don't offer this to tourists, but I think that you are different. Will you trust me?"

I nodded consent and he turned to rush down the hallway without further explanation. Inside my room, poor Kit was in the bathroom. Her body was expelling violently from both ends at once as she alternated which area to position over the toilet. By the time José had returned, the vomiting had stopped and I'd cleaned up the mess as best I could. He handed me a big bottle of liquid that he said had an apple flavor and instructed me to get Kit to drink as much of the stuff as she possibly could. He also gave me a packet of herbs and said to make a strong tea with them that Kit also must drink.

"I've got to go see how the rest of the group is doing. I'll be back in an hour to see how she is," he said, and left me to administer his "cures."

# San Cristobal

José's strange potion worked like a charm and Kit was feeling well enough to travel by the next morning. Once again I awoke with the sensation that I'd been dreaming about the past, but as always the memory slid off into oblivion the moment I tried to consciously recall it.

After brief stops at the ancient tree of Tule, and the Post-Classic ruins of Mitla, we continued on through the mountains. Again driving through the steep, winding mountain roads left us groaning with car sickness, except for Kit who sat in the front seat chatting happily with Vincenté. Necessity being the mother of invention, Elmer finally rigged up a web-type of contraption to hold the windows open, using the straps from everyone's carry-on bags. We spent the night at an unremarkable hotel outside Tehuantepec on the Pacific coast, grateful just to be out of our nauseating vehicle for a little while.

To our dismay our drive was more treacherous than ever the next day as we journeyed through the Chiapas Mountains. Portions of the roads had been washed out by a hurricane and we actually had to drive up the sides of the mountain to circumvent these gaping holes in the roadway. I resigned myself to destiny — if it was ordained that I should die on an obscure mountain pass in Mexico, then no amount of worry would change my fate. With responsibility for my life entrusted in the Almighty, I tried to relax and enjoy the experience.

At a brief stop at the Sumidero Gorge, José recounted the legend of the thousands of Indians who tossed themselves down the canyon, into the river, rather than to be taken by the Conquistadors. From there, we continued on through Tuxtla Gutierrez and finally arrived in the colorful mountain town of San Cristobal Las Casas where we would spend the next two days.

It was early afternoon and we had plenty of time to go off on our own to explore the marketplace. I inquired at our hotel — a quaint two-story building nestled in the town — where we could mail some postcards. The desk clerk didn't understand a word of English, but when he saw the postcards Kit was holding, he tried to explain in Spanish how to get to the Post Office. Needless to say, we wandered about the quaint Colonial town for some time before we finally found it.

Kit tried to explain to the disinterested man perched on a stool behind the counter, that she wished to mail fifteen post cards to America. In English, he responded that "This is America!" He'd obviously been waiting for the opportunity to show those *turistos* from the United States that he knew a thing or two. I realized that if I didn't step into the conversation it would take Kit forever to get her post cards mailed.

"Lo siento, Señor, she's only a child," I said, praying that the man knew more English than his "We're Americans too" speech. Kit, of course, turned to me ready to defend her intelligence. But I shot her a look that said "Just keep your mouth shut for once!" and the girl recoiled with a confused and hurt sigh.

I continued to salve the man's ego and finally he totaled up the cost of the postage and gave us two sheets of very large stamps, explaining that one of each would be required on each of the post cards. Now Kit was being pushed too far as she realized that her writing, which covered every bit of the post card's surfaces, would be completely obliterated by the enormous stamps. But I had already used up my patience on the testy postman and wasn't prepared to deal with my daughter's complaints too. So I folded up the sheets of stamps and stashed them into my pocketbook along with the postcards.

"We'll figure this out back at the hotel," I announced as I steered my daughter out the door. But a stack of flyers on the end of the counter caught my eye. They were typewritten in Spanish but a Maya-style line drawing of a Jaguar, at the top of the page, intrigued me and I took a flyer with me.

We caught up with Linda and Dave on our way back to the hotel and I showed them the curious flyer. Linda was able to decipher enough of the mimeographed notice to understand that it referred to a lecture about Indian healing rituals that was to be given that evening in a place called Na Bolom. Linda and I decided that it sounded interesting enough to find out more about it and agreed to show the flyer to José to interpret it further. When we got back to the hotel, Kit went on up to our room muttering, "Only my mother could manage to find a lecture to go to in the middle of a vacation."

We found José in the lobby engaged in a heated debate with the hotel desk clerk. Both men were hurtling their Spanish words at each other as if they were flinging daggers. But when they noticed us watching them, they quickly ended their tirade and acted as if nothing was wrong. From what little I could surmise, José was complaining about the poor service in the hotel. When he turned to us and suggested that the restaurant across the street would be more suitable than the hotel dining room for dinner that night, I assumed I was correct. While the desk clerk continued to grumble under his breath, I showed José the flyer about the lecture.

He looked at the notice quickly and explained that Na Bolom was the residence of a woman named Trudi Blom, who had spent many years studying the local Indians and had turned her charming colonial home into a museum, library and guest house for those interested in studying the present-day Maya. He suggested that we make arrangements for a cab with the desk clerk whom he'd just been arguing with.

I left that task to Linda, while I went upstairs to my room to see if Kit could be cajoled into coming with us. I found her preening in front of the tiny bathroom mirror with the woven shawl we'd purchased in Oaxaca. "You look like an Indian maiden," I cooed as I gave her an affectionate hug. But Kit was embarrassed that I'd intruded on her fantasy. She was trying so hard to be as adult as everyone else in our group pretending to be an Indian was much too childish. Of course, my condescending reaction only increased her humiliation and she tossed the shawl down onto the bed as though it was incriminating evidence.

"Why don't you come to this lecture with me and Linda?" I asked, oblivious to her embarrassment. But Kit scrunched up her face in exaggerated distaste. "No thanks, it sounds too much like school," she replied as she flopped down on the bed and resumed fussing with the shawl.

"Well, would you mind if I went without you?" I asked. "I'll arrange for someone from our group to come and start a fire for you and when I get back we'll go across the street for a late supper." I kicked at the remains of a charred log in a small arched opening in the masonry wall near the door.

"I hear it gets pretty cold here at night and we're going to need a fire to keep warm," I explained. Already the heat of the day had begun to abate and the sun still hadn't set. Even so, it was hard to imagine that it would get so cold that a fire would be necessary. Nevertheless, I recalled a conversation with some travelers in Mexico City, who'd recently come from San Cristobal. They'd complained about the bitter cold nights of this mountain town.

Kit complained that she didn't want me leaving her alone and she also didn't want to let anyone else into our room to fix the fire. But there was no way she was going to submit to the torture of sitting through a lecture. Finally, after some playful bantering, she agreed to stay at the hotel and to let Elmer in to start a fire if it happened to get cold before I returned.

There were no telephones in the hotel rooms, so I had to run down to the front desk to find out what room Elmer and Bill were sharing. There I met Linda who assured me that a cab would be arriving to pick us up in a few minutes. Although I'd become quite familiar with the span of time "a few minutes" could encompass in Mexico, I nevertheless raced up the winding steps to Elmer's room and arranged with him to get a fire going in Kit's room. Elmer was more than agreeable, but scoffed at the thought that it would actually get cold enough to make a fire necessary.

Our cab was an old beat-up Volkswagen that grudgingly puttered the few miles to our destination. As the cab driver pulled up to a dark, foreboding building with huge, double, wooden doors, Linda and I looked at each other skeptically. The shadows of enormous, old, ceiba trees made it seem as dark as night, even though dusk was just beginning. "Are you sure this is the right place?" Linda asked the driver as I surveyed the Gothic eeriness around us. But he seemed to understand only three English words. "Three Thousand Pesos," he said without expression and held out his hand.

"Here," I said as I counted out three thousand-peso bills into his outstretched hand. "You'd fit in just fine back in New York. Would you mind waiting un momento while we make sure this is the right place?"

The driver stared at me blankly and the moment the two of us had stepped out of his cab, he sped away. "Just great!" I exclaimed as I shook my fist at the departing car.

Linda laughed nervously. "This could turn out to be more of an adventure than we bargained for. You know we forgot to tell him what time to return for us."

"As if we could count on him to come back," I said sarcastically. "We're better off calling for a cab from here when we're ready."

Linda looked around for a door bell and then pulled a string hanging from over the door. "How Baroque!" I laughed as a bell lightly jangled on the other side of the door. After several moments we could hear someone unbolting the door. A plain, fair-skinned young woman, who looked like a left over from the hippie era, welcomed us inside and assured us that we were at Na Bolom.

We followed her through an open patio that was encircled with rooms, or rather with closed doors that one would assume led into rooms. Along the walls were stark black and white photos of Indians with long black hair and woven white tunics that fell to below their knees. One particular photograph immediately captured my attention. It portrayed a handsome, mature woman sitting cross-legged beside a shrewd looking old man whom I guessed to be her husband. The two people looked at each other with such profound admiration and love that I couldn't help but comment to Linda, "It doesn't matter how they're dressed or where they're sitting, those are two of the most dignified people I've ever seen."

The woman who had let us in, whispered almost reverently, that we were looking at a portrait of the t'o'ohil of the Lacandon Mayas that Trudi Blom had been studying for over forty years. She led us around the courtyard to a set of double doors that opened to a large room with chairs set up "school style" for the lecture. Several people were already seated and a young man was toying with an old slide projector in the back of the room. "It'll be a few minutes before the program starts," an elderly gentleman in the front of the room explained with an accent that seemed to be German. As I slid into a row of chairs and took my seat, I noticed the collection of artifacts that covered the walls of the room and waited enthusiastically for the program to begin.

As it turned out, the lecture was more boring than even Kit could have imagined. The subject matter was more about accommodating modern medical procedures to the Indian's way of life, than about the Indian's own healing methods. "So much for my ability to translate Spanish flyers," I thought as I tried to follow the monotonous dissertation in English, with a pause every few sentences while a young man translated into Spanish. Meanwhile, slides that were flashed on the wall behind the speaker, seemed to have absolutely no correlation to what was being said.

As the minutes wore on, I became aware of an increasing feeling of distress in my intestines. The group was too intimate for me to leave unnoticed, and the presentation was so poor that I was sure my departure would be interpreted as disapproval. But finally I had to answer nature's unrelenting demands and I slipped out of the room as quietly as possible.

Once I was out into the dimly lit patio area I realized that none of the surrounding doors were marked in any way that would indicate that they opened to a rest room. I could hear voices coming from somewhere, but none of the closed doors looked any more promising than the next. Gingerly I turned the knob to one door and peered inside. There, in almost total darkness, I saw a tiny old man dressed in a long white tunic, with a sparse mustache and dark hair that fell past his shoulders. He motioned for me to enter the room and I hesitantly moved a few steps inside.

"We've been waiting a long time for you," he said. But I realized that he hadn't actually spoken. Slowly his words poured into my mind like a stream of chanting, and yet no sound actually came from the man. I could easily understand him, and yet I realized that I was hearing a language completely foreign to me. In my mind his words sounded musical and enchanting. He seemed to be telling me the same thing over and over but in a different way. It was as though I was listening to a Picasso painting, hearing every facet of the message from all sides — forewords, backwards and sideways all at once. What he said, if it could be spoken in English, would have sounded something like this:

*This is the message you have come to hear,*
*This is the reason you have returned.*
*You must listen to the voices within you,*
*You must hear perfectly what is said.*
*The Ancients speak within you,*
*The Ancients summon you now,*
*Only the pure of heart can hear them,*
*Only the true people can understand.*

*Soon your purpose will become known to you.*
*Soon your past will be remembered.*
*It is the past of a holy bacab*
*It is the purpose of the holy bacab*
*All of the universe awaits,*
*All of humanity awaits,*
*For this, the message of Kahwil*
*For this, the message of your fathers and mothers.*

*Know now the calling of your birth,*
*Know now, the destiny of the jaguar-sun.*
*This is the wish of the ancients,*
*This is the prayer of the true peoples,*

*This is all that is certain*
*That change is inevitable*
*That change is predictable*
*That the cycles continue infinitely,*

*As above, so below*
*As below, so above,*
*Even the smallest of the small.*
*Even the largest of the large.*
*Listen to your dreams, Ahow of Te'nab,*
*Listen to the voices of the cave,*
*Listen to the words on the stone,*
*Listen to the cries of your ancestors.*

*The time is here for your remembrance,*
*The portal opens for you now,*
*You will dream well only if you remain pure in spirit,*
*You must dream well, pillar of the true peoples.*

As he completed his message he pointed his cigar toward me as a parent would motion to admonish a child. The darkness of the room increased and the image of the old Indian appeared to move further away. I moved toward him in an effort to see him more clearly, but as I approached him I realized that I was only looking at a photograph on the wall. The old man stood frozen in the framed picture, looking directly at me, his cigar poised between two wrinkled old fingers.

I rubbed my eyes, attempting to focus on the image in the unlit room, certain that my mind was playing tricks on me. Slowly I backed out of the room. My stomach no longer ached for the rest room, but I felt extremely tired. I turned at the sound of the doors to the lecture room opening and watched as the disenchanted audience shuffled out to the patio.

"Where did you disappear to?" Linda asked. "I was getting a little concerned, although I must admit that I was tempted to leave, myself. So tell me, what have you been up to for the past hour and a half?"

"Hour and a half?" I asked, surprised that Linda should think I'd been gone that long. "It just goes to show you how time can crawl when you're bored. I only left a few minutes ago."

Linda looked as if she was about to argue the point but decided against it. She glanced at her watch. "I can't wait to get back. I'm starving. Do you think everyone went ahead and had dinner without us?"

I looked at my own watch. It had been two hours since we arrived. That meant that I had been listening to the photograph of the Indian for over an hour. I didn't dare tell Linda what had happened and Linda didn't seem to notice the puzzled expression on my face. She asked one of the men who had been at the lecture, where we could call for a cab and he pointed out a doorway across the patio. We followed his direction and walked into a little office where the pleasant young "hippie" girl, who had let us in earlier, called a cab for us.

While we waited, I nonchalantly asked the girl if any of the local Indians were staying at Na Bolom that night.

"Not tonight," she answered cheerfully, "although often we do have visitors from Naha. But tonight there's no Lacandon here."

She assumed my question was one of curiosity about the small, isolated Indian community that some believe are descendants of the Maya of Palenque and showed me several books about them. I purchased a book which had some of the photos I'd seen on the walls, but not the one that had "spoken" to me. Then I hurried after Linda for our cab back to the hotel.

The desk clerk at our hotel informed us, in an obviously disturbed tone of voice, that our friends were across the street having dinner. We crossed the narrow cobblestone street and stepped up the foot-high curb to the doorway directly across from the hotel. Inside, a narrow stone stairway led up to the second floor. A handsome European man with a French accent directed us to the two tables where our group was in the midst of dining and laughing over one of Bill's corny stories.

When he saw us, José told me that Kit was still in her room. "I stopped by to invite her to join us but I think she is afraid to go out without her Mama," he said in a fatherly tone.

I thanked him and hurried back to find Kit sound asleep and curled up under every blanket in our room. The temperature had been steadily dropping and the room was now uncomfortably cold. I tried to awaken her but she couldn't be roused. Answering my questions with a sleepy "yes" or "no", she clearly had no intention of leaving the warmth of her bed or her sleepy state of consciousness.

It appeared that Elmer had attempted to start a fire in the fireplace, but the slightly charred log had gone out. I went down to the front desk to inquire about getting some kindling and a few more logs and was glad to see that the disgruntled clerk that José had been arguing with, had been replaced. The lobby was open to the bitter night air and the Ladino behind the desk had several woolen shawls wrapped around his head. Holding his hands under his armpits in a effort to keep warm, he struggled to understand my broken Spanish. He directed me to a young boy in the lobby who seemed decidedly under-dressed for the temperature, but who eagerly carried a bundle of firewood and shavings to my room. When I handed the youngster a tip of two thousand pesos, he was so overjoyed that he returned a few minutes later with bottled, purified water. Then, noticing that I was struggling to start the fire, he motioned that he could help. In minutes he had arranged the shavings and logs in such a way that a brilliant orange-red flame was dancing around the firewood. I was so pleased I offered him another two thousand pesos which he accepted with a dramatic display of gratitude. I asked him in English if he wanted to warm himself by the fire for awhile, but he seemed to be unable to understand me, and hesitantly went on his way.

Sitting on the bottom corner of Kit's bed, which was nearest to the fireplace, I warmed myself and thought about the strange vision I'd seen at Na Bolom. The Indian's words stayed clearly with me, mysterious and yet familiar. I considered how all of my life I had felt different in some way from those around me. I enjoyed things that no one else seemed to care about, like astronomy and ancient mythology, while often feeling that some of the concerns of my peers were frivolous and silly. Was this difference, that had always left me feeling alone and misunderstood, something that made me special? Had I actually once been a Maya ruler who for some reason, chose this time and place to return?

For a long time I watched the flames flicker and change color in the fireplace. As I relaxed, bits of the strange dreams I'd been having every night since we'd arrived in Mexico seemed to flicker in the fire. "Listen to your dreams," the old man in the vision had said.

But once again my physical needs demanded my attention and I realized that I was ravenous with hunger. I tucked the blankets close around Kit and whispered to my innocent sleeping daughter that I was going across the street for something to eat.

"Do you want me to bring something back for you?" I asked the child buried beneath a pile of brilliantly patterned blankets. But Kit only groaned in her dreams. "Dream well," I said, quoting the old man. Wrapping Kit's shawl around my head I quietly locked the door behind me and headed over to the restaurant.

Only José and the Weinsteins remained at the table and José seemed about to leave when he saw me walking towards them. "Ah, the Señora has returned!" he exclaimed as he pulled out a chair for me.

"You look like you could be one of the natives with that scarf wrapped around you," Andy commented. "How is the little one? All tucked into bed, I suppose. She missed her Mommy tonight, did she?"

I nodded to his questions, suspecting that Andy didn't ask questions because he cared to hear an answer, but because he was in love with the sound of his own voice.

"Did you get a fire started for her?" José asked in a soft, concerned voice that was further softened in its contrast to Mr. Weinstein's.

"Yes, a boy from the hotel did a wonderful job of it," I answered.

"Oh, that little ruffian!" Andy quipped. "He's a devious one! Tried to soak me for a fortune by bringing the wood to me in three separate bundles and expected a tip each time!"

I could just imagine Andy reluctantly parting with a meager fifty peso coin each time he sent the poor boy for another bundle of wood. I cringed to think that the boy would think our whole group would be so stingy. Janet seemed annoyed by her husband's remark and gently suggested that perhaps he'd had a bit too much to drink. "Why don't we get you off to bed, just like dear little Kit," she said in her usual motherly manner as she got up from her chair. Andy bid his farewell to me and José and mumbled something about José being "one smart Indian", apparently referring to some previous conversation, as he stumbled towards the door.

By now his wife was beside herself with apologies to José, whispering that Andy hadn't meant anything malicious but, "He just says things all wrong when he's drunk. Come along now dear," she said to her bumbling husband as she ushered him out the door.

José didn't seem to be disturbed by the Englishman's thoughtless remark but I had allowed him to irritate me once again. "How can you put up with people like that?" I stammered.

"Oh, there's one like that in every group. I just have to ignore them and think about the money I'm making. Actually I feel sorry for him. He misses so much of the good things — the things you notice. Do you know what I mean?"

I nodded.

"You must be starving. Aren't you the one who likes to eat dinner so early? They have that Sopa de Lima that you like so much."

I was surprised that José had noticed so much about me. "You don't miss much yourself, do you?" I quipped and motioned for the waiter who was standing at the bar, to take my order. "Sopa y Tortilla, por favor," I said using up my entire repertoire of Spanish.

"You can speak in English," the waiter laughed.

"Good," I sighed playfully. "Because I don't know how to say 'I'm starving so make it as fast as you can,' in Spanish." The waiter nodded knowingly and hurried off.

"I'll have another tequila," José called after him and then explained to me that it was only his second. "I don't usually drink on tours because I can't afford not to feel good the next day. But tonight I am feeling very lonely and the drink will warm me. You would do well to have one yourself on such a cold night. Do you drink tequila?"

Again I nodded and he called out to the waiter to "bring one for the Señora too!"

"You know, for once Mr. Weinstein was right. You looked beautiful when you walked in just now with that shawl around you. But more like a princess than just an ordinary native." José's voice was soft and his accent made his words sensuous. I realized that I was just too tired to keep up my defensive attitude towards him. He reached over for one of the tortillas piled on a plate the waiter had just brought to the table with my soup and folded it and dipped it into my soup.

"This is how it is done," he whispered as he held the sopped tortilla to my lips. As I took a bite, he seductively explained to me that it was an Indian custom, that when a woman fed tortillas to a man, she was consenting to marry him.

"Then I'll be sure not to feed you any tortillas," I laughed. But José put the remainder of the tortilla in his mouth and said slyly, "Ah, but you have already done so."

I tried to remind myself that José probably treated at least one woman on every tour this way, but as the tequila began to relax me, my perspective began to change. The many sensitive things he'd said and done during our journey began to replay in my mind.

"Would you like to take a walk so that I can introduce you to my friends? It's chilly, but I think I can keep you warm. No?" he asked so quietly that he was barely audible.

"You have friends in San Cristobal?" I asked, trying to avoid his suggestion and his eyes that were looking directly into mine.

"Not only in San Cristobal. Actually they follow me everywhere I go. That way I do not usually feel lonely when I am on a tour. My favorite is Sirius. Maybe you cannot see him from New York."

Suddenly I realized that he was speaking about the stars. "Of course I can see him from New York! This time of year he's just below Orion in the early evening." I felt my adrenaline race as I realized that here was someone I could speak to about one of my favorite interests — the sky.

"Seen from Mexico, the brightest star in the heavens follows behind Orion, not below him," José explained, quick to pick up on my enthusiasm. "Come outside and I'll show you." He helped pull my chair out for me and I tried to act as if such chivalry was commonplace to me. Then he lifted my shawl up from my shoulders and placed it around my head and brought me close as though he was going to kiss me. But instead, he only stared into my eyes saying nothing.

"Come with me," he finally whispered and guided me down the stairs to the street. "It's only a few blocks to the Zocalo. Do you feel like walking there?"

I was eager to see the sky, but not much was visible from the narrow street. "Sure" I said as I pulled the shawl closer around my face. It was hard to believe how cold it had gotten. "I should have brought a winter coat," I stuttered, trying to speak without shivering. We walked briskly in an effort to keep warm and reached the open square in only a few minutes.

Except for an old man huddled on a bench, the square was deserted as we took turns pointing out familiar constellations and stars. The first thing I noticed was the unfamiliar angle of the stars. "This is just the way the sky looked in a dream I had a few months ago. I dreamt that I was looking up at a solar eclipse and just when the sun was completely blocked out, this is exactly what the sky looked like… just like this, with Orion on his side and Sirius following behind. I must have been looking at the sky from here!" Suddenly I stopped talking, afraid that José was probably thinking I was some kind of weirdo. But he wasn't looking at me as if there was anything strange about me at all.

"You know much more than you let anyone know," he said. "Much, much more. You are like a Shaman. You can heal and you can dream of the future too."

I realized that José was referring to his neck which he'd claimed was somehow cured when I touched him in Monte Alban. "I don't know if I'm dreaming of the future or the past," I explained. "Maybe it's the same thing; the future, the past, the present… Doesn't it bother you that I might be…" here I paused looking for the right word.

"Gifted?" José offered.

I looked at him, grateful that he hadn't used a word like "peculiar" or "weird". As I looked into his dark piercing eyes, I felt his hands on the sides of my face pulling me close to him. He kissed me very differently than Charlie. Not strong and deeply, but gently pulling my lower lip into his mouth and alternately increasing and decreasing his hold of it until shivers of excitement began to rush up within me. My first impulse, to pull away, was quickly replaced by a desire to never let it end. As he gradually loosened his pressure on my lips, he pulled my face away as gently as he had brought it to him and looked at me with eyes ablaze with passion.

"I have wanted you since the first moment I saw you," he whispered hoarsely. "I feel as if I have always known you, and always wanted you. You arouse in me something unlike anything I have ever known before... a passion that has awakened me every night of this trip; like a memory of somehow knowing you and desiring you before.

"I know you think that I am one of those men who lure every woman they meet into their bed. Once, yes, I was like that. But not for many years now. I've grown weary of the emptiness. I haven't slept with a foreign woman in many years. And the Mexican women I've had only fill the physical need. My attraction to you is very different... very, very powerful!"

Suddenly José seemed embarrassed by his outburst of emotion and I'm sure that the look on my face clearly indicated to him that he had said far too much.

"Let's go back to the hotel," he suggested and as we slowly walked, he apologized far less eloquently than he had just propositioned me. Yet when he put his arm around me, he must have noticed that I didn't resist. I was fighting a war in my mind. I could never let José know how tempted I was to succumb to his seduction. What would that make of my relationship with Charlie? Was it possible to feel this attracted to someone if you were in love with someone the way I was with Charlie?

When we reached the hotel, José summoned the firewood boy and paid him to start a fire in the blue-tiled fireplace at the end of the little sitting room off the lobby. There we sat for what seemed like hours, just talking. The tequila had loosened my tongue and I felt comfortable enough to tell José about the strange vision I'd had at Na Bolom that evening. I half expected that my story would frighten him away and I wouldn't have to face the dilemma of my attraction to him. But as I revealed all the mysterious events that had led to my trip to Mexico, José seemed to be all the more attracted to me.

Again he kissed me as he had done in the Zocalo, and again I felt a quiver of excitement rush through me. I had to admit that I would have found it difficult to resist him had he chosen to continue. With his arms around me, I struggled to explain to him that I had a wonderful relationship with Charlie that I could never betray. I explained that Charlie had given me and Kit the tickets for our trip.

"If I were to fall for someone else while I was on a trip he'd paid for, I wouldn't be able to live with myself," I insisted.

But José was undaunted even by my profession of love for Charlie. "I will not be responsible for influencing you to do something you don't think is right," he softly replied. "You think about it. Think about the way you feel now, tonight. Think about this." And again he kissed me. As I melted in the passion he aroused in me, he stood up and pulled me up from the sofa towards him. He put his arm around my lower back and pulled me close against him.

"You will think about this tonight, no?" he asked as he pulled me away from him. I couldn't speak. Tears welled in my eyes as I tried to deal with the confusion he had stirred within me.

"Destiny has brought us together," José said, looking straight into my teary eyes. "That is not something to cry about. Long ago my father had predicted that the ancient one whom I had wronged would return... that I would have the chance to do right by them... You spoke the words yourself, `I forgive you — there's no more need to suffer.' You'll see. You'll see. Good night. I will dream of holding you, my love."

With those words, he turned and walked away and I sat back onto the sofa in the quiet room, lit only by the dying fire. "Charlie, I wish you were here," I said half aloud. "I know that the only reason I feel this way is because I miss you so much." If there had been a telephone in the hotel, I would have called him, in spite of the horrendous cost. I closed my eyes and tried to imagine Charlie beside me. But the only thoughts that came to mind were of José. His melodious accent still echoed in my ears as I slowly climbed the dark, winding stairway up to my room and tip-toed inside.

All of our blankets were piled on top of Kit and I debated taking one for myself. But instead I quietly put on another layer of clothes, added another log to the fire and crawled into my cold bed.

# The Open Portal

I awoke before dawn to the sounds of people and animals moving on the street below. Braving the cold, I peered out the window to watch the pre-dawn arrival of the farmers and their families bringing their goods to market. They seemed in a festive mood for such an early trek. As for me, I decided I was too cold and sleepy to start my day and returned to bed to await the warmth of the sun's arrival.

When morning actually did arrive, we spent it exploring the marketplace in San Cristobal. The air was still cool as we set out towards the center of town, retracing the steps of the earlier procession of Maya farmers. But it warmed so quickly that the woven canopies that covered each vendor's display of wares offered a welcome relief from the glare of the sun. The market area, covering the equivalent of a city block, was rich with the smells, sounds and sights of an adventure movie. From their booths, vendors hawked fruits and vegetables; nuts; yard goods of cotton prints and colorful woven wool; high-backed leather sandals; flowers; meats and fish; and even live poultry. I was surprised to see that the meat was displayed uncovered and open to flies — it stood out in stark contrast to the overall cleanliness of the market. With the exception of a few tools and plastic buckets, here was a world devoid of packaging, artificial ingredients, or factory made items. I noted that no one I saw seemed the worse for it.

In the square outside the pale, rose-colored, baroque church of Santo Domingo, tiny Indian women, their babies secured at their breasts with woolen shawls, offered colorful woven belts, purses, ponchos and satchels for sale. Their colors and designs were seductive... the innocence of their creation made them irresistible. Most of the women wore a folded rectangular cloth on their heads that extended past their foreheads for a few inches, apparently shading their eyes. But when I noticed one woman arriving with her wares piled high in a net sack that she carried on her back suspended from a strap across her forehead, I realized the very practical function of a cushion that their strange headgear provided. This method of portage, used by both men and women for carrying surprisingly heavy burdens, is called a tumpline.

Most of the women wore their long black hair twisted into a knot at their forehead, which also seemed to help hold their head shawls in place. They sat in groups that could easily be recognized as representing different villages by the color of their shawls: some royal blue, some a light magenta and others black. The men also seemed to be costumed according to their clan — some wearing ponchos of a pin-stripped magenta and white, others wearing solid black or deep blue.

After lunch we loaded up our bags to continue our journey, first stopping at some Indian villages before going on to Agua Azul. We passed through several villages, each distinctive in the colors its residents wore — almost like uniforms. I remarked to Kit that she was seeing what could happen when people take "being in style" too seriously. I couldn't help wondering how someone of a more rebellious, independent nature would survive in a society that seemed so rigidly structured. I presumed, if everyone dressed identically, this was an indication of a general attitude of strict conformity in all aspects of life.

Just as I was considering how impossible it would be for me to exist in such a society, we arrived at the village of San Juan Chamula. Watching several young girls tending a flock of sheep in a beautiful pasture just outside the village, I envied the beautiful simplicity of their lives. What could one possibly ever worry about... there was only the day you woke up to, doing what was expected of you, breathing clean air, resting your eyes on the luxuriant vista of the countryside, no worries, no challenges... I could endure it for a least a day!

As we drove into the center of town, Vincenté explained that the inhabitants didn't fancy the intrusion of the touristas and we should be very careful not to insult them. José had gone over to the Village Hall to obtain permission to visit the church and when he returned with our permits he cautioned that we were not allowed to take photos in the town.

"The Indians believe that if you take an image of them, you are taking a part of them as well," he explained in an almost reverent whisper. As we followed him to the church he warned that this would be unlike anything we'd seen before. "A priest has not been to this church in many years and these people have reverted back to many of the old ways. Inside you may see some things that will surprise you, but I must insist that you keep your opinions to yourself. These are a very proud people, and if you insult them they will think nothing of throwing all of us out of town."

The outside of the church was a simple, Spanish-style architecture except for the colorful archway of flowers painted over the entrance. But as much as José had tried to prepare us for what we would see inside, it was still a shock. There were no pews and pine needles were strewn about a floor covered with clumps of hardened wax from melted candles. Fabric banners with fancy cut-outs were draped across the ceiling, lending an Oriental feeling to the place. Along the walls were life-size statues of saints, encased in glass and wooden shrines. Each statue was draped in woven fabrics and trinket ornaments adorned their heads. Most of the statues had mirror pendants hung about their necks along with garlands of fresh flowers.

People gathered, chanting in prayer in small groups before some of the saints. On the floor before them, the flicker of thin candles added an eerie light to the dimly lit church. The color of the candles represented the nature of their prayer, white for rain, black to overcome fear, blue for peace and harmony, and green for the fields. Occasionally one of the men would take a drink of a potent sugarcane liquor from an old soda bottle and chase it down with a swig of cola. The combined fragrances of burning candles, fresh flowers, pine needles and burning incense were so overpowering that I thought, like many of the praying women, soon I too would be swooning.

I watched, awestruck, as an old woman cried out a prayer as she stretched a black chicken from its feet to its head on the floor before her. Swiftly, she snapped its neck and passed the dead chicken over her family's heads as if anointing them with the life force she'd just released from it, chanting emotionally all the while.

Andy couldn't handle that! "Good God," he whispered loudly enough to be heard throughout the church, "These poor devils are savages!"

José grabbed his abrasive charge by the arm and nearly dragged him from the church. "What's wrong with you? Didn't you hear me explain that you must not remark about the customs of these people!" he exclaimed in a whisper almost as loud as Andy's. I thought the two men were going to resort to throwing punches instead of insults when José suddenly threw his hands up in the air and called to God to rid him of this idiot.

Andy stood arrogantly looking at José, his hands on his hips, his chin proudly jutting out. "Leave it to the Spanish to think they could civilize the lot of you," he proclaimed as he pivoted seriously away and strode back to the car.

"Señora Rossi, would you and your daughter be so kind as to change vehicles with the Weinsteins. I will not have that fool in my car!" José said to me as I walked out of the church.

I suspected that José had other motives for changing us around, and I was sure the rest of the group thought likewise. But I agreed to continue our journey in José's old tan station-wagon, wishing that we'd changed before that nauseating journey through the Sierra Madre mountains.

Before leaving we walked through the small market area just outside the church. I couldn't help noticing how happy the children were and commented to José that I couldn't recall ever hearing a baby cry or a mother scold her children in any of the places we'd been in Mexico. He proudly explained that their children are extremely important to the Mexican people.

"They're important to everyone," I replied, but I wondered what it must be like for children to spend the first three years of their lives always at their mother's side. It had to have a very different effect than bottle-propping and nursery schools.

I watched a little girl, no more than five years old, pulling wool from a bag as one continuous strand, guiding it to her grandmother, sitting beside her, who twisted it into thread and wrapped it on a spool. Other women wove at looms secured around their backs, the opposite end pulled taunt from a post. It was such a simple contrivance, and yet from it they produced absolutely magnificent shawls, skirts and huipils, the ornate blouses worn by the Maya women.

Everyone seemed busy doing something — and content. Once again I found myself envying the harmony and sense of being in the right place that these people seemed to possess.

While looking through a pile of shawls in one booth, I watched as two teenage girls combed out their just-washed hair. They ran pretty, carved, wooden combs through their long, silky black tresses, giggling about something — maybe the silly gringa that stood watching them. In the next booth a little albino girl, with white skin and hair and pink eyes, clung to her mother's skirts and eyed me cautiously. I tried to reassure her with a gentle smile, but I couldn't help wondering how a child who was "different" would fare in a society so obsessed with conformity. She didn't appear to be suffering for her uniqueness.

José summoned me from across the courtyard to prepare to leave. But just as I started towards him a very old man came out from the booth with the Albino girl and put his hand on my arm to stop me. He only stood as tall as my shoulder. His skin was dark and more wrinkled than anything I'd ever seen before. But his grip was intense, almost fierce. When he was certain that I wasn't going to run he released my arm and slapped a small pouch into my hand.

"Recordar" he proclaimed, pointing to my head.

I thought he was trying to sell me a headache remedy.

"No, no, thank-you. I don't need it," I gently responded, attempting to hand the pouch back to him.

"Recordar" he repeated more vehemently, refusing to take back the pouch.

I resigned myself to this unusual sales technique and reached into my pocketbook for some money. "How much?" I asked resignedly, first in English and then in Spanish.

"No, no! Recordar!" he replied, motioning with his hands that he didn't want any money, and seeming to grow impatient with my failure to understand.

I slowly put the pouch into the pocket of my skirt, puzzled, wishing I knew what was expected of me. Slowly I backed away from the man, sensing that many of the people around us were now staring at me. I sensed that I had done something to offend them, but I had no idea what. The man motioned with his hand that I should go, saying over and over again "Recordar".

José, Kit and the rest of the group had already gotten into the cars when I walked out to where they were waiting. As I had expected, only the front passenger seat was vacant in the station wagon. I momentarily forgot the old man and his gift, while I pretended not to want to sit up front with the "Don Juan of San Cristobal". José seemed to be hurt by my teasing, which bothered me because I still couldn't accept that I wasn't just another conquest, in spite of our encounter the previous night.

The drive to Agua Azul was long and the roads were in a terrible state of disrepair. I noticed that the smell of fumes was as bad in José's car as it had been in Vincenté's bus and began to suspect that it had something to do with the kind of gasoline they used. We'd driven for over an hour before I remembered the pouch the old Indian had given to me and pulled it from my pocket to examine it. It was woven in a delicate, lacy pattern that seemed to represent a jaguar. I could see through the small openings in the weave that it encased dried herbs, but the pouch was sewn all around and apparently wasn't meant to be opened. I held it to my nose to smell it and was pleasantly rewarded with a rich, sweet pine-like fragrance. There was something addicting about it because I repeatedly brought it up to my nose to inhale its perfume.

"What's that?" José asked when he noticed me holding the pouch to my nose.

"Oh, something I got in the market. It sure smells a lot better than this car!" I commented thoughtlessly.

"What's wrong with my car? I put in an air freshener," he retorted defensively, pointing out the pine tree shaped freshener dangling from his mirror.

"That's useless against the gas fumes. I guess everybody down here must be used to it." I replied, noticing that José seemed unusually sensitive to my remarks. This seemed remarkably different from his arrogant teasing when our journey began. I wanted to tell him that I hoped that our encounter in San Cristobal wasn't going to ruin a perfectly good sparring team, but I didn't want to mention it in front of Dave and Linda and Kit, although they all appeared to be dozing in the back seat.

I thought about the old man in the market again and asked José nonchalantly, "What does recordar mean?"

"To remember," he answered. "Why?"

I didn't explain, but continued to inhale the fragrant pouch as we progressed toward Agua Azul. I started to feel queasy and light-headed and attributed it to the gas fumes.

"I guess it wasn't any better traveling in this car than in the bus through the mountains," I sighed, holding my face to the open window and wishing the uneasy sensation in my head would go away.

"Are you all right?" José asked, noticing the change in my voice. "We're almost there. Can you hold on for a few minutes more?"

I nodded, holding the scented pouch close to my nose in an effort to overpower the fumes. "I'll be all right," I replied, more to convince myself than him.

By the time we pulled into the parking area of Agua Azul I was feeling desperate to get out in the air. I could never have picked a better place to recover! This was paradise! Hundreds of cascades flowed into little pools and one another, all an extraordinary aqua color. The air was cool and sweet smelling and I sucked it into my lungs like a tonic.

"I'll be fine now!" I exclaimed, certain that the cool, fresh air would revive me. Kit, who seemed none the worse for the drive, eagerly joined the group for a hike upstream to a village. I tried to keep up with them for a few minutes, but after reassuring myself that they would be taking the same route back in a few hours, I suggested that I would rest at a grassy spot alongside one of the more picturesque falls.

I wandered over to a tall tree near the water's edge and lazily watched the brilliant blue water rushing down the cascade into the whirling pool below. But the dizzy feeling I'd felt in the car only seemed to increase. When I closed my eyes, the sensation grew more intense, as if I were drunk. I opened my eyes again and tried to focus on the waterfall and the scenery around me, but the need to close my eyes was too compelling, despite the dizziness it provoked. "Is this what it feels like to die?" I wondered as I felt myself being drawn into the dark, terrifying orifice of the underworld.

# BOOK THREE
# The Memory

# Hanab Pacal

Sleep overtook me like a sorcerer's spell. Images began to fly past my mind's eye like an incredible collage of hundreds of thousands of video snippets — each running at a fantastic speed, and each a replay of an entire lifetime. I knew at that moment that I could recount, in precisely accurate detail, each of those memories.

Then as quickly as it began, the cascade of images ceased and I saw a handsome young man, dressed in only a loin cloth, motioning for me to follow him into the jungle. As I approached him I noticed that he held the fruit of a miniature avocado in his hand.

"This is the favorite of the quetzal, My Lord. I'm certain that if we climb up a little further into the cloud forest we might be able to capture a bird and pluck its tail feathers," he exclaimed.

I was Hanab Pacal, the proud young ruler of Jaguar-Sun, enroute to the home of my chosen bride. I knew that I didn't have to warn my servant, Kan, that the penalty for killing a "flying serpent" was death. As young boys we had learned the trick of luring these magnificent birds into a trap, plucking their prized tail coverts and releasing the sacred bird unharmed. It was the beginning of nesting season and Kan and I knew that most male quetzals would soon loose their coveted, blue-green iridescent coverts in the process of their nesting duties, anyway. Their plumes would regrow before the next mating season, in time for their undulating dance of seduction, so it was safe to assume that the gods would not take offense if we helped ourselves to their splendid plumage before it was damaged.

I followed Kan into the brush, envisioning a handful of quetzal plumes to accent my marital headpiece. We left the merchant, Bol, to set up camp alone and hurried deep into the cloud forest.

Kan paused to point out the dangerous leaves of the weeping tree which could burn your flesh with only a careless touch. Although I was the Holy Bacab of Jaguar Sun, I was dressed, like my servant, in only a loin cloth. It would have been much too dangerous to travel in an attire that would identify my royal status. A captive of divine blood was a cherished prize for any warrior. And while it wasn't considered honorable to take a captive outside of battle, Bol had warned that, with planting season approaching, the honor of securing a Holy Bacab to sacrifice for the fertility rituals could outweigh the disgrace of how I was acquired. At Bol's suggestion, I dressed for our journey as a young man in service to a merchant.

While I carefully avoided the weeping tree, Kan plucked another type of leaf and rolled and split it, then held the opening to his mouth and blew to produce the sharp "tak-teek" call of the quetzal. Suddenly, in the distance we heard a hoarse reply, "wac-wac-wac-."

Kan raced exuberantly off towards the sound while I tried to keep up with him. Again he paused and blew his shrill summons through his leaf. For a moment there was nothing. Then directly overhead we saw the flash of the sacred red belly. Kan quickly pulled out his knife and slashed a nearby sapodilla tree. Almost immediately it began to bleed its latex blood. Breaking a number of small sticks from the brush around him, he turned their ends into the sticky ooze and set them into the ground in a cluster with only the distance of a man's fist between them. I watched with amused anticipation as he paused to call the male again. "Tak-teek, tak-teek," reverberated through his leaf whistle.

"Wac-wac-wac-wac-wac," the male called back enthusiastically. Now we could see him clearly through an opening in the jungle canopy; his red belly swooping up and down, his magnificent tail swirling behind. I could feel his energy and zest for life even before I could see his extraordinary beauty. While I admired the revered creature, Kan was busy placing the hard, pale-green fruits of the miniature avocado on the ground between the gooey posts.

Now he pulled me back into the trees and repeated his call to the bird. This time the male flew in close to us, seeking the mysterious female he heard beckoning him. As he swooped down to the ground he caught sight of the fruit Kan had carefully positioned, but then he swooped up again above the canopy. I knew that usually a quetzal would grab his food on the fly, rather than perching to feed, and we waited silently for his return. Sure enough, we saw his brilliant red belly descending again towards us. "Wac-wac-wac-wac-wac," he screeched as he headed for the trap. The startled creature wailed as he realized his predicament, entangled between the posts.

We had to move quickly before the bird injured himself or damaged his precious coverts in his panicky efforts to free himself. Kan raced up to our captive and snatched him gingerly from the sticky snare. He deftly yanked the four shimmering feathers from his rump and released the frenzied bird.

I watched as the poor creature struggled to a sapodilla branch and perched to pluck the remnants of resin from his feathers. He would be forced to spend the remainder of the season without his magnificent plumage, while I would sport those plumes with pride for many seasons to come. "You would have lost them soon anyway," I called up to the smitten bird. I wondered if he would ever fly again with such unchecked exuberance, or rush to the call of a female quite so enthusiastically again.

My sympathy for the quetzal was quickly replaced with my exuberance for our prize. Kan had managed to extricate the bird before any of the latex had touched the coverts and they shimmered now with magical perfection in his hand. The light from K'in, now low in the sky, caught the feathers, changing their color from blue to green to golden as Kan moved them through the air, recapturing the movements of their former owner.

We raced back to our camp, hooting loudly in triumph. When he saw us, Bol shook his head with the feigned disapproval of a parent, but then he saw the feathers we held aloof and his expression immediately changed to pleasure.

"Perfect, perfect! he exclaimed. We'll put them in the proposal bouquet. Great Jaguar will know you are truly a great ruler with such a treasure to offer!" he exclaimed. I fell easily to the mat Bol had set near the fire and held the feathers aloof so that the firelight made them glimmer. I hadn't considered relinquishing my prize to entice my bride, but then, if we failed to win her, there wouldn't be a need for a wedding headdress after all.

"Tell me again about this girl chosen for me, Bol. Is she as beautiful as these feathers?"

"Beauty is not the measure by which she was chosen, My Lord, although beauty is hers," replied Bol in his typically evasive style.

"Come merchant, I'm not an old woman in the marketplace buying shells from you! Answer me directly or I'll have you tortured!" I cried out in jest.

Bol shook his head seriously. "Take care with your words, My Lord. There are those who will scurry to enact every bidding you utter, unable to distinguish sarcasm from a command." He looked about us as if, even in this isolated spot, one of my over-zealous subjects was waiting to inflict some horrendous act of abuse on him.

I knew he was right in his admonition. My mother had warned me of the responsibilities of power, and the repercussions of carelessness, many times before. But my adventure with Kan in the forest, dressed so humbly, had left me feeling more like an ordinary young man, than a responsible leader. For a moment I'd disregarded the hundreds of guidelines and rituals that regulated every moment of my life, but I would take care not to let it happen again. I was the Holy Bacab of Jaguar Sun, the son of the divine Lady Resplendent Egret. The survival of my ancestors, my lineage and all the people of Place of Jaguar-Sun depended on my careful adherence to the codes and requirements of the gods. Bol's words sobered me quickly. "Good merchant, tell me of this woman that has been selected for the Holy Bacab. If not for her beauty, what qualities did my mother direct you to search for?"

As he'd already done many times during our journey, Bol began to reiterate the extraordinary lineage of my bride-to-be. Her father is a wise man from the place in the West where the first true people were created. His name is Great Jaguar, and he serves as chief advisor to the Holy Bacab of Tikal. The girl's mother, according to Bol, was Ixtab, the Moon goddess, a fact that he confirmed when he saw her. "Her skin is the color of the moon, and so is her hair. Her eyes are like the pools here in Place of Blue Waters," Bol whispered in reverent awe.

I tried to imagine such a woman and secretly feared her. I knew that I too was of divine lineage, my mother had taught me the names of the long list of my ancestors who were descended from the "Three-Born-Together" gods. But my chosen bride was actually the daughter of the Moon! Such a union would dispel any doubts about my appointment as Holy Bacab. But, I worried, what if she was more powerful than me? I dared not reveal my fears about the woman, even to Kan and Bol. After all, I was the Holy Bacab.

~

Our journey to Tikal was uneventful. Bol had traveled the route many times before. Unencumbered with the trappings of my position, we traveled quickly and easily. Since I was the only one in our trio who was not stooped over with the weight of a loaded tumpline, I was the first to notice Tikal's tallest temple, still under construction, towering like a vision above the forest canopy. We were still almost a day's journey away, but a paved limestone causeway made the final leg of our journey quite pleasant. As we approached the city, many people filled the road, going both to and from the city, and carrying all sorts of bundles on their backs. We stopped in a marketplace just before the plazas and temples. Nowhere could a plot of uncovered earth be seen. Bol had cautioned me and my servant not to look about like two awestruck foreigners. "Tikal is teeming with thieves and hucksters who prey on naive young men," he'd warned. But, despite his admonition, it was impossible not to gasp with wonder.

The marketplace was alive with vendors offering all kinds of food and goods I had never seen before. Men with features very different from anyone I'd ever met, offered us furs and feathers and woven goods with exquisite patterns. Pottery and baskets were either brimming with something for sale, or in one booth, it was the pottery and baskets themselves that were being sold. There were more people in the market than I had imagined lived in all the world, and Bol explained that this was only one of several marketplaces in Tikal!

Bol summoned a young boy standing near the basket stand and promised him a cacao bean if he would inform the Its'at that visitors awaited him in the market. The boy scurried off and Kan pointed out a shady spot for us to wait. Bol gave him a look to remind him not to publicly show deference to me, lest someone recognized my position. "Some of these thugs wouldn't think twice to sell you to the Chief Warrior," he whispered under his breath.

As I sat in the shade, waiting for the arrival of my father-in-law, my thoughts were not about seeing the young woman chosen to bear my legacy. Instead, I was thinking about how precarious my legacy was. I had often questioned the sanity of sacrificing captives of divine blood. How could the gods be pleased with the blood of those born to preserve the sacred mysteries necessary to serve them, I wondered. Of all my ancestors, I alone survived to carry on my lineage. How could my sacrificial death please the gods? It was madness — a madness that had haunted me since my childhood.

I was so absorbed in my thoughts that I didn't noticed the giant man lumbering toward us until his shadow blocked the sun. Bol and Kan quickly bowed low in respect before the man of obvious important status. Meanwhile, I found myself in the awkward position of knowing I should never bow to anyone, yet aware that in my guise as a merchant's apprentice I was expected to show respect to an Its'at. I bowed quickly, hoping the strangers around me would not notice that I had not lowered my gaze. The Its'at, I knew, would be astute enough to see that my deference to him was not genuine. In turn, he briefly glanced downward, secretly indicating his recognition of my superior position. "Follow me," he said quickly, then forged through the crowded marketplace toward a group of brightly painted stone buildings.

There was a festive camaraderie among us as we followed our imposing host through the maze of courtyards and homes. Everywhere the aroma of cooking tantalized our appetites. Mingling with the warm, familiar smell of tortillas sizzling on stone griddles and beans bubbling in clay pots, there were less familiar but equally enticing aromas of roasted game, baked squash, and broth steaming with herbs and fowl — perhaps a turkey or a curasow. From the fragrances that teased us as we hurried past softly lit doorways, keeping astride with our lumbering guide, it was clear to me that these were times of prosperity for Tikal.

Great Jaguar pointed out various improvements that had recently been made since the confidence of the residents of Tikal had been restored. For almost fifty years he explained, they had been denied access to their gods and confusion had reigned without the rituals and traditions that once were the backbone of their society. Crops had failed, and many of the hungry, disenchanted populace had moved on to other communities, where a more stable leadership had assured them of their place in the universe. Every May was taught as a child, that only by maintaining a cooperative relationship with the gods could they expect to enjoy prosperity.

"Civilization is such a delicate balance," Great Jaguar explained. "Without the structures provided by the divine royalty, the common people were confused and frightened. Many of them simply left. And without farmers and workers Tikal fell apart. Lord Water didn't have to destroy the entire population, all he had to do was destroy the structure," he said with a sweep of his hand as if he was wiping the city away. I understood only too well what he was saying.

"This is why it was so important to reactivate the temples; to restore the rituals. When we brought the gods back to Tikal, we brought back the whole civilization," he proclaimed. He slowed his pace and put his hand on my shoulder. "Now we will do the same for Place of Jaguar-Sun," he solemnly assured me. I dared not show my surprise that this stranger was aware of the problems in my homeland. Did he also understand the urgency of my mission—if the lineage of the Jaguar-Sun dynasty were to end with me, there would no longer be a Place of Jaguar-Sun. It was up to me to maintain the traditions, to nourish the gods; to implore their blessings and discourage their wrath. Only those of divine descent could read the sacred books that record the cycles of the sky and determine the times for planting and harvest. Without this, farming would be impossible, and without maize, people would return to the jungle, as the monkeys did in the Last Great Cycle. This is what it meant to be of divine blood— we were the caretakers of civilization.

As we reached the eastern-most end of the residential area, Bol noted the unusual architecture of several of the buildings. "This is a style of building I've seen in places far west of here," he exclaimed, obviously impressed. Just then Great Jaguar stopped at the doorway of one of the strange buildings and held up his hand, indicating for us to wait outside. He ducked his generous frame into the doorway, and reappeared only moments later, grinning like someone who knew a wonderful secret. "Go ahead in," he motioned to me. "My daughter has been expecting you."

Keenly aware of my importance, I strode past Great Jaguar into his home. Once inside the torch-lit room, I immediately forgot that the old man and my companions were behind me, watching with mischievous delight. There, on a mat beside the cooking fire, sat Hel. She was exactly as Bol had described her— her large blue eyes glistened with warmth and her wordless smile spread her full lips across her face in a way that made my heart race. A finely woven huipil fell from her shoulders over perfectly rounded breasts to where her brocade skirt cinched her narrow waist and spread over full, womanly hips. Rather than the white of an old woman's hair, tresses like the strands in maize before it's dried softly framed her mysteriously light face. A bluish tattoo decorated her neck and ears, just touching the edges of her cheeks, and the pattern was picked up in the woven design of her blouse. I recognized the pattern — it was the intricate Path of Bolom Tzacab that my own mother had explained to me as a boy.

Instead of kissing the ground in the usual woman's greeting, Hel rose up to meet me face to face. I was glad to see that she was slightly smaller than me, considering that I was shorter than most men of the Jaguar lineage. As she moved closer towards me, I recognized the musky fragrance of acoté and it increased the excitement that only seeing her had aroused in me. There seemed to be no need for words between us. She had been expecting me and understood what she was to do — who she was to be. We seemed to be able to communicate by only looking into each other's eyes. My concerns about being intimidated by her disappeared in the passion that her delicate appearance aroused in me. I turned back to Bol and nodded my approval — he could begin the customary marriage negotiations.

Great Jaguar ducked his large frame through the doorway with

Bol following behind. I sat back on a bench near the wall where I could continue to observe Hel, standing near the only window. Like a magician, Bol had pulled our bouquet from his pack—two quetzal feathers surrounded with an assortment of white flowers he'd purchased in the market. He extended our offering out to the girl's father, who had taken advantage of Bol's distraction to settle his body onto a mat in the center of the room. "Would the father of Hel explain for the Holy Bacab of Jaguar-Sun, his own lineage and how it came to be that Ixtab is the mother of your daughter?" Bol asked, cleverly putting our host on the defensive.

We listened as Great Jaguar began recounting, in a sing-song chant, the incredible story of his ancestors, the True People of the third creation. His story gracefully unraveled about those who peopled the earth when the last Great Cycle was about to end. Although I'd heard many versions of the tale, this was the first time I'd actually heard it told by a direct descendant of those who were believed to be the oldest tribe.

Between long, sensuous puffs on his cigar, and a frequent rumble as he cleared his throat, Great Jaguar's story flowed in a smooth, repetitive cadence of couplets. He told how the gods had looked with disappointment upon their creation— the humankind, that they had made for companionship. They had the gift of vision and could see and speak with the gods, but they were lacking in both compassion and wisdom. These people were like wooden toys without spirits and would not kneel in worship to their creators. So, to the very few among them, who were True People, the gods had warned, "Get yourselves from this place quickly. Soon earthquakes and floods will destroy everything you hold dear." Great Jaguar's ancestors were instructed to fell the four giant mahoganies that grew in each of the corners of their world.

"Make of these sacred trees, four kaxtlan chem— mighty canoes. Store safely within them the sacred bundles of your ancestors; the sacred books of the counting of the days and the journeys of the stars; the holy statues, the pih of the gods of your lineage, through which you will worship and communicate with us, for, except for a chosen few, you will neither see nor hear us again," the gods had warned.

"And these few true people did exactly as they were instructed" explained the enormous man after another puff and a liquid cough that made his massive frame tremble. "They set off in the four canoes in the four directions and looked back with great sadness and many tears to see their homeland falling into the sea.

"Those who followed the sun into darkness came to the place of the Jaguar, Lord of the Night. These were my ancestors, the people who began the new Great Cycle. The venerable old man's voice became sad and ominous as he described the fate of his ancestors. Their children were the maize-growers who, except for a few, could neither see nor speak with the gods. As it had been divined, only a few remained who could conjure the gods and speak with their ancestors in their dreams.

The old man paused in his chanting to study me. And I, likewise, returned his stare. My story, although most unusual, had not been transformed by the storytellers into a chant so beautiful that children of countless generations would listen spellbound until they had committed the entire tale to memory— to repeat it to their offspring, word for word, without deviation from the way it was originally told.

"Your lineage is most impressive," Bol spoke, drawing the attention of The Learned One of Tikal from me. But how is it that your daughter is also the child of the Moon Goddess, Ixtab?" he asked.

Great Jaguar attempted to sit up. Finally he resigned to a reclining position on the mat, his fleshy face propped with one chubby brown hand, his brocade robe hopelessly entangled around his cumbersome body. Only his feet, shod in high-backed leather sandals, and his round, dark face protruded from the woven mountain before us. An elaborately carved jade ornament pierced the septum of his nose and his ear lobes were decorated with ear-spools of obsidian worked to such delicate thinness that they were translucent. I noticed that the tassel of hair that extended from the jade ring in front of his jaguar-skin turban was not smooth and straight, but rather flared in all directions, like a brush made of the bristle of a peccary. The almost obsidian color of his skin and his round facial features clearly marked him as a foreigner. His full lips were characteristics of the First True People from The Place of Creation.

Selecting another cigar from a woven basket beside him, Great Jaguar rolled it on the mat methodically as he contemplated where to begin his story. He seemed to be savoring my curiosity as much as the tobacco he was preparing to smoke. Perhaps, I thought, he was trying to form the tale into a chant. As I silently waited, he placed the cigar in his mouth while touching the tip of a strip of acoté pine to the lighted censor pot. It immediately sizzled with a flame.

"Thank-you for this bit of fire, mighty Hunab," he mumbled around the thick cigar in his mouth. Holding the flaming torch to the tip of his cigar, he sucked in quickly several times until it lit. Finally, he was ready to speak and looking directly at me, instead of Bol, he began.

"These things I will tell you, I have spoken to no man before. Listen carefully, for you will be the one who will tell these things to my grandsons.

"When I was only slightly older than you are now, I was commissioned to a colony two months journey southeast of my homeland. There I was directed to teach the most recent advances in architecture to the builders of that great new center of trade. It was a wonderful experience for a young noble who was bright and full of the enthusiasm of youth. There was plenty to do and plenty of prosperity and recognition to be enjoyed.

"I had freed myself of the distractions of young men, replacing those fathering instincts with my love for my trade; spending every sunlit moment supervising the construction of the magnificent stone mountains of my dreams. There was so much to be considered in building a new center and a lot of my time was spent listening to the wisdom and advice of the wise ones— astrologers, mathematicians and scribes. The days grew into years before I knew it, and I had become an old man who had fathered no heirs.

"Then one day, as I was inspecting a burial chamber that was being constructed deep within a sacred cave, I noticed a strange young woman standing in the shadows of a dark corner. She was unlike anyone I'd ever seen before, with skin so light it seemed to glow in the darkened chamber. I thought that she was a cave goddess who, like a plant that had been kept from the sun, had grown without color. Her eyes were exceptionally large and seemed to reflect the shimmering green of her quetzal feather cloak and headdress. She was radiantly beautiful and more sensual than any woman I'd ever known.

"She summoned me to follow her deeper into the cave, but not with her voice. It was as if I could hear her thoughts and she, mine. We communicated in this manner for a time that I could not measure, while I followed her for a great distance through a maze of passageways. With only the light of her torch, we came at last to a chamber that appeared to be sectioned into three parts. A soft, misty light came from some distant opening far above us. She pointed out inscriptions to me that had been painted on the walls and silently explained their meanings; instructing me in the sacred mysteries of the ancestors; showing me how to use the magical powers of numbers; and sharing with me the deeper meanings of our rituals.

"Then she directed me to journey to a holy place, ten days north, where all building and ritual had ceased under the reign of a brutal invader who had desecrated the temples of the ancestors. I was to assist in the reconstruction of the sacred portals to the gods so that the lineage of the True Peoples could be empowered and the gods would once again be properly venerated.

"Sitting beside her, listening to a voice that made no sound, I learned how to summon the power of the gods. I was able to absorb everything she was teaching me as effortlessly as a child learns to suckle its mother. But at the same time I was feeling a fire in my groin that all the hard work and dedication of a man's entire life could not suppress. As I've told you, she was capable of knowing my thoughts, yet she seemed pleased with what she knew I was thinking. Then, as casually as if she were handing me food to eat, she reached over and removed my loincloth.

"She was so tiny and delicate that, at first, I was afraid to touch her. But soon that concern was overcome by the complete, unbridled release of passion that she aroused in me. I confess that my position and wealth have allowed me to know many women in a most intimate way. But I've never known a woman who could bring me close to what I experienced deep within that burial cave. When at last I'd laid back, completely satiated, she spoke her first words aloud to me.

"'My purpose here is complete,' she said. 'You have listened well and you have learned well. Take this sacred bundle and protect and nurture it. Within it is wrapped the holy pih of Kahwil. But remember that the power of the Third Son of the First Mother belongs not to you. You will give it to the daughter of Ixtab when she comes to you. She will be the mother of Kahwil. She will be the one who nourishes and protects his pih.'

"She handed me the sacred bundle and that was the first and last time that I ever saw Ixtab, the Moon Goddess. When I walked out of the burial chamber, I was astonished to find out that thirteen days had passed. I was almost a thin man!

"This is the place where she had directed me to go. Tikal had been oppressed for many years by the barbaric Lord Water who had destroyed their temples and most of the descendants of the divine Jaguar-Paw dynasty. Those few who survived had been in hiding for two generations, keeping the memory of their ancestors alive and protecting the bundles of their lineage. But without access to their sacred mountains they were unable to call up their gods and they remained powerless to the problems that beset them. Finally, after two katuns (forty years), Lord Water took the terrible road down to the Underworld; down to face his trials in Xibalba. (And what horrible trials I would hope they would be). His eldest son's only interest in Tikal seems to be in the fine clothing and ornaments and the beautiful young girls they send to him in tribute.

"Surreptitiously, at first, and then brazenly in the open, Shield-Skull, the rightful heir of Tikal, began reconstructing the holy mountain shrines and opening their sacred portals. He replaced the pihs on their altars and worshipped and nourished them. Then the gods spoke to Shield-Skull, advising him of my arrival.

"For over twelve years I served as Its'at and First Advisor to Shield-Skull of Tikal. The sacred knowledge taught to me by Ixtab in the burial chamber has made me a prosperous and respected man. But as clearly as I recalled every detail of the Sacred Mysteries that Ixtab explained to me; as reverently as I practiced the rituals she'd taught me; I continued to wonder about the ecstasy of our encounter and often wondered at the 'purpose' to which she had referred before leaving me with the sacred bundle. Every day I placed fresh flowers on the altar where I kept the bundle enshrined. Each night I burned copál and prayed to Kahwil to pardon the humble home where I'd hidden his pih, wondering when his mother would arrive, as promised, to relieve me of this awesome responsibility.

"Then, one morning, almost three years ago, I had my answer. Ixtab appeared in my dreams to say 'Your daughter, Hel, the mother of Kahwil, is ready to join you. Prepare her for the one who will take her to the Place of Jaguar-Sun; to the Holiest Shrine of Kahwil.' I awoke to see, sitting on the floor beside my sleeping mat, a young girl with skin as fair as the clouds and the round, generous features of my peoples. When I saw her eyes of blue water, I knew she was the child of Ixtab.

"What an awakening to a man who once considered himself wise and knowledgeable! Hel has the intellect and the knowledge of the gods. She divines with the red seeds and crystals, and interprets the lightning in her blood more accurately than any shaman I've ever known. No one can take offense with the advice or direction of this strange young woman— such is her way of charming people. In the three years she's been with me, I've achieved more than in the twelve years prior!"

I studied Hel's father with the curiosity of a child. I knew very little about my own father's background, other than the fact that he was an Ahow of the Sky-Snake clan that had provided consorts to

the royal family for many generations. He was one of those chosen
few who could speak with the ancestors in his dreams and his
advice was sought by many. I knew of the red seeds and crystals of
which Great Jaguar spoke— many were the hours I'd spent watching my father sort and arrange these seeds, noting the count when
he felt his blood pulse. This was the way the gods spoke to their
shamans— those seers chosen by their birth to advise, heal and
intercede for the True People.

No one had ever questioned the fact that Yellow-Macaw, the
shaman of the Sky-Snake lineage, who could bargain with the gods
for health and prosperity, could also father the child of the Divine
Lady Resplendent Egret, Holy Bacab of the Jaguar-Sun dynasty. But,
while I had inherited my father's aquiline nose and unusual height,
as well as his ability to conjure the gods, he had remained reverently distant with me. After all, I was divine and he was not — very
much like Great Jaguar, who had been privileged to father Hel.

It was because my divine lineage had come through my mother,
rather than my father, that Bol had deliberately put Great Jaguar on
the defensive in his negotiations. He was, after all, very skilled in the
negotiations of a merchant. But now, Hel's father asked the question
I'd been dreading. "Tell me now how this young man claims to be
divine," he bluntly asked Bol, nodding towards me.

Bol remained standing, carefully piecing together his words in a
way that would make his tale as impressive as the one Great Jaguar
had told. He understood that it was the way a story was told that
indicated its veracity.

He explained that I was the only child of the Divine Lady
Resplendent Egret. When I was still a young boy, warriors from the
east attacked my homeland and carried away my uncle, Turtle-
Maize the Holy Bacab of the Jaguar-Sun dynasty, along with all the
other males of divine blood. I alone survived because my mother
had been warned in a dream to hide me in the mountains.

Our oppressors had attacked just after harvest and ransacked
most of our stores of maize. But they weren't satisfied with taking
our leaders and leaving our people to starve. They feared the power
of our gods and returned four months later to desecrate our mountain shrines and to shatter the pih of our gods in Te'nab, the holy
cave of our ancestors.

When these horrible things were happening, the gods marked my
mother as the embodiment of the First Mother by transforming her
face to look like that of a jaguar. The people of Place of Jaguar-Sun
recognized this as a sign from the gods and enthroned her as Holy

Bacab of their shattered land. They reassembled the fragments of the pih of Bolom Tzacab and attached them to a headpiece which she carried in rituals as the Protector of the lineage god. Then, when I was twelve years old she passed that sacred emblem on to me, designating me as Holy Bacab of the Jaguar-Sun dynasty. "Now it is Hanab Pacal, who must protect and nourish the gods, continue the lineage and beseech the ancestors for the prosperity of our people," Bol explained.

He went on to describe our homeland, a beautiful ledge between the earth and the sky— perhaps the most beautiful place in this world— about a six-day journey from Tikal, towards the setting sun.

"He is all that remains of the divine Jaguar-Sun lineage, so you can see how important it is that he produce an heir. Without descendants to worship them, the ancestors of Jaguar-Sun will cease to be, and their stars will fall from the sky," Bol stated, as if to imply that there was no need to assure Great Jaguar of the credibility of my lineage as much as there was an urgency for me to continue that lineage.

Great Jaguar paused to savor his cigar, and then leaned his pudgy hands on his knees. "These things Hel has already prepared me for. She's read them in the quickening of her blood and the sorting of the seeds. Pray with me now that the gods are good to the mortals who bless this union. Then, if Hel chooses to serve you tortillas and balché, she has agreed to be your wife," he explained with an unmistakable glint of mischief in his eyes.

# Hel

Upon hearing her father's words of approval, Hel walked shyly towards me. She would not look into my eyes again and instead asked quietly, in the traditional way of a Maya girl, "Would you care for something to eat?"

But I couldn't compose myself enough to trust my voice to answer her. Instead I persisted in staring at her for what seemed like an unendurably long time. Hel finally turned to the fire just outside the door at the back of the house. "Come have something to eat," she said as she pushed some of the logs in towards the fire, increasing the flames that licked up around the edges of the round, flat, stone griddle. She sat gracefully down on the mat beside the fire and pinched a chunk of corn dough from inside a large gourd and rhythmically slapped it between her hands until it had become thin, flat and round. I watched as a child would, seeing something done for the first time, as she let the tortilla fall expertly onto the griddle, then quickly pinched another piece of dough from the gourd. Within minutes she had several tortillas on the griddle and many more keeping warm in another hollow gourd on the floor beside her. Absorbed in the fluid sensuality of her movements, I forgot the three men standing behind me in the doorway.

When the pile of tortillas rose above the sides of the gourd, Hel checked on several other things that were baking in pottery crocks near the fire. I watched her move about with the graceful dignity of a well-born woman. Yet, now and then, I thought I caught a sly twinkle in her eyes betraying the spirit of a playful child. I ached to pull her close to me, to feel her restraint melt, to release that impish child.

Finally, she rolled out an intricately woven mat on the patio and arranged the bowls of foodstuffs on it. Last of all, the large, decorated gourd, brimming with tortillas, was placed in the center. She motioned for me alone to be seated, but our audience also moved from the doorway, anxiously waiting to be invited to join us. Hel ignored them, and sat alongside me. As she reached over the mat, she picked up a tortilla and dipped it into a bowl of chilies. I could not help enjoying the round curve of her bottom beneath the brocade skirt and the sensations it aroused in me. Hel seemed too distracted by the ritual she was enacting to notice what was on my mind.

She brought the rolled tortilla to my lips. "Would you like something to eat?" she asked playfully. I opened my mouth and closed my eyes feigning that this was distasteful to me. But Hel was not to be outdone and she continued to hold the food just beyond my gapping mouth. Not until I heard my companions roaring with laughter did I open my eyes and, grabbing my tormentor's hand, I took a bite of the tortilla. Then I guided her hand to her own mouth so that she also took a bite of the food.

The marriage proposal was complete. Now Great Jaguar was clapping in delight as our audience seated themselves around the mat and proceeded to feast with the newly betrothed couple. His enormous appetite finally satiated, Great Jaguar dipped a cacao shell into a large, three-legged vessel resting in the corner of the room. He passed the cup of balché to his daughter. "Give your husband something to drink!" he laughed and then cautioned me to keep my eyes open this time. Hel brought the cup to my lips and giggled as half its contents spilled out the sides as I tried to drink as fast as she poured. The swift consumption of the potent liquor left me swooning. Now Great Jaguar passed drinks to everyone, bellowing out a rowdy song in a language I had never heard before.

The revelry continued on into the evening until, at last, I escaped with Hel, out into the night air. My head was spinning and my feet were uncertain as we looked out over the plaza. The city had been transformed by the glowing, silvery-blue light of the pregnant moon, casting a mesmerizing pattern of shadows on the many levels of the residential compound. As we walked towards the reservoir, Hel tried to explain the reasoning behind the positioning of some of the buildings. But I was too inebriated to understand. At the reservoir we rested on a carved stone bench and marveled at the moonlight shimmering on the still surface of the water.

"Your mother is almost as beautiful as you" I whispered, but Hel seemed not to hear me. I wondered aloud about Hel's childhood; where she had grown up; if her mother really was Ixtab... but she wasn't inclined to discuss these things. It didn't matter, I knew that the gods had made her for me. Never before had I felt such desire and love for someone.

If we had been only common people, our ritualistic meal would have sufficed as our wedding ceremony and we would have joined as husband and wife that night, under the sacred light of the moon. But we were not common people, and almost everything we did was determined by tradition and ritual, and for good cause— what we did, and how we did it, and when we did it, was being closely monitored by the gods. First and foremost, it was our obligation to please them. Any action on our part that could provoke their anger could result in disaster for our entire community.

But that night, sitting beside this woman who only a short time earlier had been a stranger, I wished that for only one night I could be just a common man. I tried to imagine what it would be like to live in a simple mud thatched home; to plant and farm in the rainy season; to labor in the limestone quarry in the dry season; to never have to plan or worry—trusting someone else to determine the time for planting and the time for sacrifice. If I had not been burden with the responsibility for the consequences of my actions affecting all of Jaguar-Sun, I would have taken Hel behind the bushes beside the reservoir that night and buried myself into the warmth of her womanhood.

But I was not a common man, and in less than twenty days the cluster of stars called "Fistful of Seeds" would make their last appearance on the horizon just after K'in had departed to the Underworld. This would signal the heralding of the rainy season, and all planting had to be completed before then. The farmers of Place of Jaguar-Sun were awaiting the return of their Holy Bacab, the only one who could anoint the seeds before planting. This year the ceremony would be different, and far more powerful than ever before. Instead of performing the usual bloodletting ritual on the mound of maize kernels that awaited planting, I would consummate my marriage to Hel atop the seed pile in the Temple of Yum Kaax, bestowing the abuntant power of fertility our virginal act would release, upon the season's planting.

So I sat that night in the moonlight, savoring the feelings Hel aroused within me, as one who waits eagerly, but patiently, for the balché to ferment. We would begin our journey back home just as soon as Kan had replenished our supplies and Bol had completed several transactions of trade. Meanwhile, Great Jaguar would secure permission to leave his position as Chief Advisor to Shield-Skull of Tikal. The Its'at of Tikal would become the Its'at of Jaguar-Sun, and his daughter, Mother to the heirs.

# Place of Split Sky

I could hear the roar of the jaguar in the jungle around us as I moved closer to the fire. He was close — perhaps only just beyond the clearing where we were camped. But I had matters of great concern on my mind and resented the interruption to my thoughts more than I feared the attack of one of the Lords of the Night. "Go back to Xibalba you loathsome beast!" I hissed into the darkness and lay back on my mat to study the stars.

Our departure from Tikal had been delayed for an additional three days while Great Jaguar assembled the entourage of servants and goods that he insisted were necessary for our journey. My intentions to travel unnoticed had been completely undermined. Now, in addition to my concerns about reaching home in time for the blessing of the seed, I was also worried that I was now vulnerable to capture. Great Jaguar had assured me that the five warriors he had secured to accompany us would provide adequate protection from attack, as well as securing game for our dinners. He also had insisted on bringing three women to prepare our meals. In addition, twenty strong young slaves were required to carry the huge henequen sacks stuffed with items that Bol had bargained for in the mesmerizing marketplaces of Tikal along with pottery, headdresses and ritual costumes of his lineage which Great Jaguar brought.

Concealed from view within her litter, Hel carried her sacred lineage bundle with the carved statue of Kahwil. She would not be separated from this precious burden entrusted to her safekeeping, until she saw it safely ensconced in the mountain shrine of Jaguar-Sun known as Toctan.

Our progress had been much slower than I'd anticipated—encumbered as we were by all of the accouterments required by my new father-in-law—and nightfall had overtaken us before we reached the settlement at the eastern end of the Egret Lake. I continued gazing at the sky as I thought of how simple our journey to Tikal had been in comparison to this. With only Kan, Bol and myself, we'd traveled swiftly, and completely undetected, down the Monkey river to Tikal. But now it took eight strong slaves just to carry Great Jaguar's ornate litter and another four for Hel's and four for mine. I'd insisted that even with my limp, I could move faster than the four lazy fools who transported me. But Great Jaguar wasn't concerned with speed. His many years in Tikal had conditioned him to expect the trappings of power and position.

As I stared into the night sky, I wondered what Great Jaguar's reaction would be to Place of Jaguar-Sun where we still worshipped in caves— albeit powerful, magical caves— but crude in comparison to the grandeur of the temples of Tikal. I resolved that one day we would make Jaguar-Sun even more grandiose than Tikal. With Great Jaguar's knowledge and skill I was certain it could be done. Hel's father could be almost as critical as she was to fulfilling my mission.

I stood up and paced around the fire as I recalculated the days remaining before Fistful of Seeds would herald the time for planting. We had to be in Place of Jaguar-Sun in fifteen days. The journey to Tikal had taken us only six. But it made more sense to return by way of the Xocal Ha, which flowed northward towards Place of Jaguar-Sun. The problem was getting to the great river—the only route being overland, first south to the lake, and then west to Place of Split-Sky.

"Oh, Almighty Ek Chuah, Protector of Travelers," I cried out into the darkness, "Bring us good fortune on this journey!" I bent to the ground and touched my face to the cool earth in supplication, repeating the action in each of the four directions. "Oh benevolent Chacs, be merciful to these humble travelers," I prayed.

Still restless, I walked through our encampment, surveying the slumbering slaves, their naked bodies sprawled on mats, unprotected from insects and snakes except for the foul-smelling, black ointment they had slathered all over themselves. Closer to the fire, Hel slept, sheltered in a small makeshift hut made of mats propped against poles. I imagined her soft, white body covered with finely woven blankets, and longed to lie beside her. Then I remembered the sacred bundle that she must protect, even in her sleep, and I murmured an apology to Kahwil for desiring to take his place.

Beside Hel's hut, a much larger contrivance housed her father. I listened to the rhythmic rumblings of his sleeping sounds, not unlike the sounds of the contented Jaguar. While he professed to being mortal, I suspected that this majestic man had somehow acquired that mysterious trait that made one divine. It was my good fortune, indeed, to return with these two precious people, even if they did require an awful lot of baggage.

Too anxious to sleep, I finally sat down on my sleeping mat near the fire and studied the movement of the stars across the heavens, waiting for K'in to emerge from the bowels of Xibalba. All at once I heard the sound of slow, stealthy movement in the trees, just beyond the clearing. There, in the darkness, two brilliant eyes of a jaguar appeared moving steadily closer, heading directly towards me.

I tried to reach for my spear without taking my eyes from the terrifying stare. My fingers groped the ground where I remembered laying it down, when suddenly a whizzing sound passed within a hair's breath of my cheek and the jaguar, never making a sound, fell to the ground, a spear between his eyes. There was Kan, standing behind me, grinning proudly. "A new ex, My Lord?" he asked, dryly referring to the handsome loincloth the great cat's hide would provide.

"Oh Kan, I'm forever in your debt," I cried out, forgetting the restraint expected of one of my position, as I rose to hug my brave companion. For only that small token of my affection, I sensed that Kan would have faced every jaguar in the world.

"You should sleep, Ahow. Even a god needs to close his eyes once in awhile," he suggested. "And I, who am not even the least bit divine, require some sleep as well. But how can I rest while My Lord paces so anxiously?"

"I'll awaken a couple of slaves to skin the cat and keep watch. Then let's both steal some rest from this worrisome night."

I nodded agreement, still shaken by the sudden turn of events. Wrapping my *pati* loosely around my head and body, I lay down on my mat by the fire. Kan shook his head in disapproval.

"Great Jaguar is right, it's time you demanded to be treated more like a ruler than a slave. Tomorrow night I'll prepare you a hut like his."

"Whatever makes you happy, Opossum" I laughed, referring to him with the endearing nickname a husband uses for his old wife. But the taunt failed to disturb Kan. In fact, he seemed to enjoy it.

As for sleep— it eluded me that night as, over and over the gruesome horror I'd narrowly escaped, of being torn to pieces by a Lord of the Night, replayed in my mind.

~

The following day we passed through the outskirts of the settlement on Egret Lake where we should have spent the night. A group of women and young girls, standing in the water, their white cotton underskirts pulled up between their legs and caught at the waist, stopped their laundering to stare at the passing train of strangers. I had to admit that we made quite an impressive sight.

Much to Great Jaguar's dismay, I'd chosen to walk, instead of enduring the ride in that obscene litter. Bol, who had hurried on ahead, to make a few shrewd trades with the villagers, now joined me at the head of our group. He grinned proudly, holding open a large sack to display its contents—brilliant, red, macaw feathers!

"For your marriage cloak, Ahow! Aren't they magnificent! And for only ten cacao beans!"

I imagined the breathtaking *pati* the feathers would make, especially draped over the new jaguar skin the slaves had already begun to prepare. Such attire would surely impress the gods! Bol noted my look of pleasure and strode proudly beside me, past the curious villagers.

We would journey for four days through the rain forest to Place of Split-Sky. Fortunately, by the second day we were moving along at a more reasonable pace. Great Jaguar's determination to instill in me a respect for protocol kept things lively and unpredictable, and the slaves were placing wagers on the extent of his patience. But, to their surprise, Great Jaguar was a man of remarkable tolerance and humor. It never became necessary for Kan to prepare a hut for me because we managed to arrive at a village each evening, where even the slaves slept under a roof and ate warm tortillas and hot chilies.

On the sixth day of our journey, our festive group arrived at the eastern banks of the Xocal Ha. Directly across from us rose the breathtaking temples of Place of Split-Sky, a city almost completely encircled by the mighty river. Along the flatlands of the riverbed that surrounded the hilltop city, pure white limestone patios and ball courts glistened in the sun. Ceiba, mahogany and sapodilla trees shaded the perfectly manicured gardens that decorated the pristine limestone and painted stucco stepped walls. Even Great Jaguar had to admit that his beloved Tikal did not enjoy the talents of such skillful gardeners, nor such a dramatic location. From our distant vantage point, we could see the graceful staircases that led from the banks, up the hillside, to the awesome red temples that towered above them.

Kan and Bol went on ahead of us to barter for canoes and experienced canoeists to navigate the unpredictable Xocal Ha, but they

returned looking worried and upset. "Every canoe has been con-
scripted for battle," Kan moaned. "Holy Bacab Bird-Jaguar has allied
himself with Tikal's enemies for an attack on a nearby city. The warriors will be departing tomorrow and there's nothing to be done but
to wait for their return."

My hopes, that we could use this journey to establish an alliance
with the Holy Bacab of Split-Sky, were dashed. Not sure how this
new alliance would affect his loyalties towards Jaguar-Sun, it
seemed wiser to avoid going into Split-Sky altogether. Worse than
the political disappointment was our more pressing logistical problem—how would we return to Jaguar-Sun without canoes. Only
seven days remained before Fistful of Seeds would be planted.

"We must be in Place of Jaguar-Sun on time!" I yelled in panic,
"Even if we have to swim!"

Hel, who had been listening from behind the curtains of her litter,
called to me to explain what was wrong. "How long will it be before
the canoes have returned?" she asked calmly.

Kan and Bol looked at each other hesitantly. Finally Bol offered
"Who can say how long a battle will last. It could be many K'ins, My
Lady, many suns."

"And have they taken all of the canoe builders along with them to
battle?" she queried further.

"Why, I'd seriously doubt that a craftsman would be allowed to be
lost to the enemy. No god would be so greedy as to demand the
blood of one with talent and skill," Bol replied a bit indignantly.

"But even if Split Sky is fortunate enough to have several canoe
builders, it will take weeks to build a fleet large enough to transport
a traveling party of this size. And then we would still have to wait
for the return of the canoeists!" Kan moaned. He spoke directly to
me, ignoring the feminine voice in the litter.

But Hel continued, "Why not set all the builders available to building just one canoe. Kan and Bol obviously are skilled as canoeists
since you traveled by river to Tikal. They could take you, me and my
father on to Place of Jaguar-Sun, while the rest waited for the return
of the warriors of Split-Sky.

It was such a simple solution, yet I realized that in my panic I had
been unable to think if it. I addressed my two companions as if the
idea was my own. "Take the dugout back to Split-Sky now and
round up all the canoe builders. Tell them there will be a bonus if
they can build the canoe in a day!"

The two men didn't conceal the fact that they were annoyed to
have been outdone by a woman, but nevertheless, they hurried off

to expedite my command. Hel sensed that she had antagonized the two of them and made a note of it. It would be important for her to keep Kan and Bol as allies in the days ahead. In the future she would be careful to present her ideas in such a way that they seemed to come from me.

Although it would have appeared weak to me to openly acknowledge it, I knew at that moment how valuable Hel would be for me and my success. Where I was short tempered, she was calm; where I was impulsive, she was thoughtful; where I was stubborn, she was flexible; where I was outspoken, she was sensitive and tactful. What I didn't know then was that my downfall would come the day I let passion and pride deprive me of her wisdom and diplomacy.

# Kan

We prepared to spend the night encamped on the riverbed across from Place of Split-Sky. Great Jaguar readily agreed that, because of their alliance with Lord Kan, it would be unwise to go inside the city, and he alerted his warriors to maintain a watchful vigilance throughout the night.

Since most of our party would be staying at this spot for quite awhile, the slaves set about constructing huts with some semblance of permanence. First, an oval frame was constructed with saplings strung together. Then a thick mortar was made of mud from the riverbed mixed with dried grasses and this was plastered over the saplings to form walls. Finally, palm fronds were woven into a round roof that rose to a point. By nightfall several of these huts had been constructed. Hel and her father shared one with the three cooks and I shared another with the two warriors Kan had assigned to act as my bodyguards in his absence.

It had been dark for some time when I heard a raucous commotion outside and looked through the doorway of my hut to see torches coming across the river. From the robust sound of their singing, I could tell Kan and Bol had found more than canoe builders in the plazas of Split-Sky. I started out towards the riverbank to greet them and was annoyed when both warriors jumped up to follow me. "I'm not some helpless woman!" I hissed angrily at them. "Go back to sleep — both of you!" The naked men stared at me, confused in their sleepiness, as to whose direction they should follow: Kan, who had ordered them not to let his master out of their sight; or the Master himself, who obviously detested their presence. They decided to stand watch from a distance and hesitantly followed me towards the riverbank.

Kan tossed his torch to me as his little boat slipped up onto the riverbed.

"Ho there, Ahow! You shall have your canoe tomorrow! A crew of builders will be hacking away at the mighty mahogany throughout the night. In fact, even I had the chips flying in all directions, when I took a turn on the hull. It's going to be a magnificent vessel—like the kaxtlan chem of the ancestors!" He tripped out of the boat into the mud. "Ho!" he cried out again as I reached down to help him up. "You should have seen that place, Ahow. What a site!" exclaimed the drunken, muddy messenger.

I was loosing patience. "Where is Bol?" I asked, peering into the darkness for the merchant.

"In the arms of a dog." Kan smirked, leaving no doubt of his disdain for Bol's lusty reputation. "I know I'll be subjected to all the disgusting details tomorrow." He paused, then peered sideways at me and added, "But I've got a story of my own this time!" Kan laughed, looking impishly at me to see if he'd captured my interest. He'd succeeded.

I hadn't seen Kan in this condition since I'd known him, but I hoped that the young man was about to tell me that he'd finally experienced the pleasures of his manhood. It was believed that Kan was conceived during a lunar eclipse, a night of the "darkened moon," because his sexual identity fluctuated with the phases of the moon. Usually his mannerisms were more feminine and nurturing, and he tended to mother me; sometimes even dressing in the huipil and skirt of a woman. But on the night of the full moon, the one night when the moon mimics the sun, rising up out of Xibalba and traveling completely across the sky, then Kan would assume the ways of a man. I doubted that he had ever actually been with a woman in the way that a husband is to a wife, though, even during the full moon. But this was the night of the "dead moon" and the possibility that Kan had taken on his male role this night intrigued me.

"Come inside and tell me all about it," I whispered as I took his arm and led him towards the hut. The warriors froze in fear as I noticed them standing not far behind me. "Shoo, get away!" I called to them, making a brushing motion with the arm that wasn't supporting Kan, as if they were a swarm of annoying insects. They looked towards Kan, who had instructed them earlier that evening to protect his master, but he was too inebriated to pose any threat to them. Grumbling, they positioned themselves outside the hut and watched warily as we entered.

"My Lord, come see what I've got!" Kan whispered proudly as he crouched down on his mat. He pulled a woven pouch from his loincloth and carefully untied it to reveal its contents. I brought my torch closer to the pouch to see several awl-shaped objects. The handles were made of deer antlers, ornately carved with symbols of the god of war and tapered to hold a sting-ray spine.

"I'll bet you never saw anything like this before!" Kan proclaimed proudly, his speech suddenly clear and awed by the objects spread out before us.

"Do you understand what these are for?" I asked nervously, eyeing the red stains on the spines.

"Bloodletting!" Kan almost hissed in delight. "I actually watched as the warriors pierced their penises with them, never so much as flinching from the pain. The bleeding was magnificent! Oh, the gods surely were impressed with such bravery. See this," he said pointing to the barbed edges of the spines. "It's the puncture that draws the blood, but removing the spine, that brings the pain! Imagine, My Lord, the courage to endure such pain! I've never seen anything so impressive in my life!"

I studied my friend seriously. I knew that he suffered deeply from the insinuations of others that he was not truly a man. But I wondered why such a gruesome ritual would have such a tantalizing effect on him. I noticed that just talking about it had caused him to have an erection and I remembered Kan's tearful admission that he had been unable to achieve this important precursor of manhood. Why would the excitement of pain cast such a spell on him, when the sensuous lures of women had failed?

I watched as Kan caressed the bloodstained edges of the spines as lovingly as I longed to touch Hel's soft skin, and I tried to understand how the physical and emotional distance between us, since my accession, had affected him. But what concerned me more, was hearing that the most sacred of all rituals, which was meant to be practiced only by those of divine descent, in a state of extreme devotion, was being recklessly exercised by the warriors of Split-Sky. If Bird-Jaguar, the Holy Bacab of Split Sky, had advocated this practice, then he was tampering with very dangerous powers indeed—powers that should never be put into the hands of the common man, even warriors.

"Kan, this ceremony that impressed you so much, do you understand its purpose?" I sternly asked. I was anxious to know how Bird-Jaguar had rationalized this sacrilegious divulgence of sacred knowledge.

"Oh yes, the gods want blood. If the warriors spill their blood now, the gods will not demand it of them on the battlefield. My Lord, we should teach this to the warriors of Jaguar-Sun so that they too will be spared in battle," Kan replied.

I could feel myself loosing patience with this confused young man for failing to realize what a blatant abuse of knowledge this was.

"The braves of Jaguar-Sun will never exercise the sacrosanct rituals of the Holy Bacab! How could you be with me all this time and not understand how serious this is? The gods don't want the blood of ordinary men. Don't you realize that Bird-Jaguar is a fool to put this power into the hands of wild, ignorant young warriors! Has he done this so that they will rush fearlessly into battle to capture more slaves to feed his gluttonous need for power? He knows that young men have no desire to endure pain, that the prospect of suffering is frightening to them.

"But a Holy Bacab knows the teachings of the ancients. He knows that men fear only that which they do not understand; that once something becomes familiar, then it is rendered powerless. This is one of the most powerful of the sacred mysteries of the gods and Bird-Jaguar has given this power to his fighting men! He's created an army of warriors with no fear of pain—nothing can stop them!

"You don't know how much it grieves me, Kan, that tonight the young braves of Split-Sky became fearless *holcan* with this ritual. It was a forbidden glimpse into the secret knowledge of the forces of the gods—forces that the *holcan* can now use, not only to rise above pain but to destroy the balance of civilization!

"Bird-Jaguar knows that the *holcan* of Split-Sky must never know that the power they have learned to harness tonight is the same power that makes him a god. So instead, he's told them this story of the quota of blood the gods require.

"My dear, dear Kan, don't you see? There's no need to risk divulging these secrets to those who lack the training and wisdom to respect the power they can unleash. It's not necessary to enslave people when there's a true understanding of the nature of power. A vast collection of peoples in servitude will never equal the value of a small following of inspired, loyal subjects. Perhaps Split-Sky is grandiose, but it will never be inspirational. I will build a center unlike any ever known before. A place that will raise the spirit and instill a sense of harmony in all who see it. And I will do it with the labors of a people driven by a love for beauty and a desire to please the gods—a people of a higher mind than the slaves of Split-Sky, or Tikal or anywhere else in the world."

I sensed that my words were falling on deaf ears and began to pace the room searching for a way to make Kan understand. Finally, in exasperation, I grabbed the pouch and it's contents from Kan's lap and threw them outside. At first, he started to protest, but I stopped him short. Spinning back into the hut, without the words to reason with him, I stood in the doorway for a long time glaring at the confused, young man squatting on the mat across the room. Kan alternately returned my stare and looked down as if he was studying the pattern woven into the mat.

I said firmly and resolutely, "Bloodletting is for those that speak with the gods. It will not make you more of a man. Compassion and the courage to be different—these are the things of greatness; the qualities I have always admired in you."

My sermon complete, I extinguished my torch and lay down on my mat, turning away from the reprimanded young man. But Kan continued to trace the woven pattern on his mat with his finger in the darkness. I didn't realize, at the time, how his heart was screaming inside with hurt and jealousy; how much he needed my approval; how much he resented my obvious enchantment with Hel.

My thoughts lingered on the image of warriors with the power of gods. I had answered my own questions about the wisdom of offering royal blood to the gods. For some reason, the perfectly reasonable practice of personal bloodletting had degraded into substituting the blood of captured royalty. Whereas a ruler's personal offering of his own blood brought him closer to the gods, the offering of the blood of our divine brothers would eventually destroy those lineages with the wisdom to lead, to pass on the ancient knowledge, to organize and inspire men to accomplish such awesome feats as building the towering temples we saw in Tikal, and to carry out the rituals necessary to appease the gods. It was this obsession with securing and sacrificing captives of divine blood that had shattered and nearly destroyed my own lineage. And, even though I would myself, sacrifice Pomona captives in future ceremonies, I sensed that this practice would weaken and eventually shatter our world. That night I had nightmares of a world where no one could read the sacred books, or count the days, or decipher the movements of the gods in the night sky.

As for Kan, when he was sure that I was asleep, he slipped outside and retrieved his prized bloodletters. Slipping them back into their pouch, he quietly tied it around his waist and tucked it under his loincloth.

~

Kan may have consumed too much balché the night before, but he had been correct about the canoe. Before K'in had even cleared the tree tops, Bol arrived with our vessel. It was the length of five men with a canopy stretched over a frame in the center to shade its passengers. In addition to contracting for the canoe, the shrewd Bol had struck several deals while in Split-Sky. Sacks of goods, from woven cottons, to pots of salt and copál, were packed into the hull. Most of these items were unloaded, to be brought on to Place of Jaguar-Sun when the remainder of our party returned. Hel added a small bundle of herbs she'd been collecting during the overland portion of our journey. A muscular slave also carried out two large sacks containing Hel's belongings and those carefully selected items that her father couldn't bear to be without, and added them to our cargo.

The five of us ate a hasty breakfast of toasted tortillas left-over from the evening meal, which we washed down with posol, a milky drink made of corn dough dissolved in water. Bol gave some last-minute directions to those who would remain behind, concerning the items he had traded for throughout our journey and, at last, we resumed our journey home.

"So now you have it your way after all," joked Great Jaguar in reference to our rugged traveling arrangements. He settled his huge frame into the center of the canoe, adding, "I hope you've packed enough posol to keep us fed for the next few days." The stately man bellowed with laughter at his preoccupation with food, as he patted his prominent stomach. I assured my father-in-law, with amusement, that he wouldn't starve on our journey, pointing out a sack stuffed with corn paste, squashes, dried meats and chilies in the hull.

Hel sat facing her father under the canopy, clutching the sacred bundle to her breast under her woven wrap, as a mother would hold an infant. I sat behind her while Kan and Bol manned either end of the boat with their oars. As we moved downstream from Split-Sky, the river drew our canoe swiftly through narrow rocky stretches. I was astonished by its swiftness considering that the rainy season had not yet begun. I could see Kan and Bol tensed with anticipation. Apparently they also were taken by surprise by the lively spirit of the Xocal Ha. They had heard many horror stories the night before about the perils that awaited us on this unpredictable river. As for Hel and her father, they appeared to be unconcerned, as they watched crocodiles basking in the sun along the rocky banks, and rows of red-eared slider turtles sleeping on floating logs that mimicked the crocodiles.

I closed my eyes for a moment and savored the sensation of K'in's warmth on my face. Soon the rains would come and day after day we would feel only the inescapable discomfort of the humidity and steamy heat. Parrots screeched and howler monkeys roared their disdain of our intrusion into their jungle paradise, but it would soon prove to be the river itself that resented our presence the most. Even before the hilltop temples of Place of Split-Sky had fully disappeared from behind us, the elusive spell of tranquillity was shattered as boiling rapids and swirling whirlpools began to speed us ruthlessly downstream. It took us all by surprise, and Great Jaguar cried out to the gods for mercy as his daughter flung herself and her bundle into the safety of his grasp. The angry river tossed about our staunch canoe like a child's toy as we were swept helplessly past the treacherous Vulture Falls—a wall of water that crashed violently down into the Xocal Ha from steep cliffs along the riverside.

Then, just as I had commended my spirit to the Gods of the Underworld, our defenseless vessel was tossed into a long stretch of calm, open water. Shaken, and grateful to still be alive, we continued on towards the ominous Place of Dark-Canyon.

Bol had been advised by returning traders in Split-Sky to stop at an embankment opposite, and just before, the boulder-strewn beaches of this notorious center where captives were said to regularly become human sacrifices after suffering the most tortuous of deaths. While we posed neither threat nor opportunity to the rulers of this bloodthirsty realm, there could be no assurance that a visiting dignitary would not be taken captive. We would be safest to pass the center under the shroud of darkness and to camp well past the danger of their heinous scouts.

K'in was already beginning his descent into the Underworld when we reached the stop-off described by the traders. Without slaves to help him, Great Jaguar had suddenly became quite proficient at helping himself and, in a surprisingly short time, had assisted Hel in gathering firewood and preparing our meal. All the while he reminisced aloud about the journeys of his youth. Obviously he had not forgotten the lessons of survival he had acquired in those days.

Kan was spooked by the gruesome tales Bol had shared with us that afternoon of the poor captives of Dark-Canyon who'd had their jaws ripped off, or worse yet, had their still-beating hearts carved from their chests. He startled at every sound from the forest beyond the embankment, certain that at any moment, the monstrous holcan of Dark-Canyon would descend upon us. Then, just as dusk was throwing long, ominous shadows from the jungle across the rocky

embankment, Kan noticed the rustle of movement originating from
a well-worn path into the forest. He grabbed me by the arm and
pointed with his spear at the colossal shadow that preceded the
noisy intruder. Stretched across the flat rocks was a dark silhouette
of a long snouted creature the length of three men!

Kan held his spear tense with anticipation, certain that one spear
would never bring down such an enormous beast. Slowly the animal
responsible for the shadow emerged from the forest. By now, Bol
and Great Jaguar had joined us to see what had caught our attention. But as the old tapir strolled out into view, following his usual
route to the river for his nightly bath, we all howled in laughter with
relief. The sound of humans startled the harmless beast and he
crashed blindly back into the jungle. But his departure was abruptly stopped when the near-sighted creature collided with a large
sapodilla tree and knocked himself out!

By now, everyone, even Hel, was choking with laughter. Kan
quickly regained his composure and raced up to the unconscious
animal to pierce him through the heart. "We'll have meat for dinner
tonight," he proclaimed as he proceeded to butcher the thick-
skinned animal. Hel wasn't too certain how the fresh meat of this
strange beast would taste, but she accepted the roast Kan carved
from the animal's hunches and brought it to the fire.

It wasn't dinner that Kan was thinking of as he carefully cut away
the tapir's tough hide. He was thinking of his responsibility to get us
safely past Dark-Canyon. Recalling how the warriors he had
befriended in Split-Sky had demonstrated how their tapir-skin
armor could thwart even the sharpest obsidian spear. Now he took
the heavy, bloody hide down to the river and washed it off. Without
any further preparation he girdled his torso with the stinking thing,
using leather strips to tie it in place.

After dark our party quietly boarded our craft. Bol dismantled the
canopy and directed us to lie low. We wouldn't take the chance of
creating even the slightest noise with our oars and, instead,
allowed the river to take us soundlessly downstream, past Place of
Dark-Canyon. Once he was certain we were safely beyond the dan-
gers of the center, Bol slipped his oar into the water and steered in
towards the embankment. We made a quick camp under the shelter
of an immense Ceiba tree and all but one of us fell quickly to sleep.
Kan sat alert and ready beside the small fire. He didn't seem to
notice the stench of his armor, nor mind the insects it attracted. He
was the personal *holcan* of the Holy Bacab of Jaguar-Sun and no
one would ever harm his beloved master. "That" he thought to him-

self that starless night, "is far more important than anything a wife could ever do."

The following day we continued downstream into Smoking Waters. Here the waters of a tributary plunge the depth of fifteen men into the river, generating great clouds of spray amidst a deafening roar. As we moved blindly through the canyon, Kan and Bol thrust their oars out into the cloudy mist, sensing boulders and rocks as we approached them rather than actually seeing them. Thanks to their skillful maneuvering, we continued unharmed on into a calm, clear stretch of river where the waters became so deep that Kan was convinced there was no bottom. He speculated that if he were to fall in, he would fall directly into the realm of the Lords of the Underworld.

With K'in directly overhead, our canoe slipped into a dark passage between awesome cliffs that seemed to reach into the heavens. The distant roar and menacing winds whipping through the canyon served to warn us to hold on tight. Bol warned that we were approaching the most treacherous part of our journey. He checked to secure all of our goods in the hull, including Hel's precious parcel, while Kan dismantled the canopy and fastened ropes to each passenger's waist. As our craft was pulled helplessly into the rushing current, white water splashed violently about us. Everything we had experienced before this was only training for this brutal passage. Moments seemed like eternity as Kan and Bol fought the water's persistent efforts to overturn us. I lay flat on the bottom of the front half of the canoe, alongside the terrified Hel. Her father's body lay face down, filling the stretch of boat behind us. I could hear him chanting prayers for deliverance, punctuated by occasional curses, each time the canoe slapped violently down from a swirling crest. Just when I was certain that I would suffer the embarrassment of loosing the contents of my stomach in front of Hel, the rapids suddenly smoothed out and we were thrust into a sparkling, sluggish river. As our bedraggled group struggled to sit up, Bol, the only experienced traveler among us, pointed out the tributary to our left that we would take. From here our journey would continue overland, two, maybe three days, to our final destination — Place of Jaguar-Sun.

# Place of Jaguar-Sun

The remainder of our journey was uneventful, but difficult, since we were forced to continue northward overland. Kan and Bol bore the remainder of our cargo in tumplines. Stripped to their loincloths and slathered with ointment to repel the insects, the sight of their strong bodies, climbing the rocky paths through the hills—their muscles swollen with the weight of their burdens, must have pleased the gods. It was a most important obligation for us, the beings of the third creation, to provide beauty for the gods to enjoy. This was why True People labored to build and to decorate magnificent places where the gods can rest their eyes. But each man and woman was also taught from childhood to keep their bodies beautiful; to bathe and decorate the flesh the gods had bestowed on them, so that when the maker of all things chanced to glance in their direction, he would find satisfaction in his creation, and he would express his pleasure by bestowing good fortune.

These were my thoughts as I watched the young, energetic Kan, and the mature, but strong and lean, Bol climb before me, followed by the most exquisite creature of all the world. Hel was truly the finest work of art the gods had ever modeled. In those few rare moments when she lifted her eyes from their modest, downward gaze, it seemed that the air around her sizzled with energy. I thought to myself that it was good that such vitality had been given to a woman who, with her discipline, could contain and control its power. The gods were wise to confer such remarkable energy to one of such restraint. And they were generous to give her to the Holy Bacab of Jaguar-Sun. I would always revere and respect this woman chosen to bring the pih of Kahwil to Place of Jaguar-Sun and to bear the sons of the Holy Bacab.

It was late in the day when the path began to grow familiar. I knew the stream that ran beside us—it was one of several that flowed down the mountains into Jaguar-Sun. And then at last, like seeing an old friend, I recognized with fondness the great Ceiba tree that marked the entrance to the shallow cave known as Toctan. This was the cave where I had hidden for two years while Jaguar-Sun was under the siege of the Pomona warriors. Kan turned to me with a warm smile of remembrance as we approached the mouth of the cave, so well hidden by the sacred, ancient tree. "This is where I first served My Lord," he announced with reverence and pride to the rest of our party, leaving it to me to explain the special meaning of the place.

I indicated to Hel the side of the tree where the moss hung thickest and explained that Kahwil, the "Trickster" had seen to disguise this shrine with a mantle of green. "It is here that Kahwil, Most Holy Third-Brother of the Three-Born-Together gods, protected me—the last survivor of my ancestors, so that I could carry on the divine lineage. It is here that the pih of Kahwil will rest for all time, safe and protected, to be worshipped and revered by all my heirs.

"Protector of Kahwil, come with me," I said to Hel, indicating that she alone could follow me into the cave. I led her, with her sacred bundle held close to her breast, into the cave opening where a small earthen pot of copál marked our path. Chanting the words of the prayer of empowerment, I began the ritual that would transform this ordinary cave into the Sacred Shrine of Kahwil.

*Pardon my sins, Maker of All Things*
*Pardon my weakness, First Grandmother, First Grandfather.*
*Come into your holy house, Kahwil, the Magician,*
*Come into your holy shrine, Kahwil, the Snake,*
*Come into this sacred temple, Elusive One of Fire,*
*Third-Son, Third-Brother of the Three-Born-Together.*

I stopped my prayer to lead Hel to the carved stone altar at the back of the cave. Standing behind her, my hands resting on her shoulders, I presented her to the god we were about to enshrine.

*Most Holy Kahwil, pardon this humble place,*
*This protection place, this powerful place.*
*Here is your protector, the Ahow of Toctan.*
*She will feed you the white food, the yellow food.*
*She will dress you in the white cloth, the yellow cloth.*
*She will worship you on the Ahow days, on the kept days.*

At this point in the prayer Hel removed the beautiful jade statue of Kahwil from its several layers of white and yellow cloth and gently placed it on the stone altar. This was the first time I'd actually seen this sacred idol of her lineage, entrusted to Hel's care by her mother, the goddess Ixtab. In the dim light that seeped through the moss-covered entrance, I studied this most sacred object with reverence. It was the size of a man's head, carved of solid jade, inlaid with other stones and shells. Kahwil, the third son of the first mother, was depicted in a sitting position, one leg bent to rest on the other, which took the form of a snake dangling before him. His face staring menacingly towards us. His hair was made of human hair shorn from a sacrificial victim, pulled to the top of his head and secured with the sacred yellow knot, the signature of his divinity. A polished obsidian mirror, attached to the front of his headband, was positioned at his forehead. Protruding forward from the mirror was a small obsidian cone with red feathers extending from it to represent fire. This was the hallmark of Kahwil, the elusive god of fire and magic. Other small mirrors decorated his arms and legs and a string of beads extended down his neck, to his spine and down to the back of his snake-leg, portraying his notorious ability to take the form of a snake and to slip silently and undetected, anywhere— even into one's thoughts.

Hel continued the ritual prayer as she arranged pine needles she'd gathered earlier, around the base of the statue. At the appropriate time, I smashed the pot of copál on the stone altar, signifying the end of the previous purpose of the cave—having once served as a hiding place for me in my precarious childhood. Speaking directly to the cave, I instructed it in its new role as the Temple of the Divine Kahwil. Taking three broken pieces of the pot, and arranging them on the altar in front of Kahwil as saucers, I lit the copál offering. The cave was now assuming its new identity and no one except its Ahow would ever again be permitted within it. Chanting additional prayers of respect and adoration, I backed out of the entrance, leaving Kahwil with his Protector, the newly appointed Ahow of Toctan.

It wasn't commonplace for a woman to have the responsibility of protecting and nurturing a god. My own mother and grandmother had taken this responsibility only when no male heirs were available. That responsibility had been passed on as soon as an appropriate male had come of age. In my case, my mother had taken me into Te'nab, our Ancestral Cave, as soon as all danger from the warriors of Pomona had passed, and there, twelve years from my birth, she had appointed me Ahow of Te'nab. From that day on, I alone could enter the cave; I alone could nurture the pih of Bolom Tzacab, First-Brother of the Three-Born-Together gods.

I had fasted and prayed alone within that holy cave for four moons, listening for the voices of my ancestors. Then finally the voice of U-Kix-Chan, First-Great-Grandfather of the Jaguar-Sun dynasty, spoke to me from the depths of the cave. He commanded me to lead my people from their oppression and to once again make Place of Jaguar-Sun a place of beauty for the gods to behold. One by one my ancestors revealed themselves to me and taught me the sacred mysteries—those secrets that had been lost when the Pomona warriors had sacrificed my uncle, Turtle-Maize, Holy Bacab of Jaguar-Sun.

As I waited for Hel to come out of the cave of Toctan, I remembered the day that I had finally emerged from Te'nab. It was the hottest, wettest day I could ever remember. I was weak with hunger, having subsisted for forty days on only sips of posol which I made by mixing maize paste with the sacred water of the cenoté. My eyes were blinded by the light of K'in and my body was overcome by the heat, after spending so many days in the cool darkness of Te'nab.

Two slaves who had been posted at the entrance to wait for me, carried me, weak and exhausted, to where my mother, Divine Lady Resplendent Egret had been waiting; praying those forty days that the ancestors would acknowledge me. Kan, the young slave, who had been appointed to care for me during my two years in hiding, was beside himself with joy when he saw me being carried to my mother's home. He brought fresh cloth and washed me down and anointed me with fragrant herbs. He held a cup to my lips with a curative drink of cacao that quickly revived me almost instantly, all the while exclaiming his delight with my return.

A large crowd had gathered outside the hut as word spread that the ancestors had chosen the next Holy Bacab of the Jaguar-Sun dynasty. Hanab Pacal was chosen to lead the True People of Jaguar-Sun from the confusion and despair that had ensued since the attack of Pomona. Considering the magnitude of my responsibility, I'd knelt before my mother. bringing my head to the ground so that she could shave away the traditional band of hair from across the back of my head—a reminder of the separation of body from mind that was expected from me. This was the mark of a shaman—and now I was to be the Shaman of Shamans. She gathered together my hair from the front of my head into a forelock and I held it tight while she secured it with a knot of yellow cloth—for my ancestors had confirmed that my blood was the blood of the gods. Then, one by one, chanting the ritual prayers of accession, she handed me the ornaments that had belonged to my uncle, Turtle-Maize and to the many Holy Bacab who had preceded him: the jade pendant with the cut-out of Ik the god of the wind, that would rest on my chest, signifying that my breath was the breath of the gods; the translucent ear-flares of jade, with a front weight of sapodilus shell, and a rear counter-balance of jade beads; the cuffs of long, narrow, jade beads, edged with the bone fragments of my ancestors; and the wide belt of narrow, jade beads on which the carved jade faces of the Three-Born-Together gods were fastened.

I walked to the doorway of the hut for the completion of the ritual. It was important that the people for whom I was now responsible, should witness the event to follow. The crowd outside had grown to hundreds of men, women and children. When I appeared before them there was an immediate hush as they fell to their knees, their right arms grasping their left shoulders in respect. A small platform had been constructed nearby where all that remained of Turtle-Maize's royal trappings—the doubled-headed jaguar throne—was positioned. I walked proudly up the few steps of the platform and sat cross-legged on the throne, nodding for my mother to approach. Beside her, Kan, disguised in the mask of the fox, carried the sacred bundle of our dynasty. Divine Lady Resplendent Egret waited while her husband, Yellow-Macaw, and his priests lit the incense burners at the four corners of the platform and chanted the ritual prayers of accession. The crowd remained motionless as she opened the bundle carried by Kan and took out the white headband with the face of Bolom Tzacab attached. She held it draped across her outstretched hands before me.

I remember fearing at that moment, as I reached for that holiest emblem of power, that I was an impostor—that I was in no way different from the people who watched me with wonderment and trepidation. I brought the headband up to my forehead and reached back behind my head to tie it just below where Kan was holding up my hair, revealing the newly shorn Band of the Shaman. Then something incredible happened; something even more wondrous than hearing the voices of my ancestors in the cave of Te'nab. Just as the emblem of Bolom Tzacab touched my forehead I could feel the rush of his power within me! Suddenly I comprehended the magnitude of my responsibility. From that moment on, I lived only to serve my gods and my people.

My mother held up the headdress with the reassembled head from the pih of Bolom Tzacab attached to the front and I could see that she was crying. She never explained those tears to me—were they tears of regret because she would never again be the one to hold the pih; or were they tears of pride in her successful continuance of the lineage; or was it an expression of love for her son, for her pih, or for her people whom she had saved from obscurity? Perhaps they were tears of compassion, for only she could possibly understand the trials and isolation that awaited me.

~

My reverie was broken by the breathtaking sight of Hel holding aside the moss as she emerged from the cave of Toctan. It was time to take her to Place of Jaguar-Sun. I held my hand out for her and she took it without speaking, walking regally beside me to where my companions sat waiting. Kan and Bol tucked their heads into the harness of their tumplines and we resumed our journey in silence, each consumed in their own thoughts.

We hadn't traveled for long when we came to the crest of a hill that overlooked a flat, grassy plateau. We were standing on Quetzal Mountain and just to the west was the sacred hill that encompassed my ancestral cave, Te'nab. From our vantage we could look out northward, beyond the plateau, to the alluvial plains that stretched all the way to the great waters of End-of-Earth. Like a nest crowded with baby birds, their mouths open in desperate expectation, those fertile raised beds awaited the seeds we had returned to anoint.

To the west we watched mighty K'in falling into the jaws of the Underworld. His magical priests had painted the sky and clouds with brilliant red cinnabar for his nightly burial ritual. The view was breathtaking! "This," I proclaimed proudly, "is Jaguar-Sun!" I pointed to the west where the last bit of K'in could be seen disappearing behind the anticipated silhouettes of hut groupings and turned to enjoy the reaction of my guests. As I had hoped, they were obviously impressed with their first view of my magnificent homeland. As for myself, I was delighted that the gods had timed our arrival to just this moment so that Hel and Great Jaguar could see why this place was called Jaguar-Sun—here was where K'in died each night, amidst all of the pomp and splendor befitting the death of a god. Throughout the dark night the sun would struggle to overcome the trials of Xibalba. Empowered with the prayers and sacrifices of the True Peoples, he would defeat the menacing Lords of Death, and finally rise in triumph from their world of horrors to light a new day.

We rested on Quetzal Mountain until K'in's majestic burial ceremony was completed. Kan mixed the last handful of maize paste into a miserable posol that we each shared with wistful conversation of the feast that would accompany tomorrow's wedding ritual. Great Jaguar groaned with anticipation as Kan described the great pit where many deer, dogs and peccary would be roasted. Even I found myself salivating at the thought of the tantalizing dishes of squash and beans and avocado spiced with fiery chilies and herbs! Too many days had passed with nothing but posol, posol, posol. I didn't care if I ever tasted that milky, mushy drink again! "These have been kept days for no reason!" Great Jaguar complained, referring to the days prior to Period Endings and Solstice days when a fast of only posol and herbal waters was required of all True People, along with a strict abstinence from sexual relations and all arguments.

"We could consider it a preparation fast for Hel's appointment as Mother of the Lineage," I suggested.

Hel smiled in agreement, "It did us no harm to fast. I think of it as a purification for the anointing of the shrine of Kahwil today," she added, in her quiet, demure way.

She had spoken so little during our journey that the feminine sound of her voice took me by surprise. I thought quickly of something more to say, that would inspire her to speak again.

"Look, Bolom Tzacab follows his brother into Xibalba," I said pointing to the bright star that either announced his twin brother, K'in's emergence from the Underworld at dawn, or followed him into its horrors at dusk.

"Yes, and Fistful-of-Seeds is close behind. You were wise not to linger in Split-Sky, planting can't wait any longer," Hel replied.

I tingled with the excitement she aroused in me and the anticipation of our joining on the following night. One could shave a band across the back of their head, but there was no way to sever the physical desires of a man from his thoughts, I mused as I stared at her shy, enticing smile. Suddenly I was aware that everyone was quiet and watching me. Had they been able to know what I was thinking? Regretfully I pulled my eyes away from Hel and lit an acoté torch in the fire.

"Let's hurry. Soon the jaguars will emerge from Xibalba and lay their claim to the jungle," I warned, resuming my posture of command. I lit and handed additional torches to each person in our party, but Kan and Bol were obviously uncomfortable with this small act of servitude from me. I made note of their reaction and the advice of Great Jaguar echoed in my mind. It was time for me to put away the behavior of a common man and to assume the role of the Divine Mah Kina Hanab Pacal, Holy Bacab of Jaguar-Sun.

Our weary group moved carefully down the mountainside to a bridge over the near-dry river. Soon the rains would swell this stream, that fed one of the prettiest waterfalls in Jaguar-Sun. Just on the other side, a slave greeted us with a deep bow of submission. "Mah Kina, Holy Bacab! Your mother, The Divine Lady Resplendent Egret awaits you and the Lady Hel at the Ancestral Cave," he proclaimed. Pointing out a well-lit clearing just to our west he added, "It is her wish that I accompany your other guests to their accommodations."

Kan and Bol knew that they were not permitted anywhere near the shrine of Te'nab. In fact, they feared the terrible power of the place. There was no known end to the cave, which was believed to lead directly into Xibalba. Tree-stones grew from both the floor and ceiling of the entrance, giving the appearance of gapping jaws, and mighty Ik, the god of wind, often emerged in a fury from its horrible throat. Sometimes the magical Kahwil would follow, concealed in a smoky mist. The fear of this place was so prevalent, that the duty of keeping guard here, especially at night, was often threatened as a punishment to slaves—for many were rumored to never return from that dreadful assignment. This was a place of nightmares and the fearful unknown; a place far different from Toctan, where we had just anointed Kahwil. It was in the bowels of Te'nab that I had been left alone, as a boy, to seek the blessing of my ancestors; entering as a terrified young prince and emerging transformed as a brave leader of men.

But Great Jaguar did not share this fear, for he had been privy to the secrets of caves since he was a young man. According to his story, it was in such a cave that he had fathered Hel. Obviously slighted by the slave's inference that he could not accompany us to meet my mother, he announced that Kan and Bol could go on, but that he intended to stay with his daughter.

Without warning, I was suddenly confronted with one of the most wrenching decisions of my life. Great Jaguar was not a man I wanted to alienate. His knowledge and skill were of great value and I had hoped to avail myself of his talents as soon as possible in the design of a great temple at the mouth of Te'nab. If I were to deny him access to this shrine, how would he be able to help in the design and construction of its temple? In fact, I realized that at some point I would also have to extend access to the laborers who would have to construct the temple and the artisans who would complete its decoration.

But, on the other hand, this was not an appropriate time to provoke a confrontation with my mother. She was a woman of frightening power, who could still invoke the wrath of the gods. While I was certain that she would never do anything to harm me, I also knew that she would never understand that my decision to allow Great Jaguar access to the shrine was anything but a deliberate act of defiance. I was painfully aware that, while I had been conferred the title of Holy Bacab, it was still Resplendent Egret who made and enforced policy. Her wishes were still the will of a god. It was her strength and wisdom, after all, that had saved me from the hands of Pomona's butchers. And it was her unrelenting diplomacy that had convinced the shattered populace that I, Pacal, though not of patrilineal descent, had been ordained by the ancestors as rightful heir of the dynasty.

I could feel myself choking with the pain of my words as Great Jaguar looked to me for approval. "Only those of the Jaguar-Sun dynasty may approach the Holiest of Shrines," I said, hoping that my tone explained the regret I was not permitted to express. But I could tell immediately from the expression on Great Jaguar's face, that I had insulted him irreparably. And I knew at that moment I had lost a great ally. I also realized that my magnificent temple would never be built while my mother was alive.

I couldn't look at Hel as I turned away from her father; I couldn't bear to see the hurt in her eyes. "I am the Holy Bacab. You are to be the mother of my heirs. My words are the words of the gods, my wishes are to be obeyed without question, for they are the wishes of Mah Kina," I said without emotion. She followed behind me and I felt an enormous sense of relief. I don't know what I would have done if she had followed her father instead. The proud, old man turned away from both of us, and the slave as well, and walked defiantly alone into the dark jungle. It would be some time before I would concern myself with his whereabouts. As for Hel, I'm certain he never left her thoughts.

Resplendent Egret stood alone at the entrance to Te'nab. Hundreds of torches had been lit around the gaping hole, casting eerie shadows on the tree-stones within and the imposing woman who had positioned herself theatrically in their midst. She didn't move in the slightest until we were directly in front of her. Then she nodded to Hel, indicating silently that she wished the timid young woman to kneel in submission. Hel quickly fell to her knees, obviously frightened by this imposing woman.

Resplendent Egret knew how to command respect and the gods had given her the features to do it well. In the years since she had appointed me Holy Bacab, her face and hands and feet had been slowly enlarging. Her fingertips and toes had grown to puffy nubs that gave her the appearance of having paws rather than hands and feet. Her jaw was large and strong and her tongue had swollen to the point of making her speech almost unintelligible. It protruded from her open lips in a most disarming manner. Her eyes were nearly hidden by the puffy flesh that encircled them. The long, purposefully etched scars, that extended from each corner of her mouth, back towards her enormous ears, were exaggerated further with the red pigment that underlined them.

She was wearing a decorative collar over her huipil, that was a construction of three layers of jade squares with Kan-cross cut-outs with a large Ik pendant across the front. On her headdress was a fabrication of a large white egret head, with a small representation of Kahwil perched in its crest and hundreds of white egret plumes fanning out from behind.

A glimmering obsidian blade was clasped in one of her paw-like hands. With her other hand Resplendent Egret forced the head of Hel down and grabbed her hair as a warrior would to take possession of his captive. For one awful moment I thought she was about to sacrifice the poor, terrified girl. But instead, she expertly shaved the Band of the Shaman from the back of her hair. Without letting go of her clutch of Hel's hair she motioned to me to pick up the yellow cloth strip that was draped across the altar beside her. I pulled it around the fistful of tresses and secured it tightly into a forelock. Adorned with the yellow knot, Hel had been recognized by my mother as both a priest and a god; her power was almost as great as mine. That this ceremony was performed at the entrance to our Ancestral Cave meant that Hel had been reborn as one of the Jaguar-Sun lineage. In essence, tomorrow I would be marrying my sister.

Now Divine Lady Resplendent Egret struggled to utter only one word. "Ahpo" she slurred and then repeated with determined clarity, "You are my daughter, Ahpo."

"Rise up, Lady Ahpo Hel, mother of the divine lineage," I now commanded, adding the name my mother had given her—her Jaguar-Sun name.

Ahpo Hel slowly rose to face my mother, her face expressionless, careful not to reveal her thoughts. But I suspected the she was wondering how she would survive in this strange place. I think that we both knew that we would never see Great Jaguar again. Perhaps, in the dark of night, when she heard the roar of the jaguar deep within the jungle, she would wonder if her father had joined with his animal companion and was calling to her. Ahpo Hel had the gift of vision and perhaps, even then, she knew that no one else, including myself, would ever love her as much as her father did. If I had truly loved her, I would have never brought her to this place where she would have to compete constantly for my attention; where everyone around me would view her as a rival; where the power and the title my mother had bestowed upon her would be her condemnation to a life of isolation and loneliness. This was the burden we had both been condemned to bear. The rest of our lives, from our marriage to our burials, would be a series of public rituals. Everything we did would be for one purpose—to intercede with the gods for the survival of our people. Nothing we would ever do or say would be considered private, or frivolous or without consequence.

Final preparations for our marriage ceremony were made throughout the night. A shallow pit had been dug and lined with stones as soon as word of our arrival reached the cooks. Already the game that would be served to commoner and nobleman alike was roasting in these earthen ovens. The balché had been fermenting for days in anticipation of our arrival and was now ready for the final addition of allspice to be added by the shaman. The new god-pots were arranged around the entrance to the temple of Yum Kaax, the maize god. Some would burn copál, its black smoke representing man, while others would burn dried pine needles, which would produce a white smoke representing woman. These incense burners were arranged in such a way that their smoke would combine just as Ahpo Hel and I entered the temple. Makeshift huts formed a wide swath around the solidly built nah of the residential compound, as the influx of visitors expanded the village population by many-fold.

I spent the night in the company of the shamans at a small godhouse on the hillside, after first purifying our bodies in the stone tubs of the ancient bathhouse. Through the night we prayed for prosperity and fertility, with offerings of balché to Yum Kaax, which we alternately poured on the earth or drank in one, breathless gulp. Embellished with the smoke of our potent cigars, we shared stories of our encounters with the gods and our dreams of the ancestors, until finally, in a dazed stupor, we fell asleep on the floor of the temple, hearing the voices of the ancient teachers in our dreams.

As the first rays of K'in appeared across the vast planting fields that Place of Jaguar-Sun overlooked, young women hurried to put the finishing touches on the garments and headpieces we would wear. Several women accompanied Ahpo Hel to the steam bath where she performed a pre-nuptial purification ritual. Her body was then painted with red achioté, symbolic of rain, and the women proceeded to dress her in the attire of her mother, the goddess of the moon.

Meanwhile, I also sought purification in a steam bath, after which Kan smudged my body with the black soot of burned copál. I wrapped the new jaguar ex around my waist and secured it with a large jade clasp. Elaborate jade spools were anchored into the loop of my ear lobes with front weights of carved bones. Bracelets of jade, amber and bone covered my arms and ankles and an intricate bead pectoral held the royal cloak of the red macaw feathers that Bol had traded for outside of Tikal. I marveled that such a work of art could have been constructed in only one night and Kan explained, as he attached an amber nose-piece to the bridge of my nose, that many women had labored under the torch-light to complete it in time.

The sun was past midday when Divine Lady Resplendent Egret arrived at my hut to present me with the jaguar-deer headdress of Bolom Tzacab. Traditionally it was the bridegroom's father who would do this, but my mother assumed this role to emphasize that it was through her that the blood of the Jaguar-Sun dynasty had been passed on. She was dressed in the manner of the Holy Bacab, the only difference in her attire from mine being that her ex was longer and wrapped higher to cover her breasts. Her hair was arranged in the way of a male, pulled up into her white egret headdress, with her hair beneath clean shaven Band of the Shaman clipped short at her neck.

Kan helped me to securely position my headdress so that my forelock, which was held with a yellow bead, appeared to emerge from the jaw of the polished jaguar skull. A deer hoof extended from it's snout and shells were inlaid in the eye sockets. Kan pulled the remainder of my hair up through an opening in the top of the skull and I tied it with the yellow knot of divinity. As always, Kan babbled like a young girl when he was dressing me for ceremonial rituals. He seemed to find great delight in the color and pageantry of preparing me.

"I'm sure the gods will find your appearance most pleasurable, My Lord," he laughed as he fastened shell and bone ornaments into my hair. "The sight of you most certainly overwhelms me!"

I patted him on the head, as one who expresses love to a child. Though I was only a few years older than he, Kan would always be a child to me. In this way I was free to feel great affection towards him and to enjoy the innocent exuberance he often expressed when he was around me.

Satisfied that my costume truly personified Bolom Tzacab, the god of my ancestors, I led the crowd of men of privilege, who had gathered outside my hut, in a procession to the center of the maize field where the Temple of Yum Kaax stood. From the opposite end of the village, Ahpo Hel also began her walk to the maize field, accompanied by musicians and all of the women and children of the village. The vision of her approaching evoked a gasp of admiration from the men around me. Her skin, transformed to a luminous rose by the achioté paint, was lightly covered with a long huipil into which white egret feathers and a delicate blue cotton had been woven in the traditional pattern of the Tzolkin. A jade-beaded sash was wrapped around her waist and hundreds of tiny, bluish, jade beads were combined with white shells in her necklace. Her white shell ear-spools seemed to reflect the reddish hue of her painted face in a way that I found most tantalizing. As she moved closer to me, I could smell the fragrance of the orchids that adorned her headpiece and my manhood responded to her allure. One part of my body began to secretly protest that there would be several hours of ceremony to endure before I could finally take her into my arms.

My father, Yellow-Macaw, led the shamans in their invocations to the long list of deities who held influence over our lives. Each of the priests addressed a different god, begging for abundance and harmony in whatever realm of the universe they had been assigned responsibility. They repeated their prayers over and over, in ever varying ways, to ensure that they were understood perfectly. Indicating the end of each phrase with a rap on their turtle carapace drums, or a shrill on their bird-shaped whistles, they continued for hours in the merciless heat of the sun. If a prayer was not answered by the gods it could only be that the request was not rightly put; therefore, it was the responsibility of the shaman to state their prayers in every possible way. I understood the rational of this because I understood that the power of the gods rested within the one who prayed. This was one of the mysteries taught to me by my ancestors during my initiation in Te'nab.

When the invocations were finally completed, the music and festivities began. We sat in a large circle with Ahpo Hel and the women on one end, and myself and the men on the other. Fantastic dances were performed that were tests of physical endurance as well as enactments of the teachings of the Tzolkin. Young men dressed as the feathered serpent, Kulkukan, threw themselves on the ground and brought their legs up behind them in a slow serpentine movement that required great strength, dexterity and concentration. Two strong young warriors, one painted black and the other white, locked legs and spun faster and faster using only one leg each, in a magnificent display of the power of harmony. All the while, young girls brought us dishes of foods and saucers of balché.

Finally it was time for me and my bride to ascend the steps to the Temple of Yum Kaax. The musicians shrilled their whistles and pounded their drums in a wild crescendo of excitement, while the crowd repeated their fertility chant over and over, with increasing intensity. As we climbed the steep steps together, I allowed my hand to brush against Ahpo Hel's finely woven dress. My need for her had grown so great that even the feathery texture of the brocade sent quivers of excitement running through the back of my hand. I sensed her body tensing slightly to our almost imperceptible contact and I wondered if her response was one of fear or anticipation. The incense pots arranged along the temple opening at the top of the steps released billows of fragrant smoke that seemed to consume us as we disappeared within.

I gently took my bride's hand and led her through the cloudy shroud into the temple. There were thirteen narrow steps downward into the hollow interior, to the top of the maize pile that would now serve as our nuptial bed. The incense, combined with the fecundity of the maize crop, intensifying my arousal. My need to hold my bride grew ever more irresistible as the rhythmic sounds of the musicians and chanters outside continued unabated.

I allowed myself to gaze unabashedly at my bride. She truly was a goddess, with her round face encircled with orchids and feathers. Her breasts seemed to quiver with each breath, causing the hundreds of beads in her necklace to move ever so slightly. I hesitantly reached for the embroidered sash that encircled her waist. My unpracticed hands fumbled with the knot, but she made no effort to assist me. The sash loosened and, slowly, as though unveiling a work of art, she allowed her huipil to fall from her shoulders to her feet. A gasp of approval escaped my lips as I watched her bend foreword to spread her dress out over the maize. Then, sitting in the center of the blue and white pattern, she reached up and took my hands and brought me down to her.

Outside the music pulsed faster and ever more intensely, but I was listening to my own inner music as I touched Ahpo Hel's face and neck. Her response told me that time had come to anoint the seed of Jaguar-Sun.

I must confess that what we shared, that first night together on our bed of maize, was not the spiritual ritual of fertility we'd been appointed to perform. We discovered a realm of physical pleasure that somehow, I think we both sensed, would provide us with a means of enduring, so that between the many prescribed abstinence's, the ceremonies, the sacrifices and prayers, the gods would allow us these sweet, brief moments of pure happiness.

# Resplendent Egret

Ahpo Hel leaned forward and spilled her handful of red seeds and crystals onto the woven mat spread out onto the floor before us. She placed her right hand over the pile and mixed them in a circular motion, chanting a plea that her blood would speak. "K'in will survive," she whispered and I knew that she had felt the quiver of the gods in her right arm.

She then picked out ten crystals and placed the largest of them above the pile, addressing it as the Wise One. She placed two crystals on either side of this one, to be the priests. The remaining five crystals were assigned the duty of protectors and were lined up in front of the first five. Now she blew quickly into her hand and grabbed a handful of seeds from the pile. Pushing the remainder of the pile aside, she quickly distributed the handful into rows of six clusters of four seeds each. The last row ended evenly with exactly four seeds in the last cluster.

"A good omen," I said aloud while my wife continued her divination. Ahpo Hel glanced towards my mother, searching for some small indication of approval. I didn't need to turn towards the Divine Lady Resplendent Egret to know that she would never relinquish even the smallest sign of pleasure to her daughter-in-law. The disappointment and disdain my mother held for both of us hung in the room like a rancid, rotting mold. The stench of her contempt seemed to grow with each moon that Ahpo Hel's body signaled that no seed was growing within her.

The flicker of torch-light threw haunting shadows across the floor as we waited for Ahpo Hel to determine what divine power would rule the new cycle of days that would begin at dawn. Addressing the first pile of seeds by the number and spirit name of the approaching day, she commanded, "Come here, One-Ahow you are being spoken to." She continued to summon the spirit of each pile as the name of each succeeding day: "Two-Imix; Three-Ik; Four-Akbal; Five-Kan; Six-Chikchan." Suddenly she stopped, as once again she sensed the quiver of her blood. This time she motioned that the prophetic sensation was sensed in her right thigh.

"The snake wishes to be born," she declared, interpreting the spirit of the day Chikchan with the meaning of the tremor in her thigh.

This was the way the new Period, 9 Baktun—10 Katun, began. Before K'in returned from his nightly trials in Xibalba, we knew that the next Katun would be held in the spell of the Snake. But I wondered, as I'm sure the others in the room did, if the Snake, who would control our destiny for the next twenty years, was the beneficent Sky Serpent, or the devious magician, Kahwil. We silently watched and waited as Ahpo Hel continued her divination. "Seven-Kimi, Eight-Manik, Nine-Lamat, Ten-Muluk, Eleven-Ock," she continued, identifying the piles and waiting for the revelation that would come in the mysterious movements of her blood. She continued naming the piles to the last cluster and then resumed with the first, this time with the name Four-Etznab. Once again she halted, noting the twinge in her right foot.

"Etznab is the cave of mirrors, of the illusion, the realm of trickery! It is Kahwil, the magical snake, who bids us our fate in this new katun," she prophesied. I held my breath, fearing that Divine Lady Resplendent Egret would object. Even though she had scrutinized Ahpo Hel's every movement during this ritual, she was certain to suspect that my wife had used trickery in order to manipulate the outcome, so that her own lineage god would be named ruler of the new katun. But to my surprise, the same woman who, for the past seven years had allowed me none of the power of my title as Holy Bacab, permitted my barren wife to empower her own god as omnipotent ruler for the next 20 years!

"Toctan," the old woman slurred from her mat on the floor. Toctan was the shrine where Ahpo Hel had nurtured her lineage idol since the day she first arrived in Place of Jaguar-Sun.

I quickly motioned to the four slaves who waited at the door, to carry my mother to her litter. We would have to arrive at Toctan before dawn, to assure Kahwil of our devotion before he began his reign. Ahpo Hel gathered her seeds and crystals back into her divining pouch and passed the pouch three times through the smoke of each of the three new incense pots.

I studied her smooth but deliberate movements, sensing a change in the way she held herself—the relationship of her head to her shoulders no longer apologetic. While she continued to hold her eyes modestly downward, the torch light caught a glimmer in her eyes I hadn't noticed in years. Was it hope that I saw there or that first sweet taste of conquest? It was no secret that Ahpo Hel resented her domineering mother-in-law. For too long we'd both cowered under Resplendent Egret's oppressive shadow. We'd been nothing more than mouthpieces for her commands. Our failure to produce an heir had provided her with the rationale for retaining her stranglehold on the power of Jaguar-Sun. Yet, somehow, despite Resplendent Egret's progressive disfigurement as absolute affirmation of her divine authority, tonight Ahpo Hel appeared to have stolen some of that power for herself. It wasn't like Resplendent Egret to relinquish so easily. "Don't smile yet, my shrewd wife," I thought to myself, "She'll use you and your god if it will get her what she wants. Don't imagine for a moment that you are in control." But if Ahpo Hel could read my thoughts, as often she did, she gave no indication of it this time.

I summoned Kan to place the incense pots in woven satchels that Ahpo Hel, and I and my father would carry alongside Divine Lady Resplendent Egret's litter, as we traveled the steep trail to the mountain shrine of Kahwil. As our small procession headed east in the torch-lit night, I studied the pre-dawn sky for a sign of what to expect in the coming years. How strange that Kahwil should lay claim to this Katun, I thought, his spirit light was nowhere to be seen in the heavens. There on the distant southeastern horizon, just above Toctan, I noted the bright light of the spirit of First-Father-One-Hunter. Slightly above him, towards the south, was the light of the twin brother of K'in, Bolom Tzacab, the First of the Three-Born-Together and the god of my lineage. Almost exactly aligned with these two important gods, was the spirit of Yum Kaax, the maize god. It was a clear, moonless night and one could see millions of spirits in the sky; those of the thirteen divine lineage clusters along with the millions of other souls who clung to the skin of the sky serpent in a milky band across the heavens. Almost directly overhead I could easily identify the form of the jaguar, the cluster of spirits who were my ancestors.

A knot of anxiety clenched my stomach even as I admired the souls of my ancestor in the sky. The six bright points that formed the curve of one jaguar ear, were clearly visible, along with the outstretched paw that ended with the bright glimmer of a claw. When I was only a small boy my mother had pointed out that glimmer as the soul of my grandfather, and namesake, the first Hanab Pacal. What would happen to the spirits of my ancestors if I failed to produce an heir? The incense pot I carried felt heavier and heavier as I thought about the seven years I had tried to father a child, praying every morning in Te'nab; listening to the directions of the shamans; fasting and abstaining when they prescribed it; and planting my seed within Ahpo Hel whenever the moon was unborn. But while the belly of the moon had swelled each month, no life had grown in the womb of Ahpo Hel. My inability to produce offspring, male or female, had become more than a matter of shame, it was a failure of horrendous consequences. At my death, there would be no one of divine blood in Jaguar-Sun to carry on the rituals of devotion; the rituals that nurtured my ancestor's spirits and appeased the gods. Without heirs there would be no bodies for my ancestors' spirits to re-enter when it was time for them to return. One by one, each glimmer in the Jaguar cluster would grow dim and disappear, until, one day not only would there be no one of the Jaguar-Sun dynasty here on earth, but there would no longer be that magnificent constellation of the Jaguar in the sky. My mother was justified to be so obsessed with my infertility. How could I claim my right to rule, when I failed so completely in my primary responsibility!

I felt an overwhelming sense of grief and despair as I walked along the well worn path towards Quetzal Mountain. We would not stop at Te'nab this morning. Only a short time remained until K'in would announce the new Katun and we had to be with Kahwil before then, or suffer the wrath of his anger for many years to come. As we passed the turn in the path for Te'nab, I whispered the prayer I always chanted to the pih of Bolom Tzacab each morning, along with my apology for my absence this morning.

Ahpo Hel, walking almost gaily beside me, was obviously pleased that her lineage god would be the ruler of the next Katun. I couldn't help but resent her display of happiness when I, myself, felt so wretched. Our failure to conceive a child had put a bitter distance between us. For as much as I desired her affections and enjoyed her company, I had begun to prepare myself for what was soon to become necessary—I would have to find another woman of divine birth to bear the sons of Hanab Pacal. Enjoy your moment of happiness, I thought. Kahwil or not, soon I will have to publicly blame you for this failure. Soon you will have to step aside while I choose a fertile woman to be First Companion and Mother of the Heirs.

Ahpo Hel seemed to know my thoughts, but instead of resenting me, she put her hand on my arm and smiled. "It will be all right now," she whispered warmly. "Kahwil will be good to us. I've worshipped his pih diligently these many years. I've never missed an Ahow day.

I've never let the flowers on his altar die, nor let the incense stop burning. He will show us his gratitude this Katun. You'll see."

If we were not in procession beside my mother I would have responded in a loud, angry outburst. Was she implying that I had not properly served Bolom Tzacab, my lineage god, these past seven years, and the many years before she had ever even come to Jaguar-Sun? Did she assume that her relationship with her god was more powerful than mine? That our lack of offspring was all my fault? I could feel myself burning with a fury I could never express within ear-shot of Resplendent Egret. There was only one thing I feared more than the wrath of my ancestors, and that was the anger of my mother—if that was what you could call this deformed creature that was being carried on the litter beside us.

Lady Resplendent Egret had grown more grotesque with each passing year, and her cantankerous nature had disintegrated into an irrational madness that would explode at the slightest provocation. The healers had explained that the enlargement of her skull was causing pressure inside her head and this in turn had transformed her nature, as well as her appearance to that of a terrifying beast. Her physical transformation into what many suspected would soon be a Lord of the Night was almost complete.

My resentment seemed to grow even as I walked beside her. I was thirty years old and had been permitted to do nothing as leader of my people. I'd built no temples, nor had I erected any tree-stones. I wasn't even been permitted to let blood in my ancestral cave in order to induce the mystical trance that would invoke the voices of my ancestors! For almost eighteen years I had been the Holy Bacab in name only, denied all of the duties and privileges of my title. Until I succeeded in producing an heir, nothing else I did or said was of any value! What if it was all my fault? What if my seed never grew in any woman? The thought horrified me, not only because of the waste my life would become, but because of the unthinkable consequences. If Resplendent Egret were to take the road into Xibalba knowing that no legacy existed for her spirit to return to, she would never survive the trials that awaited her. Her spirit, and the spirits of her predecessors would simply cease to exist. Over and over I contemplated these things as if somehow, with my thoughts alone, I could force my wife's belly to swell.

We came at last to the giant Ceiba tree that marked the entrance to Toctan. Ahpo Hel had indeed kept this shrine well. I noticed many potsherds piled around the opening of the cave—an indication that the people of Jaguar-Sun frequently visited this shrine. While no one but Ahpo Hel was permitted to enter, it was obvious that many people had made this site part of their ritual pilgrimages. Ahpo Hel knelt to my mother in submission, requesting her permission to bring the pih of Kahwil to the mouth of the cave, where we could worship him. Resplendent Egret nodded her approval and then made an unintelligible sound to Kan, indicating with her swollen hands that he was to bring something to her. While Ahpo Hel went into the cave, Kan quickly brought an old, frayed pouch to my mother and then hurried back into the woods to hide with the slaves before the terrifying idol of Kahwil was presented.

I walked up to the cave entrance and held back the damp moss drape, swinging my incense burner towards the opening. As Ahpo Hel came towards me I fell to my knees and averted my eyes from the sacred idol she held out before us. Divine Lady Resplendent Egret had hobbled, with the aid of her husband, to stand boldly before the powerful effigy. Yellow-Macaw seemed to know what was coming next, because a look of terror had overtaken his aging face. He now held the pouch Kan had delivered to Resplendent Egret moments earlier and as he pulled the antler handled sting-ray spine from it, I suddenly recognized the bloodletting implements Kan had taken from Split-Sky many years ago.

Without hesitation, Yellow-Macaw grabbed my mother's swollen tongue and pierced it with the spine. Blood began to spurt from her mouth in frightening quantities. But while Yellow-Macaw had been able to insert the tortuous tool quickly into his willing victim, he was horrified to discover that he could not pull it out. Tears welled in his eyes as he slowly ripped the barbs back through his wife's tongue, tearing it to shreds in the process.

But Resplendent Egret was oblivious to the miserable mess of bloody flesh that hung from her mouth. Her gruesome face was beaming with ecstasy as she caught the blood that flowed profusely from her mouth onto paper strips in a bowl she supported with her outstretched forearms. Kahwil wouldn't have to wait for the blood soaked paper to be burned in order to receive this sacrifice. His statue was already covered with bright red blood from the spurting the initial piercing had induced.

It wasn't difficult to understand Resplendent Egret's last desperate attempt to beg Kahwil's help in bringing her a grandchild. I only wished that I had been permitted to make such a noble sacrifice. But a male was expected to endure this bloodletting ritual in the loose flesh of his male organ, and this would be a risk no god would respect from one whose primary obligation was to produce an heir.

I helped my father hold Resplendent Egret up, as the loss of blood weakened her. But just as it seemed that she would pass out, we felt her shudder violently and knew that the gods had deemed her sacrifice worthy. I had heard the voice of the gods coming from a human only once before, as a very young boy, when my uncle, the Holy Bacab Turtle-Maize, had let blood at Te'nab. But the voice that spoke with my mother's bloodied mouth, was very different from the deep, thunderous sound I remembered of Bolom Tzacab.

"You honor me, Hanab Pacal," hissed an eerie, barely audible voice. I knew that it was the voice of Kahwil.

*"Your son shall be the incarnation of Kahwil,*
*Third Brother of the Three-Born-Together gods,*
*These are the things you must hear,*
*These are the things you must know*
*You must not plant your seed again*
*until First-Father has moved across the sky,*
*You must not plant your seed then*
*until First-Father journeys through Xibalba.*
*Wait for the day he rises up from the Underworld,*
*Watch for the day when Ixtab bears a male child,*
*Plant your seed on that Kimi day.*
*Plant your seed on that male moon day.*
*Every day until then must be a kept day.*
*Every day until then you must not spill your seed.*
*Every day you will pilgrimage to Toctan*
*Every day you will burn copál at my shrine.*
*Then the Ahow of Toctan will swell with life.*
*Then Kahwil will be born as your son."*

Resplendent Egret shuddered again and collapsed in our arms. Her dead weight was almost too much for Yellow-Macaw and myself, as we struggled to drag her to her litter. Ahpo Hel stood in the cave entrance holding her blood-drenched idol, gaping blankly in shock. "Bring him back inside!" I ordered her.

"Return Kahwil to his altar!" I pleaded, trying to rouse her. Ahpo Hel slowly turned into the cave, the moss falling behind her. I looked around me and realized that it was no longer dark. The first day of the new Katun had begun with the promise of Kahwil himself that I would have a son!

I turned to my mother, her garments and ornaments covered with blood. Her eyes slowly opened from behind the puffy flesh that threatened to soon obscure them, and I saw, for the first time in many years, a flicker of warmth. She couldn't speak, and I knew that she would never speak again. But as I held the cloth my father had dampened in a nearby stream, onto the shredded remnants of her tongue, I knew what her eyes were saying. I had not betrayed my heritage, her spirit and the spirits of her ancestors would not cease to exist. "Hanab Pacal will bear fruit!" I cried to her and tears flowed from the narrow slits of her eyes. "You will have your grandson," I whispered, as I gently wiped the blood from her face

Ahpo Hel came around to us with a handful of herbs, which she crushed in her palms and pressed onto my mother's ravaged tongue. Resplendent Egret flinched, then let her head fall back on the pillows Yellow-Macaw had propped behind her, as the herbal compress stopped the pain.

I watched as my father gently wiped the perspiration from her face and wondered at their strange relationship. No husband had ever suffered more than he—never the master of his home; kept always in the position of one who is subservient. I couldn't remember ever hearing her express a word of gratitude or affection toward him. I wondered how it was that he had come to father me, and if he had ever known the pleasure of a woman's softness, as I had known with Ahpo Hel. Still, he touched her now with true gentleness and respect. I wasn't sure if I felt admiration or disdain for him. I feared his willing submission to this strong and powerful woman and his warmth and patience with her. I feared that with Kahwil as ruler of the katun, Ahpo Hel could seize power, as my mother and grandmother had done. Would the son, promised to me today, one day see me as I saw my own father? This is what I feared most in my father—my propensity for becoming him.

I called to Kan and the slaves to help us, and soon we were on our way. By now, day had fully blossomed, and we passed many people on our way back to the residential compound. To each of them that stared with frightened curiosity at our bloodstained bodies, I explained proudly that their Divine Lady Resplendent Egret, mother of the Holy Bacab, had let blood for Kahwil, and in return there would soon be an heir to the Jaguar-Sun dynasty.

To this announcement, my people expressed their happiness by crying out with joy. It was then that I fully realized how important this child was to their survival, as well as the survival of my lineage. They understood that, without their divine leaders to intercede for them, they would be at the mercy of a mind-boggling list of frightening and powerful entities. We were all that stood between them and hunger, disease and chaos.

# Kahwil

It had taken almost two years for First-Father to complete his journey across the heavens and his long disappearance into Xibalba. I'd begun to fear that he had been defeated by the demons of the Underworld and would never again appear on the eastern horizon, to herald the moment I would impregnate Ahpo Hel. Many of the people of Jaguar-Sun had taken to joining me during those days of waiting, on my daily pilgrimage to Toctan, to pray for the reappearance of First-Father and the conception of the heir. Our morning procession grew to include hundreds of worshippers — men, women, and children, pleading for the timely release of First-Father from the dark unknown, an event of the greatest importance to the survival of Place of Jaguar-Sun.

I had kept those many days, as Kahwil had directed, remaining celibate and fasting on posol; watching the eastern horizon night after night; waiting for the sign that would indicate the time for the promised conception. First-Father had finally appeared just above the shrine of Kahwil, and Ixtab, the moon, was swollen with child directly overhead, just as Kahwil had foretold. There had been as much merriment and festivity that night as there had been on the first night of our marriage, as once again, after what had seemed like an eternity, I brought Ahpo Hel with me into the Temple of Yum Kaax, and planted the seed of Kahwil.

~

The seed had grown, and the male child had been born, as promised. As was the custom for the first-born male, when fifteen moons had passed, Ahpo Hel dressed in the costume of Ixtab and took our son alone to Toctan, to present him to the pih of her lineage. It was rumored that during this secret ritual, Kahwil himself had spoken through the boy, and chosen his name—Little Jaguar. Kahwil's promise, that my son would be his incarnation, seemed to be known and accepted by everyone. Perhaps some shaman, during a secret ceremony, had revealed the prophecy. More likely, word had spread of the child's six fingers on each hand and six toes on each foot—a sure sign of divine appointment. I'm sure, as stories go, many mysterious or unexplainable events were attributed to the deification of the son of the Holy Bacab, because it was generally accepted that a gift to Little Jaguar was as good as a gift to Kahwil himself. Offerings of everything from finely woven cloths to intricately worked stones were presented to the baby almost daily, from petitioners and worshipers from as far away as Simojovel in the west and Jonuta in the north.

Six harvests passed; six plentiful harvests that reassured the growing population of Jaguar-Sun that this was a place that basked in the beneficence of Kahwil. Satisfied at last that the lineage she had fought so desperately during her life to preserve, could survive without her unrelenting control, Resplendent Egret had finally taken the road to Xibalba. After twenty-five years, I was finally free to be the Holy Bacab in actions as well as title. I planned to do things very differently from my mother.

Waiting all those years under her tyrannical rule, I had the opportunity to observe how people behaved differently in Resplendent Egret's presence than in her absence. Even I was often guilty of scheming secretly in order to do things my own way, avoiding the futile frustration of disagreeing with her. I'd noticed that, just as Great Jaguar had chosen to storm off into certain death in the jungle that night many years ago, rather than submit to Resplendent Egret's unreasonable demands and control, many of the most talented and intelligent people had chosen to remain obscure, sacrificing the opportunity to use their skills to please the gods, so as to remain free from her insensitive domination.

But I felt no need to manipulate and control, perhaps because my own creativity had been stifled for so long. I was determined to make Place of Jaguar-Sun a haven for the most talented artisans and craftsmen in the world. Here they would have the freedom and opportunity to perform their greatest work, whether designing buildings, carving monuments or painting murals. Already word had begun to spread that a man of artistic skill would be treated with respect, and allowed creative expression, in Place of Jaguar-Sun.

I envisioned the entire plateau area covered with limestone plazas and terraced gardens even more colorful than those I'd seen in

Place of Split-Sky. Temples would be built to each god and the most magnificent would be for the ancestors of Jaguar-Sun. In that Temple of the Divine Lineage, I would record the whole history of the Jaguar-Sun dynasty. It would be more beautiful than any temple ever built, so that no god could overlook the sincerity and purity of the sacrifices performed there. I would construct the temple to completely encompass and protect the entrance to my lineage cave and my own tomb would be secured within it, just as I'd seen in the temples of Tikal.

In the center of the plaza I would build a colossal platform where all matters of administration would be addressed. Here I would welcome visitors from all parts of the world. I imagined myself, attired in magnificent costumes, accompanied by my wife and son, conferring with the leaders of all the clans of Jaguar-Sun and the sahals of our many tributaries. Hundreds of artisans would present their wondrous creations and report on the progress of the temples under construction, while merchants from distant places would eagerly bargain all manner of goods for our world-renowned art.

I imagined these things as I led the procession on this Nine-Akbal day—the day that Ahpo Hel had divined to present my son to his ancestors and to acknowledge him as rightful heir. It was the first of the five kept days that preceded the Summer Solstice, so there would be no dancing and music, nor copious drinking and feasting for the presentation ritual of Little Jaguar. But still the crowd that followed us in procession to Te'nab, my lineage shrine, numbered in the thousands.

Not permitted to approach the shrine itself, they waited on the glistening limestone plaza, that had only recently been completed, in the area just north of Te'nab. Now, as I started on the secluded trail towards Te'nab, with my young son beside me, followed by only Ahpo Hel and my father, the old and nearly crippled Yellow-Macaw, my thoughts were of the blessings Kahwil had bestowed on Place of Jaguar-Sun. With his continued good graces I knew that all the things I'd dreamed of doing, could happen. There would be no problem finding the labor—people were already clamoring for the chance to show the gods their gratitude.

As I continued down the path, treading slowly over the leafy patterns of shadows and light, it occurred to me that this would be the perfect opportunity to open the area surrounding my lineage shrine to those who would be needed to build the temple for my ancestors.

I turned to face the crowd that stood watching us from the plaza and proclaimed, "Good people of Jaguar-Sun bear witness to the

160

presentation of my son. Humble servants of Bolom Tzacab, join us at his holy shrine!"

My father shook his head in dismay knowing that Resplendent Egret would have never approved of such a bold breech with tradition. But my wife beamed in approval. "A wise decision," she whispered as the crowd shuffled hesitantly towards us. Ahpo Hel knew how important it was to me to build my lineage temple and she understood how difficult it would be to secure the enthusiastic efforts of talented craftsmen to a place they had been long forbidden to enter—a place tainted with frightening stories that were meant to keep men respectfully distant.

The crowd silently filed behind us, keeping a measured distance, obviously fearful of intruding onto the sacred grounds of the patron god of their Holy Bacab. But follow they did, and when I had arrived at the mouth of the cave, I turned to face them, my son standing in front of me. Deliberately, I waited until everyone of them had reluctantly filled the clearing before me. I thought of how my mother had once positioned herself in the gaping jaws of this cave, the night I had arrived with Ahpo Hel, and I imagined that to my frightened audience I appeared just as imposing. Only after the crowd had settled in a reverent silence before me, did I begin to speak, with the sound of my voice reverberating from the cave walls, lending a power and authority to my words.

"Behold this place of the resting of the bones of Jaguar-Sun. This is the holiest of all shrines, the place of the Great-grandfathers and Great-grandmothers. The home of the pih of Bolom Tzacab, god of our ancestors. Here we will build a temple to the ancestors of Jaguar-Sun."

With these words I hoisted my son up to the throng and turning to face the opening to the cave I proclaimed, "Here my Grandfather and Grandmothers is the true son of the Holy Bacab, heir of the Jaguar-Sun dynasty, Little Jaguar." As I carefully set the boy on his feet I nodded to Yellow-Macaw to hand me the pot of blue paint he carried. Exaggerating my movements so that everyone in the crowd could understand what was happening, I spread the blue pigment over Little Jaguar's face and chest, marking him as one of divine blood. He stood proud and motionless, puffing his belly forward with regal pride. Now I took the headdress of Kahwil that Ahpo Hel held out for me and placed it on his small head. Little Jaguar looked up to me, waiting for my approval, his eyes bright with an intellect far beyond his years. I burned with pride as I nodded and watched him stride fearlessly into the cave. Following behind him, I held a torch to light his way past the tree-stones that grew downwards and upwards like teeth, to the altar that was positioned at the beginning of the narrow, dark passage with no end.

But to my sudden horror, Little Jaguar boldly reached out for the drum-shaped headdress with the reassembled pih of Bolom Tzacab, without stopping first to bow in submission. He seemed oblivious to his mistake, despite the careful instructions I'd given him. Instead he took hold of the sacred object and turning, handed it to me. This was not what we had discussed. He was doing it all wrong!

"My son," I pleaded in a voice so soft I prayed the gods could not hear, "You must pay homage to the god of your ancestors."

But instead Little Jaguar reached up and removed his headdress. I realized now that the replica of Kahwil that was attached to the front was actually the sacred idol of Kahwil that had been enshrined in Toctan. Ahpo Hel must have replaced it! Terror gripped my throat as I watched my son usurp the god of my lineage and replace him with the pih of Kahwil. He bent to the floor in submission before the newly enshrined Kahwil and then turned to me and smiled with pure innocence.

"Father, it is Kahwil who blesses the Jaguar-Sun. We will worship him now as the god of our blood," he firmly stated without emotion, in a voice that did not match his tender age.

I stood frightened and confused between him and the crowd that stood outside. I'd been aware for some time that many of those who stood in the clearing behind me had already begun to pay greater homage to Kahwil than to Bolom Tzacab. It was he, after all, who had answered their prayers. Perhaps the Third-Brother god had overcome his brothers, I thought. Perhaps Bolom Tzacab was no longer empowered. Could a new god simply lay claim to a dynasty? What would happen to Bolom Tzacab if we stopped nurturing his shrine? I looked at the fragments of the old pih that I held in my hands and suddenly understood what I should have realized long ago, that the warriors of Pomona had destroyed the power of this idol long ago. That was why it had taken so long for me to father a child.

Slowly, like one who has been blindfolded, the light of comprehension began to clarify the situation. Bolom Tzacab had abandoned the people of Jaguar-Sun way back when the Pomona warriors had sacrificed my uncle, Turtle-Maize, and taken our lineage god for their own. That was why the warriors had returned to shatter our pih, they had stolen our god! No wonder the Lords of the Night had taken possession of Resplendent Egret; she had only a powerless, broken statue to protect her!

Little Jaguar stood silently grinning as he watched me slowly coming to grips what had happened. I looked at him in the dim light of the cave and for a moment I thought I saw Kahwil. Could it be possible that he was indeed Kahwil? He had a wit like no child I had ever known; easily comprehending complex thoughts and quick to poke fun at things that made no sense to him. He had learned the intricate patterns of the Tzolkin already and could form many words with a brush in both their simple and ritual forms. Surely these were not the ways of an ordinary child, even one of divine descent.

"I will present Kahwil to his people," I said as I put the powerless idol of Bolom Tzacab on a stone pedestal nearby and walked towards the altar where the jade idol of Kahwil sat proudly, his snake foot pointed directly towards me. But Little Jaguar intercepted me and held out his hand. I understood and picked the boy up in my arms and carried him to the cave opening. When the crowd saw me standing there surrounded by the smoke of the many incense pots they had placed just outside the cave, they fell to the ground in reverence.

"This is Kahwil, the god of Jaguar-Sun," I proclaimed to my people. I looked over towards the radiant woman who stood on the other side of the incense pots. She was the child of Ixtab and the mother of Kahwil, and I suddenly felt powerless and insignificant. Hanab Pacal had only been a tool of the gods. For better or worse, I delivered my people into the hands of Kahwil.

Sadly, I set my son, the god, on his feet. Looking down at his aristocratic features, I realized that he would never again seem small, vulnerable and innocent. Turning back into the cave, I picked up the defrocked idol of my lineage, and the pine torch I had earlier set into a notch in a tree-stone, and walked, as if enchanted, down the dark passageway into the bowels of the earth. I walked to where the light of K'in never reached, past the chambers where my ancestor's bones rested, past the mound where my mother's remains were entombed, past the dark river and the long hall of tree-stones, to the sacred water-place where I had heard the voices of my ancestors when I was only a boy of twelve. I looked around for the things that had become familiar to me then—the altar I had made from a large flat stone with a well-like depression in its center, where I had burned copál; and the narrow depression in one wall where I had slept, hidden from bats and snakes and other demons that slipped up from Xibalba. I listened for the steady sound of dripping water that echoed throughout the chamber and heard it's reassuring plop, plop, plop. Everything was the same as when I had left it, over twenty-five years ago.

Everything is the same except for the weary heart of Hanab Pacal, I thought. I was uncertain what to do next as I placed the powerless statue on the old altar. "Everything is the same and nothing is the same," I said aloud in the darkness. My words returned to me in an echo.

This was the moment I'd waited for all those many years under Resplendent Egret's restraints, when I would make a blood sacrifice as Holy Bacab; to petition the ancestor who would return in the body of my son, to reveal himself. But how could my predecessors enter the body of one who has already proclaimed himself to be the embodiment of Kahwil? What was I supposed to petition for now? I knelt before the old pih and spoke to it like a wayward friend. Smoothing the feathers on its drum-like frame, I asked for an explanation. "Have all my petitions for intercession these many years been made to a lifeless, broken, old statue with no more power than a rock in the forest?" I cried.

I remained there, weeping before my impotent idol for a very long time. My pine torch had been long burnt out before I could finally bring myself around to the ritual I was there to perform—the divine sacrifice that would open the portal to the gods. This was the ceremony I had been denied until it was certain that I had produced an heir that was acceptable to my ancestors. Now that obligation had been accomplished and I was, at long last, free to experience this most sacred of sacrifices. When I'd strode in procession earlier, I'd been so sure of myself, so prepared to endure the suffering that would accompany this intrusion into the realm of the gods. But that bold self-assurance was gone.

Hypnotized with fear, I pulled the satchel from my shoulder and removed its contents: a large, flat-bottomed bowl decorated with images of the Lords of the Night; several rolls of narrow bark-paper strips; white cloth; a ball of copál; a cigar of magical herbs; and a freshly slivered shard of obsidian. I placed the incense in the depression of the altar then realized that I had nothing with which to light it. That meant that I would also be unable to light the cigar that would dull the intense pain I was about to inflict on myself.

In a daze of despair, I decided to continue the ritual despite my lack of fire, and began the long, empowering chant of preparation. At each prescribed part of the prayer I proceeded as I had been taught many years ago, following each step exactly as my ancestors had, since the beginning of time, except that when I was supposed to pass my blade through the smoke of the incense, I simply passed it over the unburned copál, and when I was supposed to stop to draw the smoke of the cigar deep within my body, I put the unlit roll of herbs to my lips, and imagined that I was feeling its inebriating effect.

Ritually I removed my loin cloth, chanting the ancient words of sacrifice. At the appointed words I pinched a small section of the loose skin of my penis tightly between my thumb and smallest finger and ran the narrow blade completely through it. The pain was blinding as I groped for the first paper strip and threaded it through the slit before loosening my grip on the pierced flesh. Clenching my teeth, I slowly forced myself to pull the paper through, so that half its length hung from each side of the slit. Tears of agony filled my eyes as I released my grip and allowed the blood to be drawn onto the paper. Almost immediately I could feel the entire length was saturated with my warm blood.

I grabbed another section of flesh slightly further up my member from the first cut, and quickly pierced it, afraid that I would soon be too weak to complete all three of the required cuts. The pain was excruciating as I threaded the second paper strip through and released my hold. Once again I quickly pulled the flesh of my penis up and pierced it. No longer able to restrain myself, I screamed in anguish as my hands mechanically pulled the last strip of paper through my tender flesh, and allowed the blood to be released.

In the total darkness of the cave, I felt for the saturated strips of paper draped between my legs and cried out as I realized that I would be unable to burn them with the incense, as required. "I have no fire!" I screamed as my head swam with the overwhelming pain and weakness. And then, suddenly, the pain stopped, and it no longer mattered that I had no fire. The cave was lit with a red glow and Kahwil stood before me. He took the paper strips in his hands and they were so saturated that they fell from my wounds. Placing them in a pile on the altar, Kahwil set them ablaze!

"Now we will talk" he said to me in the same eerie hissing voice that I had heard come from my mother when he'd manifested during her bloodletting.

"These are the things you must teach your son," he began. "First, you will instruct him in the many skills of the scribe. He is the chosen one who will record the story of your ancestors, not in the perishable, folding, bark-paper books, but in the everlasting medium of stone and stucco," he commanded.

"He will preserve the stories of the ancient ones, of creation and destruction. And he will transcribe those mysteries that I will teach you now, that you will in turn teach to him."

On and on the god of magic went, filling my mind with so much enlightenment that I thought I would explode. Each explanation he provided seemed so simple, that I found myself exclaiming, "But why didn't I realize that myself!" For instance, this is the way he demonstrated that there is no beginning or end to time—just a constant repetition of cycles with only slight variations as we grow in our understanding.

"Which of these things would you say happens first?" he had asked. "Does the avocado fall from the tree? Does the rat devour its fruit and bury the nut? Does the nut sprout roots and grow into a tree? Does the tree bear fruit? Not one of these things could possibly happen without the thing that precedes it happening first.

"It seems very simple," I sighed. "But tell me why these things are so clear to me now?"

"Think of the caterpillar," he quickly replied. When he crawls around on the ground the world seems so vast and strange. He can see it from only one place—below. To him a field of grass is the limit of his knowledge. His whole life consists of nothing but munching leaves and avoiding the birds that want to munch on him. Then one day he ventures up a tree and out onto a branch, and he can see for a great distance and realizes for the first time that the world extends beyond the field of grass. But he is very weary from all this climbing and learning and he falls into a deep sleep, as you have done now. When he awakens he is a beautiful butterfly with wings that can carry him everywhere the birds can go. Then he realizes that what he thought he knew when he was only a crawling creature was really nothing. And spreading his wings he sets out to learn everything all over again—this time from the vantage of the gods.

"So you will return, Hanab Pacal, to the field of grass, and try to explain to those poor lowly creatures that there is something far more wonderful than they can possibly comprehend. If you succeed, then you will be remembered for all time as the one who inspired men to create that which is godly and wondrous."

I wanted to assure Kahwil that I had listened well. I wanted to tell him of my dreams to build many temples to all the gods and to inspire the talents of the most skilled artisans in the world. I wanted to proclaim to him how honored I was that he had chosen me to be the father of his human embodiment. But my voice could utter only one word over and over. "Kahwil, Kahwil, Kahwil," I muttered like an awestruck simpleton!

Kahwil cautioned, "The test of one's true greatness is in his ability to put aside his pride and forgive. You have a very great test before you Hanab Pacal. Kahwil can work great magic, but I cannot protect you from your own pride. Remember that the power of magic is in the way one looks at things, what we fear most is usually our own reflection."

With these words Kahwil's eerie form moved away from me, dissolving into the darkness of the cave. As his image grew smaller and more faint, the pain in my groin increased, until it seemed that my genitals had been ripped apart by a ferocious beast. But just as I was about to cry out in agony I felt the relief of a cool compress being applied to the fiery pain, and opened my eyes to see Kan kneeling beside me, treating my wound with astringent herbs and damp cloths. When he saw me looking at him, he quickly brushed tears back from his face and exclaimed, "I thought you were dead, Ahow! You were making the sounds of a man on his way to Xibalba!" Tears now streamed from his eyes as profusely as the blood that had poured from my penis.

"What are you doing here!" I scolded. "No one is permitted within these chambers except the Ahow of Te'nab! Go quickly before Bolom Tzacab devours you in anger," I tried to warn him.

But Kan smiled nervously and replied, "Bolom Tzacab must want me to save the life of his protector, because he hasn't eaten me yet and I've been here for a long time.

I looked at my slave in confusion. "A long time?" I questioned. How long have I been speaking with Kahwil?"

Kan nodded. "Yes, I thought it was Kahwil. I thought I heard you call him several times. But I was confused. What of Bolom Tzacab?" Kan stopped himself from babbling as often was his way, and returned to my question?

"How long? Oh My Lord, K'in passed through Xibalba twice and still you did not return from the cave. The Lady Ahpo Hel feared that Bolom Tzacab had been angered and punished you for allowing Kahwil to take possession of his shrine. She feared that if she went into the cave, Bolom Tzacab would devour her as well, for bringing Kahwil to Place of Jaguar-Sun.

"I told her that I would go after my holy master. I'm not afraid of the wrath of Bolom Tzacab," he explained in a most humble voice. "If he had dragged you into Xibalba, then I would join you there. I would help you outwit the evil ones so that when you rose up into the heavens you would permit me to accompany you. I'm certain that spirits need slaves as well as Holy Bacabs."

"You will not join me in Xibalba as my slave, cherished one," I replied, realizing that Kan's unselfish courage had saved my life.

"The man who carries me from this place will be a Sahal."

"Oh, but I am happy to serve you as your slave, Ahow," Kan stammered, resuming his weeping. "A Sahal must live in a faraway place and I don't wish to be parted from you. Please don't send me off to some foreign place to collect tribute and think you are doing me a favor."

"Send you away? I would never send away the one who loves me most. You shall be the Sahal of the Household of the Holy Bacab!" I proclaimed, delighted that I had contrived a way to honor and still retain my most treasured companion. "You can see to the needs of my family and I will tell all the slaves that they must answer to you. And in addition, I entrust the care of my son to you. Is that too great a responsibility? You will be the Protector of Little Jaguar, because you have proven your courage and devotion as no man in Jaguar-Sun ever has."

Kan knelt beside me and kissed my hand, his tears falling relentlessly. I noticed that he was wearing a huipil and smiled to myself that one who had been considered such a fool should have such a capacity to love. I reached over and touched his hair with my other hand and admonished him to stop crying. "A Sahal cannot wear a huipil, you know," I murmured in an effort to lighten the mood. It worked. Kan smiled and started to help me to my feet. He was an exceptionally strong and handsome man, showing little sign of aging. As I allowed my full weight to be borne by his shoulders I thought of Kahwil's parting words and wondered what terrible trials awaited me in Jaguar-Sun.

# The Shaman

I had walked the distance from our new stone residence to Te'nab more times this day than I had fingers and toes to count. Even if Little Jaguar had been beside me to count with his extra fingers and toes, I would have paced this distance more than that as well. "The second child should not take so long" Kan cried to me from his post outside the doorway to my home. It was the first time since he had helped me from the bowels of Te'nab, over three years ago, that I'd seen him wearing a huipil. I suppose it was his way of empathizing with the agony that his mistress was enduring.

If I hadn't been so preoccupied with my concern for my wife's life at that moment, I would have noted with relief the change in Kan's attitude toward Ahpo Hel. Instead of resenting her, Kan had made the Holy Mother of Jaguar-Sun his ally. Together they had planned the decoration of our new house and had directed the planting of the flower gardens and orchards that surrounded the pleasant lime-stone courtyard that fronted our royal residence and the nearby stone buildings that housed those I'd chosen to assist me in the administration of Jaguar-Sun. Kan had taken his responsibility as Sahal of my household very seriously, and I was sure no ruler had ever enjoyed such domestic harmony and peace.

But, while the women of Jaguar-Sun had come to accept this gentle, unassuming man in their midst, who brought them frothy cocao drinks as they sat weaving in the courtyard, and carried their firewood, surprising them with bouquets of fresh flowers and baskets of fruit, and entertaining them with tales of his youthful adventures with the Holy Bacab, today was different. They refused him access to the room where Ahpo Hel had cried out for almost two days now, with the agony of giving birth.

"Come with me to Te'nab," I said to him, putting my arm around his shoulders to tear him away from the stone wall he'd been leaning against since morning. "Neither of us can do anything for her here. Come with me to pray to Kahwil. He has blessed us and showered us with good fortune. Surely he will let nothing happen to the woman he has chosen to be his mother."

"Perhaps he resents this new child," Kan responded hesitantly, as he joined me on the well worn trail. The expression on his face seemed to be horrified by his own words, as soon as he gave voice to them. He wasn't the only one to consider the possibility that Kahwil didn't want Ahpo Hel to bear another child. I had been more than a little surprised when my wife informed me that her sign of the moon had not come. But ever since my vision in Te'nab, I was certain that nothing occurred at Place of Jaguar-Sun without the approval of that mysterious Third-Brother of the Three-Born-Together gods.

"He awaits his temple!" I exclaimed, suddenly remembering the promise I'd made when Kahwil had first spoken to me. "I must begin immediately! Of course, that's why Ahpo Hel suffers. I've built my own house and not his." I was certain that I'd identified the problem and immediately sent Kan back to the twilight enshrouded plaza to summon the Ahow of the Chosen Council to meet me at Te'nab. "We'll hold a meeting just outside the shrine of Kahwil so that he is certain to hear us planning his temple. Don't worry, Ahpo Hel will give birth tonight!" I called to Kan as he hastened to notify those men of exceptional talent and intelligence whom I'd chosen from the oldest families of Jaguar-Sun.

I hurried on to Te'nab to assure Kahwil that I'd realized my error. A wall the height of a man, made of the potsherds used to burn incense, encircled a shrine that had been positioned near the mouth of the cave. Hundreds of flowers adorned this outside altar and were also strewn around the wide cave opening. It was clear that the populace of Jaguar-Sun had accepted this new god wholeheartedly. As word of the beneficent power of Kahwil had spread beyond Place of Jaguar-Sun, to the many outlying compounds, even as far as Pomona, I worried for the safety of our pih. Two warriors were posted to guard this shrine at all times, having learned all-to-well how valuable and vulnerable a powerful pih was, to the survival of a lineage. No one would ever again rob the people of Jaguar-Sun of our god!

I nodded to the guards and they looked at me expectantly for any word of the birth, as they had done many, many times this day. But I shook my head, "Nothing yet. The Ahow of the Chosen Council will be arriving shortly. Tell them to make their offering to Kahwil and I will join them soon." With these instructions I hurried past the guards into the dark cave. Grabbing a torch from it's notch, I moved briskly into the dark narrow passage the Ahow of Te'nab alone was permitted to enter. The light of my torch threw ominous shadows onto the living stones that grew from the floor and ceiling in the narrow tunnel where the river of Xibalba stretched like a snake. But I didn't linger to study the reflections in its dark waters this night. I rushed on to the sacred cavern where the pih of Kahwil was enshrined.

Falling to my knees before the altar I'd reverently tended for the past three years, I kissed the snake foot of my holy benefactor. The voice of Kahwil had counseled me many times since that first vision. It had been Kahwil who described to me how to divert the waters of the west river so that it would not flood the maize fields. And it had been Kahwil who had advised me on my selection of administrators to manage the sudden influx of new residents who had heard of the good fortune of Jaguar-Sun. This katun had begun as one of abundance and prosperity. My responsibility to keep our merciful new god happy weighed heavy in my thoughts. But the days had passed all too quickly and Kahwil's temple was never begun.

Lighting the incense in the four god-pots that stood at each corner of the altar I prayed, "This very night, Most Loved Benefactor, I will begin your god-house. I am your humble servant, please show me the way," I repeated my prayer slowly and deliberately many times, waiting for the voice that came so easily these days.

"You honor me with your humility, cherished one," the voice of Kahwil hissed from the dark recesses of the cavern. "But it is perfection, not haste that I require of you. Tonight a warrior is born and to the god of warriors you will build your first temple. Build it on that place Ahpo Hel makes holy with her blood, for the gods must always have a more beautiful home than those who were created to worship them.

"The Temple of Kahwil will not be your first, but your final gift to the gods. You will first build four great temples, Hanab Pacal, and I will bless you with much time to learn from your mistakes. But more than a katun will pass before you know in your heart how to build that which holds the light of K'in and the breath of Ik and the strength of the four Chacs. Only then will you begin the temple to Kahwil, the god of your lineage shrine. Only after knowing great sorrow will you have the wisdom to build the most beautiful temple in all the world." Having spoken his wishes in his usual foreboding manner, Kahwil disappeared into the darkness of the cave, to the unknown places that even I would fear to go.

It's hard to explain the way I felt each time I emerged from Te'nab, after hearing the voice of Kahwil. I was exuberant, yet drained, exhausted and energized at the same time. But always that sense of enlightenment and understanding dimmed almost as quickly as the image of the Sacred Third Brother. By the time I'd walked down the narrow passageway, out to the now-dark entrance, the instructions of Kahwil seemed more like an old lesson from my boyhood, than words just spoken to me by a god. I knew that it was important to repeat his instructions as quickly as possible, so that they would not slip from me forever. The words of a god must never be forgotten.

So when I saw the men of my Council waiting for me outside the cave, I rushed to them reciting the most recent directives of our god.

"We must build a temple to Chac-Xib-Chac on the place where Lady Ahpo Hel gives birth!" I proclaimed. But as the words came from my mouth I realized with horror that Kahwil had not mentioned whether Ahpo Hel would survive the ordeal of giving birth. I surveyed the expressions on my companions' faces searching for an indication of the welfare of my wife. But they seemed to have forgotten what they were about to say as they tried to comprehend the directive I'd just handed to them. "Is she alive?" I asked, without trying to disguise my sudden sense of panic.

"She's borne you another son!" the group replied in unison and then each began to babble on his own about the large, strong child who had emerged into the world one foot first. I didn't wait for them to stop, but rushed past them down the path towards my home. I'd heard the stories of what happens to women when their children are born backwards, and now the words of Kahwil pierced my mind like obsidian blades "Build it on that place Ahpo Hel makes holy with her blood." Did Chac-Xib-Chac require the life of my wife to anoint his temple? Couldn't he be appeased with something less?

I searched the horizon for a sign and saw the sliver of the Baby Moon slipping into Xibalba. Following close behind was the spirit of Bolom Tzacab. It was the old god's first appearance since disappearing into Xibalba many nights before. Had he returned tonight only to avenge his neglect in Jaguar-Sun? "You left us! You forgot us! I never abandoned you, all those many years, Most Holy First-Brother," I cried as I hurried as fast as my bent foot would allow.

I met Kan half-way, running towards me. "Is she all right?" I called. "How is Hel?"

"They won't let me near her!" he cried out. "She's losing much blood."

I ran beside him to the large stone house with many people standing around it. Kan pushed them away, sure of himself, now that he was beside me. He hesitated at the door, then followed behind me without looking at the women who had denied him entrance earlier.

Ahpo Hel's eyes were barely open, and she smiled weakly at me as I knelt on the mat beside her. Her coloring was always light, but now she seemed to be ghastly. I hardly noticed the child she held beside her, until he let out a holler that filled the room. He was indeed a very large baby, as Little Jaguar had been. It was the blood of Great Jaguar, of the ancient Jaguar Peoples that made such big children. But that such a large child should be born backside first could only mean that Ahpo Hel was torn open in the process. I held her hands in mine, but they were cold and limp, and I feared that there wasn't much time before she would bleed to death.

Kan wasted no time rushing to the aid of his mistress. Disregarding the taboo of touching a woman in her place of shame, with one hand he held a compress of herbs on the place where the child had emerged, while kneading on her stomach with his other hand. Calling out orders to the women who surrounded him, to get clean cloths, or this or that herb, he seemed to have been somehow transformed into a healer. I searched his face for the confidence that my wife would survive, but saw only a fierce determination to resist the cruel forces who desired her blood.

Moments upon moments passed, as I watched Kan battle the spirits. One woman brought him a broth he had demanded, and I held the bowl to my dying wife's lips for her to take tiny sips. Then another woman positioned a god-pot at each corner of the mat, and Kan lit a handful of incense in each of them, chanting a prayer for mercy. He anointed Ahpo Hel with ashes from the pots, and we alternated our prayers with sips of the powerful broth, throughout the night, until K'in finally rose triumphant from the Underworld. As the soft light of dawn fell across her ashen face, Ahpo Hel slowly opened her eyes. Her dry lips parted and a faint voice asked for her baby. In a dark corner of the room, a young woman had been nursing and cradling the newborn, throughout our long vigil of prayers and offerings. I'd forgotten that the child even existed. Now, as I watched her bring him to his mother, I wondered how I could ever love him. How could I ever forget the price he had almost cost to exist? Kan brought me the cloth with the child's spirit chord, to be buried in Te'nab with my ancestors. I decided instead, to bury it under the floor of this house.

"He is the child of Chac-Xib-Chac, and his spirit chord will be buried in the temple of the one he was born to serve."

Reassured that Ahpo Hel would live, I turned my attention to the directives Kahwil had given me the night before. I explained to my administrators, who had kept the night-long vigil just outside our house, that it was the wish of Kahwil to build four great temples before beginning his temple. "Kahwil's temple must hold the light of K'in, the breath of Ik and the strength of the four Chacs," I told them.

We sat on woven mats in the courtyard, in the delicate morning light, and pondered these mandates. All at once, I felt a flash of inspiration. The temples I had seen in Tikal, and other places, had small, tiny rooms, because their heavy roofs required such thick walls to support them. These roofs had been assembled in much the same way as one would construct a palm thatch roof. Starting at the uppermost edge of two opposing walls, each successive layer of stones was gradually widened to extend towards the center, until the two sides met at a peak on the inside. But unlike a thatch roof, the stones rose vertically on the exterior. The result was a roof composed of massive, opposing, triangular sections, entirely supported by the walls from which they rose. The burden those walls carried was even further increased by the weight of a latticed wall that rose from the center of the structure, and forming the framework for a large stucco display.

"What if we lightened the roof by using a central wall to distribute its weight?" I proposed. In essence there would be four, smaller, triangular, stone lengths, instead of the bulkier two.

As my companions considered my suggestion, something remarkable began to happen. It was if the expression of this one new idea gave birth to a whole family of concepts. Throughout the morning the men around me expounded on other possibilities, ideas that each of them may have considered in the past but never expressed before now. Their imaginations, released like birds who'd been caged, offered solutions so simple, yet brilliant, that I was certain the gods themselves sat in our midst, whispering into our ears. Each new suggestion nurtured the next until something so extraordinary had been designed, that I was certain we had transgressed into the realm of the Hunab Ku—the Origin; the Creator; the One-Being.

So it was that we planned the Temple of Chac-Xib-Chac, with a roof that was lightened not only by redistributing its weight, but by further hollowing its thickness with tri-lobed hollows cut into the sections. With less weight to support, the front wall could be reduced to a group of piers, straddled with stone lintels, so that the light of K'in could easily fill the interior. Openings could be left in the walls in the "T" shape of Ik, so that his breath could cool and ventilate the front and rear rooms.

We had come incredibly close to realizing the specifications of Kahwil, and this was only the first temple. By the time K'in had reached directly above us, Kayam, the scribe, had filled an entire bark book with drawings of our ideas, and old Iguana, the stone mason, had already tallied the number of men that would be required to begin working the next day. All that remained now was to see if it would work—if such a temple would have the strength of the four Chacs!

"I understand now why Kahwil wants his temple to be my last project. There is indeed much to learn," I sighed as I sipped from the gourd of cool spring water a young girl offered to each of us. I looked about me at the men who sat in the hot courtyard and realized that Kahwil had brought me the brightest and most talented people in the world. The excitement I felt when our ideas were bursting forth was as close to rapture as I would ever know. From the expressions on their faces, it was clear that my companions shared my excitement. We were about to create something more beautiful than any god had ever seen. The pleasure it would bring to our divine observers would certainly assure Place of Jaguar-Sun many years of good fortune.

"Bol will be returning from Split-Sky with Little Jaguar any day now," I told the men around me. "I want you to include him in every step of the planning and constructing of this temple. It is more important that you include him than even myself." I noticed that the men seemed pleased by this directive. Even though Little Jaguar had not quite reached his tenth year, already he had gained the respect and admiration of the people of Jaguar-Sun. They truly believed that the heir apparent was the embodiment of Kahwil. And there was no denying that Kahwil had been most generous to them since the day I'd presented Little Jaguar to them. But many of the adults who were around me had also come to respect my first-born son because he had already shown the wisdom and dignity that commanded it. Beyond that, they enjoyed his company, and he in turn knew how to charm them.

Work began on the new temple almost immediately. I had arranged for Ahpo Hel and her infant to live with the old wife of Bol, until the merchant returned with my son. He had taken Little Jaguar with him to Place of Split-Sky, at my insistence, since it was important that the boy observe first-hand the ways of the True People in other localities.

The night that followed the birth of my second son, I lay awake for a long time, contemplating my feelings towards Ahpo Hel. Ever since Little Jaguar had replaced the pih of Bolom Tzacab with that of Kahwil, I had regarded my wife with a measure of distrust. But this feeling had been tempered with the realization that I was beholden to her for bringing the powerful Kahwil to Place of Jaguar-Sun. Still, my pride had been seriously hurt in the manner with which she had maneuvered to use the presentation of my son as the means to impose Kahwil on my lineage.

After reviewing the good fortune Kahwil had bestowed on us, I had to ask myself if I would have ever acknowledged the power of this new god, or permitted the virtual abandonment of Bolom Tzacab, if my wife hadn't arranged for Little Jaguar to devastate me in the manner in which she did. Had it been necessary to use my son, whom I loved more dearly than anyone, to shatter my belief in the god of my lineage? Had my ever-diplomatic wife tried prior to that terrible day, in less painful ways, to enlighten me to the failings of the god I'd been chosen to nurture and protect? Had I refused to listen? These are the questions that had plagued me for the past three years—the questions I couldn't answer—the questions that had forced me to keep the bright, gentle woman I had brought from Tikal, at a cold and careful distance.

Strangely enough, I never allowed the events of that experience to change my feelings towards my son. It wasn't the memory of watching with horror as Little Jaguar enshrined the pih of Kahwil that haunted me, but the memory of the humiliation I endured that day, as I watched his mother through the clouds of incense, standing outside Te'nab.

But when it seemed that Ahpo Hel was about to die, the resentment that had festered so long within me, suddenly seemed foolish. Ahpo Hel was no longer the protector of Kahwil. It had been to me that Kahwil had revealed himself, and I was the Ahow of Te'nab, to whom Kahwil had spoken many times since then. I stood in the doorway of my hut and stared into the darkness, in the direction of the maize fields where I knew rows of bent dry stalks still stood, minus their valuable harvest, and thought, "Had not Ahpo Hel been used by the gods as much as I? Hadn't she risked everything when she instructed Little Jaguar to replace Bolom Tzacab? I thought about the expression on her face when I had watched her through the smoky screen that separated us that day, and for the first time I understood what her eyes were trying to tell me. She knew how much I'd been hurt, but hers had not been a decision that allowed for any consideration of the pride or dignity of one man—even her husband—even the Holy Bacab.

Ahpo Hel's priorities had been determined by the order of the events that sanctioned her. She was first the protector of Kahwil; second the Mother of the Jaguar-Sun dynasty; and only then, the companion of Hanab Pacal. Was this the test of pride that Kahwil had warned me about? I whispered a prayer of thanks to Kahwil for teaching me this lesson without taking my beloved wife away forever.

Early the next morning I hurried to Bol's thatched hut to check on the well-being of my wife and newborn son. It took me a few moments to adjust to the lack of light, as I ducked into the modest house. While I could easily see through the back doorway, to the rear yard, where Nuk, Bol's wrinkled old wife, bent over her grinding stone, inside all was blackness. "Hel?" I whispered, using only my wife's childhood name and straining to see where she was in the room.

"She sleeps," I heard Kan whisper in a strained voice and I faintly made out his form squatting on the floor not far from me. As I gradually became accustomed to the darkness, I could see the many gourds and pots hanging from the roof poles above me, and off in the far end of the room the pile of mats and blankets where my wife and child were sleeping. I squatted beside Kan and tried to see his face.

"Why do you sit here in the center of the room?" I asked trying to ascertain the meaning of his expression, which I could just barely see. "What's wrong, my friend?" I questioned, unable to determine if I was seeing fear or anguish.

But Kan bent forward to his knees and groaned without answering. I reached out to him and could feel the heat of his body before my hand even touched him. "You're filled with fire!" I gasped. Again Kan groaned, as he lowered his shoulders to the floor, curling his body even tighter into a ball. It was apparent that Kan was seriously ill.

I should have expected this—he had done the work of a shaman, but he didn't know the ways that a shaman protects himself from the spirits that he releases from his patient. I'd been so wrapped up in my thoughts about Ahpo Hel and my ideas for the temple of Chac-Xib-Chac, that I'd completely forgotten about Kan. And now, as I cradled his trembling body in my arms, I realized that I could lose him just as I'd almost lost Ahpo Hel.

Was this some scheme that the gods had planned, to make me realize that I'd become so consumed with myself that I'd forgotten about those that I loved? Suddenly I thought about Little Jaguar, who should have returned from Place of Split-Sky by now. Had the gods put him in jeopardy as well? Was everyone I loved at risk? I struggled to carry my friend out of the dark hut to the sunlit plaza. But he was far heavier than I could manage, especially with his burning body curled into a tight, trembling ball.

Near panic, I called to several young men who were gathered around my stone house that was already being covered with rubble to form the pyramid base of the new temple.

"Help me carry the Sahal to Te'nab!" I commanded. They quickly brought a litter and I tried to place my sick friend on it. But Kan had wrapped his arms tightly about my shoulders and looked at me now with terror in his eyes. "Do not leave me, My Lord," he pleaded. I sat on the litter holding Kan in my arms like a child and commanded the four young laborers to carry us to Te'nab.

With Yellow-Macaw two years in the Underworld, and Ahpo Hel precariously clinging to life, I alone remained to serve as healer to my people. While my father had begun the training of several young priests, none had completed the rigorous initiation of the shaman— none were qualified to heal my dearest friend. As Holy Bacab, I was the Shaman of Shamans, yet, while I had learned the ways of the shaman as a boy, I had resisted assuming the role of healer, even the day before, for my own wife.

The regimen a healer was required to follow to insure that the angry spirits he released from his patient would not enter his own body, was in itself exhausting. A true healer, as my father, Yellow-Macaw, had been, led a life of strict discipline, void of all pleasures and comfort. This was not the life I wished to lead. It was enough that I spoke with Kahwil and brought his blessing on my people with my blood sacrifices, I had rationalized. I would leave the rigors of the healer to someone else. But today there was no one except myself who could save Kan.

When we arrived at the mouth of Te'nab I ordered the laborers to bring me cushions and blankets, incense and a fat, lively curassow. I reassured Kan that I would soon rid him of the spirits that tore at his insides, and he released his terrified grip and allowed me to lower him to rest on the litter. Not waiting for the young men to return, I began the litany of chants that implored the ancestors to release Kan from the grip of the evil ones. It was a long, repetitive prayer that summoned the spirits of each of the known ancestors of the Jaguar-Sun dynasty and was repeated in each of the four directions of the world. While my lips spoke the prescribed prayers, my mind wandered to thoughts about Kan.

It was suspected that Kan was born of divine blood. His mother had reportedly presented him as an infant, in offering to Turtle-Maize, during his accession ceremony. But the details of his parentage were mired in rumors and the gossip of old women. There were many reasons why a peasant mother would give her child to the Holy Bacab. Perhaps she already had too many mouths to feed, or perhaps no man would acknowledge the baby as his child. Sometimes, when a family was beset with terrible problems they would offer the gods a child in the hope of gaining his blessings.

But the story that had been told of Kan's origin was that during an eclipse of the moon, a Lord of the Night had disguised himself as the husband of a young woman, and had impregnated her. Convinced that the child would bring her only misfortune, the young woman had left the newborn in a basket, with the many other offerings that had been left on the steps of the small temple where Turtle-Maize was anointed Holy Bacab. That was a time, before the attack of Pomona, when the divine Jaguar-Sun household was blessed with many sons and daughters, aunts and uncles and cousins.

The infant had been gathered up, with all the other gifts, and the women of the household fed and cared for him, and raised him, not as a son, but as one who had been designated to live his life in servitude to the living gods. Since it was the women who undertook the training of this young slave, Kan learned to perform the tasks that were the responsibilities of the women. He collected firewood, and ground maize, and spun cotton fibers into thread. No one seemed to mind when the women entertained themselves by dressing the young boy in their huipils and laughing at the way he mimicked their feminine mannerisms.

Kan never learned the ways of men. He never had a Hetzmek Ceremony, where he would have been given a name and a purpose to his life. He never completed the initiation rites of manhood, that were required before he could take a wife. When I was seven years old and hiding in the cave of Toctan, Resplendent Egret had assigned Kan the duty of bringing me food and fresh cloth. She knew that the boy's presence or absence was so insignificant, that the warriors who besieged Jaguar-Sun would never notice when he disappeared into the jungle each morning and slipped back into the royal compound under the cover of darkness.

Back then, young Kan brought me more than sustenance each day. For two years he was my only human contact. He would share with me the gossip of the village women, whom he mingled with in the market, and recount the horrors at the royal household, where the surviving women of the Jaguar-Sun dynasty were left to the merciless whims of the barbaric savages of Pomona. Somehow he had scavenged brushes and bark-paper, and together we would struggle each day to copy the characters and symbols we saw in the sacred books of my lineage, that had been hidden in my cave. I didn't mind that Kan dressed and acted like a girl. I still was young enough to miss the nurturing of my mother and Kan's gentle friendship was a welcome substitute.

When it was finally safe for me to return to Jaguar-Sun, my mother had made it clear that it was necessary that I put my childhood behind me. The survival of my people depended upon the appointment of a male heir. I remember thinking how my mother had grown hard and cold during those terrible years, while I'd enjoyed the safety and solitude of Toctan, and the warmth of my friendship with Kan.

The warriors had not harmed the strange woman who had the face and hands of a beast, and the medicine man who was her husband. My father, Yellow-Macaw, had survived the slaughter of the lineage males because he was of the Sky-Snake clan and the warriors were wary of the powerful medicine that those of his lineage where said to command. But my parents had been virtual prisoners in their own home during those years, guarded at all times, and helpless in preventing the suffering and abuse of their people. Only the secret knowledge that their son, the only survivor of the divine lineage, was alive and safe, had given Resplendent Egret and Yellow-Macaw the strength to endure the nightmares they witnessed during those horrible years.

The end to their suffering came, not from their prayers to Bolom Tzacab, but from my father's exceptional talent as a daykeeper. Yellow-Macaw had studied the ancient books and listened to the movement of his blood and carefully counted his piles of seeds and crystals. He had divined the coming of the day when just as K'in rose above the eastern horizon, the Lord of the Night would return and devour him. My father secretly sent word to the last remnants of the Jaguar-Sun warriors, that when the jaws of Xibalba reached out and reclaimed K'in, and Bolom Tzacab and Chac-Xib-Chac appeared in the blackened morning sky, that they should also reclaim the land of their ancestors from the barbarians of Pomona.

I'd often repeated the story to Little Jaguar and the young men training to be warriors, of the day when I watched the sun disappear, as I sat outside my mountain cave—the day when the brave holcan of Jaguar-Sun stormed the royal residential compound and slaughtered our Pomona captors who stood by dazed and terrified by the sudden death of the sun. But K'in had not really died. Even as the last brutal savage was being taken captive, the god of light and warmth reappeared. The eclipse my father had foreseen, had served to restore Place of Jaguar-Sun to my people.

Now, as I chanted the prayers for Kan's recovery, I remembered the expression of delight he wore, the day he raced to Toctan to tell me Place of Jaguar-Sun was freed from the control of Pomona. Had he realized then, that we would never again share the innocent intimacy of our many days together, perhaps he wouldn't have been so jubilant. But then, considering Kan's nature—how he never expected anything in return for all that he gave—perhaps he would have been happy just the same.

I didn't realize the uniqueness of his intellect at the time, anymore than I appreciated the depth of his devotion to me. Kan had no trouble learning to read the symbols and sound-signs recorded in the sacred manuscripts. But, as a boy, I had assumed that everyone possessed these abilities. Only now, was I certain that Kan's exceptional abilities were an indication of his royal parentage.

We were at the point of the healing ritual where I would demand that my ancestors reveal the source of the sickness that was afflicting my patient. Motioning to the men who gathered around me to position Kan on the pillows and blankets, so that he was comfortable, I placed two god-pots at his head and two at his feet, and dropped a handful of copál into each. The resinous incense hissed as it fell on the hot coals inside each pot and the sweet fragrance carried my prayer up to the gods. Quickly I grabbed the large, squawking fowl from the farmer who had brought it, and, in one swift twist, snapped its neck, as I held it over Kan's stomach where the angry spirit was residing. Chanting a command to the evil spirit, to leave Kan's bowels and enter the curassow, I tore the head from the bird and let its blood drip into each of the god pots. As the steamy, red life-force of my sacrifice fell into the god-pots, I listened carefully for the voices of my ancestors.

Kan was visibly more comfortable now, his eyes open wide, in anticipation of the message I was about to reveal. The men and women who had gathered around us, fell to their knees in anticipation of the arrival of the ancestors. I listened for the voice of the spirits, as I'd never listened before. It seemed that I could hear every sound in the world, even the sound of my own heart beating, and my own blood running through my body, like a river. I listened and waited for what seemed like all of time. And then suddenly I was no longer Hanab Pacal.

The spirit was not speaking to me, but through me! I knew that my voice was speaking, but I was unable to hear it's sound. My ears were filled with only the rushing of my blood; the beating of my heart. I was trapped within my heart, while the gods used me to proclaim their wishes. So this is what it feels like to be chosen as the voice of the gods, I thought to myself. But I was lost in the warm, pulsating darkness of my own body. I'd always believed that when a Holy Bacab conjured a god, it would be the most exhilarating experience of his life. But instead, I was trapped within a terrifying sensation of absolute, helpless possession, in a state where time and place did not exist, and I wasn't certain if they ever would again.

Gradually my senses began to return. I could see the crowd of kneeling people before me, many with their hands covering their faces. Those few faces that I could see, were staring in terror. Kan also was kneeling before me, his face press against my feet, his arms wrapped around my ankles. I stood in silence for a long while, uncertain what had happened, but careful not to reveal my ignorance.

Finally, at a loss for what else to do, I reached down to Kan and directed him to stand before me. He was no longer feverish and his body seem strong and without pain, as he rose before me. But his eyes would not meet mine, and his gaze remained fixed on his feet.

"Go home now," I commanded our dumbfounded audience, anxious to be alone with Kan, so that he could reveal what had transpired in my "absence".

"Go Home!" I commanded again, more insistently. "And speak to no one of what you have seen." I knew I might as well have commanded them to stop breathing, as to expect them to return to their homes and keep the day's happenings a secret. Hesitantly the crowd shuffled away, until only Kan and I were left standing in the long shadows of the afternoon.

"My friend," I said in a deliberate, unemotional tone, careful not to disclose the terror I felt. "I must know what has happened? Did I conjure a god?"

Kan looked up at me in surprise and then narrowed his eyes, apparently confused by my ignorance. "It was One-Death, the Lord of the Night," he whispered meekly, but looking me straight in the eyes so that I would know he spoke the truth.

"One-Death!, One-Death?" I repeated. "But a Lord of the Night never speaks through the Holy Bacab!" I was horrified to think that I'd been the oracle of one of the spirits of the Underworld. It was the role of a Holy Bacab to deliver the wishes of the gods to their people. Never before had I heard of a Holy Bacab being used by the fiends of death and disease.

"What did he say?" I cried, not sure I wanted to know.

Kan fell to his knees weeping, unable to respond. I pulled him back up by his shoulders and held my face directly in front of his. "What did he say!" I roared.

Kan tried to gulp back his tears and shook his head. But when he opened his mouth, no sound would come out. I shook him violently, suddenly impatient with such an obvious display of weakness in a man. "Tell me what he said!" I commanded, spitting the words in his face.

My abusive treatment evoked a sudden, defiant bravado in Kan. A look of carefully contained fury filled his eyes, and his voice resonated loud and masculine as he replied. "He said that I have displeased the Lords of Xibalba, by stealing the daughter of Ixtab from them. He said that I am condemned to know only grief and misery for the rest of my life, my Lord, for having saved this woman's life— this woman who has taken from me the affections of the one I love most."

I knew, as I faced the frightened and angry face of my friend, that Kan would never be able to disassociate the voice of the demon who had spoken through me, with Hanab Pacal. I, myself, wondered if in some way I was angry with Kan for saving the life of my wife—if somehow, it was I, who had placed this curse on the only person who had never hurt me. It was impossible! I was not some monster that rewarded love with punishment!

"It's clear that the Lords of Xibalba fear you, Kan," I explained. "You have shown great power as a healer, to snatch such a valuable prize from them. Surely you can understand how this would anger them. But grief and misery are not diseases that the Lords of the Night can inflict on you—they are the fruits of anger and fear.

"You have been chosen to be a shaman, my friend. It is well known that when a man or woman is chosen by the ancients, to nurture and heal the bodies and spirits of the true peoples, that they can no more escape that responsibility than an Ahow can ignore the calling to nurture and protect the pih of the gods. You must begin at once the training and initiation of a shaman. Kan, you were not meant to be a slave. The mother who gave you to Turtle-Maize acted on the wishes of the gods. She must have known, as I know now, that you were destined to play a great role in Place of Jaguar-Sun.

"Come with me, I commend your education into the hands of the woman you have saved. No one is better prepared to teach you the ways of the shaman, than Lady Ahpo Hel. Follow the path the ancient ones have set before you. The blessings of the gods of Jaguar-Sun will protect you from the curse of the Lords of the Night."

# Yellow Knot

I didn't have to wait long before my fears for the safety of Little Jaguar were allayed. The morning after I channeled the Lord of Death, there was an uncommon commotion in the main courtyard. I peered into the heavy mist that enshrouded Jaguar-Sun each dawn, to see the shadowy figures of old Bol and Little Jaguar striding regally towards me. As soon as my son realized that it was his father, standing at the opposite end of the courtyard, he broke into a spirited run, and called out to me in the manner of any young boy who'd been away from his family for many moons.

I caught him in my arms and embraced him, feeling a tremendous weight lifted from my mind as I held him close, and realized that he was safe and healthy. It was not until I held him at arms length, to at long last savor that bright sparkle of energy that his eyes and smile always projected, that I realized how he had grown in the time he'd been away. I'd bid farewell to an enthusiastic, but unsure child, six moons ago. Now, a young man stood before me—self-assured, spirited and a good hand taller! Though we exchanged no words, I signified my approval of the metamorphoses with a glowing nod. He understood, and smiled with his eyes, but not his lips. I thought to myself with pride, he already possesses the control and stature of a great leader.

"Your mother awaits word of your return," I said and pointed to Bol's house. Little Jaguar turned to look at our stone house at the opposite end of the courtyard, already half-buried in rubble. He turned to me with a look of puzzlement, but it was Bol who voiced the question, "What's happened to your house, My Lord?"

"It is no longer my house. It's the house of Chac-Xib-Chac," I replied, offering no more explanation. I again pointed to Bol's hut and directed Little Jaguar to hurry to his mother. He strode quickly towards the humble home and I watched his lean, dark body move with the grace of a deer across the courtyard. Dressed only in a simple white cotton loin-cloth, and no ornamentation to mark his divine lineage, other than the white jade bead that held his forelock, there was still no mistaking his noble lineage.

Bol, realizing that I was admiring the boy, said reverently, "I am humbled to have been in his company, My Lord. It is surely questionable who was the teacher on this journey."

I acknowledged his compliment with only my silence, as I proudly watched my son disappear into Bol's hut. "I will go to Te'nab and thank Kahwil for the safe return of Little Jaguar," I whispered, and headed toward the ancestral cave, barefooted and dressed in only my loin-cloth. Bol hurried off to his hut to greet his wife. I was sure that Nuk would tell both Bol and Little Jaguar about the difficult birth of Eleven-Ahow and how Kan had saved Ahpo Hel. No doubt even Nuk had heard about the curse One-Death had pronounced, through my own lips, onto Kan. As I walked through the misty forest, I wondered what Little Jaguar would think when he heard that his father had conjured a Lord of the Night, instead of a god. I wondered too, what Kahwil would have to say about it, this morning.

The entrance to Te'nab was completely concealed by a dense fog, and I was almost face to face with one of the warriors stationed at the cave, before I saw him. He must have heard my approach and, unable to distinguish who I was, he grabbed me by the hair, and forced me to my knees.

"You dare to humiliate the Holy Bacab!" I roared as I sprang to my feet, the moment I felt his grip loosen. The warrior fell to his knees, trembling as I grabbed his spear and held it to the back of his neck, poised to sever his spine in one powerful thrust. For the first time since I had tied on the headband of Bolom Tzacab, I experienced an incredible rush of power, as I realized that I could easily end the life of the man who cowered at my feet. There would be no repercussions, no one to question the wisdom or reason for my action. I turned to see the other warrior watching me, expecting that his companion was about to die, and making no indication in his defense.

Insight comes at the most unexpected times. A man can spend his whole life in study and contemplation of the great mysteries of the ancestors, and never really comprehend what he thinks he's learned, even though he can recite it perfectly. How many times had I studied the directive, that restraint truly harnesses power? But not until that moment of hesitation, before I would have slain an insignificant man, who had accidentally provoked my anger, did I comprehend, that true power is expressed when one does not succumb to the reflexes of a wild animal.

"The Holy Bacab gives you your life," I declared, as I pulled the young man to his feet by his hair, and handed him back his spear. "You will never forget this, and the obligation to me that my generosity has cost you." The young brave stood bent in humility before me, his right hand clasped to his left shoulder, his eyes reverently downcast. I noticed a jagged scar, or tattoo, running along the side of his face, from his forehead to his chin. "Lighting-Bolt," I dubbed him, "I give you your life, and your reason to live, to protect Hanab Pacal."

I strode past the grateful warrior into Te'nab. Grabbing a torch from it's notch I stopped at the front altar to revere the pih of Kahwil. As often happened, a strong wind, the breath of Ik, was blowing from the narrow tunnel behind the altar, causing the flame of my torch to dance towards me menacingly. I lit incense in the god pots at each corner of the altar, positioned my torch in a crevice in the front of the altar and began my ritual prayer to Kahwil in gratitude for the safe return of Little Jaguar.

Chanting the same words of thanksgiving that had been sung by my ancestors through the many generations of Jaguar-Sun, I moved slowly in a rhythmical dance of celebration. My footwork was slightly modified from traditional dance to accommodate my clubbed foot. Slowly rising on the toes of my left foot, but being unable to lower my weight onto my right heel, I compensated, by lowering my right hip. With elbows bent to bring my forearms up to my chest, and touching each thumb to my second smallest finger, I rotated my hands so that the palms faced inward and outward to the smooth cadence of words. The breath of Ik seemed to blow from the cave in time with my movements, so that the torch also danced to the rhythm of my song. As I repeated the joyful words of gratitude, I felt my body growing lighter. It was a sensation that was becoming familiar to me, that moment of complete release of control, just before Kahwil would show himself to me. What I didn't realize, at the time, was how critical that willingness to relinquish control was, to my ability to produce the vision. There was no need to analyze how I was able to summon the god at will, it happened easily and naturally—the only way it can happen, I was to learn one day.

Kahwil showed himself to me this time, as a magical snake, with bands of brilliant colors and a feathered headdress, dancing in the flame of my torch, hissing in his usual eerie way.

"You have acted wisely with your power, Shield of Jaguar-Sun," he wheezed though his smoky breath. "Now I will share with you a magical secret that you must teach to the first-born, who returns to you today. Watch and listen and learn well, for this is the magic that makes what we see beautiful, what we hear, melodious, what we feel harmonious…" the voice continued. His shape changed within the flame, to that of a flat rectangle, as he explained that everything that we see, hear and feel is known to us by the way it relates to everything else we see, hear and feel. The rectangle grew larger and smaller, but retained it's proportions. As was usually the case when Kahwil explained something to me, there was no need for him to go into detail about what he was teaching; a few words and I seemed to comprehend the whole of the lesson. I began to think about the temple I would someday build for Kahwil. Everything about it would have to be in harmony, not only with its surroundings, but with itself.

I felt compelled to look at the way I was holding my hand. Kahwil was saying, "See how the four are divided by the thumb. There is one finger and one half finger on one side, and one half finger plus two fingers on the other. Keep this relationship in all things and you will achieve perfection."

Suddenly there was a great gust of wind from the tunnel, and the flame of my torch was devoured by Ik, along with my vision of Kahwil. I bowed in reverence, then slowly left the cave. This time Kahwil had given me a tangible way to remember his lesson—it was as close as my own hand.

Too busy considering the significance of the revelation Kahwil had shared with me, I barely noticed the warriors at the entrance as I left Te'nab. I strode back to the residential compound as quickly as I could, and rushed to Bol's hut. Little Jaguar was sitting between Kan and Bol, on mats in the patio, enjoying the morning warmth of K'in on their faces. My son was smoking a cigar and conversing with his two companions, as if he was already a man. His features were those of a man. The large nose and drooping lower lip of his mother's people, gave him the appearance of being much older than his ten years, although looking somewhat awkward on the face of a boy. But when Little Jaguar looked up and smiled, to acknowledge my appearance, the vitality and intelligence that showed in his expression made him appear handsome enough.

Bol and Kan bowed to greet me. "Kan has been telling me about his calling to be a shaman," Bol stated in a scratchy but clear voice. Bol had more wrinkles on his face than anyone I'd ever seen.

Though he still walked straight and tall, and moved with the agility of a younger man, Bol was the oldest man living in Place of Jaguar-Sun. Even so, his mind remained sharp and his cunning was unmatched.

"When the gods call you, there's no choice but to heed their beckoning," the old merchant continued. "When I heard the voice of Ek Chuah, the god of the traveler, I was a young man; just married, with a little milpa and dreams of a family. But Ek Chuah commanded me to be a wanderer; to travel to strange places where my goods may not be wanted, where my efforts to negotiate may not find favor. Always alone, always uncertain where I would find food and haven for the night—this was not the life I wanted."

Bol sighed a long wistful sigh. "But it was the life chosen for me by the gods. Like you, Kan, I became very ill. The daykeeper, Turtle-Sky, studied his seeds and told me that I'd been chosen to be a merchant. What was I to do? I knew nothing of the ways of the merchant, only that he must never accumulate wealth for himself and must act in the manner of an ambassador, serving the gods by bargaining for the goods that those with the blood of the ancestors require.

"I said good-bye to poor Nuk and set out for Tortuguero," Bol recalled. I knew that we were about to enjoy one of his memorable tales and joined the men on the mat, lighting a cigar and facing the sun.

"That was my first endeavor, and perhaps my greatest success," Bol continued. "The grandmother of Hanab Pacal, Divine Lady Maize-Wind, ruled Jaguar-Sun at the time. Never before had a woman been Holy Bacab, that I know of. She was a magnificent woman, both beautiful and persuasive—in a very different way than her daughter, Resplendent Egret, would be. And she was determined to keep the territories of Jaguar-Sun in line. Tortuguero had not sent tribute in all the ten years that her brother, Snake-Jaguar, had ruled. I'd heard stories that Snake-Jaguar had been of a more effeminate nature—that he never took a wife, nor produced an heir—so he never commanded much respect. All of our colonies apparently ignored their obligations to us during his reign.

"Anyway, Divine Lady Maize-Wind sent me off to Tortuguero, with the directive to return with ten years of tribute. Now, Tortuguero doesn't have anything special to offer, except for their people. People! Great Ik, they have plenty of them! They're a squabbling lot. Can't seem to agree among themselves about anything. Which is probably why they need the Holy Bacab of Jaguar-Sun to run their city for them. I'm sure the gods were as exasperated with them as My Lady was. But the gods have blessed that wild, prolific clan with the most beautiful, enticing women that ever walked the earth. I don't know if their incredible fertility has to do with the irresistible beauty of their women, but I've never seen so many children in every family!

"So it was children that I brought back from Tortuguero as tribute. Beautiful children, and young men and women who would have been children ten years earlier, when they should have been contributed to Jaguar-Sun. Ooooh, that was when I cried out to Ek Chuah for mercy! Coming back to Place of Jaguar-Sun with all those children, crying for their mothers; and young braves who I'd forced to leave their homes and friends, to serve the lords of Jaguar-Sun; and beautiful, young woman, who wept endlessly in dread of the husbands that awaited them here — that was a journey I would never want to make again!

"But Ek Chuah has rewarded me abundantly for following his command. I've served four Holy Bacab of Jaguar-Sun in my long lifetime." Bol sighed as his wife came to sit beside him, rubbing her back to his, like a playful, young ocelot. "I have lived to be an old man, and I have seen most of the world. And each time I return, no matter how long I've been away, my wife brings me tortilla and balché, and we behave like two young newlyweds!"

We all laughed as Bol returned his wife's affections with a nuzzle, and Nuk giggled like a young girl. "So you see, Kan, you must follow the directive of the gods, no matter how much One-Death might squeal about it. His power is no match for the gods who summon you to serve them."

Watching Bol and his wife, made me long for the few times that Ahpo Hel and I had enjoyed the freedom to enjoy each other. Our lives had become so defined by tradition and ritual, that the opportunities for spontaneous affection had almost ceased to be. My wife would live in Nuk's house until her bleeding stopped. Not until the Hetzmek ceremony of our new son, would we again live under the same roof. But I would let blood during the Hetzmek ritual. Needless to say, it would be many days after that sacrifice, before I would be capable of performing as a husband.

But it was something more than the actual sexual encounter that I sometimes longed for—it was the playful affection that I watched the old couple sharing. Ever since I'd returned from Tikal, my life had been subjected to constant scrutiny. Everything I said or did was seen as an act that would please or displease the gods. And every misfortune or calamity to befall the people of Jaguar-Sun, was ascribed to my shortcomings as the one who must nourish the gods. There was no place for lighthearted foolishness in my life—the gods had chosen me for the most difficult of roles. I envied Bol and Kan— their callings still permitted them a robust laugh; an occasional lapse of duty; even a failure now and then. Who would suffer for their weakness, except they themselves?

As I walked into Bol's hut to visit my wife, I felt as if I was carry-ing the weight of an entire temple of stones on my back. Ahpo Hel was lying on her side, her head propped up with her hand, the baby lying beside her, nursing. I squatted down on the floor beside her and touched the child's cheek. The v-shaped head-boards that would mold a pleasing slope to his forehead, were held firmly in place with cotton wrapping. Otherwise, the baby was unclad and unadorned. He could have been the child of any common woman, I thought. But the child of a common woman is not taught, from their first breath, that they are born to serve the gods; that the survival of their people rests with them. Already Little Jaguar had the bearing of one who is divine, one who would never know what it meant to be a child.

As usual, Ahpo Hel seemed to sense my thoughts. "Little Jaguar has come home a man," she whispered proudly. I nodded. "I know that he hasn't yet undergone the rites of manhood, but still he seems too grown now to stay with me, during my time of confinement. Don't you think that he should sleep in your hut?" she suggested.

The idea brightened my spirits immediately. "Of course, the com-pany of my son would be wonderful!" I exclaimed.

My wife smiled with satisfaction. "I know how lonely you've been," she said. "No one else will ever understand, as I do, how iso-lated power and responsibility can make a man feel. I think you've missed your son more than you admit. He is exceptional, isn't he?" she whispered.

"He'll be the most powerful Holy Bacab there ever was," I replied quietly, noticing that the infant had fallen asleep. "I only wish that I could be alive to witness it," I added, knowing that Little Jaguar would not rule until I was enduring the trials of Xibalba.

"And what of this one, my wise and perceptive wife? What awaits the second son of the Holy Bacab?" I asked.

Ahpo Hel's expression suddenly turned chagrin. "Kan tells me that Bolom Tzacab showed his spirit for the first time when he was born. And Kahwil has told you that he is born to serve Chac-Xib-Chac. I fear that this child is chosen to be a warrior. When I am well, I'll count the seeds, and determine for certain his calling. But with the stars that greeted his arrival, his destiny seems certain."

I tried to imagine the helpless creature, who lay sleeping between us, as a grown man, dressed in the cotton armor tunic of the warrior, dancing with the shield and sword, wearing the headdress of Chac-Xib-Chac. I remembered tales of the ancestor brothers of Tikal, one a divine ruler and the other a fearsome warrior. Together they extended the reign of Tikal to include many, many colonies, bringing wealth and prosperity to the city.

"Perhaps one day this child will avenge our siege by Pomona?" I speculated.

"Would it not be enough that he protected the people of Jaguar-Sun from ever again suffering such humiliation and destruction?" Ahpo Hel responded. "What purpose would it serve to spill the blood of our son in revenge? We enjoy great prosperity and peace now. Our few territories pay tribute eagerly, in exchange for our divine intercessions to the gods in their behalf. And they too have enjoyed the wealth and happiness that peace brings."

"Sometimes, because of your wisdom, I forget that you are only a woman," I said lightly. "But when you speak like this I know that it is the daughter of Ixtab, and not the son, who advises me. If the son of the Holy Bacab is born a warrior, do you think he will be like that pathetic creature who stands guard at the mouth of Te'nab? Never! He will be a fierce holcan; not one to be satisfied with merely keeping watch! Chac-Xib-Chac will see to that. If this child was called to serve the god of war, then the days of peace are not destined to last forever in Jaguar-Sun. That I can promise you."

The expression of my wife's face clearly told me that she found my words unpleasant. But I did not attempt to soften them. If her divination of the seeds confirmed that our second son was destined to be a warrior, then she would be better off resigning herself to his fate, than resisting it. There was no arguing with the gods about destiny — of that I was certain. Thinking about destiny, I remembered Kan's calling to be a shaman.

"You've heard about the curse of One-Death?" I asked my wife.

Ahpo Hel nodded seriously. "Nuk has told me that Kan has been called to be a shaman. Do you wish me to teach him?"

"I know of no one better qualified," I replied. "He has shown himself to have a great gift. And I know, from our childhood together, that he has the intellect to learn the hundreds of chants, and the meanings of each quiver of the blood and each counting of the seeds. But do you think he has the fortitude to endure the initiation?

Sometimes he can be so… like a bird that flits around without any discipline. Do you know what I mean?"

"What he lacks in self-discipline, he makes up for in loyalty," Ahpo Hel replied. If Kan believes that what he does, or doesn't do, will affect your opinion of him, then he will be able to endure the most difficult regime. You will never know anyone to love you more than Kan. Even my love pales, beside the devotion he has for you. Kan will become a fine shaman because he believes that it will bring him closer to you. He will gain your respect. For that he'll face the threats of One-Death and all the loathsome beasts of Xibalba. Tell him I'll begin his training as soon as my days of confinement are complete."

Ahpo Hel eased the child's mouth from her breast and lay back on her mat. I longed to touch her breasts, to put my lips to the moist nipple she'd left exposed. I sat watching her, with her eyes closed, breathing softly. I needed to hold her, but even more, I needed to be held by her. "Kan doesn't need to become a shaman to gain my respect," I whispered. "He has already given me the most precious gift I could possibly want — your life."

Without opening her eyes, Ahpo Hel responded, "Has he not earned the honor of speaking for this child at his Hetzmek?"

"A splendid idea! Yes, I'll tell him right away!" I bent to kiss her gently and hurried out to the courtyard. There was much to be discussed today, but I would be certain to speak first with Kan about his new title. He was already the Sahal of the Household and Protector of Little Jaguar, and now, he was to become the Godfather of the second son of the Holy Bacab.

~

The days passed quickly as we prepared for the ceremony that would give Eleven-Ahow his divine name, and proclaim his destiny. The base for the temple of Chac-Xib-Chac was almost complete and I decided to hold the ceremony on its summit. Ahpo Hel had repeated her counting of the seeds several times, and each time the results were the same — this child would be a warrior. Kan was delighted with his responsibility to speak for the child and had gone to great lengths to select the nine objects that would represent his future calling.

When it was four moons since the birth of Eleven-Ahow, we began the ritual of his Hetzmek. Before dawn, Ahpo Hel joined me in my hut and assisted me in donning the ceremonial attire that was required for a public bloodletting. I had already covered my body with the blue paint that signified the divinity of my blood. Now I wrapped a short jaguar skin kilt over my loincloth, and held it in place, while my wife encircled me with the heavy ancestral belt of symbolic, carved jade and bone ornaments. She fastened it at my groin with a jaguar-head clasp. Already weakened by three days of strict fasting, without so much as a sip of posol, the belt felt extremely heavy. But this was only the beginning.

With my wife's silent assistance, I put the ornate beaded cape over my shoulders, and draped the pendant of Bolom Tzacab on my chest. A long string of beads was attached to this necklace, at the nape of my neck, that hung down my back to counterbalance the weight of the impressive pectoral, while symbolizing the scales of the Sky Snake. Ahpo Hel attached the two ends of a chain made of carved bone, to the front of my belt. An effigy of Chac-Xib-Chac hung suspended from these chains, at the back of my legs. Next, I laced the harness across my torso, that supported a back-rack with the white egret headdress of my mother.

I could barely remain standing from the weight of the costume, when Ahpo Hel summoned Kan to assist her with my headdress. As with the rest of my attire, except for the back-rack, which changed with each ruler to the headdress of his predecessor, this costume was as old as the history of my people, and worn for only the most sacred of all events — public bloodletting and the conjuring of gods that usually accompanied such an act. This was to be the first time that I would let blood in a public ceremony, and it was the first time I wore this venerable attire.

Because it was constructed to last for many lifetimes, the base of the headpiece was made of wood, instead of woven reeds. This made it much heavier than most ritual headgear. Its decoration was an elaborate composite of symbolic ornaments, including the head of a heron with a fish in its mouth, one of the earliest symbols of our clan. The most important feature of the headdress, was the cluster of the five symbols of the Holy Bacab: the stingray spine, symbolic of the exclusive responsibility of the Holy Bacab to nurture the gods with his blood; the four-petal emblem of Mah Kina, symbol of the ruler's authority as equal to that of the sun; the crossed bands emblem, symbol of the heavens where the spirits of our ancestors live and guide us, and the maize plant, symbolic of the prosperity that can only be achieved if the gods are well served by the Holy Bacab.

I had to lean on Kan for support, while Ahpo Hel adjusted the headdress so that the upper jaw of the snake-mouth of Kahwil, protruded just above my forehead. She brought the side bands down over my ears, and fastened the strap under my chin. On the strap was the lower jaw of the snake, so that my face appeared to be emerging from the throat of Kahwil. This way, when, in trance, I spoke the words of the god, it would appear as if the god himself was speaking. Finally, Ahpo Hel adjusted the brilliant quetzal and macaw feathers that flared out from the top and sides of the headpiece, and secured my jade beaded cuffs on my wrists.

Ahpo Hel was wearing a simple woven skirt, that wrapped high enough to cover her breasts. A belt of narrow jade beads held it in place. Over her skirt was a delicate mesh of crisscrossing beads, and her cape was composed of a similar arrangement of beads over plain white cotton base, with a red feathered fringe. All of her hair was pulled up to the crown, revealing her clean-shaven Band of the Shaman. The white band that secured her hair was adorned with fresh red flowers.

I was feeling so weak, that my wife seemed to come in and out of focus, and I whispered to her that I was afraid I would be unable to walk up the long flight of steps, to the altar that was positioned where the temple to Chac-Xib-Chac would soon be built. Ahpo Hel reassured me that she would be beside me throughout the ceremony, and took a bottle-gourd from the table, where my attire had been laid out, and held it to my lips. It contained a bitter herbal mixture that was prepared especially for public bloodletting ceremonies. With just one sip, it strengthened me and yet filled my head with a buzzing, as if I'd just swallowed a hive of bees.

Kan helped my wife to guide me out to the courtyard, which was still enveloped in a heavy morning mist. I knew that the plaza before me was filled with people, but the herbal drink had begun to effect all of my senses, including my vision. I felt my wife's hand on my elbow and allowed her to guide me through the mist, to the base of the unfinished temple, not actually seeing the brilliant red steps of the new pyramid, until I was right before them. Carefully I brought one foot up to the first step. I was more aware of how the heavy, jade effigy of Chac-Xib-Chac, suspended behind my legs, swayed rhythmically into the back of my knees, as I ascended each step, than I was of the procession that followed me. Just behind me, I was sure Little Jaguar walked with the pride and stature befitting the heir apparent, but, even if I was more certain of my balance, my attire rendered me incapable of turning to see him. I also knew that Kan followed behind the young heir, and he, in turn, was followed by the eight Ahow who served as my Chosen Council. Behind them were the many Sahal who represented our territories. Alongside our procession, young boys carried incense pots in loosely woven sacks, and venerable priests recited the chants imploring the voices of the gods.

I could hear the cry of my infant son coming from above me, where the stairs ended, but I was unable to see Nuk standing behind the altar, with the child in her arms, until I'd reached the pinnacle of my climb. As the light of K'in rose up from the underworld, filling the sky with a rose hue, I walked toward the red stone altar and faced my newborn son, screaming in Nuk's embrace.

"Give the son of the Holy Bacab to his godfather," I commanded the old woman in the loudest voice I could evoke, given my condition. Nuk bowed and handed the baby to Kan. With the self-assurance of an expert, Kan placed the child astride his hip, and paced the perimeter of the platform. Stopping to pick up one of the objects laid out on the stone altar — an ax with a handle covered in snakeskin and a blade of flint — he held it before the baby and explained, "This is the ax of Chac-Xib-Chac. You will carry this into battle and secure many captives."

Again Kan encircled the platform atop the pyramid, holding the baby astride his hip, this time pausing to pick up a shield from the altar, with the face of the Lord of Death inscribed on it's leathery cover. "This is the shield of the warrior. Remember that in battle a sharp ax, and in life, a sharp mind, will give you far greater protection than a shield," he explained to the child. He continued repeating his path around the platform, and after each trek he stopped and showed the baby another of the tools he would require in the fulfillment of his destiny: a ritual blade of flaked chert, the powerful stone made from lightning; a tunic of cotton armor with the emblem of Jaguar-Sun woven into it's border; an obsidian tipped spear with blood-stained cloths knotted along its shaft to represent each of the captives slain with this ancient weapon; a finely polished obsidian mirror; the headdress of Chac-Xib-Chac and a jaguar skin kilt with the tail attached. With each item, he explained its relevance. Finally Kan picked up an old worn pouch and pulled from it the carved antler awls with the stingray spine tips that he'd acquired in Place of Split-Sky. "These are bloodletters. A true holcan, a holcan of divine blood, will make pain a familiar experience, that he will never fear," Kan proclaimed, recalling his experience with the holcan initiates that night, long ago, in Split-Sky.

Almost as if he understood, the child responded to this last explanation with a loud howl. Kan turned to me, no doubt uncertain as to how I would react to this final part of his presentation. But, by this time, I was incapable of forming any thought of my own. The combination of fasting, along with the potent concoction I'd drunk earlier, and the cumbersome weight of my costume, had put me into a transfixed stupor. My mind held only one thought — that it was now time for me to perform the ultimate act of sacrifice.

I began reciting the prayers that implore the gods to find nourishment in my gift of blood, and to find me worthy to speak their voice. Silently I also prayed that the dreadful One-Death would not return. Ahpo Hel held the bowl before me with the necessary implements. With my back to the crowd of people, who watched from the plaza below, I held aside my loincloth and quickly pierced myself with the obsidian shard. This time, I had followed each step of the ritual, exactly as required, and I felt no pain as I watched my blood flowing into the bowl of bark paper, that Ahpo Hel held before me. I watched the paper turn bright red and waited — waited for the sensation of helpless possession to overpower me... waited as the buzzing sound in my head grew louder and louder, blinding me with it's sound. Suddenly I had no strength and no sensation.

~

When I awoke, it was dark, but I couldn't tell if it was the night of the day I'd let blood, or another night of an uncertain number of days from then. I felt the soft warmth of flesh on my mat, beside me, and before I was even certain where I was, I knew that Ahpo Hel was with me. I reached to her and let my hand follow the smooth curve of her leg until it stopped at the wonderful, moist tuft of hair that hid her womanhood. "I don't think you'll be wanting to provoke any excitement in yourself tonight, my love," my wife whispered, as she turned fully towards me, and touched my face.

I reached down to touch myself and felt the compress on my wound. Although I was aware of a mild discomfort, it was nothing like the pain I'd experienced in Te'nab the first time I'd let blood. As my sense of time and place slowly returned, I remembered how I'd been dreading the ritual, not because of the pain, but because I was afraid that I would again conjure the voice of One-Death.

"Did the gods speak? Did they name the child?" I asked the warm, soft woman who had positioned her body to fit perfectly alongside mine.

"It was Chac-Xib-Chac himself who named our son," she whispered. His voice was like thunder when he summoned the child born to serve him. He said he shall be called Yellow-Knot."

"Yellow-Knot? But that is the sign of divine rulership. I've already acknowledged Little Jaguar as heir. Why would I want to call the second son Yellow-Knot?" I puzzled.

"If I did not know for certain you were a man, I would say you speak the words of a woman," Ahpo Hel said with a playful tease. "Aren't you the one who insisted that we must never question the will of the gods?"

"I suppose that it's just a name," I mused. "It probably has nothing to do with being destined to ruler. There was an ancestor with that name — Yellow-Knot-Peccary. He was the father of two brothers who were each successively the Holy Bacab. Was the name only Yellow-Knot? Are you sure there wasn't more?" I asked.

"Yellow-Knot. That was all."

I was finally alert enough to realize that Ahpo Hel's response was in retaliation for my admonition to her, four months earlier, to accept what the gods demanded. "I shouldn't have been so harsh with you... about accepting destiny. You've never been wrong in your advice, in all these years. Hel, in my entire life I will never make a wiser decision than the one I made when I hurried off to Tikal for you. A more intelligent, sensitive woman never lived.

"In your own way you will be remembered as more powerful than even my mother or my grandmother. The seed of Jaguar-Sun has produced extraordinary women, but you, the daughter of Ixtab, will surpass them. Perhaps that's why Resplendent Egret accepted you as her daughter, even before she anointed you as my companion."

I rolled over to hold her close to me, but as I responded to the sweet sensation of my wife's body, I suddenly knew the worst pain one could possibly imagine!

# Koh

We were sixteen and one half years into the Katun of Kahwil. It had been a time of peace and abundance. No tragedy, no devastation, no war had occurred in these years, to mar this period of harmony and growth for the people of Jaguar-Sun. From my stone bench, on the newly constructed Administration Plaza, I could look west over my burgeoning realm, and feel great pride and satisfaction. On a jaguar-skin cushion to my right, Little Jaguar sat as heir apparent, and the living embodiment of Kahwil, himself. On my left, stood the tall and handsome Kan, now Chief Advisor and Shaman to the Chosen Council of the Clans.

Often, during a gathering of the Council, Ahpo Hel would accompany me, sitting beside me on a carved stone bench, modestly offering me her advice and wisdom. But this was the beginning of the Solstice Rituals and my wife was still the Ahow of the Shrine of Toctan. She would spend the day and night making the prescribed sacrifices and performing her rituals of divination at the shrine. Too late, I would learn that she foretold the coming reign of Ik, the powerful and fearsome god of wind and hurricanes, while she counted her divination seeds at the mountain cave.

As I waited for the arrival of the members of the Chosen Council, I looked over the pristine expanse of the red painted, limestone plaza with proud admiration. Without a doubt, this was my greatest accomplishment to date. Located in the flat expanse of land just north of Te'nab, I had personally directed the construction of this spectacular platform to encompass the cluster of stone buildings that were previously on the site. By not filling in the original structures, as was the usual practice, they retained their usefulness as a storage place for our abundant harvest of maize, squashes and beans, along with the many items taken in tribute from our colonies, who also shared in the good fortune of Kahwil's blessings. Woven goods, cacao, precious stones, honey and more filled the chambers, safely enclosed beneath the plaza.

The previous year, heavy rains had swollen the nearby river, one of five that flowed from Quetzal Mountain into Place of Jaguar-Sun, and the storage areas beneath the half-completed plaza were in danger of being flooded. In a dream, Kahwil had shown me how to build a vaulted tunnel for the river to follow. This tunnel diverted the river beneath the plaza, so that even the river had become my servant, providing both water for drinking and steam baths, and a system of disposing of waste.

Because access to the tunnels and subterranean storage areas was only possible from a stairway on the plaza, not only was the wealth of Jaguar-Sun safely protected from the destructive heat of K'in and damage from wind, rain and animals, but I alone controlled its distribution. The Holy Bacab truly had the power of life and death, as never before in Place of Jaguar-Sun. Those clans, and their appointed Sahal, who served me and our gods well, were rewarded with abundance; while any who dared to withhold their service or respect, would watch their families starve. Fortunately, that situation had not occurred. The swelling populace of Jaguar-Sun was all too eager to express their gratitude for prosperity to the gods and to their Holy Bacab who had so successfully interceded on their behalf. An almost limitless source of eager laborers and craftsmen had been available to build this magnificent structure during the dry days between harvest and planting.

I'd already begun plans for the first stone god-house to be built on the Plaza. We would use many of the new techniques we'd experimented with on the Temple of Chac-Xib-Chac, back in the old residential compound. But, for now, only a simple god-house of pole and thatch, with all sides open, was positioned near the wide, main staircase, on the western side of the Plaza.

As the administration and control of Jaguar-Sun had become more complex, I'd appointed an Ahow to represent each of the eight original clans, on the Chosen Council. In consideration of the service and tribute they provided, each clan was assigned an area in Place of Jaguar-Sun, where they built their residential compounds around a god-house, to the god of their lineage. Each compound usually consisted of stone houses for the Ahow and his family, surrounded with the traditional pole and thatch homes for the clansmen, and communal homes for the slaves and laborers. These were often men from other places, who had either voluntarily offered themselves to these households, in exchange for the opportunity to one day raise their families in the safety and prosperity of Jaguar-Sun, or they were skilled craftsmen who had been sent here by our colonies as tribute. The latter were usually artisans of exceptional talent, who had vied for the honor of serving in Place of Jaguar-Sun, as word spread of the opportunities for artistic expression that prevailed in our prosperous community.

Each clan excelled in the area that was controlled by their respective gods. While the clan of the Ahow of Yum Kaax was responsible for agriculture, all men, except shamans and those of divine lineage, were expected to work during planting and harvest, in the vast grid of raised fields that stretched northward from Jaguar-Sun. But the men of the Yum Kaax lineage were responsible for planning and supervising the system of canals and raised gardens, and the terraced flower beds and orchards that adorned the hillsides to the south, and steep escarpments to the north. They were also responsible for the rituals and sacrifices required by the demanding god of agriculture, Yum Kaax, at his temple — one of the oldest structures at Place of Jaguar-Sun.

Young braves born or assigned into the clan of the Ahow of Chac-Xib-Chac, were raised to be warriors. They would sharpen their skills with the ax, the spear and the blow gun, by hunting for deer, monkey, peccary and jaguar, as well as all kinds of birds and fowl, to be used to nourish both gods and men.

The men of the lineage of Mam, studied the ancient books of the daykeepers, and determined the times of fortune and the days to be wary. Similarly, those of the lineage of Itzamná were sky-watchers, who studied the movements of the heavens, noting the comings and goings of the gods through the thirteen clans and interpreting the meanings of their positions. It was their responsibility to advise the Chosen Council of the celestial events that required preparation and sacrifice, such as the present Rites of Solstice.

Bol was the Ahow of Ek Chuah and although his clan was small, he had begun the training of ten young merchant apprentices, who already were successfully supervising the collection of tribute and its distribution.

The men of the clan of the goddess Ix Chel, maker of rainbows, were expert at securing and preparing pigments for all purposes, from the painting of stucco, to the ritual decoration of bodies. Just as all men were expected to labor in the fields during planting and harvest, women from all of the clans were expected to become proficient weavers. But it was the women of the clan of Ix Chel, who produced the most spectacular designs. When a young girl of anoth-

202

er clan showed exceptional talent as a weaver, her parents would arrange for her marriage into the clan of Ix Chel, since the honor of creating the garments to be worn during rituals, and the clothing that adorned the sacred stone effigies, belonged to only the women of this clan.

Kayam, the Ahow of Hun Batz and Hun Chuen, the first twins of First-Father, was the Master Scribe. When it was determined at birth, that a boy was destined to be a scribe, he was sent to live with Kayam, almost as soon as he could walk. The art of recording in painted strokes, that which was spoken, and even that which was only thought, was so complex, that the education of a scribe had to begin at a very young age. Students of Kayam would practice their skills on folding books of bark paper and pottery vessels. But only the most talented would be called upon to paint, on stone, the outlines for carvers to follow, and to impress their fluid strokes into the pliable stucco medium that would become the hallmark of Jaguar-Sun.

Kayam had a way of inspiring his students to excellence, but more importantly, he was able to convey to them the sense of harmony and balance he seemed to understand instinctively. Several years earlier, when I had tried to explain to him the magical proportions Kahwil had described to me in Te'nab, he drew a long box on the ground before us. Dividing it so that one portion was a square, he then divided the remaining section into two parts, of which one was square. He continued to divide the non-square section of each division until his boxes were too small to portion further. When I noted that each non-square box had the same shape as the original box, Kayam held his thumbs to his grandfather fingers and said, "See, the one and one half to the two and one-half that Kahwil showed you — it is the same. This is the magical shape we will use to build Jaguar-Sun."

Unfortunately, Kayam wasn't the man who would actually build the temples of Jaguar-Sun. That honor fell to the Ahow of Kauwac, the highly respected god of the firmament. A bawdy and abrasive old man, Iguana's family had worked the stone quarries from ancient times. He alone held the secrets for cutting and transporting the limestone slabs and blocks, to be used for all the new public buildings being built in Jaguar-Sun. And he alone seemed to understand what the stone was capable of accomplishing, and what was impossible or doomed to failure. While Iguana's obstinate nature made it difficult to convince him to try something new, there was no denying that his instincts were always correct.

It had been a struggle to get Iguana to consider trying some of the innovations we eventually used on the Temple for Chac-Xib-Chac. I thought, at first, that he would die laughing when his eager young apprentice, Seven-Kimi, had first suggested that the tri-lobed hollows be cut into the roof sections. But the next morning, Iguana had come back with a modification of the young man's design, which he assured us would work. And when Iguana declared that something was feasible, no one dared argue. I'm sure that many of the laborers, whom he instructed to chisel out the hollows in the new temple roof, believed their master had gone mad. But Iguana was right. The Temple for Chac-Xib-Chac stood soundly; the roof held strong, supported by a front wall of only piers, straddled with stone lintels. Just as Kahwil had instructed, the light of K'in filled the front room of the new temple.

As each of the Ahow of the Chosen Council arrived on the plaza, they bowed to me in respect, and joined their brothers in the shade of the thatched roof of the god-house, alternately drinking balché and chanting pleas to K'in to resume his journey south. For two mornings in a row, the sky-watchers of Itzamná had noted that K'in had risen from the Underworld, at the exact same place on the northeast horizon. It was a dangerous time, the rains had ceased, and the half-grown crops seemed to gasp in thirst. If K'in continued moving north towards the great waters, the rain might never return, and every man, woman and child would be set to work, day and night, carrying water to the fast wilting plants. Eventually, even the five rivers that flowed from Quetzal Mountain would dry up, and the fertile plains would become a labyrinth of dry, cracked mounds and parched trenches.

I was enacting the Solstice rituals without much concern. Kahwil had proven his affections to my people for many years. It seemed certain there would be no problem with K'in returning, as he always did before, since the beginning of time. And the precious rains also would resume, very soon. Nevertheless, I adhered to the requisite fasting and abstinence from sexual relations during this time, as dictated by tradition, even though my heart was not anxious and my prayers were half-hearted.

When Bol arrived, accompanied by two warriors who were dragging the fat Sahal of Tortuguero between them, I was grateful for the distraction. At a nod from Bol, the young braves dropped their obese charge before me and hurried away to the main stairway of the plaza. Bol bowed to me, then turned to acknowledge the other members of the Chosen Council, who sat with me in the god-house.

"Holy Bacab, forgive me for my late arrival. The journey from Tortuguero was delayed, because this scoundrel refused to come of his own accord."

I looked at the bruised and tattered Sahal, who knelt before me, shaking with terror, and laughed aloud. "Bol, have you made some kind of mistake? What could possibly be the crime of this Sahal? Has he forgotten to fast this Solstice!" I laughed, turning to my associates to share in my amusement.

"He has refused to relinquish the very tribute required of all the people of Tortuguero!" Bol announced, as he gave the accused a swift kick in his well padded ribs. "His first born is seventeen years old and still lives with him. She should have been sent here five years ago. But the dog insists that he has kept her as a favor to us! He claims that she is possessed by the Lords of the Night, and would only bring us harm. That's why, five years ago he substituted a slave girl in his daughter's place!" Bol proclaimed.

I looked down at the pathetic man who cowered at my feet. For many years he had enjoyed a life of comfort, in return for his duties of securing the required tribute from his clansmen. Now he was being accused of withholding the very sacrifice that he'd extorted from his own people.

"Has not Tortuguero enjoyed the peace and plenty that I have secured for you from the gods?" I commanded.

The man nodded meekly.

"Have I not welcomed you to this place as a guest, and sent you home laden with gifts and honor for your loyal service?"

Again the man nodded.

"Is it true, as you have been accused, that you have kept your first-born, who is rightly the property of Jaguar-Sun?"

"But for good reason," the man whimpered. "She brings sorrow to everyone who knows her." The fat man glanced about suspiciously and whispered, "I have seen her at night, Most Holy Bacab, dancing with the jaguars! It is for this reason I have kept her hidden; to protect you from the grief she would bring you."

The man's story seemed as feeble as his person. I found myself sickened more by his terrified, whimpering excuses, than by his crime.

"What kind of man asks from his people more than he is prepared to give himself? You have insulted me by your failure to perform as one who has been chosen by the Holy Bacab. Where is this child, whom you claim I must be protected from?" I thundered sarcastically.

Bol motioned to the warriors who waited near the stairs, and they, in turn, summoned their companions in the courtyard below. I waited, half amused, half annoyed, for the girl and her escort to ascend the steep stairs. First, the feathered headdresses of two braves appeared at the point where the stairs met the plaza, then their faces, trained to show no expression, came into view, and finally, the face of the young woman between them, rose from the stairway. Unlike her guards, her feelings were clearly visible — in all my life I've never seen such fiery defiance! The body that followed the face was physically much smaller than the two strong young men who held her arms, but her expression and bearing was one of extraordinary strength and nobility. That such an incredible beauty could have been the offspring of the disgusting creature before me, was one of life's great mysteries.

"Is it necessary that these men hold you so securely?" I asked the girl, careful not to frighten her with my tone. She didn't answer, but looked at me with proud resignation, as if to say, "What could I possibly do anyway."

"Release her!" I ordered.

I addressed her father, "She doesn't appear very dangerous to me. Have you educated her?" The Sahal appeared to be startled by my question.

"In what way?" he asked

"In the rituals of a woman who will serve the gods? Is that not what the daughter of the Sahal is destined for?"

Her father shuddered, surprised that I should know what had been foretold for his daughter at her birth. I was surprised, myself, by my pronouncement. But from the moment I saw her, I knew this was no ordinary woman. There was something about her eyes that enticed me; something about the way she held her head, and moved her hips. She exuded pure, unbridled sensuality, and yet, an innocent vulnerability that made me feel both helpless and powerful at the same time.

"What is your name?" I asked hoarsely, my mouth suddenly dry. Moments passed, while she seemed to consider the answer to my question, all the while her eyes never leaving mine; never losing their expression of proud defiance.

"Koh" she responded, the single sound leaving her lips like a challenge to grasp her in my arms and dare to possess her.

I tried to tear myself from her stare, suddenly conscious that I was on the verge of making a fool of myself. Forcing myself to concentrate on her father, I repeated my question. "Have you educated her?"

The bedraggled, old man looked up at me like one who is about to meet his death. "I beg you not to take her, Most Divine Holy Bacab. She will bring you sorrow, as she has brought to me," he cried.

"Have you educated her?" I demanded again, impatient with his ominous warnings, when my entire body ached for the beautiful creature, who brazenly continued to stare at me.

"She has been educated in the rituals of a woman who will serve the gods," her father sighed. "She knows the days to keep, the patterns to weave, the herbs to prepare, the chants to pray. But she cannot be taught to serve, anymore than I can be taught to stop eating. It is not in her nature. You cannot teach a jaguar to obey, as you can teach a dog. This one is owned by the jaguars! I warn you, she will never serve you." He broke down and started crying convulsively.

"Get him out of here!" I called to the warriors. "I will tend to him after K'in moves back to the mountains. As for the child... the girl... Bol, bring her below, into one of the storage rooms. Let her contemplate her destiny, surrounded with the other items of tribute, of which she is now one. And station a guard at the stairs. See that she doesn't go running off to find her father. Then come back here, to help us finish our prayers."

Bol looked at me suspiciously as he took Koh by the arm, and led her to the stairway that gave access to the subterranean chambers below us. Just as they reached the stairs, Koh turned and caught me still watching her. For an instant her expression suddenly changed to one of seductive invitation, and then just as quickly, she resumed her look of stoic insolence. Had I just imagined it?

I turned to see Kan, looking at me with concern. "Her father's right. That one is trouble. I would advise you to send her back to Tortuguero. Let her continue to torment her own family. That would be fitting justice."

"I have not asked you for your advice, Shaman!" I proclaimed. "Be certain that you do not speak from jealousy. It doesn't suit one who calls himself the friend of the Holy Bacab."

"The friend of the Holy Bacab wishes only to protect you," Kan replied and bowed respectfully.

"Good! Then let us resume our prayers!" I proclaimed and tried to shake the thought of Koh's departing glance from my mind. But as the endless afternoon wore on, with each series of chants followed by generous rounds of balché. The only thoughts that filled my mind, were fantasies of the mysterious enchantress who awaited me, in the dark chambers below. K'in began his journey into the underworld, but our group continued the endless series of prayers.

On into the night we prayed and drank, until, one by one, the Ahow of the Chosen Council collapsed on the floor of the god-house, in a drunken sleep. Even Little Jaguar fell victim to the power of the balché. At last there was only Kan and myself awake, but Kan showed no signs of sleepiness.

I could wait no longer. "I'll return soon," I whispered to Kan, as I stumbled toward the stairs that led to the rooms beneath us. But I felt his firm hand on my shoulder. "It is Solstice. You must abstain. All of Jaguar-Sun depends on you," he said, as clearly as if he'd drunk nothing but water throughout the long day and night.

"Of course, I have no intention of taking her tonight. I just want to... speak with her." My words were slurred, despite my efforts to match my friend's sober advice.

Kan looked at me skeptically, while I tried to assure him. "You have my word. I will not break the abstinence," I declared, and grabbing a torch from the wall, I hurried down the narrow stairway, as one who is being helplessly drawn to their doom. At the foot of the stairs, stood the warrior Bol had assigned to the duty of guarding this tantalizing captive. I recognized him immediately — he was the brave I'd almost slain outside Te'nab, several years ago. The lightning bolt scar on his face was even more pronounced in the flickering torch light.

"Hand me your torch. Now, wait at the top of the stairs, and see that no one comes down here," I commanded. The warrior quickly moved up the steps. "Speak of this and I will make a sacrifice of your tongue," I called up to him, hoping that Kan wouldn't hear me. I knew, even then, despite my oath to Kan, that I was powerless to resist the temptation I was throwing myself into.

I stumbled noisily past rooms filled with sacks of dried maize and beans, and chambers lined with gourds of honey and herbs, and stacks of folded woven goods and pottery and baskets brimming with cacao beans and precious stones and all the abundance of Jaguar-Sun of which I was so proud. I considered calling out for Koh to reveal herself, but feared that I would appear weak or eager. Instead, I proceeded to peer into each dark vault for the elusive creature, uncertain what my intentions were, once I'd found her.

I imagined myself grasping her by her hair and forcing her proud body into submission. Never before had I experienced such a need to feel complete control over a woman. It was more than lust that lured me deeper into the musty bowels of this structure; it was the need to dominate a spirit that challenged my supremacy, from the moment I saw her. I held my torch into each narrow room, searching its shadows for her form, promising myself that tonight I would only touch her, smell her, savor her beauty. I would prove to her that I was the most powerful man of all the world, by reducing her to the point of submission, and then rejecting her, without breaking the abstinence of Solstice.

I imagined how her fragile brown body would look, as I forced her down on her back beneath me; how her eyes would implore me for gentleness, as her legs would spread and finally resign to the thrust of my masculinity. But I would not enter her tonight. I would only take her to that point of submission.

Where was the wretch! I looked among the baskets of resinous balls of copál, their fragrance intoxicating me further. Then, finally, in a tiny alcove I saw her, nestled among sacks of feathers. The light of my torch dramatically outlined the fine features of her face and her delicate form. Her eyes sparkled like stars in the night. For a moment she seemed to be pleased to see me.

"You are comfortable?" I asked dryly.

"As comfortable as the corn and the squash" she snapped.

Her arrogance aroused in me an uncontrollable need to possess her. I tried to remind myself of the limits I must impose on my actions, but, at the same time, I found myself moving helplessly towards her. I imagined tearing at the knot that secured her simple cotton wrap at her firm, round breasts.

"I have only come to assure myself of your comfort and safety," I lied, never taking my eyes from the curves that tantalized me from beneath their sparse concealment.

"You have come to be served as a god, by the one who was born to serve you," she replied without fear, her voice soft and seductive. She knelt before me and without any instruction from me, wrapped her arms around my legs, burying her face in my groin. There was no way to deny that she had aroused me completely, and I stood helpless as she pulled aside my loincloth and drew me into her mouth.

"This is not actually a sexual encounter, in the sense that is forbidden tonight," I tried to rationalize to myself, as the extraordinary sensations of her mouth reverberated throughout me. "I have not spilled my seed, nor have I touched her place of shame. The gods will not punish me for this," I reasoned, as I struggled to resist the incredible tension that was building in my loins. This is truly the ultimate pleasure, I thought, as the woman who had only moments ago defied me, now knelt before me in complete submission to my needs. Never before had I experienced such ecstasy, such power!

But as the fire of her mouth continued to pulsate around me, I soon lost all ability to think. There was no power that could contain the imminent release of the fire she'd drawn from me. Then suddenly, just as I was near exploding, she pulled her mouth from me and turned away, kneeling on all fours before me, her wrap falling to the floor. I plunged mercilessly into her, releasing my seed in a wild, seething explosion, into her place of shame, crying out in helpless ecstasy.

The moment it was over, I was suddenly sober and aware. I'd done exactly what I'd promised myself I would not — exactly what I knew I never should have done. Not only that, I'd taken her as an animal, from behind. Hanab Pacal, the Holy Bacab, the divine ruler of Jaguar-Sun, had succumbed to the lowest form of behavior, at the worst possible time!

I pushed the still kneeling woman away from me, and vehemently pinned her face to the floor with my foot, certain that the only way to redeem myself of this pitiful act of weakness, would be to sacrifice her on the spot. But the light of my torch, that somehow had remained in my hand throughout our encounter, revealed a terrifying mark on the buttocks of my temptress. It was unmistakable; a thick vertical line, the size of my thumb, crossed at the top with a horizontal stroke. She'd been branded from birth with the mark of Ik! Suddenly I understood the warning of the loathsome Sahal, this was a messenger of Ik! It was not me, but the vengeful god of hurricanes, whom she was born to serve.

I stood shaking in the moist shadows of that dungeon, and for the first time in my life I felt total, irrepressible panic. If I were to sacrifice this woman, I would surely provoke the wrath of Ik. If I allowed her to live, I would have to face the consequences of breaking the fast. I shook with fear as I prayed that the gods had been unable to see what had happened within the darkness of this stone cavern.

As soon as Koh felt me release the pressure of my foot on her, she slid from me and pulled her wrap around her body, in a futile attempt at modesty. She knew I'd seen the mark, she'd planned it that way. She also knew that I understood its implication. There was no fear in her voice as she spoke. "I alone can intercede with Ik for mercy, for the Holy Bacab," she stated coolly. "But first, you will name me publicly as your companion, and you will recognize my children as your heirs." Her voice grew softer, almost apologetic… almost seductive. "At my bequest, Ik will bless you even more abundantly than Kahwil. He will protect you from the anger of the gods. Your weakness will remain unpunished, as long as you serve the

Lord of Hurricanes," she continued, emphasizing one of the more devastating aspects of her god.

I knew I had no choice, but to follow her instructions. I was in no position to ask Kahwil, or any other god, for help against the rage of Ik. In one moment of drunken weakness, I'd placed the survival of Jaguar-Sun into the hands of this tiny, beautiful, treacherous woman.

"As you wish," I whispered, trying unsuccessfully not to reveal the despair that was engulfing me.

Koh rose gracefully, like a flower unfolding, her eyes bright, her lips turned slightly up on the ends in a sweet smile. She looked nothing like the manipulating beast I felt choking me from within. "You will know pleasure with me that only the gods deserve," she cooed. "You know now, how I have been 'educated' to serve you."

For one brief moment I allowed myself to recall the delicious pleasure her delicate mouth could deliver. But I wasn't foolish enough to believe Koh would ever serve me. It was I who was now enslaved. I turned from her, and made my way back through the dark tunnel, toward the stairs. I knew she was following behind me, but I wanted her to be gone. I wanted to just awaken in the god-house, and realize that this had only been a nightmare. Isn't that how things were supposed to happen, first there was the dream— the warning. I would awaken from the dream and learn from it. I would be prepared. I wouldn't succumb to temptation.

I held the torch close to my face and could feel its heat. Touching the walls, I felt their smooth, damp hardness. I listened to the footsteps of the woman following behind me. It was all too real to be a dream.

When I reached the top of the stairs, I saw Kan, standing beside the warrior, Lightening-Bolt. Both men looked at me anxiously, but I tried to meet their eyes without expression. Then they saw Koh ascending the stairs behind me. Lightening-Bolt's face tightened, certain he would be slain for witnessing this event, but Kan's expression was one of devastation. Neither of them could possibly know the anguish I was feeling, as I gave Lightning-Bolt this command.

"Take this woman to the royal residential compound. She is to sleep in the house next to mine tonight."

Then I turned to Kan. "Tomorrow, I will proclaim Koh as Companion to the Holy Bacab of Jaguar-Sun. She will sleep in my house and her sons will be acknowledged as heirs of the divine Jaguar-Sun dynasty."

Kan was speechless. He stood on that spot without moving for a very long time. Tears filled his eyes. Of all the people of Jaguar-Sun, he alone had the power to admonish the Holy Bacab, with only his condemning silence. I walked stoically past him, to my throne in the god-house, and sat watching the men of the Chosen Council sleeping on the floor around me. I had betrayed them all. And my son, Little Jaguar, who rested so peacefully among the leaders of Jaguar-Sun — had I just jeopardized his future? What of his mother? How would I explain to her, that she would now share her household, and her husband, with this devious young woman?

I sat waiting for the return of K'in, hoping somehow things would not look so hopeless in the light of day. For the first time, I wasn't sure K'in would even return. I was no longer so certain that he would begin to journey south again, bringing the precious rain. I turned to Kan, who still stood rigid at the stairs, watching me. "I must go to Te'nab. Will you accompany me?" I asked more meekly than a Holy Bacab should ever speak. He nodded, and silently followed behind me, down the west stairs, to the courtyard. We walked in the darkness without speaking, towards the shrine of my lineage.

I hoped that I would be able to beg Kahwil and my ancestors for forgiveness. The gods expect that occasionally their True People will succumb to those weaknesses they've given us, to simply prove to us that we are not equal to them. But I had no such expectations for Kan, I knew that I'd lost the respect of my friend—perhaps for forever.

# Sandals Full of Stones

I prayed deep within the dark, sacred chambers of Te'nab, for what seemed like eternity, waiting for the voice of Kahwil. Uncertain whether K'in had yet returned to light a new day or if he had resumed his journey northward, I pleaded to the pih of my god, for mercy and forgiveness. Finally I heard the faint, but familiar hiss of Kahwil, seeming to come from within my own body.

"I could put only one pebble in your sandal, Cherished One, and you would be quickly crippled," his barely audible voice whispered with angry menace. "This easily I could destroy the weak one who dares to summon me. But Kahwil does not forget that you have nourished me with your blood these many years. Instead, I will fill the sandals of Hanab Pacal with many stones. The weak one will walk for two katuns, with the pain and burden of his failure. Expect no more from your god, Cherished One, than the longevity required, for you suffer sufficiently, to redeem yourself and your people."

The sliver of hope I'd held, that the gods had not seen my sin, dissolved, along with the voice of my god. I left Te'nab burdened with a disgrace I'd been cursed to bear alone, and for the first time in my life I knew the clutch of despair. Without the help of Kahwil I would be at the mercy of Koh's god, the ruthless and destructive, Ik.

Outside, a drizzle darkened Kin's halfhearted attempt at morning. At least the rains had returned, I thought to myself. Kan was nowhere to be seen and I walked alone in the rain toward my home. Drenched and miserable, I crept noiselessly past the small hut where I'd instructed Lightening Bolt to bring Koh. There was no sound from within, and I wondered what kind of woman would dare to sleep after dawn. The wrinkled old cook, Three-Deer, was at her grinding stone, in the open-walled cooking hut of my compound. But Koh was not among the daughters of Three-Deer, who were dropping tortillas on the stone griddle.

The familiar sizzle and aroma of the tortilla gave me no comfort, as I felt no appetite.

I was glad to see that Ahpo Hel had not yet returned from her rituals at Toctan; it allowed me some time to consider how I would break the news to her, that I would be taking another wife. While it was permissible for any man to have more than one wife, if he could support them and their offspring, I was certain that Ahpo Hel would resent sharing me, especially with a young, beautiful woman, like Koh. But more than that, Ahpo Hel was astute enough to sense immediately what had happened with Koh. She had the gift to see into the soul of a person, and she would know without any words from me, that Koh's spirit was wretched, and mine was disgraced.

I decided not to deny whatever she could perceive, but I would offer no further information, nor any explanation. I was the Holy Bacab, and would humble myself to no one, not even my wife. Alone, I waited in the damp, unlit, back room of my home, for the familiar sound of Ahpo Hel's footsteps, rehearsing my announcement over and over again. I would inform her in a cool, detached voice, befitting my position, that Koh was to be my Companion, equal in all respects to Ahpo Hel, and her sons would share the privilege of my heirs.

The downpour outside disguised the sound of my wife's approach, and suddenly, without warning, she was standing in the doorway. In the darkened room I watched as she peered towards me, her eyes quickly adjusting to the lack of light.

"There is great trouble ahead, My Husband," she warned somberly, as she moved into the room, to sit before me. "My blood speaks of only ill fortune." She buried her face in her hands and sighed deeply, then slowly looked into my eyes and I knew she was seeing my soul.

"It has begun already, hasn't it?" she asked with despair in her voice. I nodded, unable to remember even the first words of the speech I'd carefully planned. How could I hurt her with such cruel detachment? Once again, I considered the possibility of slaughtering Koh. But it wouldn't solve anything — the gods knew of my sin and Kahwil himself had condemned me to a long life of suffering. Here now was the first of the stones he'd filled my sandals with — I would break Ahpo Hel's heart and loose her love and respect, as I'd already lost Kan.

As I struggled to piece together my words, Ahpo Hel cried out, "I must tell you something I've kept from you for many days, My Husband. I dared not believe the counting of the seeds, and so I had

Kan try for me, and when he came to the same conclusion, I swore him to secrecy, until I'd heard the same prophecy from each of the shamans who worshipped at Toctan." Even in the dim light I could see tears rolling down her cheeks and fear in her eyes. "I carry another child, and from this child the lineage of Jaguar-Sun will flow."

"What kind of foolishness is that!" I screamed, as soon as the words left her lips. "Little Jaguar is heir, he is chosen by Kahwil himself! The lineage will flow from him!"

Ahpo Hel was sobbing convulsively now. Between almost panicky gasps for air she stuttered to explain her fear that this prophesy implied that her sons' lives were in danger; that neither of them would live to produce descendants."

"That's nonsense! Kahwil would not let anything happen to Little Jaguar. He has acknowledged the boy as his own embodiment. He will be the greatest Holy Bacab that has ever lived. My wife, you have made some mistake in your interpretations. If this child you carry threatens the life of Little Jaguar… and his brother… then it would be better that it was never born."

As soon as I spoke the words I regretted them. I remembered how Ahpo Hel had almost died with the birth of Yellow-Knot. This new child in her womb, that provoked such ominous prophesies, could destroy her. Would this too be one of Kahwil's cursed stones!

Suddenly, what little light there was in the room, disappeared. I looked up to the doorway, to see what was blocking the few pathetic bits of light that the dismal day offered, and saw the delicate silhouette of Koh's figure. Ahpo Hel turned and saw her too. Koh, realizing that Ahpo Hel was crying, assumed that I'd broken the news to her about taking a new wife.

"Your tears will not change the will of Ik," she said clearly and coldly. "I will be named Companion to the Holy Bacab today, with or without your blessing, so do not waste our husband's sympathies with your groveling."

Ahpo Hel's back snapped straight and rigid. She looked at me with ferocious anger. "What is this child talking about?" she pleaded, her eyes begging me to declare the words of this belligerent intruder to be lies.

"I will name her my Companion today," I said as forcefully as I could, returning Ahpo Hel's look of horror with a blank stare. It was done. I'd as much as stabbed her through with a spear. The expression on her face clearly told me that this time Ahpo Hel had not read my soul. If she had, she would have known the anguish and despair I felt. Before me, untold suffering awaited, and I would be forced to face it alone, without the love of either Kan or Ahpo Hel. I dared not think about Little Jaguar. Would he also be taken from me?

Abruptly breaking myself from her shattered stare, I rose and walked past the tiny, malicious woman in the doorway, into the courtyard. "Kan, begin preparations for the Companion Ceremony," I called out to the handsome man who once was my friend. He'd been expecting the order; as Sahal of the Household, it was his responsibility to organize public rituals. Without showing any expression, he held his hand to his shoulder and bowed in respect. "It has been done, Most Holy Bacab," he replied without emotion. "Your people await you at the Temple of Yum Kaax, as the Lady Koh has instructed me."

I turned to Koh in surprise, and noticed that she was already attired in the traditional wedding huipil. "You have not been given the authority of my household!" I bellowed. "How dare you presume to tell the Sahal what to do!"

Koh glared at me, but did not respond. Again, that look of defiance enchanted me. I could think of nothing else but the delicious thrill of possessing her. I walked past her, back into my house, and allowed my hand to brush against her place of shame. Ahpo Hel noticed, but I didn't care.

"You will prepare to accompany me to the Temple of Yum Kaax," I instructed the poor, shattered woman who stood in the dark before me. "You will publicly welcome Koh into our household, and you will privately tolerate her as your equal. The survival of our sons and our lineage depends on this." What explanation could I possibly offer that would lessen her hurt, or soften her shock at this sudden turn of events. "I am deeply sorry," I whispered and turned away.

~

I stood on the north stairway of the Administration Plaza and watched the progress of the temple mound being built some distance before me, just south of the steep escarpment that bordered the rich agricultural lands that extended to the Great Sea of the North. Soon all that land would be blanketed in the smoky fires that would prepare them for planting and the building projects would cease.

We had made good progress in these few dry months between harvest and planting. In the next building season, a new temple would be positioned atop the steep, artificially constructed mound with five terraces. The stairs, ascending these terraces on the east side, were almost complete and artisans had already begun covering the rough stonework with a fine red plaster. The New Katun celebrations were still over two years away and I was certain we had ample time to complete this temple. It had already been well established that the next katun would belong to Ik and in an elaborate display of adoration to him, I would dedicate this beautiful new temple during the celebrations.

The air was warm but dry and a pleasant breeze was a subtle reminder of the more beneficent nature of Ik. I thought proudly to myself, he is pleased with his new protector, Hanab Pacal of Jaguar-Sun. If it were not for the nightmare that awaited me each evening in my home, I would have thought that Kahwil's threats of punishment had been forgotten.

Both Ahpo Hel and Koh were large with imminent childbirth. But even if their waists were as slender as young girl's, my home would not be big enough for the two of them. Koh never ceased taunting Ahpo Hel with everything from derisive remarks about her sons to the unattractiveness of her light colored skin. And Ahpo Hel was not one to keep silent when angered. She would return Koh's insults with a barrage of fiery vengeance that would have brought even the strongest man to tears. But not Koh! Impervious to her competitor's biting tongue, the young woman would glare with the eyes of the jaguar and quietly, but viciously, curse everything the older woman held dear. She would finish off each argument with the same excruciating reminder that their husband shunned the bed of Ahpo Hel.

This was not a household any man would relish returning to, and were it not for the irresistible lure of Koh's body, even swollen with child, I would have spent the remainder of my nights in the solitude of the god house, on the Administration Plaza. But my need for the passionate favors of Koh had only increased with time, and I stole to her bed each night as hungered as a man who had not known the pleasures of a woman in years. As uninhibited and remarkable as our encounters always proved to be, they never seemed to satisfy me in the way that Ahpo Hel and I had once enjoyed. There was no spiritual aspect to what we did; no feelings of love were ever aroused in the heat of our passions. Sometimes, waking before dawn, and feeling exhausted and empty, I recalled the delirious sweetness of my lovemaking with Ahpo Hel and longed to return to her bed. But Koh had made it clear that her favors would end forever if I soiled myself with the touch of the "ugly old hag with the white skin." Koh's body was as addictive as the magical herbs used to enslave sacrificial captives, and I would no more risk losing her than a captive would abandon his "Protector".

If losing the affections of Ahpo Hel was the only price to pay for my sin on the Solstice, then I would have considered myself fortunate. But the loss of Kan's love was a far more bitter punishment, and not a day passed that I did not secretly grieve that loss. Off to the east of where I was standing on the Administration Plaza, Kan and Little Jaguar were mapping out the perimeter of the new ball court, that would also be completed in time for the New Katun Ceremonies. From where I stood I could hear them clearly, as Kan explained, with poetic simplicity, how he had chosen the location. He drew the simple stepped shape of a temple mound on the ground and announced that directly beneath them was a temple of the underworld, its pinnacle abutted to the earth.

"Here we will build a mirror of that temple so that our sacrifices will be laid directly on the altar of the Lords of the Night," he explained, as he drew inverted temple steps directly above his first drawing, creating a perfect reflection, and the sign for the day, Etznab.

Little Jaguar listened to Kan with near adoration. I realized, as I watched them, that although my son was still three years from his manhood rituals, he already had the stature and bearing of a leader of men. Yet, with Kan, he seemed to still be a boy, in awe of his master. The respect and admiration shared between them, was apparent to anyone. Perhaps, if I hadn't loved them both so completely, I would have resented that bond between them — even had the foresight to fear it. Instead, I watched them with a benevolent envy, enjoying their warmth from a distance; resigned that my exclusion from such happiness was of my own doing.

As Kan continued to divine the positioning of the "upside-down" stairs that would border the ball court, presumably directly above their underworld counterparts, Little Jaguar marked each spot with a ceremonial staff. Hundreds of butterflies danced among the bright red and blue ribbons that adorned each rod, blowing gaily in the gentle breath of Ik. The sky was a clear, brilliant blue, with only the most delicate tufts of white, and the plains that stretched out before me were a vibrant green in spite of the dry weather. I turned toward the god house and began a chant of thanksgiving. Jaguar-Sun had been spared the wrath that I, alone, was condemned to suffer. The mercy of the gods could not be extolled enough. For even as a people enjoy the blessings won by the sacrifices of their Holy Bacab, they must suffer for his sins.

From the corner of my eyes I caught the movement of a young girl rushing towards the Plaza. As she neared, I could see that she was calling out something of great urgency. Her approach was curtailed by two warriors, whose duties included protecting me from the foolish interruptions of the common people. But her cries took on a panicky shriek as she tried to explain her message to the guards.

I turned to little Yellow-Knot, who was prancing about the Plaza, pretending he was a fearsome holcan. "Go quickly down to the courtyard, and find out what troubles that girl," I commanded the young boy. Delighted that he'd been given such a grown-up directive, Yellow-Knot adjusted his forelock and strode with exaggerated dignity down the west stairs. He stood looking up at the warriors, unquestionably certain of his superiority, and demanded, in an unnaturally deep voice, "What seems to be the problem here!" I couldn't help laughing as I watched the way the warriors bowed and submitted respectfully to the young heir's presence. Not waiting for her message to be relayed, the girl shouted to Yellow-Knot something about the wives of Hanab Pacal.

"Tell this common woman that it is forbidden for her to speak to Yellow-Knot, son of the Holy Bacab, and Cherished One of the Lady Ahpo Hel," the small boy bellowed to the warriors. If it were not for the bit of the message I'd caught from the girl, I would have allowed myself a fatherly laugh at my younger son's arrogance. But I feared that my wives' arguments may have accelerated into something violent. What a spectacle the household of Hanab Pacal has become, I thought, as I awaited my son's dignified ascent with his message.

Yellow-Knot rose proudly over the last step and strode before me, snapping his arm across his chest in a warrior's salute. "The wives of my father are both giving birth," he said, without seeming to comprehend the meaning of his message.

"Both giving birth!" I bellowed. "Both at the same time?" Yellow-Knot seemed upset by my astonishment, as though he personally had something to do with the message. "Go quickly and tell your brother and Kan to meet me at our house!" I ordered. Yellow-Knot strode eagerly to the north stairs to fetch his brother. I descended the west stairs as quickly as my increasingly turned-in foot would allow, and then, accompanied by the warriors, I rushed off to the residential compound.

As I walked, I started to think about the counting of the days. A child grew in its mother for one complete calendar round — each of the twenty sacred days pairing with each of the thirteen aspects, until they returned to the same aspect paired with the same day — a total of 260 days. This day was right for Ahpo Hel to give birth, because I remembered planting my seed in her, thirty days before the Solstice. But this was too soon for Koh. Her child would be born incomplete and would probably die. I remembered overhearing Koh's malicious threats that Ahpo Hel carried an imbecile, and I couldn't help feeling a sense of relief when I realized that it would be Koh's child that would not survive. Recalling the horror of Yellow-Knot's birth, I wondered in what condition I would find Ahpo Hel. I didn't care what happened to Koh.

I should have realized that Ik would not let his Protector suffer. When I walked into the hut and saw the healthy boy already suckling at Koh's breast, I wondered who had fathered this child, one month before Koh had first seduced me. Ahpo Hel's labor would not be so simple. She suffered into the night and the following day. When the infant finally emerged, it was blue and lifeless, and old Nuk held her as if she was dead. I was prepared to bury the child, with her chord, under the lineage tree, when suddenly she shuddered and exhaled a pathetic cry. Her mother was no better off, and it would be many days before I was certain that either one would live.

As the days passed, Ahpo Hel remained weak and bed-ridden. She seemed oblivious to her daughter's dull eyes and immobile limbs. With a patience I found remarkable, she force-fed her milk, into a mouth that needed to be taught to suck, cooing and singing quietly all the while. Remembering the lifeless form Nuk pulled from Ahpo Hel, I named the infant Kimi, Death, certain she would not live long enough to be named in a Hetzmek ceremony.

Koh found great satisfaction in the shortcomings of my helpless new daughter, all the while extolling each trivial attribute of her healthy son. I searched her baby's face for a clue to its parentage, certain I'd been duped into raising the son of a Lord of the Night. Hadn't Koh's father warned me that he'd seen her dancing with the jaguars? But the boy, whom she chose to call Shark, because, much to her discomfort, he was born with teeth, had no markings that would indicate he was a child of an Underworld being.

My household soon resumed its usual state of constant bickering and disputes. To escape, I would awaken before dawn, and rouse Little Jaguar and Yellow-Knot to join me in an early morning prayer at Te'nab. From there, I would go immediately to the Administration Plaza, and fill my mind with the problems of Jaguar-Sun; wonderful, tangible problems that a man could solve, and feel proud and in control. Often I would silently wonder, if the men who beckoned to my every wish, and rushed to my commands, knew that in the most precious aspect of my life, in my home, I was a miserable, enslaved fool. It was an imprisonment of my own doing — every night, despite hating myself for it, I slept in the dangerous embrace of the Protector of Ik.

# The New Katun

As I worked my way up each step of the new temple, I was painfully aware of the almost fifty tun that had passed, since the day I left my mother's womb. The weight of my ceremonial Katun costume seemed to multiply with each awkward step. My left leg had become increasingly weak, as my foot turned further inward, looking more like the snake leg of Kahwil than ever before. While this divine attribute served to enhance my authority, it had begun to seriously impair my ability to manage the steep ascent to the houses of the gods.

The Holy Bacab was required to prepare for the rituals of the New Katun with twenty days of strict fasting, while studying the sacred books, in the isolation of my lineage shrine. I had left the solitude of Te'nab each morning, to make a pilgrimage to each of the sacred shrines throughout Place of Jaguar-Sun, where I led my Chosen Council in chanting and dancing, imploring the gods for their blessing in the next twenty years. Throughout all those days, we were plagued with endless rain, unbearable heat and the merciless annoyance of the insects that thrived in that hot humidity. Still, I'd followed the prescribed rituals and sacrifices, as fervently and carefully as I had as a young boy of ten, and a young man of thirty. This time though, I had not even once heard the voice of Kahwil, nor of any other god — an ominous sign of things to come.

As I reached the precipice of the first section of steps, I paused to gather my strength for the rituals I would soon perform. I thought about Kahwil's last admonition, less than four years earlier, when he had condemned me to two katuns of penitence and I wondered how my tired body and broken spirit could endure for so long, without the guidance and blessings of the gods. Until now, no one seemed to suspect that I had brought disgrace to Jaguar-Sun, or that I'd been unable to speak with the gods. Life had gone on as usual for most people, and they were oblivious to the grief and fear their Holy Bacab carried in his heart.

I turned to watch Koh and Ahpo Hel standing to my left. They had been fasting and praying for the past five days, along with all the people of Jaguar-Sun. But they looked fresh and spirited, despite the grueling combination of rain and heat that seemed to be rotting my senses. When Little Jaguar noticed that I was having trouble with my ascent, he motioned to Koh, to bring me the sacred drink she carried with her, in a painted gourd.

Even in my weakened state, I couldn't help but notice that Koh was exceptionally beautiful today. Her light blue huipil fell gracefully from her breasts, over her belly that was again swollen with child. As with all the women of Tortuguero, she was as fertile as the maize fields to the north. She had once taunted Ahpo Hel with the promise that she would present me with a child at each harvest, and, from her size, it appeared that this third child would most likely be born along with the abundant crop of maize, that awaited being bent to dry, as soon as the rains ended.

I took the gourd Koh offered, and slowly drank its foaming, bittersweet contents — a mixture of cacao and secret herbs, that was prepared only for this important ceremony. Now I was ready to begin to call upon the Trinity of the Three Born-Together gods, who originated the divine lineage of the Jaguar-Sun people.

Alone, I ascended the last flight of stairs, and positioned myself between the two red piers of the new Temple of Ik. From beneath the shelter of the vaulted roof, I looked down upon my divine family, and the Ahow of the Chosen Council, who knelt in the rain on the landing before me. Little Jaguar held his body in a protective cover over the pih of Kahwil, Third-Brother, Ahpo Hel did the same for the pih of First-Brother and Kan sheltered the pih of Second-Brother. Before me were the most precious and revered idols of all the world, being held by the three people I held most precious to me. For the moment, I forgot all of the hurt and isolation I'd felt during the past three years, as I savored the pride I felt as their Holy Bacab. Down at the foot of the temple, thousands of people knelt in the flooded plaza, many holding the idols of their family shrines, in the same protective way as my family held theirs. It was time to end the Katun of Kahwil, and to begin the Eleventh Katun of the Ninth Baktun—to seat the Katun of Ik.

I nodded for Ahpo Hel to present the pih of First-Brother and she carefully brought before me the god she'd been appointed to protect .The statue had been clothed in the most exquisite fabrics the skilled weavers of Jaguar-Sun had ever created. I took her god and reverently placed him on the altar behind us. Now, little Yellow-Knot carried the bowl to me with the implements for the bloodletting ritual: the obsidian shards and strips of bark paper. His eyes were wide with anticipation. It was exactly one year ago that I'd presented my six-year-old son as a divine son of the Holy Bacab, at the Toctan shrine. Since then, he'd been like my shadow, quietly observing my every action, especially the sacrifices and rituals that had been performed in preparation for today. Now, for the first time, he would witness a public bloodletting, an event he'd spoken of with excited expectation for days.

Dazed by the effects of the ritual drink and my prolonged fasting, I was unable to give Yellow-Knot the reassuring wink I'd often shared with him, to convey my approval. This was not a time for fatherly distractions. Once again I felt myself being transformed into the vessel of my people's devotion — the living link between gods and men. In this lengthy and strenuous ceremony, I would offer my blood to each of the Three Born-Together gods, and finally to the god of the New Katun, the mighty Ik. As the hours of sacrifice progressed, many of the people in the plaza below danced in a crazed stupor, some even spilled their own blood, piercing their earlobes and lips. Chanting in the incessant rain, the worshipers passed gourds of the ritual drink among themselves, until the whole mass of Jaguar-Sun people was experiencing a communal ecstasy of purging and renewal.

Finally, as K'in fell into the jaws of the Underworld, and the whole sky was doused in his blood, a silence of anticipation fell on the crowd. The rain had stopped, and in the eerie stillness people knelt, their faces lowered to the earth, waiting for the voice of the god who would rule the new katun. Somehow the ceremony had rejuvenated me. I felt alert and strong as I stood before the anxious crowd, but fear gripped my insides as I wondered what would happen if I failed to conjure the voice of the god they all waited to hear. Would my divine right to rule be questioned? Would my sin be exposed? For terrifying moments I stood before my people and considered committing the blasphemous sin of impersonating the voice of Ik.

I don't know what happened first, if I heard the howl of the wind, or saw the menacing darkness that rushed towards us from the fields to the north. It happened so incredibly fast! Off to my left, I watched with horror, as our perfectly groomed fields of maize, squash and beans, almost ready for harvest, were ripped apart in the blast of rain and wind that approached us with terrifying speed. I screamed above the roar of the approaching hurricane to my family and council, to hurry into the shelter of the temple. From our pinnacle of horror, we watched helplessly, as the people in the plaza below us were pelted with tree trunks and other flying debris, that seemed to come from nowhere. The men of the Chosen Council cried out in grief, as they tried to distinguish their families from the screaming crowd. The roar grew louder, as the winds crashed around us, and we watched the pole and thatch god house on the administration plaza, get torn to pieces and flushed down the west stairs.

Most of the people in the plaza huddled into family groups, trying to shelter one another from the merciless onslaught of driving rain. Although I couldn't see what was happening to their homes, in the compounds behind us, I knew there would be nothing but devastation for any of them to return to. In the darkness, I imagined the splinters and rubble that remained, where orchards once graced the terraced hillsides to the south.

On into the night, the violent rampage of Ik continued. We watched horror-stricken, without speaking, as we sat huddled in the safety of this temple we had built to honor the ungrateful god who raged around us.

~

Sleep must have claimed us all at some point, and I dreamt of the previous day, when all of the pots had been ritually smashed in a ceremony of renewal. Ik apparently had something somewhat more comprehensive in mind. What the first light of K'in revealed, in the plaza and fields below us, was a deathly quiet vista of devastation. The fields to the north, that yesterday were ripe with the crops that had sustained my people in abundance year after year, were now a sea of muddy water studded with a pattern of tree stumps protruding, with ragged tears to mark the places where, only yesterday, healthy branches extended. The roots of each of these trees had been used to hold together the raise beds, rich with silt and mud, that had been dredged from the neat canals that bordered them. In one night, Ik had destroyed not only years of proud and careful tending, and the crops that would be needed to feed the people of Jaguar-Sun for the coming dry season, but he had also taken the very core of Jaguar-Sun's power. It had been the consistent abundance of the northern fields, that we had used to trade for the tribute of our colonies. There had been no need for warfare when Bol and his emissaries came laden with offerings of food. Tortuguero eagerly paid their tribute of their first-born, Simojovel offered obsidian, Xupa brought us pigments and Tila traded their feathers and jaguar pelts. The fertile lands to the north had been our strength and our pride. Now I looked out from the Temple of Ik and cried.

Yellow-Knot came and stood silently beside me, his arm around my leg. Even at his young age I think he sensed that Jaguar-Sun had been changed forever. It would take many years to reclaim the fields from the swamp. Somehow we would manage to feed the people of Jaguar-Sun. The maize and beans stored safely beneath the Administration Plaza would be sufficient, if carefully allocated, to get us through the dry months. But there would be nothing left for us to trade with, to insure the loyalty and tribute of our colonies.

I roused the sleeping men of the Chosen Council, and instructed them to each return to their compounds to assess the damage. They would join me, when K'in was directly overhead, on the Administration Plaza, and instruct their families to assemble in the Ball Court at dusk.

The temple stairs were strewn with wet leaves and branches, and our descent was treacherous. I was glad that no one remained in the plaza below, to observe our undignified departure. With Little Jaguar, I walked to Te'nab, to replace the pih of Kahwil. Yellow-Knot accompanied his mother to the shrine at Toctan, and Kan escorted Koh to our residential compound, and then continued on alone, to the western-most shrine, where the pih of Second-Brother was housed.

As we walked passed the rubble strewn plaza, to our ancestral shrine, I looked at Little Jaguar as he proudly carried the idol of the god he embodied, and wondered, if he truly was Kahwil, did he know of my sin, and the reason Kahwil had abandoned his people. He seemed to be oblivious to the destruction around us, his eyes focused on some unseen distance, his thoughts perfectly concealed in his expressionless face. When had the boy I loved so deeply, whom I thought I understood completely, become this strange, remote man? Little Jaguar was not handsome; his nose was far too large for his face, and his large lower lip drooped unattractively. I'd grown accustom to seeing the extra finger on each hand that was a certain mark of his divinity, but his extraordinary height still amazed me. True, I was not considered to be tall, but my first-born towered above me. This was the blood of Great Jaguar, I thought, and for a moment I wondered what had become of my father-in-law. There had not been a sign of him since the evening when he walked into the jungle, outraged to have been slighted by my thoughtless mother. It was strange that there had been no indication of his fate; no word of his living in some remote place, nor reported discovery of his remains from the attack of beast or savage in the jungle night.

"Cherished son, I'm too old to start all over again," I sighed, as we reached the entrance to Te'nab, but he did not respond. Tree branches and even parts of thatched roofs, were mixed with the rubble of broken pottery that had once been stacked so neatly outside the shrine. Now the remains of years of sacrifices to Kahwil had formed a wall of rubbish across the entrance to the cave. I pulled at the wet branches and soot-slimy potsherds, to expose a passage for us. Little Jaguar still showed no emotion, as he ducked through the opening, his arms carefully encircling his god.

Without a word, Little Jaguar placed his statue, with its intricately woven robes, on the back altar. Within the cave nothing was changed. The home of Kahwil was spared the ravages of Ik, protected by the wall of brush that the god himself seemed to have positioned at its door. I knelt before the pih as Little Jaguar lit the incense in the god-pots and together we chanted the prayer of adoration to the god of our lineage. Once again I felt a bond of great love for my eldest son. Here, within the womb of my ancestors, there was forgiveness and peace. I did not hear the voice of Kahwil, but I felt his strength and wisdom. I would lead my people from this disaster and we would be greater for it. The words I would speak to assure and strengthen them, came to me, and for the first time since my sin, I felt hope.

"We will transform this nightmare into greatness!" I proclaimed to my son as we crawled over the rubble, back out to the disaster that awaited us. "We will transform Jaguar-Sun into something so beautiful that the gods will never again wish to destroy it. This will be the vision I will instill in my people today and it will strengthen them, just as it has strengthened me!"

For the first time, my son smiled. "You are a great leader, beloved father. Your words have the power to inspire even the most oppressed people. When you were much younger than I am now, you led your people from the despair of years of oppression under Pomona. You are not too old to start again. Kahwil has promised you a long life, and this is only the beginning."

I stopped dead in my tracks, and stared at my son in disbelief. He knew! Only Koh and Kan knew of my sin, but no one knew of the curse of Kahwil. No one except Kahwil! Little Jaguar looked at me with what seemed to be sympathy. Had he planned those few words to reveal his knowledge of my secret at just this moment? Did he know because Kahwil had spoken to him as once he'd spoken to me? Or was he, in fact, the Third-Brother of the Three-Born-Together gods — Kahwil, himself? Did he, at that moment, when his eyes showed only non-judgmental love, know what other horrors the day held in store for me?

I resumed our hurried walk towards our residential compound, and tried to concentrate on the words I would use to rally my people that night. Our compound had withstood the storm with only slight damage to some of the roofs. This was less miraculous than it sounds, since most of the homes in the compound were constructed of stone. Still, Koh was quick to claim credit for the power of her influence with Ik. As I listened to her babble proudly about the advantage of Ik's affections for her, I looked at the two-year old boy who clung to her skirts, and wondered again who his father really was.

"Enough!" I cried out to her, and brushed mother and children away, as I hurried past her. Assured that my household was not in need of immediate attention, I noted the position of the sun, and hurried towards the Administration Plaza. "Come with me," I called to Yellow-Knot and Little Jaguar. "This will be the most important meeting of the Chosen Council you will ever witness."

~

All of the eight Ahowob of the Chosen Council of the Clans were waiting on the Administration Plaza, when I arrived with my sons. Nothing remained on the limestone surface, except my jaguar throne. Jaguar-skin cushions, ornate incense pots, ritual staffs of office, finely woven mats, and curtains, had all gone the way of the god house, and were entangled in the jumbled wreckage in the plaza below. The men bowed in respect, then stood around, awkwardly uncertain what to do without the assurance of the accouterments of their office. I sat on my uncushioned throne and motioned for them to sit on the floor before me.

"Ik has spoken as no god has ever done before. No one can doubt that we are at the mercy of a powerful and unpredictable god," I began. My audience nodded and mumbled in anxious agreement. "Ik has broken the pots of the old katun. He has smashed our pride, but he has not broken our spirit. Today we begin the greatest katun ever known to our people. We will win the love of Ik, and we will revel in his might. Today we will begin to build the most beautiful place the gods ever will rest their gaze upon. Throughout the world and the heavens and the underworld, it will be known that Place of Jaguar-Sun exists for the pleasure of the gods. Never again will Ik, or any other deity, find reason to destroy us!"

I watched the men's faces for a sign of the effect of my words. The confidence that seemed to cross them while I was speaking was short-lived as each of them remembered the images of devastation they observed that morning. Little Jaguar seem more disturbed than the others. He kept looking out to the west, his eyes scanning the distant line of trees at the end of the plaza. Then I realized that Kan was missing. It shouldn't have taken so long for him to return from the shrine of Second-Brother. The clan of Chac-Xib-Chac was almost as far west as the shrine, and I asked the young warrior, Chikchan, "Did you see the Shaman as you walked the road here?" Little Jaguar startled at my question, and I realized that Kan had been the object of his anxious watch. But no one had seen the Shaman of the Council since early morning, when we each had gone our respective ways. Chikchan offered the information that the western section had suffered the worst damage, because so many great trees had fallen.

The Ahow of Yum Kaax quickly refuted his claim, by describing the ravaged northern plains. This brought about a confused chorus of exclamations, as every Ahow proclaimed his area as being the most seriously devastated. I listened to the melee with patience, allowing the council to vent its anxiety and trying to decipher the conditions each man described. Finally, I stood up and signaled all speaking to cease. A hush fell over the men, and I could see from their expressions, that they expected their Holy Bacab to offer them a solution. After all, I alone could converse with the gods.

Instead, I addressed each man individually, requesting that they describe what they saw as immediate and long term problems. The Ahow of Yum Kaax presented the most obvious problem, of feeding our people. I assured him there were sufficient reserves in the store-rooms below us, to keep the pangs of hunger from all who remained loyal to the Holy Bacab. I chastised the Ahowob of Mam and Itzamná for failing to foresee this disaster, in either the movements of the stars, or the divining of the seeds. In tears, they explained that the anger of Ik could not be divined by either stars or seeds. Ik was notoriously a god of unpredictable impulses.

"Even Kahwil had not anticipated this outburst," Little Jaguar offered in their defense.

I found myself resenting Little Jaguar's obvious display of his privy to the thoughts of Kahwil. It was becoming apparent to the Ahowob of the Chosen Council that I was no longer the recipient of the counsel of Kahwil. Still, unable to fully accept that my son actually was this god, and not simply my replacement as his intermediary, I found his implications of my loss of favor with our lineage god more and more threatening.

I turned to Bol, and asked him how we would fare, when word of our crop loss reached our allies. The old man shook his head, afraid to answer me honestly. "What else do we have to offer our colonies, to keep them beholden to us?" I asked. Bol looked at me intently and slowly, humbly, asked permission to offer his advice to the Holy Bacab.

"Speak your mind without mercy!" I commanded him. "But share none your idle stories today. Out with it quickly!"

The bent and wrinkled man stood squarely in the middle of his fellow councilmen, licked his lips methodically and began, "If the sky-watchers and daykeepers saw no sign of this crushing blow in the stars, then I would venture to guess that the wrath of Ik was not felt throughout the world. The winds came from the north and smashed into the mountains to the south. It could be assumed that our allies to the east and south experienced nothing more than a storm to greet the new katun."

All of the men listened anxiously for Bol to make his point, but he was not one to be rushed. Carefully, like one who is building a new temple, he laid out the sequence of his rationale before offering his conclusion. It was a masterwork of political maneuvering. He would accompany Little Jaguar down to Place of Split-Sky immediately, on the pretense of offering gifts to the newborn heir of Bird Jaguar. But while he was there, he would negotiate Little Jaguar's marriage into that divine lineage. Before word of our plight had ever reached them, the powerful realm of Split-Sky would be bound to support us. An alliance with a lineage known throughout the world for the unmatched bravery of it's holcan, would virtually guarantee the continued loyalty of our colonies.

The plan seemed flawless! I instructed Kayam to make no mention of the rage of Ik in any of his records of the Seating of the New Katun. Meanwhile, every able-bodied man would be set to work rebuilding Jaguar-Sun. With no crops of their own to fall back on, I was guaranteed an eager and dedicated work-force. Visitors would be assured that all was well in Jaguar-Sun, and our merchants would flaunt our alliance with Split-Sky, as their reason for demanding tribute, without offering our surplus crops in trade.

Only one person seemed unmoved by Bol's strategy. Little Jaguar continued his scan of the plaza below and I assumed his lack of enthusiasm had to do with his concern for the welfare of Kan. But of everyone there, Little Jaguar had the most to gain from the plan. Place of Jaguar-Sun offered no women of divine lineage, and my son would have to do as I, myself, had done, and seek a suitable mother for his heirs from the families of other divine lineages. He was of the age when the need for the comforts of a woman was greatest, and the plan should have excited him, if only for the prospect of procuring a wife.

The thought of my son's departure secretly pleased me. The years he would spend in Place of Split-Sky, in the customary service to his father-in-law, would allow me time to regain my rapport with Kahwil, and the undivided respect of my Council. Even Kan, whose alienation had tormented me since he'd witnessed my sin on the Solstice, might be inspired to resume our friendship, if he no longer had Little Jaguar to serve. It was apparent that as much as I loved my eldest son, Jaguar-Sun was becoming too small for the two of us.

Satisfied that we had resolved the most pressing issue—retaining the status and political strength of our lineage — I went on to address the other problems the hurricane had created. Iguana, the stonemason, assured me that the vaulted tunnel he'd constructed, to contain the nearby river, had successfully protected the precious contents of the storerooms below us. His own clan had not fared so well, however. Two rivers that were usually gentle streams, bordered the compounds of the clans of the Ahowob of Hun Batz, Kauwac, Mam and Itzamná. They were already swollen to capacity from the months of rain, prior to the previous night's onslaught. Now the two rivers had joined into one huge lake, destroying most of the homes and belongings of the clans once nestled between them. Kayam assured me that his compound, which was located on the highest ground of the four clans, had already begun to drain, and it seemed certain that the others would be able to rebuild after a few days without rain.

I advised Chikchan to post extra warriors around the Administration Plaza, since the foodstuffs warehoused below were now extremely precious. Since Bol would be leaving at dawn with Little Jaguar, for Place of Split-Sky, I assigned Kayam the responsibility of monitoring the distribution of this valuable supply, to only those men who had worked from dawn to dusk, on the restoration of our land.

"Tonight we will have a great celebration at the ball court. When our people see that we're not afraid, they'll return to what is left of their homes, inspired to carry on."

I turned to Little Jaguar, who still gazed westward. "We will not send just the heir of Jaguar-Sun to Place of Split-Sky; we will send them our finest hero! Tonight, I will anoint my eldest son 'Ballplayer,' and he will wear the yoke and hacha and carry the handstone of our ancestors."

This announcement, at last, captured Little Jaguar's attention. The other men on the plaza bowed to him, in recognition of the rare honor he'd been promised. The honor of participating in the Ritual of the Ballgame was not usually bestowed on a man, unless a man had proven himself in battle, and returned with a captive of sufficient status to be offered to the gods. Although the new ball court had recently been completed, the young warriors of the Chac-Xib-Chac clan had never gone to battle. Years ago, when their fathers and uncles had beaten the oppressors of Pomona, many of the more influential captives had been sacrificed, during the Ritual of the Ballgame, on an older court that had since fallen into ruin.

"Who will he challenge?" Chikchan asked, knowing that there really would be no contest. When the challenger was of the ruling family, there was never a question who would win. Usually a captive or criminal, weakened severely by starvation and abuse, would serve as the opposition. The object was not to prove physical superiority, but to provide the theatrics necessary, to justify the brutal consequences the victim was destined to endure from the outset.

No other ritual or ceremony could unite and arouse the emotions of a crowd the way the Ballgame Ritual did. This was part of my plan. I knew that tonight, the people of Jaguar-Sun would revel in the pleasure that someone else was suffering more than they were. The formidable Ik would be appeased, with the most precious offering that could be made — human life. And Little Jaguar would be elevated to the revered status of Ballplayer — as valuable a husband as any young woman of the divine Split-Sky dynasty could ever dream to marry.

But who would serve as the hapless opponent? I had no suggestion for Chikchan. The Chosen Council looked at one another and murmured among themselves, but no one offered a recommendation. "Is there no one accused of any serious wrongdoing in all of Jaguar-Sun?" I asked them, amused by the thought. Again they murmured and shrugged, but offered nothing.

Finally Little Jaguar spoke up. "If I could identify the sinner who has brought the anger of Ik upon us, would that man be certain to suffer defeat by my hand tonight?" he asked mysteriously, looking me squarely in the eye. I sat speechless before my Council as they chorused their agreement. If such a man lived, he deserved to be sacrificed for the salvation of all those he'd caused to suffer. My mouth was bone dry as I tried to respond, certain my son was about to disclose my disgraceful transgression. I had no choice but to allow him to expose me. Without taking my eyes from him, I nodded consent, certain my face had already revealed my guilt.

"Fine," Little Jaguar exclaimed, and clamored to his feet. Forced to look up at my accuser, I waited for his words, as if he held his spear to my chest, the thrust of death imminent. "Then I will oppose the Sahal of Tortuguero in the Ball Court tonight!"

"The Sahal of Tortuguero! What has he done?" Bol exclaimed, before I'd even comprehended my escape from condemnation. The others repeated his cry of astonishment, but Little Jaguar remained silent, never taking his eyes from mine.

"The Ballplayer did not make the revelation of his opponent's sin part of the condition," I announced, my voice suddenly returned to me. "We have assured him his opponent and no further explanation is required. Chikchan, you will find the miserable slug in my compound, I'm sure. If no yoke will fit around his waist, make one with some rolled mats, and prepare him for the game!"

I pounded my staff on the floor to signal that all discussion had ended, and watched as the men of my council straggled down the west stairs. Little Jaguar sat on the floor before me and seemed to be struggling for the words to say. "Without her father's cunning advice, Koh will not be so quick to claim the blessings of Ik," he stated flatly.

"And the boy? Is his grandfather also his father?" I asked, quick to assume that my son's knowledge somehow surpassed my own. But Little Jaguar seemed surprised by my question.

"Shark?" he asked.

"She carried the child before I ever knew her," I explained. But Little Jaguar didn't seem interested in continuing the discussion. Apparently Shark's legitimacy as an heir was of no concern to him.

"I'm going to find out what's happened to Kan," he whispered, changing the subject completely.

As I watched him rise and walk towards the west stairs, I called out, "I am grateful to you, cherished son!" Little Jaguar continued down the stairs without acknowledging my thanks, leaving me to wonder still, just what he knew about me.

For the first time since morning, I noticed Yellow-Knot, who had sat quietly beside me through all of this. "Come, my brave little warrior, I'll tell you about the Ballgame Ritual your brother will perform tonight," I said, and rested my arm on his shoulder, as we walked toward the north end of the Plaza, where I could point out the various features of the ball court below us.

"Beloved father, why does my brother wish to challenge Grandfather?" Yellow-Knot asked, and I could hear fear and confusion in his voice. I hadn't realized how upsetting the night's events would be to the boy, and for the first time I considered the effect the sacrifice would have on my household. My first reaction had been of such relief, that Little Jaguar hadn't named me as the cause of Jaguar-Sun's problems, that I'd failed to consider how callused my reaction to the condemnation of my father-in-law might seem. Even as I stood there, on the Plaza stairs, Chikchan and his warriors were informing the grotesque Sahal of his fate. No doubt, they would be forced to drag their cumbersome captive all the way to the ball court. He would certainly not face his challenger with the resignation of a drugged captive warrior.

Suddenly, I was uncertain why Little Jaguar had chosen such a pathetic opponent. Did he realize that Koh's father was somehow responsible for the anger of the gods? Or had he simply chosen the easiest victim he could think of? And had he considered the chaos his choice would create?

My mind raced on, oblivious to Yellow-Knot's questions. If I allowed my father-in-law to be sacrificed, Koh would never welcome me to her bed again. Had this been Little Jaguar's motive? Was my son acting with divine wisdom, or was he merely avenging his mother's loss of power, or even assuring that Koh would bear me no more sons?

"Father, don't let him sacrifice Grandfather!" Yellow-Knot cried, tears running down his cheeks.

"He is not your Grandfather!" I roared, annoyed that the boy interrupted my thoughts. Your grandfathers were honorable men."

Yellow-Knot stopped crying and I could see that his mind was working hard, trying to somehow add my words to his perception of the world. "I will explain," I said and sat down on the top step of the stairway, looking out over the muddy lake that only yesterday was fertile, alluvial terrain. "Your grandfathers were both shamans. Yellow-Macaw was my father and Great Jaguar was your mother's father. He was an Its'at from Tikal…"

I sat on the stairs and recited for my second son the long, ancient story of his heritage, and as I spoke, my words felt comforting and reassuring. The Jaguar-Sun lineage had been through many hardships; my ancestors had fallen victim to all the weaknesses of men

— sins far more disgraceful than mine; and yet we had prevailed. We would rise up again, I knew that, in the deepest part of myself. That is the secret of the survival of the True People; we know that the cycle will always repeat itself. Even as I and my sons carried the names of our ancestors, we would carry their burdens and their dreams, and each time we played out our destinies, we would make wiser choices...

~

K'in had traveled almost to the end of the world, by the time I finished my story. Already people had begun to gather in the courtyard below, in anticipation of the evening's rituals. I heard footsteps behind me, and turned to see Ahpo Hel walking towards me, carrying my ritual costume. She was smiling! Actually, she was glowing!

"What pleases you, old woman?" I asked her. "You would not find delight in the grief of Koh tonight, would you?"

"She will not take you to her bed tonight, old man!" she replied, obviously relishing that thought.

"And will you keep me warm, if that is so?" I retorted, certain she would use the opportunity to torment me.

"There has not been a night that I would have turned you away, in all the years I have been your wife. Tonight will not be any different," she answered, as demurely as a young bride.

My wife held out the garments and ornaments for me to put on, but instead of reciting the prayers customary for a ritual dressing, we continued alluding to the comforts we would enjoy with one another that night. We both knew that I would be in no condition to perform as a husband after the previous day's bloodletting, but just the same, the tenderness and desire, we once shared, seemed to have returned. And once again, I forgot about the ever present, ever observant, Yellow-Knot. But it was good that he understood who his mother was, and how deeply she was loved by his father.

Finally attired, we descended the north stairs, to the courtyard where Little Jaguar was now waiting with Kan. "It's good to see that misfortune has not befallen the Shaman" I said to Kan, as we met them.

"Misfortune has befallen all of us," Kan sighed.

"Those are words you will not speak again!" I commanded. "Hasn't Little Jaguar explained the plans the Council made today?"

Kan nodded, apparently not pleased by what he'd been told, then changed the subject. "Soon I will hand your son the yoke and hacha, just as once I handed you the costume of the Holy Bacab."

"We were only boys!" I exclaimed, as I recalled how terrified I was that day.

"I was a boy, but you were the Holy Bacab." Kan replied. "On that day I lost my friend. Today, I will be left alone, once again."

Little Jaguar put his hand on Kan's shoulder, and led him towards the Ball Court. I watched them, and tried to understand what Kan was saying. He suddenly seemed old and tired.

The musicians began to rap on their turtle-shell drums, and shrill their clay flutes, and shake their rattles, and the procession began. I walked beside Ahpo Hel, with Yellow Knot strutting proudly before us, through the narrow expanse of the ball court, holding the staff of Kahwil high in the air. Along the top of both sloping ball court sides, Chikchan's young warriors stood stiff and proud holding their spears in one hand and their ritual shields in the other. The people of Jaguar-Sun packed the plaza to the north, where only yesterday they had cowered under the assault of Ik. I sensed their anxious mood, even though their flickering torches concealed their faces.

Holding my staff high to signal quiet, I began the words I'd pieced together throughout the day. I spoke to them of the glory that would be ours, of the strength of our heritage and the richness of our people. I assured them that the gods would never again make us suffer and that the powerful Ik would become our ally against our enemies. And as I spoke, I could feel the mood of the crowd change; their torches were held a little higher and their respectful silence was punctuated often with shouts of agreement. When I was sure that I had brought the spirit of the crowd to a crescendo of hope, I offered them their prize.

"Tonight," I proclaimed, "Ik will choose his sacrifice — either the son of the Holy Bacab..." I pointed to the tall, young man who stood at the end of the ball court on my right, "or the incestuous sinner, who took the innocence of his own daughter — a child born to serve the gods!"

I pointed my staff with contempt at the obese man being dragged to the opposite end of the ball court. The sound of surprise from the crowd was overpowered by the shouts from the accused. "It's not true! It's not true! I swear by my love for Ik it's not true!" he cried out. "It was the jaguars! I tried to warn you! The jaguars!"

That's when I saw Koh. She was being restrained by two warriors all the way over by the Administration Plaza, but I could hear her screams, even above her father's cries and the taunting of the crowd. She was hysterical with grief, and pulled at her guards with the strength of a wild cat. I turned to the crowd.

"It is for Ik to decide!" I called out, and pounded my staff on the ball court, once in each direction, to awaken the deities of the underworld on whose altar we now performed. Then I walked to the north end of the ball court and touched my son's head with my staff. Kan proceeded to position the wooden yoke around Little Jaguar's hips and inserted a hacha, in the shape of First-Brother, in the front of the yoke, at his groin. Little Jaguar's arms and knees were wrapped with heavy cotton and leather padding, and his hair was pulled to a knot on his forehead. He stood straight and sure of himself, waiting for his opponent to be garbed by the warriors who had forced him there.

A makeshift yoke had been hastily assembled with rolled reed mats, that barely encircled the Sahal's wide girth. The crowd roared with laughter as one warrior held up the *hacha* — a feathered shield used in rituals, that would obviously offer no protection to his male parts. On it had been painted the grinning face of a simpleton. Oblivious to his ridiculous appearance, the Sahal began to shout insults and threats to his opponent. Now the warriors were struggling to keep him in position as their charge spat huge globs of saliva towards Little Jaguar.

"Ik will prove me innocent!" he roared, as he pulled himself free from the warriors and rushed towards Little Jaguar.

"Ik waits to see you score," called Little Jaguar, and he brushed past the fat man and moved lightly towards the center of the court, where the heavy rubber ball had been positioned. Dropping to one knee he maneuvered his hips so that with his thigh he poked the ball into play. It rose from the ground only slightly, but Little Jaguar hit it directly with his yoke and it flew up and towards his goal. The Sahal rushed to stop it but tripped over his own feet and fell forward. He spit out a string of insults, while Little Jaguar bounced the ball off his hip to score again.

The game continued longer than anyone had expected, with the Sahal finding incredible stamina in his fear of death. Over and over he struggled to his feet, while Little Jaguar continued to score, almost completely unimpeded by his opponent. But scoring was only important to impress the gods. An honorable victory called for your opponent's collapse, from injury or exhaustion. Only then could the victor sever the head of his opponent with one swift slice of his obsidian knife.

Little Jaguar's opportunity finally came, when the clumsy Sahal took the oncoming ball directly in his chest. His eyes bulged in agony, as in one horrifying moment he gasped for his last breath, and fell backwards onto the stone court, the smack of his head echoing off the ball court walls. Little Jaguar caught the blade Kan tossed to him, and cried out a furious curse, as he grabbed the hair of his fallen opponent and separated his gruesome head from his disgusting body. He seemed as practiced as a veteran Ballplayer, as he attached the bloody mess onto the head of his spear, and held it aloft for the cheering crowd.

The effect of the spectacle was exactly as I'd planned. The crowd followed behind us in a frenzy, as the Ballplayer of Jaguar-Sun paraded his bloody trophy to the Temple of Ik. Ascending the stairs alone, he stood in the central doorway, where only last night I had offered my own blood to the insatiable Ik. "For Ik!" he shouted over and over, as he held his offering up for the crowd. The People of Jaguar-Sun repeated his cry, "For Ik! For Ik! For Ik!" I could feel the excitement of their voices in my skin and I knew the spirit of Ik had overtaken the people of Jaguar-Sun. This would truly be a new katun!

Finally, Little Jaguar set his spear into a hole in the temple floor, and descended the temple stairs, leaving his sacrifice to be consumed by the gods. The body of the Sahal had been left on the ball court, the altar of the Lords of the Night. Tonight they would come as jaguars, to claim their prize. The ceremony was complete, and the people returned to their homes, as confident and inspired as I had hoped.

~

"Beloved father, I wish to speak with you, alone," Little Jaguar said seriously, as we stood in the plaza.

"What troubles the hero of Jaguar-Sun on this glorious night!" I laughed, thinking his sober attitude entirely inappropriate.

"Alone, please, good father," he pleaded, growing more agitated.

"Come, we'll go see if the baths survived the hurricane," I responded happily, and taking a torch from one of the warriors, I led him to the platform beyond the ball court, where a bath house had been constructed in the time of my ancestors. The bath house was alongside a section of the river, that widened into what was usually a clear and peaceful pool. As we approached it, I noted that, although the waters had risen to almost the height of the platform, the baths were still in good condition. After carefully removing our respective costumes and ornaments, we eased into the welcome coolness of the stone tubs, and allowed the water to relieve us of the remnants of the day. Little Jaguar slid entirely under the water and swirled his long black hair in the dark liquid. The torch I'd positioned in the wall behind us, cast glimmers of blood-red light into his flowing tresses, as my son sloughed off the blood of the Sahal that had caked on his body.

He emerged from the water in a start and shook his head like a wild animal, then pulled himself up onto the stone ledge, his feet dangling in the water. I remained standing in the bath, savoring the way it cooled me, waiting for the Ballplayer to reveal what was troubling him. Finally the young man spoke.

"Send Yellow-Knot to Split-Sky, instead of me. He is born to be a warrior and there is no better place for him to learn than under the tutelage of the fiercest of holcan," he said in a tone of pleading rather than advice.

"But you're the heir apparent! You're the one who must father the lineage. It's time you married and there is no suitable bride here," I explained, astonished by his reluctance.

Little Jaguar studied the ripples his feet were creating as he moved them rhythmically in the bath. "I have no desire for any of the women in Split-Sky," he murmured.

"How can you know that! The last time you were there you were just a boy. The girls you may be remembering have grown into women. I'm sure there will be one of your liking," I retorted, quickly losing patience with his foolishness.

"No! I wish to remain here!" he answered, suddenly arrogant.

"There is no one worthy of you here," I said, near anger. "Don't you understand how important this union is to our strategy. We need Split-Sky as an ally!"

"Then send Yellow-Knot! I've done enough for my people with this bloody performance tonight! You act as if my life is something you can manipulate to your advantage. No one ever asks me what I want. You make decisions... strategies... with me, as if I were a slave to be ordered about, with no voice in my own destiny."

"You will be Holy Bacab!" I screamed in frustration. "You have no more to say about your destiny than a slave. You exist to serve your people and your gods, and there is no escaping it. They are all your masters. Don't you think I have longed all my life for the freedom of the common laborer? He marries whomever he wishes, he builds his hut, works his milpa in the rainy season, works in the quarry in the dry season. It's all so simple for him. And if he drinks too much, or sleeps with his friend's wife, or forgets to pray or fast, who suffers but him?

"But you are born with divine blood, my son. You are the first-born, chosen to protect and nurture the gods, as your ancestors did before you. Your destiny is not your choice, it's your obligation!"

The young man began to kick his feet, creating loud splashes in the bath. When he saw that the sprays of water were hitting me in the face he increased his wild thrashing, until I was forced to pull myself from the water. "What son shows his father such disrespect!" I screamed, wiping the water from my face; panicked by my son's strange behavior. Little Jaguar stopped kicking and rose to stand beside me.

"I'm sorry, father," he whispered in sincere repentance. "What god must I plead with to free me from this obligation. Is there nothing else I can offer the gods in exchange for a task I find so revolting?"

"What's so revolting about marrying a woman from Split-Sky? Is there someone else who has already captured your heart?" I pleaded, anxious to understand why my son would make such an issue out of such a seemingly simple thing. By his sudden change in expression I realized I'd identified the problem.

"Is she from Jaguar-Sun?" I asked, when his silence confirmed my guess. Little Jaguar looked down into the water and nodded.

"Please tell me this common woman does not carry your first-born!" I cried in panic.

"No! No there is no need to fear that!" he eagerly explained.

"Good! Then you will go to Split-Sky and take a wife of divine blood. After she has born you a son, you can take this other one to your bed, as I have done with Koh."

"As you have done with my mother!" he screamed and jumped back into the bath. His shouts echoed on the stone walls like the voices of the gods. "I will never hurt the one I love, the way you've hurt my mother! We're all sinners! We're all weak! But I'll defy the will of the gods before I'll ever marry a woman from Split-Sky!"

I was afraid the people of Jaguar-Sun would hear his disrespectful tirade, or worse, that the gods would hear his blasphemous threats. Little Jaguar sensed my discomfort and continued to shout. In exasperation I agreed to send Yellow-Knot to Split-Sky and rushed from the bath house to end his loud, humiliating tantrum.

In the modest cloak of night, I walked naked along the bank of the river, to where its water crashed violently down the escarpment that led to the flooded northern plains. The cool mud squished in-between my toes and the splashing cascades combined with the steady hum of the night insects, in a soothing song.

I sat on a rock near the water's edge, and studied the flashes of moonlight on the broken surface of the rushing water. It seemed that the past two days had been filled with the greatest highs and lows of my life. I felt exhausted and confused. I thought about Ahpo Hel's offer to hold me in her bed, and, for the first time in many years, her body did not seem so old or uninviting. Somehow Koh's youth had lost its appeal. Little Jaguar's devotion to his secret love seemed understandable, and even admirable, in the awesome loneliness of the night. In fact, the longer I sat there the more diffused my sense of right and wrong grew. The night wore on and sleep alternated with my wakeful vigil, the sounds of night melting into the voices of my dreams, and resuming once again, as a background to my thoughts.

Suddenly there was a new sound added to the, now familiar, movement of the water, and murmuring of the insects. It was the steady, almost comforting rumble of a great cat. I turned slowly to see the powerful beast poised beside me, but felt no fear. His eyes reflected the moonlight in a piercing stare, but the smooth, easy movement of his great chest conveyed his relaxed breathing. Gracefully, he stretched one mighty paw, and then the other, onto the rocks, and lowered his massive body to rest beside me, never taking his eyes from mine. I knew I was in the presence of a Lord of the Night.

I sat without moving, beside my strange companion, and wondered if his contented company could be explained because he'd just satisfied himself with the abundant offering left for him on the ball court. The blood around his mouth was most certainly the Sahal's. Was I to consider it a blessing, or a curse, to share the night with this magnificent, fearsome creature? Time took on that immeasurable nature of a dream as the jaguar continued to watch me with his penetrating gaze. Then, just as quietly as he had arrived, he pulled his great body up, and carefully picked his way over the rocky cascades, disappearing in the forest beyond. When he was gone, I rubbed my eyes, wondering if I'd been dreaming. But awake or asleep, a visit from a Lord of the Night could only mean trouble was at hand.

When I rose to leave, my bones felt old and weary and resisted being asked to move. I considered if it would have made any difference to the world if the Lord of the Night had devoured me. What value does an old man have, I thought, as I remembered Little Jaguar's arrogant accusations. Why do the young always think they know better than those who have already made so very many mistakes? If I knew what disappointments awaited me, I would have chosen the lesser pain in the jaws of the jaguar.

I walked quietly back to the bath house to get my clothing, when I noticed a torch still flickered inside. Then I heard the sound of my son's groans and thought, with horror, "It was Little Jaguar's blood I saw on the beast's face!" I raced to the bath house with the sudden speed and agility of a youth, gripped with the vision of my son's torn, bloody body. His groan's grew louder and more horrifying, until, just as I reached the entrance to the baths, he let out a piercing cry!

"Oh cherished son I'll save you!" I screamed, as I swung into the doorway.

It took me some time to realize what I had seen. At first I thought that Kan had reach the poor mangled boy before me, and was bending over him to help. It's strange how we can have an image in our minds and try to force everything we see to fit that image. That's why, at first, I interpreted Kan's expression of horror, as an indication of the extent of Little Jaguar's injuries. It wasn't until my son sprang to his feet, and faced me in shame, that I realized that his cries were not from pain, but pleasure... pleasure he'd enjoyed from the man in the huipil, who once called himself my friend!

Kan fell to his knees before me, crying for forgiveness, but my son just stood facing me stoically, without remorse. I spat at him in disgust, and grabbed Kan by his hair and pulled his face to the ground, as one holds a captive. "You've ruined him!" I screamed hysterically. "It's all your fault! For you he will not take a wife!" I could feel my whole body shaking with revulsion and hatred. "You've destroyed my son, my heir! You've desecrated my lineage! I made you part of my household. I entrusted this boy to your care! And you have betrayed my trust! I will make a sacrifice of you so horrible you cannot even begin to imagine the pain!"

At my first suggestion of punishment, Little Jaguar leapt to his lover's defense, pushing me from him. "He had no choice in this. It was my doing. I demanded this from him. You can't punish Kan for obeying the directives of the heir!" he cried. "I'm the one who should be punished," he pleaded, as Kan raced from the bath house into the night.

I turned to chase him, but my son grabbed my arm and held me fast. My strength, even enraged, was no match for his size and youth. I turned on him, but he held me immobile, while I screamed and cursed, until I was so hoarse all I could do was cry. Finally, I jerked myself from his hold, and quickly wrapped my loincloth around myself.

"Kan will be punished for this," I snarled, "And you will hear his screams for mercy for the rest of your life. You rejected your destiny for this!" I swung away from him, and taking the torch from its holder, left him in the darkness. As I raced towards my home, I cried as no man has ever cried before. My son and my friend had betrayed and disgraced me, and I had no idea what to do next.

The stillness around my compound belied the turmoil that had just struck my household. Ahpo Hel was still awake, sitting on a mat, just inside her sleeping hut, she'd been waiting for me. I walked to her like a beaten warrior, and though she didn't know how, she knew my heart was broken. I buried my face in her shoulder and cried like a child.

Finally, calmed by her, I fumbled for the words to explain what had happened. It took far less than I thought.

"I've suspected as much for some time now," she whispered, shaking her head sadly, but hardly surprised or upset.

"How could you suspect something like this and not tell me, or put a stop to it?" I cried out, trying to keep my voice muffled.

"You yourself have acknowledged that our son is the embodiment of Kahwil," she whispered. "If a god chooses these strange pleasures, how can you or I tell him he is wrong?"

"It's Kan's fault!" I exclaimed. "He's corrupted the boy. One day he dresses as a man, the next as a woman. It seemed harmless. I trusted he would never to do anything that would hurt the boy."

"This was not Kan's doing. Since you were children he has loved you, even more than I have. But never once did he even suggest that you should share the affections of a husband and wife. I can't believe he would have initiated this with Little Jaguar. Think about it… our son has never even mentioned an attraction to women."

Ahpo Hel's words stung me and I reacted like one who had been stabbed. "How dare you speak this way about your own son. Who knows how long Kan's been twisting his senses… maybe since he was a baby. Oh, I curse myself for making the monster his guardian! I'll summon Chikchan as soon as there's light, to find the scoundrel. There will be a public sacrifice that will make the death of the Sahal seem like a quiet, painless sleep!"

"Would you undo all that you've achieved today, just to salve your own hurt pride?" Ahpo Hel asked, as gently as I'd ever heard her speak. "Beloved husband, it would be better for everyone if you spoke to no one of this. If you publicly disgrace the son, whom you've proclaimed heir and god of our ancestors, you will bring disgrace to all of us, and to all of our ancestors. Let the gods mete out their own punishment. Their afflictions will be far more just and painful than anything you could do."

I was too painfully aware of the validity of her advice and willing to concede that a public disgrace would serve no purpose, but I resolved to have Kan found and secretly, and mercilessly destroyed. But even that small satisfaction was denied me. When morning broke, Lightning Bolt stood at my door with a message that he was certain would disturb me. He would never know just why, or how much. Kan had been found hanging from a Ceiba tree, dead by his own doing. This, I knew, was a death of honor. When his spirit reached the entrance to Xibalba, he would be required to wait at the door, until the time when he had been destined to arrive, had he not taken his own life. But there would be no further pain, nor disgrace, for the Shaman of the Council.

# BOOK FOUR
# The Return

# Palenque

I looked up to see my daughter, Kit, standing before me, the expression on her face obviously fearful.

"Mommy? Are you O.K.?" she stammered.

I squinted, trying to focus on her face, despite the glare of the sun, low in the sky behind her.

"Dios Mio!" José exclaimed. "What language was that. If I didn't know you better, I'd swear you were just speaking in some Maya dialect. Those gas fumes must have had more of an effect on you than I realized. Some people are more sensitive to things like that than others."

It was obvious that José was shaken up, but I was unable to comprehend what was upsetting him. While I recognized both him and my daughter, somehow I felt distant and removed from them, as if I was looking at strangers. Pulled back from my "dream" too abruptly, I wanted to just close my eyes and return to what was happening only moments earlier, in the remote recesses of my mind. The words and concerns of those around me were a tremendous annoyance and I resisted their intrusion, determined to return to my fast-fading dream. But the memory was slipping away from me even as I sat there frantically trying to preserve it. Before I was even fully awake, it had escaped me entirely.

My dreamy distance only served to further alarm José and Kit, and soon their anxious voices dominated my consciousness. Never before had I resisted awakening so vehemently. Realizing that the memory of my dream was completely erased, I felt myself shaking with the grief of one who has just suffered a tragic loss.

"What's wrong?" Kit moaned compassionately, as she touched the tears that were falling from my eyes. I sat speechless before her. It was as if the words to express my feelings had to go through some kind of translation. My brain struggled to reassemble my thoughts into a new language — a language that lacked the words to adequately convey such profound thoughts — thoughts I'd easily expressed only moments earlier. Moments that were over 1300 years ago!

Silently, I rose from the rock I'd been resting on, for apparent centuries, and joined my companions. As we walked towards the parking lot, I allowed the sound of their voices to pull me securely into the present. Still, what I saw around me reverberated with a sense of recognition far too powerful to simply be called déjà vu. I'd been there before—I knew this place! I turned to José and whispered mysteriously, "See those miniature avocados, they're a favorite food of the quetzal."

"There are no quetzal around here," José replied smugly but then he swung around to look at me with his eyes full of puzzlement. His astonished reaction delighted me and I teased his curiosity further.

"Not so!" I snapped belligerently. "I've been here before… a very long time ago… hunting quetzal."

"Don't let anyone hear you saying that!" he admonished with a slight hint of amusement in his voice. "There is a severe penalty for killing that bird. It's almost extinct."

"What's a quetzal look like," Kit asked, strangely undisturbed by my announcement of being there before.

That was when I realized that I had no idea what a quetzal looked like. By now José was laughing with delight. "Those gas fumes made your mother a little crazy," he sputtered to Kit. "But I'm glad to see she's talking again. Imagine, hunting for a bird when you don't even know what it looks like! We'd better get this crazy woman to the hotel in Palenque before she starts confessing to anymore crimes."

~

I awoke before dawn and groped quietly in the dark for my black silk robe, careful not to disturb Kit. Once again I had the feeling that I'd been dreaming about my past, but this time I sensed that soon I would be able to remember the dreams. The words of the old Indian in San Cristobal echoed in my mind. "Recordar"— to remember — he'd said. I wondered if the herbs he'd given to me had been responsible for the vivid dream I'd had at Agua Azul. I felt around the floor of the dark room for the skirt I'd been wearing the day before and found it near my bed. Reaching into the pocket, I procured the suspicious pouch.

"It wasn't a dream at all, it was a memory!" I exclaimed aloud, shaking with the excitement of this new insight.

The sound of my voice caused Kit to stir, but she didn't awaken. I sat gingerly on the edge of her bed, smoothed her long brown hair that lay sprawled across her pillow, and tried to imagine where all these strange occurrences were taking us. Was I soon to understand, not only what had driven me to go to Mexico, but perhaps even why I was born? I sensed that the answer was as close as the magic pouch that I held in my hands, it's powers so ominous that I was afraid to bring it to my nose. What if I went back to the dream and never returned?

With the first pale light of dawn on the thin voile curtains, I unlocked the door to our room and stepped outside to the misty, damp morning. We were on the second floor of the Hotel Mision Palenque, which was a relatively modern accommodation, compared to some of the more quaint and romantic places we'd stayed on our journey. On each floor, a balcony ran the full length of the building, with stairs on each end. Facing east, I watched the first red glow of the sun, just beginning its ascent, from the rolling hills that extended as far as I could see. On the grounds below, grew an enormous Ceiba tree, it's trunk ridged deeply and it's branches spreading almost to where I stood. In a cage, just beyond the majestic tree, an ocelot paced off the meager space he was allotted, stopping each time he came to the end of his prison, to gaze at the distant hills, now draped in the red light of dawn. Despite the fact that I couldn't see the poor creature very clearly in the early light, I sensed his yearning for the freedom, that was always there for him to see, but never again to enjoy.

Sitting on a small stone bench, just outside my room, I watched the sunrise, while my hands idly toyed with the Indian's pouch. I could hear the growl-like roar of howler monkeys in the distance, orchestrated with a variety of birds calls and barking dogs, as the world around me began to awaken. Suddenly, I realized that these noises were identical to the sounds of the eclipse dream I'd had, on the night following my past life regression with Reverend Blaze. Alone, watching the morning mist rising from around the giant Ceiba tree, I tried to understand the connection my faint memories of the past had, with what was happening in the present. What was it I was supposed to remember, and why?

The silhouette of a man approached silently from the far end of the balcony. It was easy to recognize José's stride, before I could see his face.

"I couldn't sleep, worrying about you," he explained, as he came before me. "You were acting like you were drugged or something yesterday. How do you feel this morning?"

Maybe that was it! Maybe I was drugged. The dream that seemed so real, yet remained so elusive, could have been some type of hallucination! "José, you know a lot about herbs and stuff like that. What do you suppose is in this pouch?" I asked, and held out the mysterious amulet for him to examine. José tried to force some of the herbs from the loose weave of the casing, but it still wasn't quite light enough for him to identify its contents. He held the pouch to his nose and took one hesitant sniff and then a longer, quizzical inhale. Shaking his head in puzzlement he seemed to be searching his memory for something remotely familiar.

"It's nothing I can recognize off-hand. Maybe rosemary? But there are many powerful herbs known to the local shamans, some that only become powerful with the spells they are endowed with by magicians — some good and some very evil. Maybe you were under some kind of spell yesterday. You certainly acted like you were."

José took me by the shoulders and pulled me up to him and encircled me in an embrace. "I wish that I could put a spell on you, that would make you fall helplessly in love with me," he murmured. The way his body felt, so close to mine, made me think that it wouldn't take too much of a spell to entice me.

"Maybe you are the one I'm supposed to remember," I whispered, and allowed him to kiss me deeply and passionately.

"Marry me!" José spontaneously exclaimed, as if he'd just thought of it. "Come live here and marry me."

"I have someone waiting for me at home," I stammered, hesitant to say anything that would end his embrace. "I love him."

"But you will love me more! Before this trip is over, you'll realize that you love me more. Just now, when we kissed, I felt as if a tremendous burden had been lifted from me. My whole life I have been looking for you... longing for the way you make me feel," he cried.

"José, we're so different," I countered. "I don't even speak the language you think in! How could we ever really share our feelings?" I rationalized, groping for an explanation to my sense that something was wrong.

"Let me make love to you, just once, and you'll know that we will have no trouble sharing our feelings. The language of love needs no translation," he replied, again pulling me exquisitely close to him.

Encircled in his embrace I could seen the caged ocelot staring out toward the hills. Would these arms, that felt so tempting, one day confine me, like that poor beast? The thought came and went, unheeded, as I savored José's affections.

But our embrace was suddenly interrupted by the sound of the door next to my room opening. We heard Andy's radio, tuned to the BBC newscast, before we even saw his bedraggled form emerge from his room, radio in hand.

"There's been a plane accident in Hawaii," our unwelcome guest announced, too loudly for the time of day. His voice destroyed both the peace of the dawn and the romance of our interlude. "Seems like the top of the plane just tore off in mid-flight. Bizarre!"

José and I quickly composed ourselves, and tried to respond to our intruder's conversation. But a plane accident in Hawaii was the last thing in the world I wanted to discuss. "I'm going to get showered and dressed," I said blankly and left José to exchange civilities with the Englishman.

~

Walking into the site of Palenque was like stepping directly into my dreams. From the moment I stepped out of the station wagon I recognized the way the air felt, the fragrance of every plant and the sound of each bird. The whole place had an aura of exquisite beauty and peace, and the comfort of familiarity. I wasn't the only one who was struck by the profound emotions Palenque evoked. David, the architect in our group, commented, after only just glancing around, that if he'd seen this place earlier in his career, he would have designed his buildings very differently — more in harmony with their surroundings. As David spoke, I recalled the anguish I'd expressed during my past life regression, about my failure to accomplish what had been the purpose of that life. Perhaps, I thought, Pacal had not failed after all. Everything around us seemed to be in perfect harmony.

Even Elmer, who had professed to traveling to just about everywhere in the world, seemed immediately taken with Palenque. He walked along nodding in approval then turned to me, about to say something, his face alight with a warm grin. But when he opened his mouth to speak, he seemed to forget what he was about to say, or perhaps thought better of it, and instead closed his lips in a contented sigh.

José led us down a path with several ruins along the hill to our right. Before he'd said a word, I recognized the Temple of

Inscriptions ahead of us. This structure had been photographed in many of the books I'd read about the Maya. Here was the first Maya temple that was found to contain a tomb. This was where the sarcophagus of the great ruler of Palenque was discovered, on the day I was born! José repeated the story of how the archaeologist, Alberto Ruz, first noticed four plugged circles in the floor of the temple. When he removed the plugs, the four openings allowed the stone slab "floor" to be removed, revealing a stairway into the temple that had been entirely filled in with rubble. It took Ruz and his team two seasons to finally clear the secret passage that led to the ornately sculptured room, enclosing the now-famous sarcophagus of the great Maya ruler.

We struggled up the steep steps of the Temple, and I tried to imagine how the small-statured Maya could have ascended these steps with dignity. Strangely, as I drew closer to the top, it became increasingly easier for me to visualize the ornately dressed ruler striding up each steep step, carefully balancing his feathered headdress, holding the staff of his lineage out before him, his entourage following respectfully behind. As usual, Kit was the first to reach the top, apparently unchallenged by the arduous climb. But as I neared the top, my body began to feel achy and tired, and very, very old. Finally, gasping for breath, I stepped into the center doorway of the temple and turned to look out over the site. To my left was a vast, stepped platform with many long buildings on it's perimeter. This was called the Palace by archaeologists and assumed to be a residence for the royal family. Beyond that, several structures lined a long escarpment that edged the plateau which the entire site was situated on. Beyond that, were lush green plains, as far as the eye could see. I wasn't sure if I was seeing water on the very distant horizon, or only the blue of the sky, meeting the edge of the earth. It was that view of the horizon that startled me — it hadn't changed in over 1300 years! I could see the ancient Ceiba tree where, throughout the year, the star cluster of the Turtle lineage would rise to the right, just barely clear the top branches, and fall back into the underworld on the left. That was the center of the world, the place where the sacred tree of life joined earth with the worlds below and above us. How many nights had I sat with Kan watching the progression of the stars and gods around that treetop! How many mornings I'd stood on this very spot and wondered if that was the tree where Kan had hung himself.

Kan? I looked back at the horizon but the tree was gone! It was a memory, as clear as a recollection of an event in my childhood, but for the first time, it hadn't disappeared. The dreams were coming to the surface at last!

I spent the remainder of the day slipping in and out of the body and mind of Hanab Pacal, Holy Bacab of Jaguar Sun. Time took on a strange character of being all-present, so that no one seemed to notice the elapsed spans when I wasn't Christina. I adroitly followed José down the dark, slippery steps within the Temple of the Inscriptions leading to the tomb of Pacal. But as I peered through the dark opening to see the dim outline of the sarcophagus cover, the room suddenly burst into brightness. This was the way it looked when it's construction had just been completed, years before the temple was built above it. I knew that this room was actually built into the opening of the lineage cave of Te'nab. This was Kahwil's temple! The one Kahwil himself had directed me to build.

Oblivious to my thoughts, José pointed out the stone duct that led from the tomb, up the stairs, to the temple above. "No one knows the purpose of this duct. It's unique in all of the ruins of the Maya," he explained.

"It was necessary to maintain contact with Kahwil, the god whose idol was forever entombed behind this shrine," I replied softly, not really wishing to explain. José continued up the dark, slippery stairs before us, apparently not hearing my perfectly logical explanation. According to José, archaeologists were also puzzled by the apparent age of the skeleton found in this tomb. It seemed to be a man of 40 or 50 years old, while, according to the hieroglyphs that had been deciphered on the site, Pacal had lived to be eighty. I made no attempt to explain the magical powers of the god who had condemned the ruler of Jaguar-Sun to such unusual longevity, to suffer until he had learned to forgive, both himself and others. Pacal didn't age physically from the day Kahwil passed that sentence on him. Anger and hatred were the burdens of punishment he was forced to carry, yet for thirty years, Pacal had carried them, and his life was filled with isolation and disappointment.

When I emerged from the tomb, I was again Christina, but I could remember everything that I'd recalled of Pacal. With each temple that we visited, new memories were evoked and retained! At the Palace I recalled the council meeting, hastily called after the devastating hurricane of Ik. I remembered adding the White Stone House on the Administration Plaza, following a battle where we'd joined forces with a group of warriors Yellow-Knot had brought back with him with from Split-Sky. There was an obnoxious *holcan* leading them, named Bolom-Te-Chac. How I despised him — yet allowed him to convince me to accompanying him in that assault on Pomona.

The memories returned in such abundance that I grew nauseous with the confusion. Names and faces... events... like the ballgame where I decapitated my prisoner, Ch'a-u-bac, to dedicate a second god-house on the plaza. I never admitted how much I regretted that sacrifice. I had grown to respect Ch'a-u-bac, during the five years he was my most prized captive. But he was a Pomona noble, and his blood was necessary to avenge the desecration his father had brought on my lineage. Or was it? The death of Ch'a-u-bac brought me only further loneliness and confusion.

As we walked among the three temples known as the Cross Group, José explained that these buildings were built by Pacal's successor, Chan Balum. I realized, as we climbed the steep path to the temple that was nestled in the hillside, known as the Temple of the Foliated Cross, that it was Little Jaguar who had actually succeeded in creating art that could be understood by any sensitive observer, not with the language of words, but with the language of the spirit. The tree-cross was clearly a tribute to the man we had both grown to love. I knew, as I peered through the iron gate that had been built to keep observers from getting too close to the carved panels on the back wall of this temple, that the face portrayed in the corn-like branch, on the left of this tree, was Kan's portrait. The bone on his nose signified that this was a memorial to someone who was already in Xibalba. The corn husk that encased him, was also his name — Kan. Linguists, epigraphers and archaeologists were at odds trying to determine if the two figures on either side of this tree-cross were Chan Bahlum and Pacal or Chan Bahlum at two different ages. But none of them would ever understand what Chan Bahlum (Little Jaguar) had secretly portrayed. This was a memorial to the selfless and devoted man-servant, friend and (for him) lover, Kan.

Unfortunately, throughout the day, while these revelations came so clearly to me, I could also hear another voice. In the background, calling "Janet, Janet" over and over, was Mr. Weinstein, summoning his wife. His voice finally became so unbearable that I tactlessly yelled to him to shut up. Andy was shocked by my outburst, but mortified sufficiently to keep quiet the remainder of the day! José heard me and came over to calm me, explaining, "There's something about that man that is more irritating than anyone I've ever met. I get the feeling that God has sent him here for the express purpose of driving me out of my mind!"

I couldn't help but wonder what all of us were doing there, together. From all parts of the world, had we somehow returned to even up the score? Was Mr. Weinstein one of the characters that sped through my mind? Was José?

As we walked towards a line of buildings known as the Northern Group, I noticed a little grove of orange trees alongside the river. All around were hundreds of butterflies, of many different colors, shapes and sizes. I remembered the story Kahwil had used to illustrate how one can look at things from a new perspective, just as the butterfly sees the world very differently than the caterpillar. Suddenly I understood why I was there. I had returned to see things from a new perspective. I could see things now as the butterfly sees them, and I could understand. It was time to forgive myself, and all those who had hurt and failed me. Was José perhaps Kan? Was this my chance to finally rid myself of the hatred and anger that had eaten at the soul of Pacal for thirty years. Was this the opportunity to love and be loved, that Kan had been denied in our prior existence?

Just beyond the grove I could hear the splash of water moving swiftly over rocks and wandered towards the sound. Kit was off with Linda and David at the Temple of the Count, no doubt being enlightened on the subtle architectural nuances of the structure. I wondered if David would remember building that temple or trembling within it that night of the terrible hurricane of Ik. He was there, I was certain, as we all were. Just who each of us was, remained to be seen.

"There you are!" José called, and joined me to sit on the smooth rocks alongside the Otolum river. "You've had a very serious look about you all day," he said, "Are you considering our conversation this morning?"

Honestly, I'd forgotten all about our conversation, but I didn't have the heart to confess it. "José, you've been here many times — how many would you say?"

"On each tour, once on the way to Merida, and once on the way back with a different group—maybe a hundred times!" he proudly calculated.

"Have you ever felt differently about this place than other sites?" I inquired further.

José didn't hesitate, "Palenque is by far my favorite stop. People always say that this place is the most beautiful of all the Maya sites, but it's more than that. It's like an enchantment that draws me to it. Still, sometimes I experience an overpowering sense of sadness when I'm here. Do you know what I'm talking about?"

I nodded, more certain than ever that José was the reason I was there. "I think that you and I were here together, in another life," I said, hesitantly testing his reaction to the idea.

José seemed intrigued. His eyes opened brightly as he slid himself next to me, so that our bodies touched. But he said nothing, waiting instead for me to explain.

"I think that once you did something that I could not forgive. I died without forgiving you," I whispered.

"What did I do that was so terrible?" he asked. "I can't imagine ever hurting you. Maybe this is my chance to make amends — to love you so much that you will forgive me," he paused for a moment, then a flash of insight lit his face.

"If you marry me, I will consider myself forgiven!" he proclaimed and grabbed me in a triumphant hug.

This time his embrace didn't feel as welcome as it had earlier. Was it possible I was still carrying my anger towards him? "José that's a ridiculous reason to marry someone!" I laughed, pulling myself from him as gently as possible.

But José was undaunted by my unresponsiveness. "I knew the moment I saw you that I wanted you. Never have I felt such an attraction to someone. I've dreamt of taking you in my bed every night of this tour. But in only a few more days this tour will be over. I don't have the luxury of time to woo you. Please, Christina, think about my proposal. At least think about my dream. Will you come to my room tonight?" he pleaded, pulling me towards him again.

"José, I must admit I feel a very strong attraction to you. But I have to be realistic. I have someone waiting for me in New York that I deeply love. My feelings for Charlie are much more than attraction. I don't think my feelings for you are anything like that. Maybe I'm just sensing an obligation for something that happened hundreds of years ago. That's not enough to convince me to move to Mexico. And it wouldn't be anymore realistic to expect you to move to New York. A tour guide is a respected career here in Mexico. Here you're important and successful, but in New York you would be just another immigrant, without a job."

The rational words were coming from my lips, but José had increased the pressure of his body against mine. Then I had to stop speaking, as his mouth enveloped mine with a deep, wet kiss. There was no rational explanation for the effect his kiss had on me. There was no Charlie, no Kit, no New York, there was only an uncontrollable need for fulfillment.

Once again Andy intruded on José's seduction. The voice I'd been repulsed by earlier, now came from behind me, like a stab in the back.

"Do I have to wear a skirt to get a guided tour of this place?" he whined.

José startled and then tensed, his voice strained with controlled contempt. "I said I would meet the group at the Museum at 2:00. You are free to stroll around the ruins as you please until then."

"To be honest, there's something about this place that gives me the creeps. I'd just as soon stay around you. I'd feel safer," Andy grumbled.

Perhaps it would have been better if I'd stayed with them, to keep the conversation light and amusing. I'm sure José was hoping I would. But Andy's presence was just too insufferable and I grabbed at the first chance to escape. "I'm going to find Kit," I proclaimed lightly and hurried off, leaving José for the second time in one day to deal with his tormentor.

# Xibalba

The Hotel Mision is located outside the small city of Santo Domingo, which is only a few miles from the ruins of Palenque. Andy had hovered near José right until the moment we boarded the VW bus for the short drive back to our hotel, leaving no opportunity for me to respond to José's request to join him that evening. José announced, as we drove up to the entrance of the hotel, that we had an hour to freshen up before meeting in the dining room for dinner. He glanced towards me anxiously, searching for some inconspicuous indication that our evening would continue together, after the meal. I was grateful that the situation allowed me to neither accept nor refuse the request in his eyes.

Actually, I was feeling extremely tired. Beyond the physical exertion of actually traversing the expansive site, and climbing countless steps, I'd spent the day in an emotional whirlpool, traveling between two worlds. I was too physically and mentally exhausted to consider the decision José had set before me.

Palenque seemed to have the complete opposite effect on Kit. She was still full of energy as she raced up the stairs to our room. "I get the shower first!" she shrieked, as she put the key into the door. I didn't dispute her claim. My body felt as if the energy was draining from it, even as I walked down the terrace to our room. "I'm going to take a nap while you're in the shower," I mumbled, feeling as if I could sleep for a hundred years. "Don't wake me up. If I'm still sleeping in an hour, just go to dinner without me," I groaned as I pushed my sneakers off with my feet and flopped onto the bed without bothering to pull down the spread. Before my head even made contact with the pillow I was asleep.

~

The young man unfolded his bark-book before me. Flipping panel after panel of columns of glyphs interspersed with depictions of Ixtab, the moon goddess and Bolom Tzacab, in their various activities and relationships. Finally he paused and pointed to one page. Ixtab was a slender young virgin, still without child, her expression one of innocence. She sat facing the lecherous old Bolom Tzacab, his hands held out to entice her.

"This is the phase you asked me to watch for," the novice sky-watcher whispered reverently. "This night your lineage god will follow the virgin moon into the underworld. If you follow him now, he is sure to be distracted by the beautiful Ixtab. You can follow close behind and enjoy the protection of his presence, without risking his wrath. The Lords of the Night will not disturb anyone in his company. He's sure to have a canoe ready at the river, where he will offer to escort the naive young goddess through the darkness. I would suggest that you slip quietly on board. Who knows, perhaps you'll even get to watch that virile old man take Ixtab, right there in the canoe."

"What if Bolom Tzacab should notice me observing such a private act?" I wondered. "It might be dangerous if I was discovered."

"There's little chance of that," interrupted the Ahow of Mam. He was almost as young as the skywatcher, but considerably more arrogant. "That old god is going to have his hands full trying to impregnate Ixtab. She's at her loveliest tonight and he's as ancient and ugly as any god ever was." The young skywatcher snickered along with him, at the thought of an old man attempting to perform sexually, with such a beautiful young woman. They seemed to forget that I was eighty years old! But who could blame them, I hadn't aged a day in over thirty years. It was part of the curse of Kahwil — to live so long, to suffer sufficiently for my sin. Just living with Koh for these past thirty years should have been punishment enough for all the sins of my entire lineage!

But now, at last, the sign had come in the heavens that it was time for my journey through Xibalba. "This is an Etznab day. Is that not the best time to make the crossing?" I asked the pretentious day-keeper.

"Most certainly! All of Xibalba is in confusion. Kahwil has his mirrors everywhere and he sits in the dark corners laughing as he watches the Lords of the Night puzzling over what is real and what is only a reflection. If you move quickly — keep up with the nimble Ixtab — you could get through the whole journey in the one night. By this time tomorrow, you could already be making your first journey across the sky, as part of the Jaguar star cluster," he assured me.

"Then summon my sons," I commanded. "Tonight I will leave all of you behind me, and go at last to be tested in the Underworld."

Koh came walking into the courtyard, as the two young men scurried past her. "The Holy Bacab has chosen tonight to die!" they called to her, as they raced down the southern steps of the Administration Plaza, to find Little Jaguar and Yellow-Knot. It was understood that Shark and Turtle-Bat, the sons of Koh, were not included in my directive. Even though both young men shared their half-sister, Kimi, as their wife, I continued to exclude them from matters that had anything to do with the divine rights of the lineage. They were Sahals and enjoyed the privileges of that title, but they were awarded absolutely no responsibilities. By denying them any opportunity to contribute to the welfare of Jaguar-Sun, I had politically degraded and emasculated them. Unfortunately, their father's contempt hadn't effected their virility, and between the two of them, my daughter, Kimi, had been pregnant almost continuously, from her seventeenth birthday.

Koh had seven grandchildren to dote upon, and spoil, and poison with her devious manipulations. As for myself, I felt no more familial connection to those children, than I would to seven slave children delivered in tribute from Tortuguero. In fact, I detested them — resented their father's blood and, more so, their grandmother's blood.

Koh's existence had been her own revenge, since the day her father was sacrificed on the ballcourt. She never ceased to remind me that my eldest son was effeminate, and his brother, although brave and strong, had proven to be infertile, even though he had taken many wives. Koh's curse had proven more powerful than thirty years of prayers and sacrifices to every god there was to beg, plead and bargain with. My sons, the sons of Ahpo Hel, would bear no fruit!

Poor Ahpo Hel went to her death, pleading with the gods of her lineage, with Kahwil, with Ixtab, to break Koh's curse. But the old Sahal of Tortuguero had been right about his daughter, she danced with the jaguars. The magic of the Lords of the Night was more powerful than anything the gods of the heavens could muster.

Koh stood before me in the courtyard, her hands on her hips, her jaw defiantly set. She'd grown fatter and uglier with each year. Her face was lined deeply, especially around the mouth and eyes. Her brow was furrowed in a perpetual snarl and her mouth was pinched together so tightly that I often thought it resembled the opening in her backside. Actually, what usually spewed forth from that opening was as repulsive and disgusting as anything that could have come from it's visual counterpart. I grit my teeth waiting for another tirade of the stinking mess to burst from those miserable lips.

"What about Chaacal?" she sneered. You can't go to your death until you've named him your heir! The boy is sixteen and you've yet to publicly recognize him as your grandson!" she screamed.

"And I'll go to my death without ever doing it!" I retorted firmly.

"How can you persist in being such an imbecile! It's obvious where Kimi gets her wits from!" she snarled. "Ahpo's sons are the end of your lineage, unless you recognize Chaacal. You have no choice, you ignorant old fool. Name Chaacal your heir, or Jaguar-Sun will perish, and so will your spirit and the spirits of all your ancestors. There'll be no one to worship you and tend that presumptuous shrine you and your female son have been building for so many years? You have no choice!" she declared again.

"I should have had your tongue ripped out long ago, you ugly witch!" I replied as calmly as I could. I'd learned long ago not to react to her verbal assaults. The calmer I spoke, the angrier she got until, red with fury, she'd storm away and leave me in peace — at least until she thought of something else to badger me about. "I do not wish to spend my last day listening to your howls. Go back to the jungle and conjure with your devils. The Holy Bacab demands peace in his last moments," I said with controlled force.

"Recognize Chaacal and I will leave you in peace," Koh replied, almost civilly.

"No! The boy will not be acknowledged by me!" I roared. "Now get away from me!"

Koh stood defiantly before me, not moving a bit, eyeing me like the underworld beast she really was. She stood like that in the bright sun, searching my face for the slightest indication of vulnerability. But I returned her stare with more hatred than I'd ever felt in my life. Our staring duel was finally broken by the appearance of Little Jaguar and Yellow-Knot.

The sons of Ahpo Hel had grown as tall and imposing as their Grandfather, Great Jaguar. Yet, even though they were already close to the age Great Jaguar was when he disappeared forever into the jungle, they remained slender and agile. I'd learned to accept, although not appreciate, Little Jaguar's sexual confusion. Too many young men had passed through his door in the night to ever hope that all of Jaguar-Sun didn't know that the heir chose to behave like a woman in bed. But long ago I stopped worrying about it. He was, after all, the embodiment of Kahwil. So who was I to criticize the behavior of a god? Little Jaguar's divine personage had become unquestionable. He had proven to be a master of any task, from reading the sky to resolving disputes between clans. But his wisdom and intellect were never more apparent than when it came to the design and construction of temples. While I, as Holy Bacab, was officially attributed with the construction of the nearly complete, Temple of the Divine Lineage, it was Little Jaguar who had been the brilliance behind it.

It didn't surprise me that Yellow-Knot was more disturbed by the news that I would depart for Xibalba tonight, than his older brother. I understood the test of patience my longevity had been to Little Jaguar. I expected that he often wondered if he would meet his death before I did. It must have seemed unnerving to him that I never showed signs of aging, never fell sick with the diseases of old men, never slowed my step, despite the inward twist of my foot. If he had been less of a god and more of a man, perhaps this long wait would have driven him to secretly hurry my demise. But never once had he indicated that he grew impatient to rule, or even suggested that I step aside in favor of his divinity and superior abilities. Even so, today he was his usual calm and detached self.

Yellow-Knot, on the other hand, was having a difficult time containing his tears as he embraced me. "What a fine son you've been," I said calmly, trying to conceal my own fears.

"What a fine father you've been," Yellow-Knot replied hoarsely.

I turned to Little Jaguar, prepared to offer him a similar parting, but to my own surprise I broke into tears. "I fear this more than anything I've ever faced before! My life has been such a dismal failure. You and your brother are already old men. What will happen to Jaguar-Sun when you also have died?" I babbled on like a silly old woman. "For the first time I completely understand my mother's painful sacrifice to secure a grandson. What will become of my spirit if no one remains to pray and sacrifice for me? Will I be forced to suffer in Xibalba for all eternity?" I stammered.

Now it was Little Jaguar's turn to embrace me. He pulled me towards him far more gently than his brother. My head came only to his chest and I didn't resist when he rested his hand on my head, as a mother would comfort a child.

"I have something to tell you that I've kept within me for thirty years," he said softly. "On that terrible night, when you believed that Kan had abused his power and deliberately corrupted me, I found him in the jungle, crying in despair. You see, it had been me who had abused my power. As heir and god, I had demanded Kan to perform for me as you saw him doing that night. I'd been requiring his services as a lover for several years. But while I had always felt such passionate yearnings toward him, Kan never really wanted or enjoyed our encounters. He complied as one who had spent his whole life in obedient submission, but I was always aware that there was no joy in it for him. I don't think Kan really felt any inclination to be sexual. What he really wanted was to be loved, not physically but spiritually. And the love he needed, and would have done anything for, was yours.

"When he realized that he'd lost that love," Little Jaguar continued in a confessional tone, "he could no longer bear living. He didn't kill himself out of fear of punishment; he killed himself in grief for hurting you."

As Little Jaguar spoke, his hand held my face firmly to his chest. I could feel his heart pulsing within him, but we were both spared the agony of looking into each other's eyes. I thought of all the years I'd wasted, wallowing in hatred for the one person who had loved me without question or expectations. I thought of the years we'd spent in the cave at Toctan... of the way he looked at me when I'd uttered the curse of the Lords of the Night... of his eyes pleading for a morsel of insight that night I discovered him embedded in the backside of my son.

"I should have told you this long ago. I am, after all, supposed to be the embodiment of Kahwil. I'm forced to admit that my reasons for keeping silent were far too human for someone of my position. You see, my father, you do not hold exclusive rights to weakness and sin. It's a heavy burden to be considered a god, a Holy Bacab. How can the future of our entire lineage rest in our hands, when we are as vulnerable to temptation as any man?"

I nodded agreement, as Little Jaguar echoed the same thoughts I had agonized over, for so many years. He released his hold on me and allowed me to look up into his face. That detached gaze he'd always presented to me was gone. For the first time I could see warmth and tenderness towards me. He continued his story.

"Kan extracted a vow from me that night. I swore to tell you, before you died, that he would wait for you at the gates to Xibalba. That he would serve and protect you in the horrors of the Underworld, to help you outwit the menacing Lords of the Night and guide you out to your rightful place in the sky. He said that you would recognize him when the beautiful young Ixtab allowed Bolom Tzacab a kiss."

I thought about the skywatcher's suggestion, that I might spy on the divine seduction tonight, and for the first time felt a glimmer of hope about my journey.

Koh had scurried off somewhere and now returned with Chaacal in tow. I turned from them and led my sons through the god-house, to the southwest courtyard, so that we could admire the nearly complete Temple of the Divine Lineage. I knew that within the nine red tiers that rose before us, was encased the magnificent tomb, where I would rest tonight. The solid limestone sarcophagus had been positioned directly over the entrance to Te'nab. The room that surrounded it, and the sides of the sarcophagus, were lined with carvings of my divine ancestors. Resting on wooden rollers, the beautifully carved, limestone cover, depicted the moment when my spirit would fall into the jaws of death. Tonight, just as Bolom Tzacab followed the moon goddess into Xibalba, I would drop into the depths of the Underworld.

"The temple will be completed in less than a year," Little Jaguar said. "Maybe you should wait until then?"

"No, this is the right time. Is the recipe being prepared?"

Yellow-Knot flinched at my mention of the poison that would first put me in an ecstatic stupor and then quietly, but predictably, choke all life from me. I touched his muscular shoulder. "I would expect a warrior of divine blood to accept death without fear," I said, thinking that this would be my last instruction to him.

"My own death, I do not fear, father. But I fear how much I will miss you," he sighed.

Little Jaguar pointed towards Quetzal Mountain. "When the Lineage temple is completed, I'm going to build three more temples in that area. They will be a celebration of the gods of the Jaguar-Sun dynasty, and of you, father. What I will build will last far longer than the son and the lineage you would have had me create."

"But after you, after your brother, who will worship in these temples?" I cried.

"The sons of Chaacal," Little Jaguar murmured resolutely.

"Never!" I shouted.

But Little Jaguar just shook his head. There was no reason to argue. Soon I would be gone and his word would be law.

Two slaves came hesitantly into the courtyard and knelt before us. Each held a bundle out to me, while keeping their faces to the ground. Little Jaguar bent to take the smaller bundle and Yellow-Knot took the larger, dismissing the boys, who hurried off.

Yellow-Knot removed the white cloth of his bundle, to reveal a magnificent mask made of hundreds of pieces of jade. The obsidian and mother-of-pearl eyes peered from the jade lids in an expression of serene composure. The thin lips were slightly parted and the large nose was smoothed to the sloping forehead, with the help of a jade ornament, identical to the one I always wore. Yellow-Knot gasped in admiration. "It's a perfect depiction of you!"

It was reassuring to know that, even when my flesh had rotted away from my face, my countenance would remain forever pleasing. I turned to carefully pull the cloth from the bundle Little Jaguar held. It revealed a small painted bowl with a perfectly fitted cover. The time had come to begin my journey. Kin was already beginning to descend behind the mountains to the west and soon all of Jaguar -Sun would be draped in his blood. Already a crowd had begun to gather at the base of the Lineage Temple.

"As soon as I drink this, I will be incapable of performing any of the necessary rituals, without your help. My spirit will begin it's own rituals almost immediately, so it will be up to you to guide my body through each step. Do not fail me in this, or my spirit will be trapped forever in Xibalba!" I commanded.

My sons assured me that they understood what was expected of them. We reviewed how they were to lead me to the summit of the Lineage Temple, where they would assist me in letting blood for the last time. Then they would carry me, still living, down into the tomb, where they would anoint and dress me, and position me in the sarcophagus. A cube of jade would be placed in my right hand, and a sphere in my left. The Yellow-Knot headband of Bolom Tzacab would be draped on my forehead, and jade spheres would be positioned at the soles of my feet. Then, while all of the people of Jaguar-Sun pleaded with the gods for mercy, my sons would listen carefully for the last rumble of breath to escape from my lips. Only then, would they place the jade ball in my mouth, and cover my face with the mask Yellow-Knot now held.

"Be certain that the grandchildren of Koh are present for all of this," I whispered, certain that Koh would be listening. "After I am dead, cover me with cinnabar. But before you roll the cover over me, I want you to make a blood sacrifice Bolom Tzacab will never be able to ignore. I want you to announce your trust that he will carry on our lineage, and then I want to offer all of the grandchil-dren of Koh to him in sacrifice!"

I heard Koh's shriek and savored it! At last I would avenge her for all the misery she'd brought me. There would be a continuation of the true lineage, or there would be none at all. Surely Bolom Tzacab would not ignore us. My sons seemed at first shocked by the idea, but Koh's cries pleased them, almost as much as they did me, and they nodded their consent.

Now the old woman was at my feet pleading. "No!, No! I beg you not to kill them. They're only children! They're your own flesh and blood!" she pleaded.

"I cannot die thinking that at the first opportunity you will have my sons murdered. Koh, if there are no sons of my sons, I curse you to eternity without my forgiveness!"

I took the bowl from Little Jaguar and drank its contents quickly.

# Uxmal

My eyes were open, yet I could see nothing, except the empty void of total darkness. The air was still and quiet and offered no clues as to where I was, or whom I was. Before my sense of touch revealed the texture of the sheets on my bed, I shuddered with panic, in timeless moments of uncertainty. Was I in Xibalba or the Hotel Mision Palenque? Was I Pacal or Christina… or neither? I jumped up in terror, before I grasped the realization that I was once again Christina. As my eyes grew accustomed to the lack of light, I could make out the faint outline of someone in the bed alongside mine. It was Kit, I presumed, but reached over to touch her, just the same. Her slender body made such a little mound under the light coverlet, and her sleep was so peaceful that she seemed not to be breathing. I held my hand to her nose to reassure myself that she was indeed exhaling.

There was no way of knowing what time it was, or how much longer I would have to wait for morning. Apparently I'd slept through dinner, as the rumbling in my stomach confirmed. I wished I was home and could simply wander into the kitchen to stare sleepily into the light of the refrigerator, scratching my stomach and contemplating on how to squelch its pangs of hunger. Instead, I felt my way toward the bathroom, fumbled for the light and opened a bottle of Agua Mineral. Perched on the closed toilet lid, sipping the purified water as if it were wine, I waited, wide eyed, for the light of dawn. If I allowed my eyes to close, I was certain the dream would resume where it had left off, with that terrifying descent into Xibalba!

~

With the first light of dawn came José's uncertain knock at the door. Once again we watched the sunrise together, while I reassured him that I was feeling fine, despite falling into a stupor-like sleep the previous night.

"We have to get a very early start today," my anxious visitor groaned, "so that we can reach Uxmal by late afternoon. You'll have to go in the Volkswagen with Vincenté, because I'm going to have to drop the Weinsteins off in Campeche. Vincenté will show you around the ruins at Uxmal, and afterwards there will be a Sound and Light show. By then, I should be at the Hacienda Uxmal, where you'll be staying. We can take a stroll together then — alone?" he stated and asked in the same breath.

As I listened to him rattle off our itinerary for the day, I was suddenly aware that our journey was coming nearer to its end. I remembered José's complaint that he lacked the luxury of time to woo me. Soon our opportunity to be lovers would be forever lost. Would this be the night I would resolve the pain of centuries past? I felt a longing to be in his embrace, that seemed to have nothing to do with past lives. It was an attraction as basic and irrational as the hunger for breakfast that my stomach was noisily declaring.

"I'll meet you tonight, after Kit has gone to bed," I whispered, "but I'm not going to promise you anything. Give me the day to consider your proposition... and your proposal. I'll make a decision tonight, I promise."

José jumped up with such an exuberance that I was afraid he'd mistaken my words for a promise of marriage. "Tonight! I'll see you tonight!" he exclaimed as he started towards the steps. He swung around and called out, "Even spending the whole day trapped in the car with Andy won't bother me now!"

"Shhhhh!" I motioned as exaggerated as I could, fearing that his declaration would be heard by the named annoyance himself. I hurried back to my room to awaken Kit. This was one morning I didn't want to miss breakfast!

During the long drive to Uxmal I queried Vincenté on his knowledge of the history of Palenque. I needed to find out what happened after the death of Pacal. Vincenté was younger than José and not nearly as well read on the more recent discoveries about the Maya. Still, he could tell me that the eldest son of Pacal, Chan-Balum, (which he said meant Snake-Jaguar,) ruled after his father's death, and that after him, a younger son, named Kan-Xul, ruled until he was captured during a battle with Tonina, a site to the south of Palenque. According to Vincenté's uncertain memory, some carvings at Tonina seem to indicate that Kan Xul was held captive there for many years, but it wasn't clear if he had been finally slain in sacrifice, or died in captivity, or perhaps even returned to his homeland.

"What happened at Palenque when the second son was taken captive?" I asked him.

Vincenté shook his head, indicating that he wasn't sure, but offered more information just the same. I began to suspect that the young man knew more than even he himself realized. "I think that someone named Xoc ran things for about tens years, but it seems that he wasn't actually the ruler. He was just in charge, while Kan-Xul was still alive at Tonina."

I watched the scenery pass by, as Vincenté hesitantly relinquished the last morsel of knowledge he possessed on Palenque. Following that last statement, an hour passed in silence, with Kit and Elmer and Bill dozing off in the back of the van. I noted the subtle differences in the construction of the Maya homes as we progressed north into the Yucatan Peninsula. The women's attire also changed. Here they wore a long white huipil that was embroidered rather than woven, with patterns around the neckline. A white slip showed beneath the huipil, bordered with a wide and ornate band of lace. While the costume changed, the people still had the same distinctive features of the Maya that were so expertly recorded in stone and stucco by their ancestors hundreds of years ago.

Inspired perhaps, by the strong resemblance of the people walking along the road, with the carvings we'd seen on the walls of Palenque, Vincenté recalled one last note on the fate of the ancient site, "There was one more ruler recorded at the site," he announced, as if an hour had not passed since his last words on the subject. "His name was Chakal and he claimed to be a direct descendant of Pacal, although it isn't clear if he was a son or grandson or maybe a nephew. He's mentioned in a tablet that was just recently deciphered by a woman who has been studying at the site — an archaeologist."

His words stung me like a smack on the face. I could feel the rage of thirteen hundred years inside me as the name of Koh's grandson was spoken. "So the curse of Koh was never broken!" I snarled with an anger that startled the quiet guide.

"Who is Koh?" Vincenté asked, frightened by my bizarre response. Aware that I had suddenly provoked the interest of, not only Vincenté, but also Bill and Elmer, who were suddenly alert and leaning forward to hear me above the constant rumble of the engine, I fumbled for a reasonable explanation. Finally I resorted to the only thing I knew — the truth.

"She was the second wife of Pacal, and she cursed his first wife's children to bear no fruit. So it was her grandson who finally took control of Palenque," I proclaimed.

"Where did you read that?" Vincenté demanded, obviously insulted that I should know more than him on the subject. "That's not recorded anywhere that I've read about. Is it something new that they discovered?"

Lost for an answer I feigned stupidity, "Maybe I'm mixing it up with some other story," I laughed. "There's so many different myths connected with these places," I shrugged.

Relieved that his superiority on the topic remained intact, Vincenté laughed and assured us that we would hear yet another new story that evening, at the Sound and Light show to be held at the ruins of Uxmal.

We arrived at the site, as José had predicted, in late afternoon, and agreed to postpone bringing our luggage to the hotel in order to see something of the ruins before dark. Vincenté assured us that this was the best time to see Uxmal, since the sun wasn't as intense. It was still so extremely hot that I couldn't imagine attempting to walk the site in the heat of midday! A vendor approached us, selling straw hats, which we gladly purchased for only 7,000 pesos (about $3). They didn't offer a small enough size to fit securely on Kit, but ever the ingenious one, she took a bright pink and blue scarf from her satchel, wrapped it snugly around the hat, and that seemed to do the trick. The change in temperature from Chiapas to the Yucatan was dramatic. Although I'd heard that Palenque could be miserably hot, we had been blessed with perfect weather while we were there.

As we walked onto the site, we faced one of the most unusual structures of the Maya. Referred to as the Temple of the Magician, its front stairs rose steeply before us, far higher than anything we'd seen at Palenque. The sides of the structure were rounded, giving it the appearance of a cone rather than a pyramid. I wondered if its name had something to do with its resemblance to a magician's hat, but Vincenté explained that it was derived from a myth of a magic dwarf that was said to dwell in the temple at the summit. Actually five temples were encompassed in the structure — four encased within it and the top one.

A thick metal chain was attached alongside the stairs, for climbers to hold onto, especially during their descent. Vincenté warned us that some people had fallen to their death from this structure, and to attempt climbing it with great caution. His advice was well founded as we soon discovered for ourselves. This was the most difficult climb we'd made yet. As usual, Kit was well ahead of us and I was only midway up the stairs when I saw her nimble body disappear at the crest of the stairway. I held onto the chain for dear life, as I struggled upward, literally hugging the almost perpendicular stones. When I finally reached the top, it took every ounce of courage in me, to actually stand up. I looked around for Kit, but didn't see her in the temple.

Gingerly, I walked around the two-foot wide ledge that surrounded the temple, my back leaning against its walls. The angle of the stairs was so steep that, from the top, it appeared that we were standing on a tower — kind of like walking around a ledge at the top of the Empire State Building! Softly I called Kit, wishing she hadn't gone around to the back, and already dreading the climb down from this frightening precipice. Again I called her, this time a little louder, but still there was no response. Linda and David finally reached the top, and I asked them if perhaps they'd seen Kit already starting down the steps. They hadn't seen her. I could feel panic only a mother can know, growing inside me. Where was my daughter!

"Kit!" I called out again. But still there was no reply. She was nowhere to be seen. "Kit where are you!" I yelled, wondering if she'd somehow been taken by the gods of this temple. I knew I had to get a grip on my imagination. People don't just disappear into thin air. How am I going to explain this to her father? I thought. I could hear myself saying, "The gods took her from the Temple of the Magician!" Then thoughts of a more gruesome and realistic variety began to emerge in my mind. Had she fallen? I forced myself to look down at the people on the ground below, who appeared to be just tiny headtops, looking for Kit's distinctly adorned hat. That's when I noticed a group of people pointing towards a ledge on the back of the structure. "She's over there!" they were exclaiming.

I envisioned my daughter's broken body strewn on the stone ledge of this temple, in the middle of the Yucatan, and couldn't bear to look in the direction they were pointing. My body froze in terror. This couldn't really be happening; it was another dream—a horrible nightmare! Suddenly I saw her, that damn hat first, then her face, rising nonchalantly from the ledge at the rear of the temple.

"Where were you!" I shrieked in relief and fury.

"My hat fell," Kit explained calmly. I went down the stairs at the back, to the ledge to get it." Not only was she oblivious to the panic I'd just endured, but she was completely undaunted by the danger of her performance. A chain had been draped across the rear stairs and a sign hung from it, explaining in both English and Spanish, that these stairs were too dangerous to climb. "For a hat worth about three dollars, you risked your life!" I cried. Kit just shrugged her shoulders, and gave me a look that suggested that she was far more reasonable than her mother. This was neither the time nor place to argue the point. Besides, we still had to face the climb down this nightmare temple.

By the time we were both safely on the ground, I was too exhausted to do any more exploring. Fortunately, the brutal heat had sapped the energy of the rest of our group, and we convinced Vincenté to bring us to our hotel.

The Hacienda Uxmal was the epitome of classic Spanish architecture, with the rooms all off verandahs, surrounding a patio garden with a swimming pool. Our room was on the second floor, and was kept surprisingly cool with only a ceiling fan. When I saw that the floor was a terra-cotta tile, I dropped our luggage on the bed and kicked off my shoes, savoring the coolness on the soles of my feet.

"Don't go falling asleep again tonight!" Kit admonished me. She had been really upset the night before, when she couldn't wake me up, and had to go down to dinner by herself. I was still too shook up by her disappearance on the temple, to carry on a regular conversation with her. Remembering our escapade, arriving in the airport in Mexico City, I began to question the wisdom of bringing her on the trip. Now I was about to tell her I was going to leave her, by herself, later in the evening, so that I could take a stroll with José. Was I acting irresponsibly? What if something were to happen to her while I was gone?

Perfectly timed to add to my sense of confusion, the phone in our room rang and the operator explained that she had a call from New York. It was Charlie!

"Christina!" he exclaimed several times, as if just saying the word was therapeutic. His voice sounded so comforting and warm. "I've been going crazy trying to reach you," he called out, as if it was necessary to speak loud enough to hear him all the way in New York. "There hasn't been telephones in the rooms of the past few hotels on your list. Thank-God I've finally got you. God! How I miss you. How's the trip? How's Kit? Are you eating all right? Is everything O.K.?" he rattled off one question after another then suddenly realized what he was doing and laughed. His laugher was so exhilarating that I quickly forgot everything that had been happening. With only the sound of his voice I was mesmerized by the emotions he evoked in me.

"Oh, Charlie, I have so much to tell you, but the most important thing is that I miss you," I cried, loudly mimicking his volume.

"Is something wrong?" he asked, his voice suddenly soft, almost frightened.

"No, everything's fine, especially now that I'm talking to you," I assured him, wondering if somehow my voice had revealed what I'd been contemplating for the evening.

"Christina, you sound worried. Are you feeling all right?"

"I'm fine, but something incredible has happened. I've been having these dreams that seem like memories of a past life... here in Mexico... just like that regression. It's too complicated to explain on the phone. When I get home we'll have plenty of time to talk about it," I explained.

"I miss you, Chris. It's terrible without you. It's been snowing and cold and just plain miserable. I can't help worrying that you won't come back... that whatever has drawn you there will keep you. I love you Chris, please don't ever forget that. I love you no matter what. I'll always love you... always have and always will." Charlie's voice was trembling.

Was it possible that Charlie had been able to detect my dilemma with only the few words I'd spoken? Or was the bond between us so profound that he could sense the possibility of losing me, even though we were so far apart? How could I possibly even consider doing anything that would hurt him? I'd never loved anyone so completely, and certainly no one had ever given me such pure, devoted love.

"Of course I'm coming back," I whispered, trying to impart as much sincerity in my words as possible. "I miss you and I love you. I can't wait to see your face the minute I get off the plane. I'm going to kiss you like you've never been kissed before — right there in the airport, in front of everybody!" I laughed, certain their was no indication in my voice that I'd ever considered not returning home.

"I'll be there! See you then," he replied, still not sounding reassured.

"See you then," I echoed and then heard the click of his departure.

What am I doing? I asked myself, as I replaced the receiver in its cradle. I'm living in three different worlds! "I don't even know what's real anymore," I cried out.

Kit came out of the bathroom with one towel around her torso and one wrapped turban-style on her head. "What's wrong now?" she moaned.

I stared at her as if she was an apparition. "And you have to go doing disappearing tricks on the Temple of the Magician! You're no help at all!" I grumbled.

"And you're turning into a weirdo!" Kit retorted nastily, as she returned to the bathroom with her clothes to dress.

I looked through the wooden shutters that opened onto the verandah, down to the patio and pool below us, and resolved to tell José I'd decided against everything when I saw him.

When Kit finally emerged, dressed and groomed, I took my turn in the ornately tiled bathroom. Even the bathtub was made of blue and white tiles! Then we joined our group for dinner in the hotel restaurant, trying yet another version of Sopa de Lima, while we unabashedly toasted the departure of the Weinsteins. I was glad that José hadn't arrived yet, when it was time for us to go to the ruins for the Sound and Light show. Although our hotel was close enough for us to walk to the ruins, we all elected to take the van, deciding unanimously that we'd done enough walking for one day.

We sat on the top steps, on one side of the quadrangle of buildings at the archaeological zone commonly referred to as the Nunnery, and watched, in the dark, as different sections of the structures around us were lit with colored lights. A recording of traditional Indian music blasted from loud speakers placed among the ruins, while a heavily accented narrator recounted the tale of a love-struck Indian princess and the battle that ensued over her. It sounded too much like a version of Helen of Troy and I very much doubted that it was even loosely based on either fact or genuine Indian lore. Still, despite the unbelievable melodramatics, I had to admit that the lighting effects were entertaining. To our left, the upper part of the Pyramid of the Magician could be seen, with the interior of the temple on top aglow with red light. Across the courtyards before us, the Temple of the Turtles was alternately lit with the Temple of the Doves and the Great Pyramid behind in the distance.

With my memories of Pacal, and what life was really like for the Ancient Maya, I couldn't help feeling sad that visitors were being fed this romantic dreck about people whose real story was so genuinely dynamic and interesting.

"That whole scenario was like a continuation of the degradation of the indigenous people of this continent," I said to José when he met us in the hotel lobby after the show. He held his hands up in the air and moaned, "Don't blame me, I didn't do it."

"But you should be disturbed by it," I exclaimed. "This is your heritage they're capitalizing on. Don't you think they should at least get it straight."

"Not everybody has been privileged to have your insight, Señora. Don't take it so seriously," he sighed and put his arm on my shoulder. "I missed you today, but I've been thinking about tonight every minute."

I remembered my decision to tell him I'd changed my mind about our rendezvous, but the feel of his arm was more tempting than my resolve. "I have to get Kit settled in," I whispered, afraid someone in our group would hear.

"I'll wait for you in my room — number eleven," José said, his face lit with a warm, irresistible smile.

I was glad Kit hadn't heard our conversation. I wasn't sure how I was going to explain to her why I was leaving her alone, but I would have to think of something soon.

~

To my dismay, I discovered that room eleven was on the ground level, near the patio bar. I had waited until ten o'clock, when Kit was almost asleep, to tell her I was going down to the bar for a short while, to meet the others for a drink. Now, it seemed I would have to do exactly that, when I noticed Linda and Dave standing only a few feet from the door to José's room.

"Joining us for a night cap?" Dave queried when he saw me.

"A quick one," I sighed. "Can't leave Kit alone too long."

They both nodded their understanding, and I asked the bartender for a margarita. We exchanged the usual polite conversation, commiserated that our trip was nearing its end, and compared some of the various sites we'd seen together. As I hoped, José heard my voice from his room — there were only wooden shutters facing the patio where one would have expected windows, offering neither privacy nor security — and joined us at the bar. It soon became a contest of who was going to outlast whom, and the margaritas started adding up. At last Linda and Dave decided to take a stroll outside the hotel, and José and I slipped into his room.

At the bar, José had been voicing his belief that Madison Avenue was to blame for the obsession with material possessions which, in his opinion, was the problem with most people in the United States and Canada. I'd taken his remarks to heart, as a criticism of my entire career. But the drinks had weakened my defenses and I'd finally agreed that maybe I was in the wrong profession. My resolve to remain faithful to Charlie had been weakened as well, and as we continued our conversation, in the seclusion of José's room, I was once again caught up in the physical attraction I felt for the charming Mexican.

When you are married to me, you can leave all of that materialism behind you," he whispered, and under the spell of the tequila, his words hardly seemed disturbing. The stress and speed of life in New York grew more and more undesirable in direct ratio to the sensual desire José was arousing within me. I tried to maintain some measure of reason, as I attempted to continue our conversation, still deluding myself that the situation would not end in lovemaking.

"Maybe there is a reason I'm in the advertising business," I offered, as José touched my cheeks with the backs of his fingertips. "Maybe Madison Avenue is the new Temple of the Inscriptions. Maybe this time Pacal will use television to deliver his message."

José changed the subject. "Maybe I will not have to wait forever to know your love?" His accented words flowed like poetry, smooth and melodious. His fingertips were barely touching the back of my neck. My whole body was tingling!

I searched his eyes for the slightest hint of remembrance. If this was Kan who was seducing me, then there was no reason to resist. This was why I had returned to Mexico. But José's eyes were half closed and unfocused and I felt nothing to assure me. I stood, helplessly enchanted, as he began to unbutton my blouse. Realizing that I was no longer resisting, José was suddenly transformed from patient seducer to impassioned lover. He fell to the bed, pulling me with him and I felt his mouth all over me, moving from my lips to my neck, to my breasts. My shorts and panties were off in moments, as were all of his clothing.

Before I could reconsider, he was on top of me, inside me, his mouth pressed so hard against mine that there was no possibility of uttering a sound of complaint. It didn't matter because I made no attempt to resist, and after the initial shock my body began to enjoy the sensations of his frenzied passion. José's sudden, almost violent, initiation, was followed by pure, unrestrained sex. With an unrelenting energy he drew from me every pleasure a woman's body could give. In the heat of passion I forgot about my love for Charlie, the memories of Pacal, and my daughter, alone in another room of the hotel. There was only the unbridled excitement, the obsession of the moment, the reckless trust that no matter what the consequences, this brief, gluttonous indulgence was worth it.

Still, while my submission to my desires was all encompassing, I remained unable to reach that peak of fulfillment — that sensation of total release and exquisite ecstasy. My body was growing limp with exhaustion and still José showed no sign of culmination.

Realizing he was holding back, waiting for an indication that I'd reached a climax, I gave him the sign he needed. My feigned gasp of wild, uncontrolled rapture, brought a similar reaction from him, until we both collapsed, hot, sweaty and stinking of sex.

Completely satisfied, José fell asleep almost immediately, while I lay beside him, wide awake, wondering what I was going to do. This was nothing like the lovemaking I'd experienced with Charlie. There was none of the gentle playfulness, no loving words were exchanged before or afterwards. I had to admit that I resented that I'd failed to reach a climax, although I couldn't blame José for it, he'd certainly held out long enough. Even so, there had been something about the experience that was more exciting than anything I'd ever experienced before. It was as if I'd taken a drug that was immediately addictive, despite the fact that I knew that it would never completely satisfy me.

José lay face down beside me, his copper body shadowed in bands by the moonlight coming through the louvers. I admired the perfect form of his body, his broad shoulders, narrow waist, and rounded bottom. There was a mark there on his buttocks, a birthmark lit by the moon and I sat up to see it more clearly. There on the crest of his backside was a perfectly formed capital T!

Seeing that birthmark aroused something in me very different than the passion I'd just experienced. Suddenly I felt as if I was going to vomit in horror. I was looking at the sign of Ik, in exactly the same place I'd seen it on Koh! Tears welled up in my eyes, panic clenched my chest, as I sat frozen with the realization that I'd fallen to the same temptation that had destroyed me, and my entire lineage, over a thousand years ago.

Oblivious to the significance of a birthmark on his bottom, José rolled over to face me, his eyes warm with satisfaction. "You were even more wonderful than I'd imagined," he sighed, as he reached towards me. I froze with his touch. "What's wrong?" he asked with a hurt expression. "You aren't angry with me are you?"

I didn't know what to say. How could I explain the horrifying significance of a small birthmark? What if it was just a coincidence?

"You're crying," José exclaimed, as he propped his head up in his hand to see me more clearly. "Did I hurt you. Please don't cry, you'll break my heart. What's wrong?"

His voice was so gentle and concerned that I felt foolish condemning him, just because he happened to have a T-shaped birthmark. I turned away from him, afraid my eyes would reveal the fear and contempt I was feeling.

"If you cry, I will die with regret for making you so sad." José said. "Am I such a terrible lover to move you to tears?"

"No," I muttered, unable to say anything further to assure him.

Just promise me this one thing. OK?" he whispered.

"What?" I sniffled.

"Promise me that you will consider marrying me. That you will think about how you feel about me, and about how I make you feel, and about living here with me. Will you promise only that... to think about it?"

There was no possibility I could ever consider it. It didn't matter whether José was the reincarnation of Koh or not. The mark of Ik was a warning. That simple T- shape represented a lifetime of regret I had no intention of reliving. But there was no way I could ever explain that to José. How could I hold a man accountable for a birth-mark on his buttocks? "I can't marry you and I can't explain why," I answered firmly.

José sat up suddenly, and held my face in his hands. "No, don't answer me now. All I'm asking is that you think about it," he pleaded.

I shrugged my shoulders, not willing to argue, but knowing I'd already made up my mind. I collected my clothes from around the bed and quietly dressed, feeling José's confused stare.

"Are you mad at me for seducing you?" he asked in a contrite tone.

"No, I wanted you as much as you wanted me," I answered, meekly honest.

"Then why are you acting this way?"

"What way?"

"Cold"

"I'm sorry," I murmured, as I buttoned my blouse. "I can't explain what's wrong, but it's not your fault. Honest, it has nothing to do with you."

I walked to the door and opened it slightly, peering outside to make sure no one I knew was around.

"Can we talk about this tomorrow?" José called softly, as I stepped out to the patio.

"Sure, we'll talk tomorrow," I reassured him and hurried quickly away. My sandals echoed noisily on the tiled floor of the dark and empty patio, and I slipped them off and tip-toed up to the second floor, to my room. On the screen of the door, two large grasshoppers were mating. I stood quietly watching them, trying to recall whether grasshoppers were an omen of good or bad luck, before risking disturbing them by opening the door. Gingerly, I turned my key in the lock and eased the door open. The grasshoppers remained attached to each other and the screen. "Everybody's fucking tonight," I groaned cynically and then startled to see Kit sitting up in her bed, awake.

"Where were you!" she demanded angrily.

"I told you, I went to have a drink with everybody," I replied, suddenly aware that it was very late. "I thought you'd be asleep by now."

"I can't sleep, because I was afraid something happened to you," Kit cried, quivering, as large tears rolled down her cheeks. "I looked outside and the bar was all closed up. I thought you were kidnapped, or killed, and I didn't know what to do!"

I hurried over to her bed and tried to console her, but Kit pushed me away. "You were with José!" she proclaimed with contempt. "You lied to me. And you lied to Charlie. I heard you tell him on the phone how much you love him, and then you went off with José!"

I couldn't believe I was standing there being lectured by my twelve-year-old daughter. But I had to admit she was right. I'd acted like an idiot. Again!

"Oh my God, I can't believe this is happening," I groaned. "Kit, I'm too damn tired to be having this discussion. I'm sorry if it seems like I've lied to you, or Charlie, but there's some things you just can't understand when you're twelve years old, so you're just going to have to trust me."

"I know a lot more than you think," Kit cried, "and I know that YOU LIED!" She slumped down in her bed and pulled the coverlet over her face, sobbing loudly.

I knew that I should have tried to console her, and reassure her that everything would be all right, but I was too exhausted. I took off my clothes, dropped them on the floor and crawled under the sheets. But as tired as I was, I couldn't fall asleep. Through the long night I worried if I would be condemned to suffer once again, for one moment of weakness. When I did finally fall asleep, I dreamt that I was home, but my house was dissolving down to the frame. When I walked into my bedroom I saw that the toilet was on my bed and it was backing up, spewing its disgusting mess all over.

# Chichen Itza

Chichen Itza was only an hour's drive and we arrived at the archaeological zone while the morning air was still relatively cool. José led us first to the famous Temple of Kulkulkan, where the sun casts the shadow of the snake-serpent along its balusters, during the equinoxes. It was almost impossible for me to concentrate on his detailed explanation of the colorful history of the site — a mingling of Classic Maya and the later-arriving Toltecs. My thoughts kept returning to the birthmark that had shattered our encounter the night before. Meanwhile, Kit had resorted to her cruelest fighting tactic, silent withdrawal. We'd barely spoken all morning.

From the top of the temple, we had a splendid panoramic view of the site, but the magic I'd experienced in Palenque was gone. This place meant nothing to me, its history and architecture felt foreign and insignificant. Chichen Itza is grandiose in scope, but something mystical was missing. I sensed that the people who had created this place were driven more by undisciplined pride than spiritual inspiration. Was the difference only a perception, influenced by the agitated state of my own mind, or something tangible that could be felt by others? I noticed that Elmer, Bill, Linda and Dave also seemed less enthusiastic about this place.

I looked around at the many groups of tourists and thought it was a shame that, for most of them, Chichen Itza would be all they would ever know about the Maya. They would never feel the purity of their spirituality, and the inner peace their rituals and discipline brought to them. They would grimace at the depiction of decapitations, and listen with horror to their guide's barbaric stories of young virgins being tossed into the sacred cenoté as sacrifices, and they would return home without the slightest understanding of the brilliance and dignity that was once the hallmark of the True People.

As the day continued and the heat of the sun grew more intense, our pace slowed, as we half-heartedly followed José and Vincenté around the ruins. I tried to avoid José's eyes, but he seemed to be directing all of his remarks to only me. Finally, with the sun directly overhead, we walked onto the ballcourt. José pointed out the carvings of ballplayers having their heads cut off. He pulled his Panama hat off, mopped his brow with a red bandanna, and sighed.

"We do not know which side was sacrificed, the winners or the losers. If you ask me, whoever had their heads cut off was the real loser," he said, his voice growing so low that we had to move very close to hear him. He looked directly at me and I thought that at any moment he was going to cry. "That is all I have to tell you about Chichen Itza. You can drive back to the Hotel Mayaland with Vincenté, or you can remain here for a while and walk back to the hotel. Go in the direction of the Temple of Kulkulkan and follow towards the Market and you'll see the hotel. I'm leaving for Merida to pick up another group, so this is adios. I've enjoyed your company and I hope you've enjoyed mine."

We were all surprised by José's sudden announcement, having assumed that he would complete the tour with us. I suspected that I was the reason for his sudden change of plans. Everyone wished him well, and then followed Vincenté back to the bus. Kit started to go along with them then turned to see that I wasn't with her. Seeing José walking toward me, Kit complained, "Let's go back to the hotel, Mom, I'm hot and I'm hungry."

"I'll be right there," I said, looking directly at José.

"Stay," José said firmly. "I need to talk to you."

"Mommy, let's go," Kit whined.

"I said I'll be right there, go on!" I replied motioning with my hands for Kit to join the others at the bus.

She hesitated, looking as if she feared José would steal me from her forever.

"Go to the bus, Kit, I need to talk to your mother alone!" Jose commanded.

"Mom," Kit pleaded, "Please..."

"For godsake Kit, I'm not leaving you. Just go back to the hotel with everyone else and I'll meet you there. I promise. You're acting like I'm going to abandon you here!" I exclaimed. How could my own daughter even imagine I had so little concern for her, I thought.

Kit finally seemed reassured enough to leave us and ran off to the bus, turning several times to look at me for encouragement.

"Christina, you must tell me what's happened to make you suddenly turn so cold toward me," José's words were controlled and deliberate like an actor speaking his lines aloud for the first time. "When we were making love, you seemed to be enjoying it as much as I was. Then, when it was over, you acted as if I'd raped you! Please be fair. If you feel guilty about last night, you shouldn't. But certainly you cannot accuse me of forcing you against your will."

"I'm not accusing you of anything," I assured him. I looked into his eyes so full of hurt and wondered if I should confess how close I'd come to handing him the reigns of my future. He was right about one thing, though — I did feel guilty about our encounter. I'd allowed myself to succumb to basic human weakness. "Why shouldn't I feel guilty?" I asked. "I betrayed Charlie's trust... I should have been stronger... I should have never gone to your room... put myself into temptation that I couldn't resist. I feel very guilty, José. I've hurt everyone, you, Kit, Charlie and myself."

"You've hurt no one!" José thundered. "Why don't you admit to being human once in a while. You want to go back to New York, to this old man you're so obsessed with, then go! But go back with a memory of sharing something wonderful with me. Don't leave feeling guilty. Don't leave hating me. If what you believe, about being here before, is true, then what we experienced last night was meant to happen. I'll never forget you Christina. You were not just an idle conquest."

José put his arms around me, and continued in a gentler tone. "Do you remember back in Monte Albán, when you touched my neck and said you forgave me?"

"Yes?" I whispered, recalling the strange words that had spontaneously come from my mouth.

"Am I still forgiven?" he asked.

Suddenly I remembered my dying words as Pacal. Poor José had come into this life still carrying that curse I'd spit at Koh. That was it! "That's why I'm here!" I cried out. "I forgive you! I forgive Koh!"

"Koh? Who the hell is Koh? Forget about Koh! How about you? When will you forgive yourself?" José cried.

His words echoed those of Reverend Blaze. "Forgive yourself!" Across thirteen centuries the words of Kahwil returned. The gods had not punished me. It had been my own pride that had made me miserable. I'd been unwilling to tolerate human weakness in myself and found it equally inexcusable in those I loved.

I remembered the words of Little Jaguar, just before I drank the potion of death, "It's a heavy burden to be considered a god," he'd said. Despite being acknowledged as divine from his birth, Little

Jaguar's homosexuality had forced him to accept his own human-ity. He knew he wasn't a god, he was only "considered" a god! Yet, even while he'd resigned himself to his imperfections, he went on to create some of the most incredibly beautiful temples ever built.

José seemed to understand how powerful his words were. He held me close without speaking, allowing my thoughts to progress. I could feel the burden of my own unattainable expectations was being lifted from me, and the sense of relief was so extraordinary that I began to cry without restraint.

"I'll never forget you, José," I sniffled, accepting his offer of a handkerchief. "And I will remember this with a smile."

"What, this old handkerchief?" he laughed.

"No, you! I'll think of you, and of last night, with a smile."

"I guess there's no hope of changing your mind about marrying me?" he asked.

"No, I have a temple to build on Madison Avenue," I answered with a grin. "Besides, you're not the kind of man who should be married. Look at poor Vincenté, always missing his wife and kids. That's not you. I suspect you have a Señorita in every port. Your *onen* is a jaguar, José. I realized that last night. It's that unbridled spirit of that wild and magnificent creature that I find so irre-sistible in you. Any woman who tries to tame you, will have her heart broken."

"I think there must be some jaguar blood in you too," José laughed. "Come, I'll walk with you back to the hotel. I think Kit is afraid I'm going to kidnap you! Do you think she's holding a grudge with me from the past too?"

"Who knows," I laughed, and reached up to touch his hand on my shoulder.

Kit was sitting on the steps that led to the huge carved doors of the entrance to the Hotel Mayaland. The moment she saw us approaching, she ran up to greet us.

"I've returned your momma," José proclaimed. "Now Señora, Señorita, I must be going. Have a wonderful journey!"

"Our trip is almost over," Kit replied like a wise old woman.

"Your journey, young lady, is just beginning," he proclaimed, and walked briskly toward the parking lot.

"Are you going with him?" Kit asked

"Of course not!" I laughed. "We have a trip to finish!"

Kit hugged me and said, "I'm sorry I called you a liar last night. I was just scared and worried about you."

"And I'm sorry I made you scared. Sometimes mothers make mistakes too, Kitten. You can remind me of this someday when you come home from a date past your curfew."

As I spoke my daughter's nickname, it occurred to me that it was more than coincidental. Although she was baptized Catelina, I'd always called her Kit, and in moments of tenderness, Kitten. So it seemed, that Little Jaguar finally got the gender he wanted, I thought. I remembered reading somewhere about the Hindu belief that we were reincarnated into our own family over and over, exchanging places with our parents and children. Pacal had been so concerned that his lineage would not survive, leaving his ancestors and his own spirit without earthly connections. Now I realized that the Jaguar-Sun lineage had survived after all, we'd just surfaced in a different jungle.

# Etznab

The dreams stopped, perhaps because their purpose had been fulfilled. The memories of my life as Pacal, became like all memories, increasingly difficult to recall — the details fading slowly, imperceptibly. I'll have to write it all down before I forget it, I thought to myself, as I stared out the window, during our flight home.

Kit, asleep in the seat beside me, looked perfectly beautiful. Her transition into womanhood had begun. I was glad we'd had the opportunity to take this trip together, before she began that painful process of severing herself from me. I was even more grateful that I'd learned something more about tolerance before facing the onslaught of her teenage rebellion that was already beginning to surface.

Soon we would be arriving in JFK. Charlie would be waiting there in the crowd. How would he look? Older? Anxious? Would he be smoking? Probably. I couldn't wait to be in his embrace again.

I thought about the continuum of interwoven cycles that regulated every aspect of Maya life, most important of all, the great cycle that began on August 11, 3114 BC. On December 23, 2012, that cycle will be complete. Would that be the end of the world, or just the beginning of the next great cycle? Sometimes it seemed as if we were living perilously close to the biblical Armageddon.

If time is not linear, but rather an endless succession of patterns, then couldn't we learn to recognize those patterns. Part of the power Pacal and other Maya rulers possessed, came from their knowledge of cyclic patterns. By studying these patterns, they could predict not only eclipses and other astronomical phenomenon, but human events, such as the birth of great individuals, victorious battles or the end of the reign of the True People.

It was this understanding of patterns that had sustained the Maya civilization for nearly 2,000 years. Unfortunately, they began to deviate from the strict discipline this knowledge had over every aspect of their lives: the rituals; the beliefs; the unquestioned responsibilities that each class accepted as their destiny. They began to engage in warfare, not for the age-old purpose of securing captives for ritual sacrifice, but to feed an unchecked lust for power. Farmers left their fields lying fallow, while they participated in the quest for power through endless battles. The will of the gods was ignored, the ancestors forgotten, and civilization crumbled.

Is collapse an inevitable aspect of the great cycle? If so, collapse this time will be a global catastrophe. Or is it possible that the Maya intelligentsia, along with enlightened souls from other great civilizations, have returned to this time and place, to prevent the destruction of the human race?

Centuries of respect for discipline and hard work are again being traded for short-sighted and selfish gains. Our heroes are no longer the brave and self-sacrificing — they're the greedy, vain and irresponsible. Meanwhile, those who could make great leaders, are dissuaded from coming forward because our political process requires an impossible purity. What hope is there for a planet where critical choices are determined by the greed of the few at a terrible cost to the many. Our enlightened tolerance and compassion for the unique qualities in each human being must be tempered with a new 3-R's: the virtues of responsibility, restraint and respect for human dignity.

I'd been staring out the window for some time before I realized what I was looking at. It was a dark night, with only a sliver of a new moon. A profusion of stars filled the sky, but there was one exceptionally bright light, just at the tip of the crescent moon. How strange that you can see a star so close to the light of the moon, I thought. Then I realized I was seeing the planet Venus. Bolom Tzacab, the Maya called him. The old god, whose first appearance on the horizon heralded a call to arms, the ideal time to secure captives for sacrifice.

But tonight, the old god was seducing the young moon goddess. The Maya still explain how each month, Ixtab reappears, slim and pure. But as the days progress, her belly grows round with child, until her son, the full moon, makes his sun-like journey across the sky.

From my window seat, I watched as the lecherous Bolom Tzacab drew so near to the young goddess, that I was sure he'd kissed her. Suddenly I felt a tightness of excitement in my chest. This was the sign Kan had promised!

Over the loudspeaker the captain advised us to fasten our seat belts in preparation for landing. We were returning to Kahwil's magical place of mirrors, where my dearest friend was waiting for me.

THE END

Because *Place of Mirrors* is self-published (published by the author), you might have trouble finding it in your local bookstore. If you would like to purchase this book, you can order it directly from Jaguar Books. *Choose from these 4 easy ways to order:*

**Fax orders:**
813-724-1677

**Telephone orders:**
Toll Free: 1-800-299-0790

**On-line orders:**
jaguar@flanet.com
or visit our web site at http://www.imas.com/tpd/jaguar.html

**Mail orders:**
Jaguar Books
30043 US Hwy. 19N, Ste. 136
Clearwater, FL 34621

_____ copies of *Place of Mirrors* @ $21.95 each.     _____

**Sales Tax:** Please add $1.54/bk for books shipped to Florida addresses. _____

**Shipping:**
Book rate: *(allow 3 to 4 weeks)*
*1st book*-$2.00, add 75¢ each additional book     _____

Priority Mail: $3.50 per book     _____

**Total:**     _____

**Method of Payment:**

☐  Check or money order enclosed *(mail order only)*

☐  Credit Card: VISA, MasterCard

Card number: _____

Name on card: _____

Exp. date: _____

**Send to:**

Name: _____

Address _____

City/State/Zip _____